KATE MORGAN

STAKING CINDERELLA
by
Kate Morgan

1st Edition Trade Paperback 2019
All Rights Reserved

Dark Recesses Press

4-462 Henrietta St.,
Ontario Canada K7G 1X7

Cover Art by Bailey Hunter
Layout and Inset design by Bailey Hunter

Library & Archives Canada
ISBN 978-1-988837-19-2

KATE MORGAN

CHAPTER ONE

A quintessential cowboy parked his truck in the packed community college main lot. The complete Scooby-Doo Gang walked past on his left, the Bob's Burgers cast on his right.

He knew he should've eaten before coming to this Halloween party. Never go grocery shopping hungry. He was old enough to know better.

A sexy nun and a sexier nurse followed the Scooby Gang. So much exposed neck. He closed his eyes and marshaled his forces. Half an hour to accomplish his objective and he could escape home and feed.

Gavin Donne, historian, costume designer and drama instructor, exited and locked his truck. At the gym entrance he took a deep breath of night air and choked on cigarette smoke.

"Fancy-boy actor's lungs can't take it." Male laughter.

"Don't be an ass, Cal." A pudgy girl patted Gavin's back. "You okay, Mr. Donne?"

Gavin spat into the barberry bushes lining the sidewalk. "Yes, thank you, Stella. I see your brother is still trying to prove his manhood."

"Hey!" A blackhead-speckled face pushed its way into Gavin's line of sight. "Wanna prove your own manhood, shithead?"

Gavin managed not to roll his eyes. "Perhaps in ten years, if you've learned to hold your liquor by then." When the blackheads didn't move, Gavin raised both hands and shoved. Cal's tailbone landed on the edge of the sidewalk.

"Shit!" He rubbed the injury, staring up at Gavin with a dazed expression. "How'd you do that?'

Stella wedged a lit cigarette in her braces and helped her brother to his feet. "Mr. Donne knows stage fighting, dummy. I take classes with him, remember?"

"Mr. Donne, how'ja like our costumes?" A reedy black girl with stuffed pantyhose on her arms and legs struck Wonder Woman's fighting pose. Next to her, a cornrowed teenager with real weightlifter muscles pumped fake weights. His form-fitting Superman suit did justice to every muscle.

The Frankenstein monster and his bride—two more of Hal's acting students—leaned against the open door. They tried to sing the *Addams Family* theme, but after the first set of "da-da-da-das" the bride started giggling and couldn't stop. The monster handed her a dark bottle and she swigged and nearly dropped it.

A husky voice said, "They're so immature." From the shadow of the propped-open door stepped a man with dead-white makeup and eyes sunk in black pits.

Gavin narrowed his eyes. This 'man' had a distinctly feminine build. "And tonight you are?"

"The nameless tormentor from *Carnival of Souls*. I'm disappointed in you, Gav—Mr. Donne. Don't you watch classic horror?"

Judith. He should've guessed. Anything to grab more attention for her goth-angst-self-absorbed world. "Quite the transformation, Judith. I'm impressed."

"I wanted you to see that one of us is worthy of your time and attention."

"I never doubt that my students pay attention to me. They know my skill with a chainsaw if they don't improve."

The bride hiccupped. "Mr. Donne, you're so queer. Chainsaws are for wood."

"And you're drunk, Lorraine. Keith, what did you steal from your parents' liquor cabinet?"

The Frankenstein monster tried to shuffle his feet and bumped, off-balance, into the bride. "Aw, Mr.—Mr. Donne, just a little Glenfiddich."

"A little what?" Gavin pried the bottle from Lorraine. "Your father will flay you." He turned to Superman. "Ray, how did all of you get here?"

"Stella and Cal picked us up."

Gavin said over his shoulder, "Stella, have you been drinking too?"

"Well, maybe a little beer, Mr. Donne."

He turned to Superman. "Ray, are you going to stay sober tonight?"

"Yeah, Mr. Donne, me and Deb both are. Our mom made us promise."

"Stella, give your keys to Ray."

"But—"

"Now, Stella. Didn't you learn anything in Driver's Ed? I'm not going to be responsible for letting you get behind the wheel again tonight."

Stella reached into her silver go-go boot and handed Superman a pink enamel puppy holding a clump of keys in its mouth.

"Ray, can you help me herd Lorraine and Keith into my truck? Judith, you too."

Her dark eyes brightened. "I'd love to."

"Judith, I'm taking you home, as well." He put a hand on both Frankensteins' shoulders. "All of you are underage. You can thank me at Monday night's class."

Gavin prodded the monster and his bride across the grass and the parking lot to his Dodge Ram.

Judith trotted next to him. "Gavin—Mr. Donne—did you buy that quad cab truck just to transport recalcitrant students?"

Gavin would've closed his eyes to hide his exasperation if he didn't need to keep the bride upright. "Judith, chainsaw sculptures require a great deal of space and carrying power. Taking an acting class on field trips is simply a bonus."

Her only response was a throaty giggle as he reached into his jeans pocket for his keys. His thumb touched the right-hand button and the locks disengaged. Opening the door with one hand, he nudged the bride into the back seat with the other. "Judith, please help with her seat belt. I'll take care of Keith."

The monster tripped into the back passenger seat and Gavin propped him upright.

He squinted at Gavin. "C'mon, Mr. Donne." A hiccup. "Just one more drink? It's good stuff."

"No." Gavin buckled his seat belt and slammed the door. When he opened the driver's side door, Judith was already buckled in next to him. The car reeked—to him—of alcohol, legal and illegal smoke, and pheromones.

Perfect. Judith was just high enough to come on to him again. Happy Halloween.

Gavin drove through mostly empty streets and hauled a semi-awake Keith to his front door. A taller version of the teenager answered his knock. Gavin propped the young monster against the doorframe.

"Good evening, Mr. Breuer. I'm afraid—"

"He raided my scotch. I was just about to go looking for the idiot." Breuer cuffed Keith. "Get to bed, Frankenstein. Hope you're ready for the hangover from hell."

He shook Gavin's hand. "Thanks for bringing him home, Donne."

"Not a problem. I have two more deliveries in the truck."

Breuer shook his head. "Stupid kids. Ah, well. We were all stupid once. 'Night."

Getting Lorraine up two flights of stairs to her apartment was more work, but Gavin did not want to be indebted to Judith.

Lorraine's mother had crammed herself into the apartment doorway, wringing her fat hands like her world had ended.

"Oh, Mr. Donne, what am I going to do with her? It's so hard to raise a daughter alone these days. And how kind you are to take an interest in her well being. Oh, Lorraine, Lorraine, get

4

inside and go straight to bed." The hands released each other long enough to clutch Gavin's arm.

"Think nothing of it, Mrs. Astley." He patted the five rings on her fingers, then pried her hand from his sleeve. Her whining voice followed him into the stairwell.

A cloud of pot smoke enveloped him when he entered the truck.

"You're so sweet to help those children, Gavin."

Something had looked different in the brief light when Gavin opened his door. After he buckled himself in, he turned to see. Judith's narrow black tie and suit jacket had vanished. The first three, no, four buttons of her white shirt were unbutoned.

"We're alone, Gavin." Her black-nailed hand snaked around his neck.

He peeled it away. "And you're going home, Judith."

She dragged on a half-finished joint, held in the smoke, and exhaled directly into his face. "Pot's an aphrodisiac, you know." She giggled. "That toke did the trick." Her hand traveled toward his lap.

Gavin slapped her away, snatched the joint, cracked his door, and threw it into the street.

"Gavin…"

He slammed the gearshift into Drive and jerked away from the curb. "Judith, for the last time, my name is Mr. Donne, I am your acting coach only, and you will respect that boundary or you will no longer be my student."

The light at the corner turned red too quickly. He stomped the brake, throwing Judith against the seat belt. She bounced back with a curse.

"What are you, a fairy?"

"No, I'm a responsible adult. Button your shirt and stop this nonsense." The light changed and he gunned the truck through the intersection.

"Cut it out. You're making me sick." Judith belched and slapped her hand over her mouth. Her voice dropped its come-hither accent. "I'm gonna puke—"

Gavin jerked to the side of the road and opened her door as the tire hit the curb. He pushed her head over the running board just as she splattered the pavement with a foul, chunky mix of beer and pizza. Her body heaved again and again, some of the vomit splashing back onto her face and hair.

In another minute she pulled herself back into the truck and closed the door. Gavin handed her a towel from the back seat.

"Open your window when you're done. The breeze will help."

"I hate throwing up." All the sultriness had left her voice.

"Then don't mix drugs, alcohol, and greasy food."

"It was a party… Mr. Donne."

"And aren't you having fun." He turned right.

"I was." She cracked the window and leaned her head against the glass. "That's cool… feels good."

Gavin drove through tree-lined streets, jack o'lanterns still burning on most porches, but not a trick-or-treater in sight. His dashboard clock read 11:24. At the next light, he glanced at his passenger. Judith had passed out, a smear of her clown-white makeup along the glass where her head fell back, exposing her neck.

When the light changed, Gavin drove straight for two blocks and turned left into the alley behind the car wash. No streetlights reached here. He stopped, turned off the ignition, and unbuckled both seat belts.

His fingers pushed aside Judith's open blouse, exposing her latest tattoo: a pair of fangs in an open, red mouth, with artistic drops of blood staining the sharp points.

Silly girl. But convenient for him.

Between one moment and the next, Gavin's incisors grew points sharp as X-acto knives. He turned Judith's head away from him and his fangs pierced the vein beneath her tattoo.

CHAPTER TWO

Judith's blood slid down Gavin's throat like mulled wine. He'd never lost his taste for mulled wine; he always managed to drink a short glass at Christmas.

The next bloody swallow nearly made him gag. He would never make a habit of feeding from Judith. Smoke of any kind polluted the taste.

A few more rich mouthfuls and he withdrew, placing his tongue on the quarter-inch slits in Judith's neck. His saliva filled the wounds as he retracted his fangs. He licked the tattoo clean and raised his head.

His mouth tasted of beer, marijuana... and birth control hormones.

So Judith was no longer a virgin. He ran his tongue around his palate again. No hint of STDs in her blood. Good. If anything still challenged his ingenuity, it was a tactful way to tell one of his meals to get tested.

He dried her neck with a clean corner of the towel and buttoned her shirt. Then he put the rest of her costume on her again and buckled her seat belt.

The dashboard clock read 10:34. An efficient and profitable use of necessity and circumstance. The hundred years it had taken to learn to survive on just half a cup of blood every four days had been well spent. Seven minutes total from starting the meal to healing the slits. He closed his eyes to savor his full stomach.

He harmed no one when he fed. Judith's body would replace the blood in a few days and the slits heal within the hour. He killed no one. Most important, he made no one an unwilling victor over death.

He reached for the bottled water in the central cup holder, rinsed his mouth, and spat into another towel. Five blocks to the west, he stopped the truck outside Judith's duplex.

Her prematurely tall, painfully thin younger brother opened the door. Judith's butt at his eye level appeared to take away his power of speech.

Gavin jogged Judith into a less awkward position on his shoulder. "Hello, Kenneth. Judith's had a little too much to drink."

"Again?" Kenneth's voice cracked. "Shit. Can you bring her inside, Mr. Donne?'

Gavin pretended not to see the peeling wallpaper and piles of laundry. He followed Kenneth's frayed yarmulke down a narrow hall and into a small bedroom draped in black cloth.

Kenneth banged the light switch. "Just dump her on the bed, would you?"

Gavin lay Judith on her black and crimson bedspread with care. When Kenneth yanked off her black sneakers and flipped the other half of the bedspread over her, Gavin moved back to the doorway.

Kenneth sniffed Judith's clothes. "Good thing dad's working double shifts all week. He'd have a shit fit if he knew she toked." His breaking adolescent voice clashed with the misery in his face.

"She threw up most of it on the way here." Gavin backed into the hall and Kenneth followed. "Do you have a good hangover remedy? She'll need it."

"I'd let her suffer if she wouldn't make my life hell, too." He slumped against the wall. "Mr. Donne, she acts like she listens to you. Can you get her to cut it out?"

Gavin shrugged. "I've mentioned something to her once or twice. Perhaps this latest incident will wake her up."

Kevin imitated his shrug. "I should be so lucky. You believe in family curses, Mr. Donne? Our Rabbi does."

"I can't see how your sister's occasional binges constitute a curse." He had better not give this unhappy young man his comprehensive insight on the subject.

"It's not just her. Our mom was a lush. Totaled her car and herself when I was ten. It was okay for awhile—I liked not getting beat when she got the DTs." He scrubbed his eyes with the back of his hand. "But Judy's gonna end up the same way. Hasn't been to Temple since mom died, either." He stopped propping the wall and strode to the door. "Sorry to dump on you, Mr. Donne. Having a bad night, I guess."

Gavin put a hand on his shoulder. "We all get them. Do you attend Temple Beth Zion?"

"Yeah. How did you know?"

"Just a guess. I helped your Rabbi with Purim costumes last year." He smiled. "Have you tried talking to the Talmudic scholar staying there? He has some interesting ideas on Divine and free will. You two might get along."

The sounds of puking reached them.

"Shit. 'Bye, Mr. Donne. Thanks for everything." Kenneth grabbed a wide-mouth vase from the coffee table and ran to Judith's room.

CHAPTER THREE

Gavin entered the Halloween party twenty minutes later no longer distracted by the array of naked necks. He sauntered through the crowd repeating "Howdy, ma'am" and "Yes, they're authentic chaps." In a brief open space he flicked his whip at the heels of a ragged zombie.

"Hey!" a thin tenor squeaked.

"Howdy, foreman." Gavin coiled the whip and hung it back on his belt. "You have greenhorns to train this fine evenin', thanks to me."

"Gavin, that is a wicked pisser costume. What show? No, wait. *Oklahoma*, of course." The zombie grabbed Gavin's hat and set it on his matted hair.

Gavin snatched it back. "Hal, you'll get stage blood on it."

"Nah. I'm dry by now." Hal King, community theater director and Serious Playwright, squatted to inspect the chaps. "Who sewed these?"

The dancers began singing along to 'Yellow Submarine.' Gavin raised his voice. "A little old lady who told interminable stories about her great-grandchildren during every fitting."

Any facial expression the zombie might have made didn't pierce his makeup. "What did you say just now?"

Gavin brushed the nap straight on his chaps. "Half of your teenage satellites are home sleeping it off."

"I wondered." The zombie pointed toward the far wall with a bloody, shredded hand. "The rest are trying to decide if they're too cool to have a little fun."

"Or wondering if their fake IDs will work in the beer dungeon."

The zombie hitched a moldy vest higher on his shoulder. "It's a rite of passage. Speaking of beer..."

Gavin shouted over the band. "Enjoy. Is your new masterpiece ready for Monday's class?"

"Not yet. This is the big one, Gavin. This play will take me to Broadway. You pick out something for class, okay?" The zombie's voice cracked with his effort to be heard without creasing his makeup.

"Got it. See you Monday." Gavin would bet money it was Hal's same 'problem play.' A distant father, an overprotective mother, a repressed older sister, and a talented but misunderstood younger son. Maybe Hal would set it in ancient Rome this time. Gavin hadn't worn a toga on stage in years. Or perhaps the early Renaissance. Would anyone notice the authentic touches only he could add? Probably not. Probably for the best.

He scanned the partygoers for his reason for being here. The college had gone all out converting the gym into multiple haunted houses. A medieval castle housed the craft booths. The dance floor jousting pavilion abutted the beer dungeon. The food stands kept with the obvious, a medieval banquet hall with hay strewn on the floor beneath trestle tables. The band was the sole anachronism: their zombie clown costumes were not cute cartoon zombies. This deterred no one from approaching them with requests.

Gavin spotted his quarry heading toward the craft booths. He followed, imagining the satisfaction of piercing her desiccated vein when he found it through her neck wattles. He'd find the perfect moment. Patience was second nature to him.

His target and her costumed chihuahua worked the crowd at every booth, like a good local bigwig should.

He stopped at a stand selling homemade pet treats. One ear listening to the yapping chihuahua, he chose a half-dozen giant beef flavored biscuits for his giant dog.

The yapping moved toward the side exit. King Chihuahua the Eighth apparently needed a modern fire hydrant.

Tinkling medieval music cut through the over-amped guitars and drums. A song he remembered form his childhood. It drew him like a zombie to fresh brains.

The tall blonde at the music box booth was a bonus.

CHAPTER FOUR

Isolde Connor turned off the music switch on a papier mâché angel. In its place she set a knitting demon on the counter and pressed its ball of blood-colored yarn. "What about this?"

Dracula raised a stark black eyebrow. "What song is that?"

"An Elizabethan madrigal called 'Phyllis sat knotting.'"

Seven dollars appeared on the counter. "My mom'll love it. Wrap it up." He took the gift bag and headed for the beer dungeon.

Isolde tucked the money in a zippered makeup bag. She set an angel playing a trumpet in the open spot on the shelf. "Noelle, the demons are selling faster than the angels."

Next to Isolde in the cramped booth, her best friend pushed a reading angel behind a tap-dancing demon. "Of course they are. It's Halloween."

"I don't like scary things, Noelle. Your costume, for instance."

"Girl, you are such a wuss." Noelle tried to loom over Isolde—impossible since she was six inches shorter. "I am Vampira. I vant to suck your blaahd."

Isolde slapped Noelle's blood-red nails away. "Cut it out."

Noelle laughed. "Listen, Ms. tall, thin, and blonde, this costume shows off every bit of my assets. I'm banking on Stephen paying our booth a visit tonight."

"Hoping your pastor will take you to a secluded place to pray for your soul?" Isolde wagged her eyebrows.

"He's too proper for that." Noelle straightened her shoulders and her assets stood at attention. "But if he thinks our ratio of demons to angels needs adjusting, I'll offer to talk to him about it in private."

Isolde leaned her elbows on the counter and watched the werewolves, monsters, and movie characters entering the gym in a steady stream. "I could use a knight-errant to show up tonight. One who'll pay more attention to my graceful gown than your cleavage."

"You're welcome to all of 'em. I'm holding out for my man of God."

High-pitched yapping cut across the band's intro to "Highway to Hell."

Noelle touched Isolde's arm. "Heads up. Here she comes."

An older woman in a navy business suit lifted King Chihuahua the Eighth onto the counter. "Miss Connor, what does your sign say?"

Isolde tried not to smile at the dog's costume. "Good evening, Mrs. Gow. It's the same sign as everyone else's: Party Till You Scream For Children's Hospital Of Boston."

"Not that sign. The one above my head." She pointed with a French-manicured nail. The dog yapped again. "Quiet, Samson."

Noelle nudged Isolde aside. "It says Angels versus Demons."

Miranda Gow turned pale eyes on her. "And what is your extremely immodest costume supposed to represent, Noelle?"

"Vampira." Noelle stepped back four paces to the cardboard castle wall and pulled green spiderweb like a cape across her plunging neckline.

Mrs. Gow crossed her arms. "It is unwise to trivialize evil. Pastor Oliver said last Wednesday—"

"I asked him about it Friday when he came to visit Mr. Putnam in the hospital's Alzheimer's wing." Noelle's smile doubled in wattage. "He said that as long as I remembered I was a child of the King, he saw no harm in a little fun for a good cause."

Isolde sneaked a look as she added a few more angels to the shelves. Miranda "my family built this town" Gow looked stiffer than Noelle's whalebone bodice.

"I must say—"

A bat with a meat skewer through its chest thumped on the counter beneath her nose.

Isolde and Noelle gasped. The dog yipped and almost fell off the counter. Mrs. Gow clutched him by the skirt and patted his shivering foot-long body.

A cowboy complete with chaps and bullwhip towered over Mrs. Gow. "I don't appreciate your little gifts, Miranda."

From within Gow's arms, the chihuahua growled at the cowboy as Isolde bent over the bat. "It's rubber, Noelle. It's not real." She looked under the cowboy's hat—not hard to do; he was at least six-five in those boots. Square face, green eyes, nice lips, thinned in anger at the moment.

Staring at him, Noelle said, "I remember you. You came to see old Mrs. Tarbell last month."

Mrs. Gow turned the manicured finger on him. "And Edith Tarbell died two days later."

"That is dangerously close to slander, Miranda." The cowboy fingered his whip. "Can't a modern Soldier of Righteousness throw down an original gauntlet? Rubber bats and silver crosses went out of fashion with Hammer films."

"God has commanded me to root out evil wherever it plants its foot."

He gave Gow's navy business suit a deliberate once-over. She shivered. He smiled.

"And you're costumed as... a politician? They could be construed as evil nowadays." He sneered at the growling chihuahua. ""I see Henry the VII has come down in the world. Or is he paying off Karmic debt?"

Mrs. Gow patted the dog and poked her head toward the cowboy. "I know what you do in that house. I know why you keep that hellhound. I only wish God had seen fit to bring you to

Newburyport in a holier age. You wouldn't be so smug when we condemned you to the flames of Hell."

A laugh burst out of Isolde before she could stifle it.

The cowboy's eyes flicked toward her, then returned to Gow. "I'm keeping Chayyliel on guard outside the house four nights a week from now on, Miranda. You're welcome to guess which four."

The band's amps let out a piercing feedback squeal. Mrs. Gow's nostrils dilated. "I shall put a stop to that immediately." She tucked the miniature monarch under her arm and stalked down the row of booths toward the platform.

Noelle applauded—quietly. "Where's a camera when you need one? Gow the Cow never looked better."

He touched the brim of his hat. "Sorry about all this, ma'am. Let me remove her toy." With a fluid movement he flung the bat into a nearby trash can.

Isolde tugged her gown straight. If she couldn't be sexy, at least she looked flowing. Maybe the cowboy wasn't a boob man. "So what does Gow have against you? She looked like Jonathan Edwards preaching 'Sinners in the Hands of an Angry God.'"

One side of his mouth twisted. "She thinks I'm a vampire."

Isolde snorted, ruining her chance at a ladylike expression. "You're kidding."

"I assure you I'm not."

"That woman was born three hundred years too late." Isolde poked Noelle. "Does she freak out like that at church?'

"She's tame on Sunday morning and Wednesday night. Darn it, I'm lisping now." Noelle wiggled her fangs with her thumb. "When I start Bible Study I'll let you know."

Isolde shook her head. "Better you than me. Cowboy—" she touched his hand. "In my professional nurse's opinion, you look as normal as anyone at this fright-fest. Gow needs a hobby. Or a psych eval." She realized she wanted to keep her hand on his and moved it, pretending to adjust her sleeve.

He watched her artifice. "I agree. The rubber bat on my threshold was tame, for her. Last week it was a crucifix draped in garlic. I sent her a thank-you note and a recipe for garlic butter."

Noelle smoothed her hands over her curve-hugging black gown. "I promise you I won't get sucked into her delusion. No offense, cowboy, but I think I'm a much better-looking vampire."

The cowboy swept off his cattleman hat and bowed. "Ma'am, you'd charm the blood from a dime-store mannequin."

Noelle tried a different fang adjustment. "You're going to make me lose the costume contest."

"Can't take a little friendly competition, pardner?"

Isolde crossed her arms and put on a stern face for Noelle. "His drawl is better than your Bela Lugosi impression, too. You'll have to practice before the midnight judging." She turned to the cowboy. "Where'd you learn it?"

"Many years on the amateur stage. This particular costume is from *Oklahoma*."

The band took a break. Dancers swarmed the Dungeon of Suds, the food stands, and the craft booths. Raggedy Ann stopped and pointed to an angel and demon standing back to back. "Can I see those, please?"

When Noelle handed her the salt and pepper shakers, the cowboy put his head next to Isolde's. "I should introduce myself after my dramatic entrance. Gavin Donne. I'm a consultant for the Historical Society. Genealogical research."

Isolde inhaled his scent: leather, mint, and a touch of something exotic—his shampoo? Her tongue tripped over itself. "Um, Isolde Connor. Pleased to meet you."

Gavin tilted his head. "Isolde?"

"Honest. My mother was a *Morte Darthur* nut. Get me started and I can recite whole paragraphs of it. In Middle English."

Noelle pocketed a ten-dollar bill from Raggedy Ann and reached under the counter for tissue paper. "Please don't get her started."

Isolde draped herself over the counter like a Burne-Jones portrait. "This is the thanks I get for playing all the songs for our music boxes? I am cut to the quick. Where is a knight-errant when I need succor?"

Gavin looked meditative. "I might have a knight-errant costume in my attic." He scooped Isolde's hand off the counter. "Milady, allow me to restore the bloom to thy fair cheeks." With another graceful movement he bent his head and kissed her palm.

With a tiny gasp, she met his eyes. Cliché after cliché tumbled through her mind. Piercing, intense, deep. And what a kiss. His lips didn't merely press against her skin. They caressed it. Her hand tingled.

She had to get a grip. Since when did she start thinking in cheap romance tropes?

"I… I sawe ye comen into the feld as ye hast been a bryght aungel."

Gavin's eyes became distant, then he kissed her fingertips. "As ye wille, so be hit. I wille be at your comaundement."

Noelle elbowed Isolde. "Going to let me introduce myself to this multi-lingual cowpoke?"

Gavin released Isolde and shook Noelle's long-nailed hand. "My apologies, ma'am. Gavin Donne at your service."

"Noelle Robins. When I'm not trivializing evil, I'm the nutritionist for the hospice and nursing home complex."

"I thought you looked familiar. I don't remember seeing Isolde the day I visited, however."

Isolde nearly said 'My loss' but bit her tongue in time. "I was probably at the nursing home. I work whichever building needs me at the moment. Bedpans and sponge baths—the glamorous life of an LPN."

Three witches crowded out Gavin as the band encouraged the dancers to sing along to "Welcome to my Nightmare." He resettled his hat and rested his hand on hers a moment. "I'll return later, La Belle Isolde."

She stared after him, totaling his "hot babe" points. His fingers added two onto her initial sum: long, fine, with a few calluses. He wasn't another rich beach bum; those hands worked for a living. How could she have missed him around town?

One of the witches poked her with a skull on a stick. "Hey, I said, can I see the angel and demon on a teeter-totter?"

Isolde turned to get it and Noelle said, "That is one hot cowboy."

She nodded. "Nine out of ten. And nothing scary about him. It doesn't get much better than that."

CHAPTER FIVE

Gavin considered sending Miranda Gow a thank you note for bringing him to Isolde's music box booth.

Clever, talented, self-effacing, Isolde's blood would be light and warm. It had been years since someone interested him for more than their blood. Forty? No, fifty since the roller derby twins. Only their penchant for LSD had marred his time with them.

He paid for two ciders and slid easily through the burgeoning crowd. Dancing next. No, music. He'd never owned a music box, not in five hundred-plus years. First he'd enjoy a novelty.

CHAPTER SIX

The band launched into "Shout" and the crowd deserted the craft booths for the dance floor. Isolde plopped into a metal folding chair.

"Noelle, have I mentioned how much spending the night surrounded by scary things creeps me out?"

"Several times. Suck it up. Ha! That was funny." Noelle fanned herself with a folded gift bag. "Venn I suck your blaad you vill discover the joy uff décolletage." She hissed in classic Christopher Lee style, but her fangs slipped again. "Rats."

"I have no intention of getting into the spirit of this." Isolde looked down at her costume. "What's wrong with my décolletage?"

Noelle pulled a mouthguard holder from a supply box and set the fangs inside. "Mother Nature short-changed you."

Isolde grimaced. "I can't help my B cups."

Noelle put her hands on her elaborate, plunging corset. "Look what this does for me. A good push-up bra can do the same for you."

"Ellie, you have an hourglass figure and skin the color of a Milky Way bar. When you emphasize your D cups, men trip over curbs."

Noelle grinned. "Then let 'em stumble over here and we'll sell every music box and ornament on the shelves."

"I'll be the willing acolyte to your pulchritude. Especially if it gets us one step closer to quitting the nursing home and selling angels full-time."

"Pulchritude. I like it. And you're a willowy blonde. Some men like that."

Isolde sighed. "That's the best adjective you can come up with? It's code for tall, flat, and pale."

"Yeah, but you have great eyes."

"Like men look higher than a woman's neck."

Gavin appeared with two plastic cups of cider. "Thought you ladies would need to bend an elbow."

"Thanks," they said in unison.

Gavin tipped back his hat. "I'd ask if you were sisters, but..."

Isolde laughed. "You mean you can't see the family resemblance?"

Noelle drank half her cider in a gulp. "We met in kindergarten and haven't been separated since."

Isolde finished her cider with a contented sigh. "That hit the spot. Not true, Noelle. You took off for culinary school in Hawai'i, ya bum." She leaned on the counter. "Gavin, would you believe she sent me photos of her surfing with gorgeous men two winters in a row? New England winters—six feet of snow on the ground, no sun for days on end, and she's wearing bikinis and drinking Mai Tais."

"You were a little busy just then, remember?"

"A true best friend would have suffered the deep freeze with me."

"I sent you leis and hibiscus plants." Noelle drained her cider. "Snap her up, Gavin. She nursed her grandmother full-time for two and a half years. She's only a few months over thirty and she's a good cook. She's the perfect selfless companion."

Isolde stepped on Noelle's foot. Hard. When she looked sideways at Gavin she cringed at the amusement on his face. "Gavin, tell me you have a wife and a dozen kids."

Gavin didn't answer for a beat. "Why?"

"So I don't have to worry about my 'dearest friend' here telling an eligible man how old I am."

She called him 'eligible' to his face. Talk about baring your spinsterhood to the world. So much for any chance with the hot cowboy. She tried for a careless laugh when she really wanted to crawl into one of the empty angel boxes and die.

Gavin's forehead uncrinkled. "Ma'am, I could spend a month of Sundays walkin' out with someone purty as you. Ain't no nevermind how old you are a'tall." He cleared his throat. "Please kill me. I'm channeling Curly McLain again."

Isolde really did laugh. "Who?"

"The character I played in *Oklahoma* several years ago. Our director insisted we 'become' our part and forced us to speak cowboy-ese on and off the stage during rehearsals. I knew this costume would be my undoing."

"I think it's charming. The costume and the jargon." *Charming, hah.* He triggered every 'grab this guy' alarm she had. Maybe she could audition for whatever production he was doing next.

Noelle planted her elbows on the counter and sighed. "If only I could get Stephen to say he'd go walking out with me."

Isolde patted her hands. "Wait until he sees you in that costume."

Gavin looked over their heads at the shelves of music boxes and Christmas ornaments. "Ladies, may I ask if you have the angel Jeremiel among your works?"

Noelle shook her head. "He's a new one on me. What's he—it—the angel of?"

"Of the mercy of God."

"Oh." Isolde deducted five points. He was a religious nut. Gow with a different agenda. Damn. Well, no worries about her leaky faucet mouth. They could take his commission and she could look for another non-scary male. "We could make one, couldn't we, Ellie?"

"Sure. Do you know what you want it to look like? We can research it on the Net if you don't."

"If you have a piece of paper, I'll draw him for you."

Isolde gestured him around the back of the booth. "C'mere. Gow's headed this way again."

Gavin dodged Dorothy and the Scarecrow, maneuvered around Scarlett O'Hara's hoop skirt, and ducked under the side shelf.

"Noelle," Mrs. Gow raised her voice over all the feet stomping to the 'Cha Cha Slide,' "I would like to see that green angel, the apricot one below it." She set the chihuahua on the counter again. "Hush, Samson. And the blue one next to it."

Isolde whispered to Gavin, "When she points like that, her nails are a deadly weapon."

Gavin smiled. "I agree."

Isolde sneaked a look at his teeth. Perfectly normal. Gow was a nutbar. And that meant nothing, because Gavin was a Jesus freak. She was not interested in him. No.

Gavin crouched by an empty box and drew with a magic marker on a piece of tissue paper. "His robe is white—pure white, no other colors. Long black hair with streaks of gold. One hand holds a water-filled chalice, like in Catholic Churches, you know the kind?"

"Yes."

"Good. The other hand holds a stalk of wheat."

Isolde frowned. "Wheat?"

Gavin nodded. "Yes. He dips it in the chalice and shakes the water, the symbol of mercy, onto the repentant soul."

Isolde scooted away an inch or two.

Noelle's contralto cut through the thumping sound system. "This one with the basket of apples is the angel of nature, Mrs. Gow." She pressed an apple near its bare foot and held it to Mrs. Gow's ear. "That's 'Morning' from *Peer Gynt*."

Mrs. Gow arched her too-thin eyebrows. "I recognize the music. Entirely too rustic."

Samson scratched at his doublet with a three-inch leg. Noelle continued her sales pitch. "This is the angel of the garden." A button beneath a tiger lily played the opening to the second movement of Dvorak's *New World Symphony.*

Isolde brought her attention back to the sketch. Gavin could draw, too. The angel was definitely male. The long hair looked elegant, not effeminate. The hands resembled Gavin's.

She leaned into his ear to be heard over the band. "Would you like it as a music box?"

Noelle said in the same bright voice, "And this is the angel of water."

Almost inaudible over the surrounding din, Isolde heard herself playing Handel's *Water Music* on the harpsichord.

Gow pursed lips as thin as her plucked eyebrows. "This one. It's more refined than the others." She snapped open her Coach bag and counted out a five and two singles.

Isolde shifted a few inches to her right, screening more of Gavin from Gow. When she caught him watching her movement, she slid her eyes toward the counter, then toward him. "I don't want any more scenes," she whispered.

He breathed near her cheek, "Thanks."

Noelle leaned over both of them a minute later. "That woman and her annoying little inbred beast are gone. I should've switched her angel for a demon when I wrapped it up." Her long, curly hair tickled Isolde's ear. "The one with flames coming out of his eyes."

"Haures," Gavin said.

"Yeah." Noelle stood. "You an angel and demon expert or something?"

Gavin rocked back on his heels. "Ouch—" He jumped up, rubbing his butt. "Forgot about the spurs." He held out his other hand to Isolde and helped her rise. "I enjoy researching obscure history and legend. Now, La Belle Isolde, about a song for my angel."

"We stick with music that's out of copyright." Noelle pressed the flaming-eyed demon and a synthesized pipe organ blared Bach's 'Toccata and Fugue in D Minor.'

A Cinderella at the counter pointed to the top shelf. "Can I see the devil playing bagpipes?"

Noelle handed it to her while Isolde stared at the curtain behind the Christmas ornaments.

"Wait a minute," Isolde muttered, "wait a minute… Repentance goes hand-in-hand with mercy, right? What's that piece by Gibbons…" She turned around and scowled at the band. "Take a break, will you?"

Like magic, the thumping bass and pounding feet ceased.

"Thank you." Isolde hummed a bar or two, shook her head, and tried a different key. "That's it. Gavin, what about this? 'Drop, drop, slow tears—' "

"We love you, guys, gals, and monsters!" The band leader stepped to one side and the drummer tossed his sticks into the crowd.

Gavin came in on Isolde's next line, "And bathe those beauteous feet…"

A *Flashdance*-style dancer caught the sticks and squealed.

Isolde and Gavin both stopped singing at the end of that measure.

"How did you know to choose that song?" He looked pleased and puzzled at the same time.

She shrugged. "I'm up on ancient music."

Not only was he charming and funny, he had a buttery, rich baritone. It was going to kill her to let him slip away.

The band leader made room for Miranda Gow, who took his microphone.

"On behalf of Children's Hospital of Boston, I want to thank you for coming to this fund-raiser."

Gavin pressed an angel holding a Christmas wreath and nodded when it played "O Christmas Tree." "Do you download the music?"

Isolde shook her head. "I play it myself."

His hands dropped to his sides. "All of it?"

Noelle said over her shoulder as she handed a bag to Cinderella, "Isolde is multi-talented."

Isolde tried not to blush. "Shut up, Ellie."

Gavin pressed two angels and a demon. "But that's a cello, a flute, and a… guitar?"

"Mandolin."

"How many instruments do you play?"

"Five." Curse the luck. He looked interested enough to ask her out. Why wasn't he an average, beer-drinking Patriots fan? "It's not that impressive. I nursed my grandmother through cancer. She liked music, and I had a lot of time on my hands."

The dancers applauded Gow's speech and the band leader took back the microphone and pointed it at them. "Are you ready to par-tay?"

"Yes!"

"I can't hear you!"

"YES!"

Gavin sketched half a bow—there wasn't room for much else in the narrow booth. "Many are the women of proven worth, but you have excelled them all." He grinned. "Proverbs 31:29."

Before Isolde could think of an appropriate comeback, the band started 'I Will Survive.'

Gavin held out his hand. "May I have this dance, ma'am?"

Should she? It'd just encourage him. But she really wanted to encourage him. She never waffled like this. She should say no.

Noelle shooed her away. "Go ahead. I can handle it here."

"Well…"

Noelle bumped Isolde with her hip. "Please scoot. Stephen just showed up." She dived into her purse and came up with lipstick and a compact mirror.

Gavin clasped Isolde's hand and she followed him under the shelf.

CHAPTER SEVEN

"Do you know the Electric Slide?" Gavin shouted as their feet touched the temporary parquet flooring.

"No." Isolde could barely hear herself. The amps overpowered this end of the gym.

"It's easy. Follow me."

They squeezed into the last row of dancers. Isolde tripped over her own feet twice and turned the wrong way once, but mastered it by the second chorus. Everyone sang. The drag queen next to her kept trying for falsetto and failing, and his boa shed hot pink fluffs left and right. She brushed two from Gavin's hat and he plucked another from her shoulder.

The guitar banged his final chord and half a dozen teenage girls in the front squealed and tried to high-five him. The drummer segued from the disco beat to a slow four, and everyone else stopped clapping and paired up.

Gavin and Isolde stared at each other. She made a movement toward the craft booths just as he caught her by the waist and grasped her right hand. And there they were, gliding in a circle to "If" by Bread.

He put his mouth by her ear. "Tell me why you shied away when I described my angel."

She bit her lips. How could she think with his thumb stroking her hand?

His breath warmed her earlobe. "Are you trying not to say 'Jesus freak'?"

"I—uh—I—"

Gavin chuckled. "Bible-thumping is the purview Miranda Gow and her ilk." He pulled her closer. "I enjoy the challenge of the hunt. There are more obscure angels and demons than you'd expect."

She leaned into his ear. Maybe her cheeks weren't as apple-red as they felt. "I guess I jumped to conclusions."

He maneuvered them toward the corner away from the booths. "When you spend every day researching the names and dates of third cousins twice removed, it spills over into other parts of your life."

The singer dropped his voice an octave and two kissing clowns bumped into Isolde.

Gavin stopped them at the edge of the parquet. The bass player began harmonizing with the lead. One of the teenage groupies ooh'd. Another sighed. Both puckered black-painted lips and blew kisses at the singers.

A fog machine pulsed sickly-sweet mist around the platform and Isolde coughed. "I hate that smell. It reminds me of the disinfectant at work."

Gavin led her off the flooring next to a life-size Angel of Death. She shivered.

"Are you cold?"

"No. I hate scary things. They give me nightmares."

He stepped in front of her, blocking everything with his leather-covered chest. "Then I'll protect you from the sight of evil." He glanced at the floor to his left. "And from the belching fog machine."

"My hero." She put both hands on his chest, intending to give herself breathing room. It was a nice chest. She wondered if it was smooth or hairy. No, that would be werewolves. Oh, she was losing it. "How can I requite thy chivalry, my lord?"

His arms weren't at his sides anymore. They circled her back. "With ease, La Belle Isolde." He kissed her.

She became incapable of rational thought. His lips made small movements on hers, firm yet soft. Her hands didn't attempt to push him away. Her right brain sneered at her left brain, but she ignored it. The tip of his tongue touched hers and all the right parts of her tingled.

The amp screeched the opening to "Tainted Love." Gavin's mouth left hers. "Poor timing." Her hands felt the vibration of his words.

"Oh—yes—but better than 'I Think I Love You.' " What was she saying? Her lips tingled too. How did he do that to her?

Gavin laughed. "Or 'We've Only Just Begin?'"

"Definitely. I should get back and help Ellie."

He held out his arm. "And give her a chance to dance with Stephen? Is that the same Stephen as the Church of the Nazarene pastor?"

She took it. "Yes. He might not dance tonight—too many old ladies to gossip about it. Halloween and all."

They skirted the dance floor and stood a moment in the breeze from the open doors.

"Stephen's been trying to ask Ellie out for a month, but we work lots of OT. His church is one of those Pentecostal ones, too."

"I didn't think Pentecostalism had issues with dating and dancing."

"His church is busy, that's the problem. Two services on Sunday, one on Wednesday, Bible studies on Monday and Thursday, the works. Tonight might be their best chance. I'm all ready to work the booth alone if she gives me the signal."

Gavin looked over his shoulder. "A linebacker who missed his calling is heading for your booth as we speak."

Isolde followed his gaze. "That's my cue." She cut through the loitering teenagers and old women with shopping bags full of gifts, scooted by a pair of pirates, and ducked under their counter. "Hey, Noelle. Good evening, Pastor."

Stephen Oliver engulfed her pale hand with his light brown one. "Glad to see you again, Ms. Connor. That's a beautiful and modest costume."

Isolde caught Noelle's blush.

"May I meet your escort?'

Isolde looked behind her—Gavin was still there. "Oh. Sure. Gavin Donne, Pastor Stephen Oliver, Newburyport Church of—"

"Of the Nazarene, of course," Stephen finished as they shook hands. "Hello, Gavin. I didn't recognize you in your get-up. Easter was such a success my parishioners are already pushing me to borrow some of your theater costumes for our Christmas pageant."

"Anything you need, Stephen. Just call me." Gavin turned to Isolde. "I enjoyed our dances."

Isolde forced herself not to imitate the band groupies. "I had fun, too."

Noelle kicked her ankle and Isolde stifled a yip. "Thanks for holding the fort, Ellie. I can take over for awhile."

Stephen smiled past Isolde. "Would you like to get some fresh air, Noelle?"

Her friend's answering smile made the ceiling fluorescents seem dim. "I'd love to." She snagged a length of green spiderweb and wrapped it around her exposed cleavage before squeezing under the counter.

Isolde opened a Christmas ornament box and filled the top shelf, one eye on Noelle and Stephen's progress. Miranda Gow stepped in their path, aiming her capped teeth at the pastor while the dog yipped at Noelle. When Isolde looked to her left again, Gavin was gone.

Should she have asked for his phone number? No—too pushy. But she needed his address to deliver his angel. Damn. Well, there was always the phone book. She turned her back to the gym and pushed all the angels just a tick in front of the demons.

The band was slaughtering Queen's "Crazy Little Thing Called Love" when a hand clasped her shoulder.

"What!" She whisked around, heart jumping.

Gavin stood at the counter, hands raised in a show of surrender. "Beg pardon, ma'am. Didn't mean to rustle your mane. But it came to mind that y'all need to know where I'm bunking."

He held out a folded orange party flyer, printed side up. "Be seein' you when you deliver my angel."

Isolde opened the paper. The top read:

'Eighteen Friedenfels Street, Rings Island. Take a left when you cross the bridge. My house is half a mile down on the right. Faces the Merrimack.'

The bottom read:

'By our first strange and fatall interview,
By all desires which thereof did ensue
For thee
[New] England is only a worthy Gallerie,
to walke in expectation.' –John Donne, 'Elegie on his Mistris.'

Isolde grinned like a loon.

CHAPTER EIGHT

Gavin closed his garage door just as the sound of the town hall clock striking midnight floated across the silent river. The lights on his house's wraparound porch sensed his motion and burst into brilliance. Chayyliel leapt into barking ecstasy.

"Yes, boy, I'm home." Gavin climbed the stairs three at a time and knelt in front of a one hundred fifty-pound Rottweiler-Shepherd mix. The vicious-faced animal knocked Gavin onto his back, sending his cowboy hat into the wicker armchair. Then he straddled Gavin and slobbered his face, hair, and shirt, quitting only when he sank his formidable teeth into Gavin's whip and tried to play Tug of War.

Gavin laughed and spit and laughed again. "Chay, you hulk, leggo. Give it to me. Come on."

Chayyliel growled and splayed his front legs, jerking Gavin by the hip across the porch and down the top step.

"Chay! Chay, down." He forced a stern face. Chayyliel dropped the whip and sat, whining.

"Come on, boy. Leave my work clothes alone. Just because I haven't been a cowboy for a hundred years doesn't mean I won't be one again." He scratched Chayyliel behind both ears until the dog bathed his hands in drool.

Gavin laughed again. "Get your towel, boy. Go on. Get it."

Chayyliel scampered to the end of his long chain and trotted back with a decrepit piece of terrycloth. Gavin grasped one end and wrestled with him until the lights timed off.

"Okay, Chay. Time for me to go in. You guard my house from vampire hunters, now."

Chayyliel barked once and settled at the top of the porch steps, alert and facing the road.

Gavin locked the door behind him and turned on only the light above the glass-fronted bookcase. The soft whish of the wind in the pines came through the bay window's upper screens. The gold jacquard curtains swelled and settled in the still-warm breeze. On the porch, Chayyliel thumped his head on the deck and huffed.

The Oriental throw rugs scattered on the hardwood floor muffled the rap of his cowboy boots. He sat on the arm of the couch and pulled them off, catching his index finger on the spurs. He'd lost his touch.

He set his hat on the couch and stood to unlace his chaps. His jeans-clad legs missed their cover for a moment, until the fresh blood in his veins warmed him again. His dog-drooled shirt clung to his chest in patches, but that didn't matter right now.

Gavin settled in a corner of the loveseat. Damn his conscience that wouldn't let him use all his female meals. Isolde's face entered his thoughts. Her long, golden hair. Her breasts. Her lips. The way she responded to his kisses. She'd give him double pleasure the next time he fed.

What would her blood taste like? Sweet, perhaps, like figs or strawberries. He had to have her. Not once or twice. No, for years. He could make it happen. He would make it happen.

CHAPTER NINE

"Wake up, wake up, wake up!"

Isolde clutched the sides of her bed without opening her eyes. "Noelle, stop bouncing me or I'll puke on your Sunday dress."

The left side of the bed sagged and Isolde opened her eyes. Noelle sat cross-legged in her flowing autumn leaves skirt and blouse, her curly hair tamed under a burnt-yellow straw hat.

Isolde yawned. "Church over already?"

"It's ten o'clock, banana slug." Noelle yanked at Isolde's flowered comforter.

Isolde clutched it. "All right." She sat up, pulling down the sleeves of her Disney Princesses pajama top. "Tell me. Gow the Cow wore fishnet stockings under her choir robe?"

"Of course not, and who cares about her anyway?" Noelle's hands clasped each other. "Stephen invited me for an early supper before tonight's prayer service."

Isolde squealed and hugged her. "What'd he say? How did he get you alone? Did he ask you before or after? Did he slip you a note? What?"

Noelle giggled like a teenager. "You know how he gets that stern look? Well, during his sermon he gave me that look a couple of times and I just wanted to crawl under the seat."

"Maybe he wondered where your cleavage went to."

"Stop it! We were in church." Noelle scooted up to Isolde's headboard and snuggled against the other mint-green pillow.

"Afterward, when I was moving the folding chairs into the small chapel for tonight's service, he asked me to come into his office. I was sure that costume ruined my chances. He kinda lectured me at the party."

"Prude."

"He is not. He has to set the example for his flock. Anyway, when he closed the door, he took my hand and said how nice I looked."

Isolde tilted her head to one side in a show of consideration. "Not bad."

"Then he said how he'd admired me for a long time, and wanted to get to know me better."

Isolde chewed the inside of her cheek so she wouldn't chuckle. "How G-rated of him."

Noelle stuck out her tongue.

"I'm joking, I'm joking. Then what?"

"Then he asked me to dinner and said he wasn't too bad a cook."

"Did he kiss you?"

Noelle sighed. "No. But you should've seen his smile when I said I'd come." She jumped off the bed. "Get up. I am so psyched that I'm going to start on your cowboy's angel right now. What instrument are you going to use for his music?"

Isolde leaned on one elbow. "I don't know."

"Well, what's he like? Funny? Serious? Were the charming cowboy manners only for the costume?"

"He's a contradiction. Furious with Gow one minute and super-romantic with me later. He quoted Malory and Donne, too."

"You got all this from one dance?"

Isolde traced shadow-stripes on the pillowcase with her index finger. "Two dances and some conversation, and, well, a kiss in the corner."

Noelle laughed. "You hussy!" She sat forward. "How's he kiss?"

"Much better than Howard."

"Ugh. What did you ever see in him?"

"He liked me." Isolde shrugged with one shoulder. "But I'm never going out with a guy again until I see his underwear drawer first."

"Now if you'd met a nice guy at my church…"

"We'd spend the first date arguing about the necessity of corporate worship and there'd be no date number two." Isolde threw off the covers. "And I wouldn't be free to date Gavin. Assuming he asks me."

The phone rang. Isolde and Noelle looked at each other.

"A buck says it's him." Noelle headed for the living room.

Isolde beat her to the phone table. "Don't touch it!" She picked up the all-in-one receiver on the third ring. "Hello?… Oh. Good morning." She rolled her eyes and mouthed, *Work.* "Again?… Of course, Ms. Emerson… No, it's not too much of an inconvenience… Right. A bigger paycheck is a worthwhile goal… I'll be there. 'Bye."

Isolde groaned after she set the phone in its charger cradle. "Phoebe called in sick again."

Noelle leaned on the uncomfortable armless chair. "In a pig's eye. She's got a hot date and she's sick of the three-to-eleven shift, that's all. You're going in?"

Isolde shrugged with both shoulders this time. "It's time-and-a-half. The property tax bill came in yesterday's mail. Did you see the total?"

"Yeah. I knew that'd happen when they reassessed us. Bloodsuckers."

"It's still better than a mortgage payment. Every time I come home to this house, I know how much Grandma loved me."

Noelle stood and took off her rust-leather pumps. "I know, too. It's the town assessor's office I can't stand."

Isolde stretched and yawned. "I'm hitting the shower. I only have—" She looked at the clock above the television. "Four hours left in my weekend."

———

"Isolde! It's for you!"

She turned off the blow dryer and opened the bathroom door. Noelle's hand appeared, holding the portable phone.

Isolde tightened the belt on her sunny-yellow terrycloth robe and took the phone. "Hello?"

"Good morning, La Belle Isolde."

Gavin's voice was just as sensual in the daytime.

"Oh, hi." She punched her head. Since when did she sound like a clueless dolt?

"I was wondering if you were free this evening."

Isolde cursed Phoebe and whichever guy she had the hots for this month.

"I can't, Gavin. I'm working the three-to-eleven shift tonight."

A pause. "You don't have weekends off?"

Her head filled with curses. "Usually, yeah, but one of the other LPNs called in sick."

Gavin's voice turned distant; thoughtful. "If I'm not being intrusive, are you working tomorrow morning as well?"

That was intrusive—and probably a come-on. "Why?"

His voice became immediate again. "Could I interest you in some late-night dancing after your shift?"

Isolde tried to moderate the pleasure in her voice. "I could be talked into that."

"Would eleven-thirty be too soon?"

Isolde thought fast. Twenty minutes to drive home, five to shower, ten to dry her hair, throw on makeup, and dress.

"Isolde?"

"Sorry, I was timing things. Quarter to twelve would be better. That's not too late?"

Gavin's voice smiled. "I'm a night person. 'Madame, grutche not to go with me, for I desyre no thynge but your own promise.'"

She could listen to him quote Malory all day. His pronunciation was perfect. "Thenne take thy waye—" A discrepancy hit her. "Wait a minute. Your quote is out of context."

He chuckled. "I'll pick you up at eleven forty-five with my Caxton edition and you can check for yourself."

"Don't think I won't. 'Bye."

The instant she beeped off, Noelle appeared in the doorway. Isolde shook the phone at her. "You listened."

"You know it." Noelle leaned against the doorframe. "You sounded pretty happy, miss."

"We're going dancing, we're going dancing." Isolde waltzed into the living room and cradled the phone.

"How are you going to stay awake?"

She laughed. "With a handsome, ripped, *Morte Darthur* scholar at my side? What do you think will keep me awake?" She headed for her bedroom. "I better set out everything now so I don't obsess about it at work."

Noelle walked past her to her own room. "I think I'll wear the crimson skirt and the brown velvet blouse." She stopped in her doorway. "What do you think?"

"Ellie, he's not going to notice your clothes."

She shook her head, curls swirling around her face. "He is. I have to look alluring for dinner, but decorous enough for prayers."

Isolde walked past her room and into Noelle's. "I'll help you if you help me. I want a plunging neckline."

CHAPTER TEN

Gavin pulled into the empty Church of the Nazarene parking lot and paused with his hand on the automatic window switch. The noon sun cut through the chill beneath the balmy breeze as he inhaled the odor of car exhaust and the scent of leaves. The last parishioner must have just pulled away.

Gavin wrote another note on the first page in his sample binder. Stephen might want the costumes from Hal King's last Ancient Rome epic. Or perhaps a progressive church would be open to unexpected costumes. He opened the binder to the Shakespeare section.

A shadow fell across the *Merchant of Venice* pages. Gavin looked up and Miranda Gow squirted cold water at him.

"What the—" He spluttered and wiped his eyes.

"Hell opens its mouth to receive you, vampire." Miranda raised a fluorescent sports bottle and sprayed Gavin's face and hair. He coughed and a shot of musty water filled his mouth.

"Miranda, you fucking bitch." Gavin wrenched the bottle out of her hand and threw it across the parking lot. "What is this?"

She laughed. "Holy water."

"Oh, Christ." Gavin groped for the clean towel he'd tossed behind the seat this morning.

"You're not dissolving." Miranda's voice lost some of its hysterical certainty.

"Of course not." Gavin's fangs wanted to descend, but he bottled his fury. "It's high noon on a sunny day, you stupid git. If you think you're Newburyport's Van Helsing, you should know that vampires can't be out in the sun. Therefore holy water isn't like acid on my skin either. Therefore you're a fucking insane bitch." He dropped the towel on the passenger seat. "If the chief of police weren't your brother-in-law, I'd lodge a harassment complaint against you."

"Spawn of Satan!" Miranda's nails raked at his face.

Gavin grabbed her wrist. She'd still piss herself if he bit her with his regular teeth. He pulled her arm closer to his mouth and she choked on her next curse.

"Miranda! Gavin! What's going on here?"

Gavin dropped Miranda's arm and she leaped backward. Stephen Oliver strode up to Gavin's truck and put his arm around Miranda.

"He's—he's—" Miranda's body shook like unset Jell-o.

Stephen looked into Gavin's open window. "He's wet."

Without expecting to, Gavin laughed.

Miranda flung off Stephen's arm. "Pastor, I will not stand here and be insulted on church property." She stalked away, her still-trembling legs not always obeying her at bumps and cracks in the asphalt.

Stephen looked from Gow to Gavin. "She's been acting erratic the past few months. I'll make an appointment to counsel her."

Gavin rolled up his window and opened the door. "No offense, Stephen, but she needs antipsychotic drugs and a padded room, not twenty minutes of Biblical comfort over coffee."

Stephen's smile faded. "I am a trained social worker."

Gavin locked his truck. "Then I hope you can get through to her." He indicated the hefty three-ring binder. "Let me see if I can talk you into some creative anachronism for this year's Christmas pageant."

CHAPTER ELEVEN

Halloween's perfect fall weather disappeared by the time Isolde parked in the nursing home/hospice parking lot. Leaves blew everywhere on a chill, damp wind that made her dark green windbreaker ripple against her back. She ran across the asphalt past the soothing blue-green Tranquil Grove sign and into the disinfectant-laden foyer.

Nuncio the college drop-out sat at the white modular lobby desk, sucking on yet another Diet Coke. His small black eyes looked over the terminal screen and he let the straw fall from his chubby lips.

"Hey, Connor. Lemme guess. Phoebe called in sick again."

"Hey, Nuncio. Got it in one." She hung her windbreaker in the closet.

"She spent all last night mooning over the Screening Room's new manager."

Isolde logged into the staff PC at Nuncio's elbow. "Doesn't he work nights too?"

"Not Sundays. She's cooking him her specialty—at her place."

"Hope he likes eggplant."

"Hope he packs a condom. Phoebe informed me she hasn't been laid in a month."

"TMI, Nuncio."

He slurped his Coke. "You think that's too much info? I couldn't get her to shut up."

"Good thing she has Mondays off. Otherwise I'd get a kiss-by-kiss description." Isolde filled in the Sunday time field and entered last week's total. "Sixteen hours of OT this paycheck."

"Get a life, Connor. You'll never catch me spending more than forty a week here."

"Gotta finance my online poker habit somehow."

Nuncio snorted bubbles through his straw. "You couldn't keep a poker face in person or online. I've seen you play gin with the old biddies in the rec room."

Isolde laughed. "Okay, I admit it. I'm saving up to live permanently at Disney World."

"Gawd. That's worse than having your relatives lock you in here before the Alzheimer's hits."

The staff lounge door opened and three chattering LPNs crowded the keyboard. Isolde got out of their way and went into the lounge to grab an iced tea. A smoke-roughened voice accosted her as soon as she entered.

"Another one kicked the bucket, Isolde."

"Aw, crap, Lee. Who?"

"Mrs. Jeffreys in 201 East."

Isolde yanked out a white plastic chair and sat. "Not Ines. She just finished rehab. What happened?"

"Heart. Least that's what Dr. Pole-Up-His-Butt said."

"She hardly ever used her nitro. Is he sure?"

Lee barked a laugh. "Hell will freeze over before he admits he's wrong. You know that."

"Yeah." All Isolde's anticipation for tonight's date evaporated. "I thought sure she'd make it to 95."

Lee reached into her pocket. "Her daughter'll be glad she popped off. That ermine coat of hers cost more that my last two cars put together."

Isolde stood and shoved the chair back against the table. "Greedy relatives make me puke."

Lee smirked. "No worries on my end. If my asshole husband shoots me one night, my sisters can fight over my DVD collection." She flipped open a semi-crushed pack of Camels. "Time for my pre-shift cig. See you on rounds."

The duty roster had Phoebe—now Isolde—taking inventory until five, then delivering supper to the second floor east wing. Snoozer. She counted syringes, checked off different sizes of bandages, and wondered if she should wear the cobalt blue silk blouse tonight instead of the Kelly green one she'd set out on her bed.

Sunday dinner wasn't much of a chore. Most families took their relatives home on Sundays. Even some of the Alzheimer patients. Only ten rooms needed supper on two east.

"Hey, there, Mr. Stafford. Suppertime." Isolde set the covered plate on the movable tray and wheeled it in front of the vinyl recliner.

"Well, well, Tinkerbell. To what do I owe the pleasure?" A frail voice emanated from a blue-and-green plaid robe and an arthritic hand tried to pinch Isolde's rump.

"You're a dirty old man, Mr. Stafford." Isolde aimed a slap at his hand, missing on purpose.

"Old but not dead, Tinkerbell. What slop are you feeding me tonight?"

"Beats me." Isolde removed the cover. "Open-faced roast beef sandwich with gravy, carrots, roll, vanilla pudding."

"At least it isn't Jell-o." One of Stafford's bright blue eyes winked at Isolde. "Unless you've got a Jell-o shooter or two hidden under the napkin."

"Not likely." Isolde avoided another pinch. "I'll be back for the tray in an hour."

Ines Jeffreys' bed had been stripped, but all of her personal items were still in place. Isolde stood just inside the doorway and stared at the photographs of great-grandchildren at Christmas and restored sepia-tone wedding portraits. An oversized tote bag stuffed with yarn leaned against the nightstand. Two pairs of knitting needles stuck out of the top.

Isolde sniffled. Why couldn't God take one of the really far gone Alz oldsters instead, the ones who just stared at the wall all day with vacant eyes? Ines sailed through rehab for her hip replacement and her youngest great-granddaughter just had her first ballet recital. She'd been shocked to learn that Isolde didn't know how to knit and had shoved fat wooden needles into her hands and ordered her to sit down that instant and learn to cast on.

"Where's my supper? It's ten past five!" The shrill, angry voice carried down the hall.

Isolde grimaced and shoved the memories aside. "You're next, Mrs. King!"

———

Isolde unlocked her front door at eleven twenty-five. Of all nights for Debbie to buttonhole her at shift change. Okay, she could shower in three minutes instead of five and still be able to blow dry her hair. No changing her mind on the clothes—no time anymore.

She closed the door with hardly a click so she wouldn't wake Noelle, and turned on the light.

Noelle bounced off the couch. "He kissed me!"

Isolde gasped. "Don't do that! I thought you were in bed—he what? When? Where?"

"After supper. I offered to wash the dishes while he dried and he gave me this chef's apron that said 'King of the Grill'—"

Isolde held up her hand. "I'm late. I've gotta shower. Talk to me through the door."

In the bathroom, she stripped off her uniform and threw it in the general direction of the hamper. By the time she brushed her teeth the hot water reached the shower, and she stepped in.

"Curtain's closed," she called.

Noelle opened the bathroom door. "So he tied the apron on me and—"

Isolde squeezed shampoo onto her hair. "Back up. What did he cook for you?"

"Chicken and rice in mushroom sauce, salad, and white wine."

"Very nice. So he's not one of those no dancing, no alcohol, no singing, no fun preachers." Isolde rinsed her hair.

"Of course he's not. I wouldn't go out with him if he was. I like fun."

Isolde lathered her body. "Go on."

"So we talked about work and his church and making a Net business with the music boxes and lots of stuff."

"Does he have connections? Like with those three mega-churches in Boston?" Isolde rinsed off all the soap. "Maybe he knows a televangelist who needs a new knickknack to fleece the sheeple with."

"Stop it, Izz."

"Sorry. Bad day at work. Ines Jeffreys died."

"Oh, no. She was the sweetest thing."

Isolde turned off the water. "I've gotta get out. What time is it?"

A towel sailed over the shower curtain rod. "Eleven thirty-eight. No wonder you're on the anti-greed wagon. Her daughter was born with dollar signs for eyes."

"I'm going to dry my hair real quick. I'll be done in a second."

Even the blow dryer on 'high' only took out the worst of the water. Isolde gave it up and belted her robe. "Okay."

Noelle opened the door. "He wants to know if you'll play your cello for Thanksgiving."

Isolde scowled in the mirror at Noelle. "Don't rope me into church, please, Ellie. You know how I get when I'm around preachers."

"I told him, but I promised I'd ask anyway."

Isolde applied concealer and base and brushed medium rose blusher on her cheekbones. "Okay, you asked. Now tell me about the romance of washing dishes. How late is it?"

Noelle poked her head out the bathroom door. "Eleven forty-three. Wait—use the brown mascara. You want a warm look. And not the pink lipstick. Too light for this hour. Use the rose with the metallic sheen."

Isolde bit her cheek. "You sure?"

"You're dancing. It's nighttime. Wholesome is for work. Alluring is for studly cowboys." She followed Isolde into her bedroom. "So I washed and Stephen dried and we talked about cooking and our favorite foods and how he misses his mother's homemade bread. When we finished and I went to untie the apron, he reached around me and held my hands there behind my back."

Isolde stepped out of her closet in her underwear and pulled on the layered silk skirt. "Sneaky devil. Did you pretend to protest?"

Noelle stared at the ceiling. "Actually, I squeaked."

Isolde laughed.

Noelle stuck out the tip of her tongue at her. "He surprised me. I'd been thinking about kissing him and wondering if I should just step up and plant one on him. I didn't want to waste the opportunity, you know?"

"You hussy." Isolde buttoned the Kelly green shirt cuffs.

"He's a little shy around women."

"He's never made a move before? No way."

"No, of course not." Noelle pushed away from the wall. "He kind of hinted he ran wild when he was a teenager, and he learned the hard way to respect women."

"What does that mean?"

The doorbell rang.

"Eek." Isolde ran one hand over her damp hair and pulled a charm bracelet over her other wrist. "How do I look?"

Noelle was already at her side. "Face me. Good. Good. Here." She unbuttoned the third button on Isolde's blouse. "Cleavage."

Isolde glanced in the mirror and ran for the door. After one deep breath she turned the handle.

"Hi, Gavin." A gust of cold wind hit her. "Brr. Come in, I just have to get shoes and a jacket. Wow, you look nice."

"Thanks." Gavin followed her through the foyer and into the living room. "A pleasure to see you again, Ms. Robins."

Noelle beamed at Gavin when he took her hand. "Don't be so formal. It's Noelle."

Isolde hid her burning cheeks in the hall closet as she slid into her metallic gold three-inch heels. Why did she turn into a babbling idiot around Gavin?

She plucked a linen jacket from a padded hanger. Style before comfort tonight. "Okay, I'm ready."

Noelle opened the door. "She's working the same shift tomorrow, Gavin, so don't worry about bringing her home late."

"Shut up, Noelle." Isolde stepped onto the porch.

Gavin raised an eyebrow as he held out his arm for Isolde. "Should I worry that someone will be waiting up for you?"

Isolde humphed. "She just does that to make me go mental. I'll get her back when Stephen picks her up here for a date."

Gavin opened the passenger door of his Ram and kept his hand on Isolde's elbow. She chose not to admit that the running board would've been a challenge in these heels without him to balance on. She should've bought gel insoles. Her toes were getting squashed, too.

When they pulled away from the curb, Gavin said, "So Noelle's romance is heating up?"

"In a chaste manner."

He turned left. "I've never had the patience for a chaste approach."

"Oh?" Isolde nearly squeaked. Served her right for making fun of Noelle.

Gavin centered his left hand on the top of the steering wheel and grasped Isolde's hand in his free one.

She turned another squeak into a cough. From the way his mouth quirked, she didn't think he was fooled.

CHAPTER TWELVE

Gavin twirled Isolde on the dance floor and she skimmed back into step with him. The abbreviated Big Band changed keys for the last chorus of the two-step.

Retro Sundays at Wild Wharf never disappointed him. Seducing women to hip-hop wasn't beyond his abilities, but he infinitely preferred Big Band. After a Lindy, the woman always laughed and fanned herself and happily succumbed to an enthusiastic kiss.

Sweat, perfumes, and pheromones assailed him. This particular mix of odors in close quarters always clogged his nose. No one ever doubted his explanation of allergies. That amused him.

The two-step ended and a singer dressed like Frances Langford began 'Sweet Lorraine.' Gavin slid his arms around Isolde's waist and her arms settled around his neck. He pulled her close and steered her through the sparse crowd.

She still wasn't relaxed. Her spine was stiff, her neck tense, her breathing a little too rapid. Although the latter could be a result of three fast dances in a row.

Gavin reaffirmed his decision not to take an initial sip from Isolde tonight. In this state she'd be unreceptive to his simple hypnosis techniques. He wanted her tranquil the first time.

A woman who must have bathed in rose-scented musk glided near them. He angled Isolde to the left. She missed a step and murmured an apology.

With a throaty vibrato, the singer finished.

Over the applause, Gavin said in Isolde's ear, "Thirsty?"

"God, yes."

He led her to the art-deco bar and smiled at the tattooed bartender. "Two Long Island Iced Teas, please."

Isolde winced as she scooted onto a polished walnut bar stool. "Mr. Donne, are you trying to liquor me up?"

"My nefarious plot is exposed." Gavin paid the bartender and sipped his drink. With his body still replete from Judith's blood, too much of any food or drink would turn his guts into corkscrews.

Isolde's toes wriggled and the edges of her mouth pinched.

Gavin looked at the digital clock above the neon-framed bar mirror. "Would you like to call it a night, Isolde? It's after two."

"Well, yes, if you don't mind." She drank deeply. "That's almost as refreshing as real iced tea."

He nudged the cut-glass bowl of mixed nuts toward her and she picked out several pecans. "Thanks."

Gavin glanced at Isolde's feet. She'd curled her toes so the balls of her feet wouldn't touch the soles. If that was the cause of her tension, perhaps he should revise his estimate of the evening. He stood. "Pumpkin time, Cinderella."

She clenched her jaw and put one foot on the floor. He heard her sharp inhale despite her thin ruse of turning her head away to put down her drink. She tried to disguise a slight limp as they entered the coat alcove and shrugged into their jackets.

The November wind slapped them when Gavin opened the door. "Come on; the Ram heats quickly." He put one arm around her and hustled her between scattered cars and into his truck.

The engine caught. "There. We'll have heat in a few minutes."

Isolde nodded and started to curl her legs onto the seat. Instead, she smacked the bottom of one foot against the seat belt buckle and hissed.

Gavin hitched sideways to face her. "Isolde, what did you do to your feet?"

She worked a finger between her foot and her shoe. "I forgot how high these heels are. Nursing shoes are built for being on your feet all day, and I'm spoiled. These are practically f—" She clamped her lips shut.

Gavin bit his own lip so he wouldn't laugh at her. "I'd love to know why an angel of mercy by day would own a pair of 'fuck-me pumps.'"

Isolde muttered.

Gavin's ears caught it, but he kept a tinge of wicked delight out of his voice. "I beg your pardon?"

"I said, I bought them for the Valentine's Day Desperate Singles Mixer."

This time he did laugh. "That's how they advertised it?"

She shrugged. "No, but that's what it amounted to." With a twist, she put her back to him. "Sorry my shoes messed up the evening."

He touched her knee. "Give me your foot."

"Gavin, I'm not playing for sympathy."

"I know you're not. Foot, please."

Isolde squirmed around till her back rested against the door and both feet lay in Gavin's lap.

He ignored her puzzled, sort-of-hopeful expression and cupped one ankle in his hand. His other hand caressed her smooth calf and her entire body sighed. A task he'd considered difficult half an hour ago opened before him like the Yellow Brick Road.

He removed her left shoe. "Shall I turn down the heat?"

"No; it's perfect. My teeth finally stopped chattering."

He ran his thumbs up her arch and touched the balls of her feet. She whimpered.

"Relax, Belle Isolde. Let me dazzle you with my skilled fingers." He pitched his voice a touch lower than normal. Laying the foundation.

"This is sweet of you, Gavin." She flinched as he pressed a reflexology point. "Did your mother teach you to be this kind to the injured and imbecilic?"

He removed her other shoe. "I'm sure your brain functions quite well."

"Ow—sorry—my feet are burning." She tried to pull away, but he held her ankle. "Gavin, admit it. The only coherent sentences I've said to you were written five hundred years ago."

"Not true. When we danced at the fund-raiser yesterday you informed me in perfect, grammatical English that you abhor all things scary."

He stroked her ankle, then her calf, continuing a few inches above her knee. Her dark blue eyes, barely visible in the parking lot sodium lights, opened wide. He set down her legs. The flat three-part seat didn't give either of them much room to move, but he still got to his knees and overshadowed her. "I'm not scaring you, am I?"

"No. Well, maybe a little." Her words had a breathy sound.

Gavin lifted her by the small of her back. His fangs begged to penetrate her. Perhaps just a sample from her full bottom lip—no. If he tasted her now, he might not want to stop. He crammed his bloodlust into an inaccessible part of himself.

"Belle Isolde." He caressed her with his voice now. "I'm an actor, remember? If I want, I can project hillbilly." He chucked her chin and drawled, "Howdy, missy."

A smile began at the corners of her mouth.

"Or a stereotyped detective." He chose Basil Rathbone. "Elementary, ma'am. The butler did it."

"I always liked—"

"Or—" He balanced on one shin and stroked two fingers over her cheek and lips, "the romantic hero."

Her lips parted under his fingertips and he increased the warmth in his voice. "'Madame, I desyre no thynge but your own promise.'" He kissed her.

His hand trailed downward, over her neck, around the top curve of her breast. Her breath trembled in his mouth and he pressed his lips hard on hers. He moved his hand to the back of her head and slipped his fingers into her hair. Her body strained up to meet him.

God's blood, she tasted sweet.

Gavin broke the kiss. Archaic oaths were a sure sign his control was slipping. But why? He studied her face. A good face, but nothing earth-shattering. Long lashes, high cheekbones, straight nose, and those full lips. He'd known hundreds of women just as attractive.

Isolde opened her eyes and he smiled. "Any better?"

"You should give lessons." Isolde's brain appeared to catch up with her mouth. "I mean, I... yes, thanks. Still throbbing a little. My feet, I mean."

He laughed. It must be her mixture of innocence and experience. Ugh, now he was quoting Blake. Bizarre poet. Impossible to carry on a sane conversation with the man.

Gavin shelved the memory. "Then let me give them a little more attention." He resettled into the driver's seat and massaged her right foot. Not a twitch or whimper. His fingertips kneaded her toes one at a time. Like so many other meals over the centuries, Isolde purred.

He finished her foot with a light touch on her little toe. "Now I'm going to take you home."

Isolde's eyes popped open. "Oh—yes. It's late, isn't it?"

Gavin pressed the 'clock reveal' button. "Nearly three."

He occupied himself with his seat belt. There'd been a flash of something in her eyes. Disappointment, beneath the sensual relaxation? No, not just that.

"Belle Isolde, do you always get off work at eleven?" he asked as he pulled out of the parking lot.

She stretched her legs toward the still-blowing heat. "The first two weeks of the month, yes. The third and fourth I work the seven am to three pm shift."

"And this week is the first." He crossed the intersection to Summer Street. "May I put in a request that you don't volunteer for overtime on Wednesday?

53

"I can honor that request, Gavin—wait a minute." Her voice dropped from thrilled to serious. "What you quoted... I've been trying to place it."

"Yes?" He turned onto Pleasant Street.

"Shoot, we're nearly home. It's not Tristan speaking to Isolde. It's something about a knight, and Tristan ends up fighting him over her." She rubbed her temples. "I'm too tired. It's not coming."

"We're here." He pulled up to the curb and parked ten feet from the fire hydrant. When he opened Isolde's door and helped her to the sidewalk, her head only came up to his chin.

"Where are your shoes?"

She giggled. "In my hand. I'm not wrecking that great foot rub."

"You're going to freeze. Perhaps I should carry you to your door."

He replayed that last sentence in his head, then almost checked his shoulders for a good angel and an evil one. There could be no other explanation for that fit of chivalry.

"I'm a big girl, Gavin. I'll be fine." She turned her face up to his. "You could walk me to my door, though, if you're my Tristan for the evening."

As he kept a gentlemanly hand on her elbow up her sidewalk, he took stock of her attributes again. How was she different enough to inspire these impulses? By the time they reached her welcome mat, he decided it was the result of sanguinal and sexual anticipation.

He kissed her again under the dim porch light. Now that he'd put the evening in its proper perspective, his fangs were content to lie in wait.

CHAPTER THIRTEEN

Isolde shuffled into the kitchen. Obscenely bright sunshine filled the room, intensified by the yellow walls and white countertops. The sunflower clock's hands pointed to ten-thirty.

Why did Noelle have to open every curtain before she left for work?

Isolde filled the teapot and set it on the back burner. The tick-tick-tick of the electric starter didn't pierce her head as much as she feared.

Maybe she didn't overindulge last night. She never finished that second Long Island Iced Tea. Those God-awful shoes had fried her feet by then. Straight into the Goodwill pile with them.

She sliced a cinnamon bagel and put it in the toaster. A note with 'Read me' on it in block letters was taped to the tea canister.

'Hey, banana slug, I finished the wire frame for Gavin's angel. Get your rear in gear and record that song he wants. I can't start the papier-mâché layers till your music box thing is ready to attach. I expect all the date details after your shift—I'll wait up. N.'

The teakettle whistled. Isolde set an English Breakfast teabag in her Ariel mug and poured. The bagel popped while she searched the fridge—out of cream cheese again. They should buy the stuff by the case.

Isolde walked upstairs to the combination music room and library, bagel in one hand and tea in the other. Her feet burned only a smidge, cushioned by her fuzzy slippers and the ancient brown shag carpeting.

Mandolin for the song? No, not mandolin or guitar. Too light. It wanted drama. That eliminated the recorders too, even though performers in the 1600s would've used them.

The heavy lace drapes kept the room in a crimson Half-light. She pulled them open and all the instruments glowed in the flood of sunshine.

"Coasters… coasters… there you are." Isolde set her tea and dish on the fruitwood music shelf. "Let's see. Madrigals… too modern. Medieval polyphony… too old. Wake up, Isolde. Find the right music book… Here we go. Palestrina, Monteverdi… Ah. Gibbons." She carried the three-ring binder to the upright piano and opened the keyboard cover.

"Right, it's in C. Easy to transpose." Isolde played the melody with one hand and held her bagel in the other. " 'Drop, drop slow tears, and bathe'—wait a minute. I can double-stop this on the cello." She bolted the last piece of bagel and wiped her hands on the napkin.

Just as she got the D string tuned, Gavin's quote from last night clicked into place. She set the cello on the fake Oriental rug and grabbed her Malory off the middle bookshelf.

"There it is. I knew it wasn't Tristan romancing Isolde. It's that weasel Sir Palomides. All that sweet talk just to trick Isolde into his castle so he can rape her at his leisure."

She slapped the book closed. So that's what Gavin thought of her. All that foot rubbing and melting kisses had been the most transparent kind of ploy to get into her pants. How could she have missed it?

She pushed the book back into its alphabetical place on the shelf. Why was she so furious? It was one date. All she had to do was say 'no thanks' the next time he called.

But he wasn't going to call. He was picking her up Wednesday after work.

Damn.

Her sweatshirt pocket buzzed. She yanked out her cell phone and flipped it open.

A wavery, high-pitched voice blared from the earpiece. "Isolde, honey, it's Erma."

Isolde rolled her eyes to an uncaring Heaven and raised her voice two decibels above normal. "Hi, Erma. What's up?"

"A new sweetie came to my back door this morning. Can you stop at the pet store on your way to work and pick up a flea collar and two bags of Ocean Fish blend?"

Isolde moved the phone three inches from her ear just as Erma's voice softened. "Yes, you are a fluffy bundle of love. Yes, you can stay with us forever and ever. You'll love him, Isolde," her voice returned to its former shrillness. "He's tan and white striped and as soft as cotton candy. That's what I'll call him. Cotton Candy."

Isolde wondered how any self-respecting cat stood for being called a 'fluffy bundle of love.' "Erma, how many does this make? Twelve?"

"Thirteen, dear. You forgot little Punkinhead came to us last month."

"Animal Control isn't going to like it."

Erma made an unladylike noise. "Animal Control wouldn't like to know how many mice my babies catch each week. That industrial laundry next door is a public menace. The Department of Health deliberately ignores the vermin that overrun that eyesore."

Isolde heard Erma start to wheeze, her reaction to any mention of that particular governmental agency. "I'm sorry I mentioned it. I know you think the laundry bribes the D. O. H."

"I don't think, dear. I know they do. My hairdresser heard it from her daughter who heard it from the uniform delivery service man at the hospital." Erma's voice grew sickly sweet again. "Now, boys and girls, I fed you this morning. No more nummies till four o'clock. Isolde, you will remember the food and flea collar, won't you?"

"I'll be there at two-thirty, Erma. Make an appointment to get Cotton Candy fixed."

"My daughter already has him scheduled. 'Bye, dear."

Isolde leaned her head against the bookshelf. She loved her grandmother's school chum, but thirteen cats? She'd better get more litter and another cat box along with the food.

Her phone read eleven-thirty. She had to tune the A string and work up a double-stop harmony. Get something out of the freezer for Noelle to cook, too.

She took a pencil and a piece of staff paper from inside the harpsichord bench.

"If I start the soprano part on middle C I can play low G for the alto. Yes. Yes…" She drew a treble clef and thick dashes for the notes with her right hand as she picked out the tune with her left.

" '…and bathe those…' no, not E. 'Those beauteous feet…' "

Her hands stopped. Feet. Gavin rubbing the aches out of her feet. Gavin charming her with Malory quotes in that cramped truck. Kissing her. Getting under her skin like she'd never been near an adult male before. Erma's Cotton Candy call had made her forget.

Isolde slammed the pencil on the staff paper and ran downstairs to the telephone table.

"Denny's, Dhalgren, Dog Dates—" her finger paused at the top of that page in the phone book. "Are they kidding? Dollar Store, Dominic, Donne. There." She held her ringing cell phone against her ear while she stuffed the phone book back into the crowded drawer. "That's right, he lives on Rings Island. His house must have a spectacular view."

"It does. Good morning, La Belle Isolde."

Isolde gulped. "Uh, good morning." She couldn't let his magnetic voice distract her.

"I can't talk long. I'm just leaving for an appointment at the Historical Society."

Good. She'd have no chance to change her mind. "This'll only take a minute. I placed that Malory quote from last night."

"Ah."

Isolde swore she heard amusement in his voice. "Any particular reason you chose Sir Palomides' devious words to charm me?"

"Did I charm you, Isolde?"

"You know you did." Isolde gripped her temper with both hands. "Just how naïve did I look to you? No, don't answer that."

"Belle—"

"Kindly put a sock in it, Mr. Donne. Thanks for an enlightening date. I'm afraid I'll be busy Wednesday evening. Ms. Robins will deliver your angel in a few days. Goodbye."

He might've protested, but she closed the phone before the sound could reach her.

All the way upstairs and into to music room, her mouth wore an angry, satisfied smile no matter how many times she rearranged her lips.

CHAPTER FOURTEEN

Gavin slammed on his brakes. Damn the woman. That was the second red light he'd nearly run. What kind of repressed workaholic dumped a man after one date because he quoted a cryptic passage from obscure literature?

He should've fed on her last night instead of kissing her. He'd wasted a prime opportunity maundering about her innocence and admiring her lips. Hal's hormonal teenage actors were more aggressive.

A car horn honked behind him. His foot hit the gas pedal and the truck jerked forward. How long had the light been green? Damn the woman.

He screeched into the Historical Society's postage stamp-sized parking lot. An hour of pawing through marriage registries from the 1700s would clear his head. Maybe the anesthetic of work would dissolve this irrational anger as well.

As he walked up the Society's front steps, he formed his mouth into a polite smile. Only then did he open the door.

"Good afternoon, Mr. Donne." The Society's secretary, a retired and perpetually happy grandmother, flashed her dentures at Gavin.

He turned on his charm without thinking. "Mrs. Rhodes, I'm sure you have a Halloween photograph of all your grandchildren to show me."

"Mr. Donne, you really need to take the first step toward making your own grandchildren."

"But where would I find a woman with your background and common sense?" Not in a tall blonde's colonial house on Pleasant Street, that was certain.

Mrs. Rhodes turned her computer screen toward him. Five children ranging from three to ten years old grinned out at him, each one dressed as a character from the *Scooby-Doo* show. A stuffed Great Dane mask perched on the three-year-old's red hair.

Gavin rose above his simmering irritation. "Adorable and clever. Did you sew the costumes?"

"Indeed I did. They trick-or-treated in a group Saturday night. My neighbors are still complimenting me." She pressed a few keys. "Now, Mr. Donne, here's where you'll find a well-connected young woman. The armigerial records of Essex County."

Gavin held up his hands. "Mrs. Rhodes, you shouldn't be matchmaking on the Society's time. What will the treasurer say?"

She sighed. "You're right, Mr. Donne. Perhaps one afternoon this week. I can transfer this to my phone and show you the best prospects." Her dentures showed again. "The Society's Christmas Ball is only six weeks away."

He wasn't going to be able to maintain his façade much longer. "I'll think about it, I promise. Now I'm off to the sub-basement." He opened the elevator cage. "If I'm not upstairs by four, send in a good-looking nurse armed with Benadryl."

Her laughter followed him into the vintage Otis elevator. When it sank below the first floor, he dropped his cheerful expression. When the doors opened onto the sub-basement's maze of boxes, he freed the anger and ran his fist into the wall. His knuckles split.

"Damn! That was stupid." He was undead, not unbreakable. He shook out the pain and licked the trickles of blood. The skin closed a minute later as he walked the rabbit trail between the boxes, every twenty feet pulling a chain attached to a bare 100-watt bulb hanging from the exposed rafters.

The First Families' record boxes covered two pallets in the southwest corner. Gavin knelt in front of them and peeled open their curling yellow labels.

"Breed. No. Carlton. No. Webster. How did you get out of order?" He squinted at the bottom boxes. "And people think blackletter was hard to read. Friar Antonius should have seen an eighteenth-century bookkeeper's hand."

He stretched his spine. "Tarbell. Wednesday for you. King. No." The corner of the next label crumbled in his fingers. "Gow." He carried the box to the scuffed oak table next to a stack of smoke-damaged oil portraits. The diary on the top contained no useful information. Neither did the horse-breeding ledgers. Underneath them lay what he sought: A set of accountants' ledgers and a water-stained King James Bible.

"All right, Miranda Gow. Let's see if your great-grandfather was a rumrunner. Or your great-grandmother was an indentured servant who ran off with the family silver." He opened the Bible and inhaled mildew and stale cigar smoke. "Better yet, I sincerely hope your grandfather was a Nazi spy."

———

Two hours later, he opened the elevator cage onto the first floor.

"Mr. Donne, I was just about to come down there and look for you." Scooby-Doo's grandmother stood at her desk, sensible tweed coat buttoned and pillbox hat securely pinned. "It's two forty-five. Did you forget we close at three on Mondays?"

"I stopped my research to make sure I said goodbye to you." He reached for her hand, and saw the smears of dust and splotches of rust from rotting leather bindings on his own. "I'll keep my distance today."

"If you had a wife, she'd know the best way to get those stains out of your trousers, Mr. Donne."

Gavin's laugh almost sounded sincere. "I'll do my bachelor's best. See you on Wednesday."

He drove through a cold rain with the radio blaring death metal. Instead of distracting him, the tuneless, angry music fed his thirst. Isolde's house was only two blocks away. He didn't need blood today, but he wanted hers. He wanted to grab a fistful of her long blonde hair and yank her head back and expose her throat. He wanted to pierce her smooth neck and hear her gasp in pain and pleasure. He wanted to gorge on her sweet, rich blood like laborers at the end of a long day savored that first Guinness on tap at their favorite pub.

The light at the corner of High and Carter turned green just as his fangs tried to descend.

He stopped them. Gavin Donne, the actor, costume designer, and genealogist knew better than this. He needed to get home and remember who he was to the world.

He breathed yoga-style at the next red light. In, hold it, out. In, hold it, out. The idling high school buses hadn't yet left the parking lot. The crossing guards huddled in their Cavalier. No teenagers waited at the crosswalk to see him fight himself.

His was the only vehicle on Bridge Road. Ten minutes later he parked in his garage and listened to Chayyliel bark an ecstatic welcome.

That made him smile. He clicked his teeth. No sign of his fangs.

He pulled down the garage door and splashed along the slate path to the house. When he stomped the water out of his hi-top sneakers onto the mat, Chayyliel's paws hit the inside of the front door.

"Coming, Chay."

Chayyliel's giant Rottweiler-Shepherd forefeet crashed onto Gavin's chest as soon as he opened the door. He stayed upright this time. "I'm glad to see you too, boy. Stop barking in my ear." Gavin scratched Chayyliel's head till his ears flapped like helicopter rotors.

Chayyliel thumped onto the floor and dragged his leash off its peg next to the boot tray. With one bound, he landed at Gavin's feet. Ears at attention, teeth touching but not biting the leather, he turned enormous black eyes up at Gavin.

He laughed. "You want a walk, boy? In this rain? A walk?"

Chayyliel gamboled in a circle, barking through the leash in his mouth.

Gavin squelched across the floor. "Just a second. Let me put this in the den." The in-box labeled 'Hist. Soc.' on his birchwood desk overflowed with printouts from two-hundred-year-old newspaper files. Rolling file cabinets lined the wall beneath the octagonal window. He opened the middle drawer on the third cabinet from the left and slid a stuffed portfolio under the hanging files.

Chayyliel's nails tick-tick-ticked into the room and his head bumped the backs of Gavin's knees.

"All right, boy. The evidence is safe now." He hooked the leash onto Chayyliel's collar and let the dog drag him to the foyer.

"Let's go, Chay. I'm soaked anyway." He opened the door. "You can be the first one on the island to hear the story of Miranda Gow's great-great-grandfather, the slave trader."

CHAPTER FIFTEEN

Gavin set eight scripts on the coffee table in his living room at five-fifty p.m. Hal and his teenage protégés would arrive in ten minutes.

Medea in the Old West. Why did he want to twist this particular knife tonight? Why not make the class butcher Congreve's *Love for Love*? Or Wilde's *Importance of Being Earnest*? Or anything by Shakespeare?

He sneered at the image of Judith emoting her way through Lady Macbeth's 'Out, damned spot' monologue. She wouldn't consent to a lesser part among her peers, of course.

Chayyliel sniffed at the windowsills at the opposite side of the room like he expected to see flying cats peeking between the curtains. Gavin pushed one set aside. "No cats, squirrels, or rabbits encroaching on your territory tonight, boy." He tugged on the dog's collar. "Come on, Chay. The rain stopped, but it's too cold to tie you out back. You're in the basement tonight. Come on, boy."

Chayyliel whined when Gavin nudged him onto the basement stairs, but he obeyed.

"It's only every other Monday, boy. At nine o'clock I'll take you for a walk through the woods. Maybe the squirrels will get careless tonight."

Chayyliel barked and Gavin closed the door on him just as the doorbell rang. The community theater director pushed his way inside as soon as Gavin opened the door. Without his elaborate zombie hair and makeup, Hal King's floppy black bangs emphasized his unfortunate resemblance to a certain talkative television horse.

"Hey, Gav, tell me that's a gallon of French Roast I smell. It's freezing out there."

"Twelve cups as a start. Sugar on the table and milk in the fridge."

"Yeah, I know." Hal kicked his knock-off sneakers onto the boot tray and disappeared into the kitchen. "The gang's right behind me. The mutt's down cellar, right? Thanks."

"He's not a—" Gavin lowered his voice. "What's the use?"

Several knocks sounded on the door. Gavin opened it on a shivering bunch of teenagers.

"Hi, Mr. Donne."

"Hi, Mr. Donne. Where's Chayyliel?"

"Man, it's cold out here."

"Yeah, Stella's teeth sound like jackhammers."

"Shut up, moron."

Gavin indicated the room with a sweep of his arm. "Come in, everyone. I built the first fire of the season for you. Hot coffee and tea are in the kitchen."

Stella, looking like an average plump teenager without her Judy Jetson costume, left her sneakers on the tray and headed straight for the fireplace. "Mr. Donne, you're a mind-reader. This is the best."

Keith and Lorraine, sober and copping 'too cool to admit we're cold' attitudes, took a long detour to the kitchen. Gavin didn't miss the detour's proximity to the fireplace.

Judith followed two steps behind Superman and Wonder Woman—Ray and his sister Deborah.

"Good evening, Mr. Donne." Judith sashayed—there was no other word for it—up to Gavin and put a black-nailed hand on his arm. "Please allow me to thank you on behalf of all your willing and unwilling passengers Saturday night."

"It was the least I could do." Gavin moved to the coffee table fast enough to leave Judith's hand hanging where his arm had just been. Or perhaps she was holding the pose to emphasize a tragic solitude. He called into the other room, "All starving artists please vacate the kitchen," and perched on a barstool at the end of the coffee table.

Ray came out after the rest of the class, carrying two matched mugs. Deborah followed with a plate of frosted pumpkin cookies.

"Awesome cookies, Mr. Donne," she said, crumbs at the corners of her mouth. "You bake them?"

"Oh, please, Deborah." Judith sat in a relocated kitchen chair, hiked her black leather skirt, and crossed her legs above the knee. "Mr. Donne is patently not the domestic type."

"Oh, please, Judith," Deborah's always-happy voice did its best to drip sarcasm. "Since when did Mr. Donne make you his spokesperson?"

Hal's fingers stroked the back of Judith's neck before plopped into the easy chair at the other end of the table. "Claws in, kittens. Gavin, what are they working on tonight?"

Gavin showed all his teeth. "In honor of the cold weather, a night of cold reading."

Everyone groaned.

"Now, now, thespians. Slackers don't make it to Broadway." Gavin picked up his copy. "This play is *The Golden Acres*, the Medea legend set in the American West, circa 1890."

Silence.

"Please tell me one of you knows the story of Jason and Medea."

Stella said in a small voice, "She gave him the Golden Fleece and he married her, but then dumped her for a richer wife, so she killed their kids?"

"Excellent, Stella. That's the bones of the story. Now, with only that in mind, I want Ray to read Ezra—that's the Jason part. Judith, you read Molly—that's the Medea role. Stella and Deborah, look at Ma Strong and Ma Forrest—Ezra and Molly's mothers. Hal, you and I will read Pa Strong and Pa Forrest." The sound of pages crackling grew louder. "Lorraine, you read Agnes, the new wife, and Keith, you get to be Preacher Creed, the Greek chorus role."

"Aw, man, Mr. Donne. Preacher parts are so lame."

"Keith, never make assumptions. Act Three may surprise you." Gavin set down his script and headed for the fireplace. Poker in hand, he moved the screen and rearranged the three central logs. "Start reading, ladies and gentlemen. You have ten minutes before the Preacher's opening line."

———

Gavin let his mind wander Halfway through Act Two. Keith's Preacher was improving, but Hal had reminded Judith twice already to act instead of merely chew the scenery.

Lorraine surprised Gavin by her nuanced reading of the Other Woman. He raised an eyebrow in Hal's direction after her first scene with the Strongs. Hal mouthed, *I know.*

The thought slithered into Gavin's mind that perhaps Hal was doing some hands-on mentoring. He'd been tomcatting since his wife divorced him last spring, but Gavin thought he limited it to the Boston singles bars.

Lorraine and Ray stumbled through the wooing scene. Snickers erupted from script-shielded faces.

"Can it, people." Hal kicked Keith's chair and all laughter ceased.

"I'm nothin' like a preaching man, Miss Agnes," Ray said. "Them right-sounding words just don't show up when I need them."

"Mister Strong, I've listened to pretty speeches from self-important men since my coming-out party." Lorraine achieved the character's necessary balance between social status and courtesy. "I take your meaning quite well."

Gavin heard his Hannah's voice in that speech. Nothing ever took the sweetness from it—not even when thieves stole half their cattle and the bank tried to foreclose on the ranch. It had taken some creative lying to account to the bank manager for the gold he 'found' while hunting a week later.

Gavin read his character's next lines without attention. He'd been wrong about himself. Four hundred years roaming Europe and America hadn't taught him not to fall in love. It had taught him subterfuge—no one but Hannah knew he was more than Gabe Daniels, the cowboy turned cattle rancher. They'd kept it from the children, too. When she died giving birth to their fourth, he let Hannah's sister take them, and they lived out their lives in happy ignorance.

Scripts thumping onto the coffee table smashed that memory. He didn't object.

"Gavin, brew me another pot, will you?" Hal sauntered into the kitchen. The class scrambled for the fireplace—except for Judith, who stared out the window toward the dark river. Lorraine and Keith made a feint at the fire before heading to the back porch.

"Gavin, I'm dying for lack of caffeine." Hal's plaintive moan was probably meant to be funny. Gavin sighed and followed him into the kitchen, measured six scoops of coffee, and poured half a pot of water into the machine. "Good thing this break isn't long enough for Lorraine to need one of the condoms Keith keeps in her purse."

"Christ, are they groping each other in the living room?" Hal rinsed out his mug.

"They went out to the porch tonight. Happily for all of us."

"Idiots. One day they'll get stupid and the world will be blessed with a miniature Keith."

"Heaven forfend."

"Yeah." Hal poured milk into his mug. "Gav, about Lorraine. She's got some talent. You heard it tonight."

"Yes." Gavin took the mug from Hal's hands and slipped it under the stream of coffee.

"She's perfect for my new play. I need you to help me get her head out of Kevin's pants."

Gavin raised an eyebrow. "They're teenagers, Hal. It'll pass."

"This is my winner, Gav. I wrote the perfect play and she's part of my perfect cast. I have to have her."

Gavin switched the pot back into place and handed Hal the full cup. "Sorry, Hal. Not my department. It'll work out. Let's get through Act Three."

Hal sputtered, but Gavin turned his back on him and went through to the living room.

Gavin paid more attention to the last act. When he told Judith to stop screeching and feel the character's emotions, she chose to listen. She impressed him by the time the Preacher recited his Greek chorus to close the final scene.

"Judith, Ray, excellent work. Ray, I didn't know you had it in you to be such a shallow, smug opportunist. Judith, the speech over your children's bodies was light years ahead of your opening speech."

"Thanks, Mr. Donne." Ray gave his twin sister a one-armed hug. "Gawrsh, Maw, you're chock full of homespun advice tonight."

Judith stood and stretched her midriff in Gavin's direction. "I saw the wisdom of your advice, Mr. Donne."

Gavin looked at the rest of the class. "That, ladies and gentlemen, was a crash course in auditioning. If any of you are thinking about acting as a career, you'll spend half your life in cold auditions."

"Right." Hal gulped the last of his coffee. "You people think I'm the worst thing in a director's chair? I'm a teddy bear. Wait'll you hit the big time."

"Even before that, wait till you audition in Boston." Gavin gave them that toothy grin. "I once designed costumes for a Roaring Twenties *Hamlet*. You've heard of the Antichrist? Well, she directs gripping drama in Boston's Center for the Arts and she eats ingénues for lunch."

"The flaming bitch who wears stiletto heels and purple eye shadow?" Hal stood and cracked his back.

"That's her. I'm sure she teases her hair six inches high to conceal the demon horns."

"Mr. Donne, you're terrible." Deborah picked up the empty cookie dish.

Judith affected a sweet voice. "It's just his sense of humor."

The girl needed an old-fashioned beating with a razor strop. Gavin took a step toward her, but Hal jumped between them.

"It's been a long day, boys and girls. Thanks for another excellent session, Gavin. We'll be back in two weeks." Hal nudged Judith toward the coat closet. "The Directormobile is leaving in two minutes, everybody. Last call."

Voices that half an hour ago dragged Gavin back to his long-vanished Texas ranch reverted to nasal Massachusetts twangs.

Ray helped Deborah with her coat. Keith helped Lorraine and sneaked in a kiss. Stella, always thoughtful, took the last of the mugs into the kitchen.

Gavin waited by the door, the ignored teacher. Hal held Judith's black wool poncho for her. Judith crouched into it and raised her arms to let it drape into place. Gavin turned his head and saw Hal's arms wriggle underneath in unmistakable stroking motions. Judith smiled. Hal ran his tongue around his lips.

And Judith was on the Pill.

Hal put one arm around Judith and one around Stella and walked them to the door.

"Gav, text me your free appointment slots. We need to discuss costumes for The Play."

"You said that with capital letters."

"You know it. Did I tell you my grandmother's going to back it?" He handed Judith his keys. "Start the SUV for me, please, Judy. I'll be right out."

Gavin waited until they were alone in the doorway. "I thought your grandmother got diagnosed with Alzheimer's disease?"

"She did. But she's not gone yet, and she's ready for me to make the family name famous."

Gavin leaned against the doorframe, arms crossed. "And who convinced her?"

"Her youngest grandson, of course, who's also won most cold call sales honors three months in a row."

"Hal, you're a born telemarketer. Sorry. A born salesman."

"I am multi-talented." The wind blew between them, smelling of more rain. "Another New England winter begins."

"I'll text you." Gavin closed the door after him and leaned his forehead against the wooden panels, "Hal, you disgusting pervert."

Chayyliel clawed at the basement door.

"Coming, Chay." As soon as he turned the knob, Chayyliel leapt into the room and sniffed the door, the chairs, the boot tray, and followed his nose to the back porch.

Gavin chose his wool-lined leather jacket from the hall closet. "Ride, Chay. Ride."

Chayyliel abandoned any interesting scents and beelined for the front door. Gavin took his keys from the hook next to the retractable leash and they headed to the garage.

Chayyliel jumped into the passenger seat as soon as Gavin opened the truck's door.

Gavin turned the ignition. "All right, boy. Let's see if Hal is king of dirtbags as well as bad autobiographical plays. Maybe we can find enough evidence to head off his hostile takeover of his grandmother's life savings."

CHAPTER SIXTEEN

Gavin yanked the starter cord and his chainsaw roared. He revved it twice, its vibrating weight comfortable in his arms. To hell with Isolde. It would have been a sin for his neighbor to condemn this six-foot stunted pine to the Newburyport Highway Department chipper. A fat brown grizzly hid inside, inviting his chainsaw to discover it.

Heavy gray clouds covered the Tuesday morning sky and leftover wind from last night's tree-bending storm beat against his faded navy surplus pea coat. His knit Patriots hat protected his ears, although his hands were already chilled. The tool shed didn't block any wind; neither did the trees behind it.

He settled his wraparound composite safety glasses tighter on his nose and raised the chainsaw above his head. The blades carved a gradual twenty-degree angle from the top of the pine to a point two feet from the ground. Bark shrapnel flew three hundred sixty degrees. He made an identical cut in the opposite side.

Yes. The bear's pot belly should start right below that near-perfect knot. He curved the shuddering blades around the lower front of his bear.

Hannah had loved the rug they'd made from the pelt of that brown bear he'd shot their first winter in the cabin. She knew an infinite number of ways to cook bear meat. Hannah was one surprise after another.

Sawdust piled around him as he separated the bear's legs. He carved one leg wider than the other to hide the stainless-steel rebar supporting the wood. Even he would take awhile to recover from six feet of unbalanced pine crashing on top of him.

Pudgy feet grew out of the two-foot high circular base.

Their unborn baby loved roast bear with apples. Every time Hannah ate it, the little one spent the night kicking her. Gavin liked nothing better than resting his hand for hours on her thumping belly.

Working the saw around the wide leg, he gave the bear a droopy rump. The wind kicked sawdust against his face and he sneezed.

He'd spent most nights that winter regaling Hannah with colorful tales from all the religions he'd encountered in four hundred-odd years. The baby decided to arrive in the middle of February, of course, when six inches of ice coated everything for miles around the cabin. Not even the god-created horses of the Aesir could forge through a north Texas winter.

He was an old hand at delivering babies, though. When little Matthew squelched into his arms and he gave him a welcoming swat on the buttocks, Gavin's rush of happiness and pride was as vivid as the first time. It always was.

"Damn you, Isolde Connor." The oath spat from his cold lips. "I would've given you the best sex of your short life and we could've had children and a good fifty years together."

He revved the chainsaw and it kicked sawdust in his face again. Now for the bear's stiff tail, to contrast with the saggy rump. A gouge on either side and four swipes out and back, and a fat tail pointed toward the screened-in porch. Gavin stepped back, released the trigger switch, and kicked his way all around the tree-turned-bear.

He cocked his head at what would become the carving's head and ears. He almost saw a long tongue licking the unformed mouth. What was making his bear so happy? Berries? Too hard to carve. A beehive dripping honey? No... the tree didn't have the right shape anymore.

The wind shoved him, smelling of fish and diesel fuel from the charter boats. Of course—the bear had caught a big, plump fish for his big, plump belly.

Gavin twisted the 'off' switch. His arms trembled as he set the hot saw on the grass away from the wood chips and sawdust mounds.

"Good morning, fisher bear. Wish I had your fur today."

Chayyliel's barking gradually cut through the ringing in his ears. Who would be at his front door at eight in the morning?

He pushed his goggles to the top of his head and walked past the row of burning bushes between the house and garage. At first all he saw was a pair of legs in beige chinos. He craned his neck to see over the porch railing.

"Ms. Robins? Down, Chayyliel."

Noelle looked into the windows and raised to her toes to stare at the patterned frosted glass on the door. Chayyliel 'ruffed' and settled on the lawn. Gavin pulled off the goggles and waved them over his head. "I'm down here."

"Oh. Good morning, Gavin." Noelle came around and they met at the foot of the steps. "I brought your angel."

Gavin slung the glasses around his neck and opened the silver gift bag.

"The button is under here." Noelle pushed down the handle of a miniature wicker basket. Vibrant cello music filled the space between Gavin's hands.

"That's… amazing."

After the recording ended, Noelle said, "Cello is Isolde's best instrument." Noelle stopped talking and stepped back from Gavin's sawdust-speckled clothes. "What have you been doing?"

"Carving a bear." Gavin turned the angel over in his hands. "It's just the way I described him. Is this real hair?"

"I cannibalized two mink paintbrushes. Carving a what?"

"A bear." Gavin touched the water in the chalice. "A piece of mirror. Clever."

"Our angels and demons will be next Christmas' Tickle Me Elmo."

Gavin looked up from the angel's flowing white robe. "That won't happen at local craft fairs. You have a Website, right? How much traffic is it getting?"

She frowned. "Not much. My cousin designed it for free."

"And it looks like it?"

Her frown deepened. "Yeah. We'll never be able to quit the old people biz if we don't get a revamp."

Gavin set the angel back in the bag. "Come inside. I have The Svengalis' business card in my office."

Noelle followed him up the porch stairs. "You know the Svens?"

He held the door for her. "They did the community theater's new website in exchange for lifetime passes." He brushed most of the sawdust and wood chips from his clothes and hair onto the welcome mat.

"We owe you for this, Gavin."

"When you email them, use my name." He scraped his hiking boots on the wrought iron spikes next to the mat. Mud mixed with sawdust fell off in clumps and he finally followed her inside.

Noelle pressed her face against the living room's side window. "A piece of advice: Don't ever date a painter. When she sees this view, she won't stop till she marries you."

Gavin called, "Why?" while pawing through his desk drawers.

"To own half of this house. The light in this room is perfect."

Gavin found the holographic card and pushed the drawers to. "Then I won't get entangled with an artist." He crossed into the living room and stood next to Noelle. "Should I be grateful to Stephen for claiming you first?"

Noelle laughed. "I'm not an artist. I'm a businesswoman." She took the card. "Besides, you're Isolde's."

Silence.

"Um, Gavin?" Noelle stuck her hands in her herringbone-wool coat pockets. "What did you say to Izz?"

He leaned against the window frame, affecting nonchalance. "Why?"

"She's really ticked. She kept going on about a quote by some knight that wasn't Tristan, but I never understood the language in that book."

Gavin clenched his jaw. Impossible to explain.

Noelle put a hand on his sawdust-speckled arm. "We've known each other for twenty-five years. She's mad, but it's not a permanent mad, like with the drug guy."

Gavin straightened. "The what?"

"From the HMO. For her grandmother." Noelle gave him a 'don't be stupid' face. "Her grandmother had a stroke and then got colon cancer. Isolde quit college to be her full-time nurse. Toward the end, the only person she saw was the HMO's drug courier."

"Did he attack her?" Gavin suppressed the anger that appeared at the thought.

Noelle laughed. "No, sir. He was a wuss, and anyway, Isolde can handle herself. He asked her out to dinner and a movie. He took her back to his apartment in between—said he had a surprise for her. Then—are you ready? He came out of his room in drag. One hundred percent—makeup, dress, high heels, and a stuffed bra."

Gavin stared at her and Noelle laughed harder. "Gives you a brain cramp, doesn't it? Izz said he looked like Helena Bonham Carter with a five o'clock shadow."

"I—what did she do?"

"Thanked him for dinner and asked him to drive her home." Noelle looked at her watch. "I need to get to work. Ask her about it. She loves to tell that story."

"I'm not sure she'd be happy to see me." And that angered him as well.

"Come back to your angel." Noelle walked to the piano and plucked the angel out of the gift bag. "She recorded this after she blew you off, not before." She pushed the button and Isolde's lush music caressed Gavin's ears.

"Take your pick: Either she played this good to shove it in your face, or she played this good to…" Noelle cocked her head and gave him a wide-eyed stare.

"To indicate her phone call wasn't her last word?"

"Whatever you said, you could apologize, you know." Noelle set the angel in Gavin's hands. "Is there an apology from Tristan you can use?"

Gavin flipped through the *Morte Darthur's* eighth book in his mind. "There might be."

"Izz doesn't leave for work till two-thirty. I have a staff meeting at nine, though. Gotta go."

Noelle left him standing next to the piano with a ten-inch papier-mâché angel in his hands. He stared at the closed door and listened to Chayyliel's goodbye bark.

Isolde's music was too beautiful. Angry hands did not touch those strings or hold that bow. Gavin stared out the windows, seeing not the February day his and Hannah's first son was born, but the December day their last child arrived. Every night for forty years after that he dreamed of the baby's wide shoulders tearing Hannah's birth canal, of the gush of blood he couldn't stop, of Hannah's fading joy as he placed their daughter in her arms.

No. No more.

Gavin strode into the backyard and yanked the chainsaw's ripcord. The bear needed bent arms to hold a fishing pole.

He would ignore her sweetness. It didn't matter she could sing and play music from his youth.

He skimmed the blades over the top of the tree to make perky ears and a round head.

She'd be his new buffet. That was all. Last night's date laid the foundation for a long-term meal ticket.

The bear needed an open mouth and an upturned snout. He'd just caught a six-pound trout and he was hungry.

Gavin lowered the chainsaw and switched it off. That was Isolde's purpose. A meal with entertainment. They would trade Malory and Chaucer quotes, he'd use her, and feed. He had more than five hundred years of survival behind him. She had—what? Thirty.

A midnight snack didn't control him.

So why was he vacillating like one of his hormonal teenage students?

He flung the chainsaw onto the grass and went back inside for his truck keys. Sawdust puffed around him as he jumped into the driver's seat. He threw his goggles into the back and hurtled onto Friedenfels Street, testing Tristan quotes in his head.

CHAPTER SEVENTEEN

Isolde neared the end of Bach's *Brandenburg Concerto No. 3*, increasing volume and resonance at the *D.S. al fine.*

It was over. No, it had never begun. It was her own fault, anyway. If she went on dates once in a while instead of working more OT, she wouldn't melt for tall, handsome weasels who just happened to know medieval lit.

Her fingertips ached. Too much Bach killed. She knew singers who'd happily exhume his skeleton for the chance to pulverize it with the *St. John Passion* libretto.

She stretched into the third position at the allegretto eighth note run—and her A string snapped. The top half whipped across her cheek and ear and she almost dropped the cello. "Ow! Son of a gun." She set the bow on the rug and touched her stinging face. Her fingers came away damp with blood.

"Stupid string." She lay the cello on its side and headed for the bathroom.

The doorbell rang.

"Great." She stomped downstairs. Any Jehovah's Witness, even a comfy-looking grandmother, was about to get the door slammed in their face.

She banged open the deadbolt and yanked at the door. "Yes?"

Gavin pushed her backwards into the foyer and closed the door behind them.

Isolde shoved back. "What do you think you're doing?"

"Adults talk through their disagreements."

"We don't have a disagreement. We don't have anything." She looked at his boots. "You're tracking gunk on the floor."

"It cleans. Listen, Ms. Connor—"

"Now it's Ms. Connor? Think I'll fall for that since I saw through your Sir Palomides routine?"

"If you'd use your head instead of your mouth—" Gavin stopped and touched her ear.

"Ow—" She clapped her hand to the injury.

"What did you do to yourself? You're bleeding." He grabbed her shoulders. "Did someone hurt you?"

"Let go of me." She jerked away. "My cello string broke, that's all."

"Is your tetanus shot up to date? Where's the bathroom?" He pulled her down the hall.

She tried to dig her heels into the carpet. "It's only a scratch. Let go."

"Here it is." He dragged them both into the half-bath off the hall. "You're a nurse. You should know about infection. Where's the peroxide?"

"Not down here." She bumped her hip against his and knocked him off-balance. "The front door's behind you."

"Stop being stubborn, Isolde."

"Not used to women who don't stay puddled at your feet?" Blood trickled over her collarbone and she wiped it with her already stained hand. "Yuck."

"Damn it, woman, if you don't show me where the peroxide and bandages are, I'll dunk your head under the faucet and wash you clean myself."

That would be funny if she wasn't so annoyed. Isolde pushed him through the bathroom doorway. "Get out, Gavin." The door liked to stick, so she didn't slam it as hard as she wanted to.

The sink was only three steps from the door, and she turned both faucets on full blast. "Probably got blood all over the collar." She dragged her sweatshirt over her head. Her cell phone bonked her nose. At least she didn't throw the shirt on the floor and break her cell on top of everything else. She grabbed a washcloth from beneath the sink and looked in the mirror.

"Good Lord, no wonder he thought I got in a fight."

Isolde lowered the pressure and tested the water. Just hot enough. One squirt of aloe vera liquid soap lathered up the cloth and she wiped the drying stream of blood from her face, neck, and collarbone. A second rinse cleaned her outer ear and the mirror showed no remaining blood. She wriggled into her sweatshirt and opened the door.

Gavin snatched her on the threshold and kissed her.

She got purchase with one heel and levered herself backward. "Are you deaf? I said, get out of my house."

Gavin moved closer. Isolde took another step back and hit the doorjamb.

He was taller and stronger and she'd gone too far.

"Shut—" Gavin inhaled slowly and started again. "Please. Shut up and listen." He glared at the ceiling and dropped his hands to his sides. "That still didn't come out right. Isolde, I don't know why you're so riled over the Palomides quote, but you're reading too much into it."

"I might be naïve but I'm not stupid, Gavin. Men say what they think will get them into a woman's pants."

Gavin opened his mouth, but closed it again.

Isolde opened both hands in a 'see?' gesture. "So, thanks again for the evening out, I hope you like your angel, and will you please leave my house?" She inhaled particles from his shirt and sneezed. "What—" More flew into her eyes and she sneezed again. "What's all over you?"

"Sawdust. Listen, please, Isolde. Yes, I wanted you Sunday night." He stepped closer still. "Present tense: I still want you."

She sneezed again. "Stop moving; you're making a cloud of the stuff."

"So what? Will you listen? I want you, but not in Palomides' way. Out of context, his line is romantic and seductive. That's the way I used it." He put a hand behind her head—gently this time. "I'm sorry."

Isolde wanted to believe him. He didn't sound silk-smooth. He sounded like he meant the apology. She admitted it to herself: She played her heart into his music box. She wanted him to come back. And here he was.

Isolde met his oh-so-emerald eyes. "When ye lyst ye may come to me."

He stared through her a moment, then brought his face down to hers. "At alle tymes erly and late I wille be at your commaundement."

He kissed her. This time she pressed against him and opened her lips to his.

CHAPTER EIGHTEEN

Gavin worked the end of the chainsaw over the fishing bear's face. Away from everyone—especially Isolde—he argued with himself and his memories of Hannah, his last wife.

He should be satisfied. He would pick up Isolde after work and bring her here. They would dissect the latest *Tristan and Isolde* DVD and he'd seduce her into submission and arousal. Then he'd slip into her veins for his first taste of many to come. His tongue curled in on itself, anticipating. The scent of the blood running down her face earlier had almost sabotaged the apologize-and-kiss script he'd rehearsed in his truck on the way to her house.

People rhapsodized about the aroma of gourmet coffee. Coffee hadn't tempted him in decades, but the aroma of Isolde's fresh blood...

She was going to taste even sweeter than his post-Revolution pâtissière. Although Jeanne's gratitude at being spared the guillotine added a zest he hadn't tasted in blood before or since.

But Isolde reminded him of sweet, sensible Hannah. Not of Jeanne. Certainly not of his wild Giacinta, two hundred years before Hannah. What a stage actress she'd been. Everything was an adventure for her, including giving him her blood. They'd explored dozens of interesting veins for him to bite.

He released the trigger switch and the chainsaw idled.

He could not get attached to her. They all died. Breast cancer withered Giacinta at the peak of her career. The local surgeons were glorified butchers; he hadn't let them near her. In the end, when she begged him to drain her, he hid his grief and gave her a quick, pleasurable death.

Pleasure. Concentrate on that. Tomorrow maybe Isolde would succumb the way all his wives had succumbed.

No. Isolde was not going to be his next wife. No.

Foreplay before feeding didn't imply commitment to her. All it meant was enjoyment for both of them. He'd start with Isolde's lips, move across her cheek, and nibble her earlobe. Then he would strip her clothes and his a piece at a time, and they'd have sex on the rug in front of the TV, and he'd feed. That seduction sequence never failed. Hannah had loved it even after ten years of marriage.

Damn. Why did he keep thinking about Hannah?

He turned off the chainsaw and set it on the grass to cool.

Isolde had given him an accurate assessment of her character: she was naïve. Well, he would use that to keep her compliant and satisfied.

And that was all.

Above all, he would not become her Philippa.

CHAPTER NINETEEN

Isolde whistled 'A Spoonful of Sugar' as she wheeled the dinner cart out of the service elevator.

"That has to be Tinkerbell." The reedy voice carried through Room 217's open door.

"Got your favorite tonight, Mr. Stafford." She whipped off the metal plate cover with a flourish as she entered the room. "Pumpkin pie."

"My favorite next to you, Tinkerbell." The old man poked a finger into the whipped topping and popped it in his mouth.

"You just say that because you think I'll break down and sneak you some of my rum balls again this Christmas." She tucked a napkin under his chin.

"You will, won't you?" The old man lost his harmless leer. "I want to enjoy things while I can still remember them."

Isolde squatted next to his chair. "You're sharp as barbed wire, Mr. Stafford, and you know it. What's got you down tonight?"

"They moved old witch Annabelle King to the Alzheimer's floor this morning."

Isolde got a chill. Alzheimer's. There was no worse fate on the planet. "I didn't think she was that bad."

He shrugged. "She got to wandering at all hours. They found her in the janitor's closet this morning trying to take a bath in his hopper sink." He stared at his dinner. "It's Wednesday, right? I still remember what day it is."

"The only thing wrong with you, sir, is a pair of wandering hands." Isolde got to her feet and shook her finger at him. "Don't make me send my new boyfriend after you."

"I knew you were whistling for a reason." He picked up his fork and sniffed at a piece of meat loaf. "You tell him I can show him the best way to pinch an attractive hiney."

"He might be interested in my mind more than my body."

Stafford cackled. "Tinkerbell, you know damn well he wants to see what's under that proper nurse's uniform." He straightened his shoulders and stuck a fork into the pie. "Make sure his intentions are honorable, or I'll come after him."

Isolde pecked his cheek. "You're my knight in shining armor."

"Rum balls," Stafford said around a mouthful of pumpkin.

Isolde's whistle picked up at the third verse as she wheeled the cart toward the elevator. It cut off when she saw the two plainclothes cops standing by the signal buttons.

The freckle-faced male spoke first. "Ms. Connor?"

"Yes." Isolde kept the cart between her and them.

"I'm Detective Morgan and this is Detective Hill. We'd like a few words with you."

"Uh, sure. I'm done serving dinner."

"Is there a visitors' lounge on this floor?"

"Uh, yes—just to the left here." She pushed open the door and flicked on the light. Police? Why here? Why her? She couldn't act nervous. They'd think she was guilty. Guilty of what?

The woman—Hill—leaned against the wall beneath the artificial fuchsia. Isolde had the impudent thought that she didn't want to wreck the knife-edge crease in her black trousers. Morgan sat in a knock-off recliner. For someone who strutted like a stud horse, he sure dressed in a lot of pastels.

"How well did you know Edith Tarbell?"

Hill made Isolde feel like she'd just been called to the principal's office.

Uh—not as well as non-Alzheimer's residents." She ordered herself to stop stuttering.

"Why not?"

"She came from one of the old-school families. Then didn't socialize with the help."

Hill's lips unbent a fraction, then thinned into a straight line again. "And Ines Jeffreys?"

Isolde smiled. "Mrs. Jeffreys was a sweetheart. She always had a story to tell me about her great-grandchildren."

Morgan, who hadn't moved during this interview, uncrossed his legs. "I understand she had a large family."

"Three daughters, two sons, eight grandchildren, two great-grandchildren. But only her youngest daughter ever showed up here."

"Yet she and the chef were planning a huge family party for her ninety-fifth birthday now that her doctor stabilized her heart regimen."

Isolde shrugged. "Do you know who her oldest son is? Jeffreys' Consulting. The ones who gave the governor that image makeover and won him reelection."

"So it's all PR?" Morgan re-crossed his legs.

"Of course. But only for the adults. She was really looking forward to a roomful of grandkids for the day."

Isolde caught Hill's eye and it hit her that she'd been flapping her yap to the cops. Everyone knew cops always took the worst view of any situation.

Hill said, "Going back to the Tarbells for a minute. Did Mrs. Tarbell ever object to being taken care of by any of the staff?"

Isolde wasn't going to throw Lee under the bus just because Tarbell hated cigarette smoke. "I really wouldn't know about that. But I'm sure Ms. Emerson, the head nurse, can help you."

Hill pushed off the wall. "We'll see if she's available."

Morgan stood. "Thanks for your time, Ms. Connor." He followed Hill to the door, but turned back at the threshold. "I nearly forgot. Could you tell me what medications both women were on at the time of their deaths?' He pulled a phone from the inner pocket of his peach blazer.

She should probably answer. Act cooperative, not let on that they made her so nervous her hands were damp. "Mrs. Jeffreys was on digoxin and nitro. Her doctor had just prescribed something else, but I hadn't administered it on my shift yet." She closed her eyes and pictured the meds chart. "Mrs. Tarbell… nitro again, plus a calcium supplement, and…" Her eyes opened. "Sorry. There were at least two more, but I don't remember. She had trouble swallowing pills lately, so her doctor had switched everything to intravenous."

Morgan's stylus was typing at an impressive rate, A moment after Isolde stopped talking, he punched a key and returned the phone to his pocket. "Great. Thanks."

Hill said, "We may be in touch again, Ms. Connor."

"You know where I work." Isolde cringed. That joke fell as flat as it deserved.

She waited till the elevator closed behind them and dropped into one of the armless chairs. Her heart drummed like all the monkeys from *The Jungle Book* were practicing on it.

"They don't call the police for two nursing home deaths unless someone thinks they were murdered." She bit her lip. "This isn't *The Jungle Book*. It's *Cinderella* before the fairy godmother shows up."

CHAPTER TWENTY

Isolde closed the front door and kicked off her shoes, then almost jumped through the ceiling at the sound of a deep male voice.

"It's eleven-twenty on a wicked cold Wednesday night, jazz lovers. Here's a hot Ella Fitzgerald number to warm you up."

She shook her head. Noelle must've left the radio on. A moment later, her nose caught the scent of cinnamon. Ellie must have left a candle burning, too. Where was that girl's head at? She groped for the living room wall switch and flicked it up.

A flustered voice came from under the bay window. "Isolde—um—you're home."

Isolde fought to keep her face neutral as Noelle straightened her sweater and Pastor Stephen Oliver's butt muscles springboarded him to an empty couch cushion.

"It's nearly eleven-thirty, Ellie. Hi, Pastor." She shouldn't tell him about the smear of Noelle's lipstick on the corner of his mouth. Really she shouldn't.

"Good evening, Ms. Connor."

"Stephen's never had my Killer Brownies, Izz, and I knew we had a package in the freezer, so I invited him back here after the musical."

Isolde hung her coat in the closet and covered a guffaw. When she came out, her face showed only mild interest. "How was church?"

"Fun. You should've seen the kids singing *Wizard of Oz* songs with lyrics about Jesus. Just adorable."

Isolde swallowed a gag reflex and plopped into the armchair. "Sorry I interrupted this necking session."

"Isolde!"

"Ms. Connor, if you'd like us to move—"

"Oh, hush. And let's ditch the formalities, pastor. Especially since I think you're going to be around here a lot. I'm Isolde."

Stephen smiled at Noelle, then at Isolde. "I believe you're right. I'm Stephen."

"Good. And don't worry about me. I'm just resting my feet a minute, then I have to change. Gavin's picking me up."

Stephen gave her a strict-teacher look. "Will you be staying there overnight?"

Isolde couldn't reply for a moment. She opened her mouth to tell him where to get off, but considered how Noelle felt about this prig and chose a 'frost them with perfect manners' reply. "I beg your pardon?"

Noelle plucked his sleeve. "Stephen, Isolde's morals are not that loose."

Isolde frowned at him. "No offense, but I'm not your parishioner. And I'm an adult. My morals are my business."

Stephen inclined his head. "Point taken. But in my experience, the initial high of a new relationship can lead to a lack of common sense."

Isolde tried to hold back, but the laugh sputtered through her compressed lips. "I'm sorry, but that smear of Ellie's lipstick undermines your chastity lecture."

Noelle grabbed his head and giggled. "Here—" She wiped it with her fingers.

Isolde stood. "Stephen, I think you're just trying to be a good pastor, so let's call it a draw. Ellie, are there any brownies left?"

"Eight or ten."

"I'm going to take a few to see us through the movie. It might be bad enough to rate the MST3K treatment."

Stephen stood and took a few steps toward the kitchen after her. "Isolde, I was being officious. I apologize."

She turned and faced him. He looked like a puppy. A linebacker-sized puppy. And she wasn't really mad. "No problem."

He held out his hand. "Thank you. Noelle says you work only till seven p.m. two weeks a month. You're welcome to come to any of our evening services. We have a small prayer meeting after the Monday and Thursday Bible Studies. I think you might like it."

Preacher-itis reared its head. Isolde had known it was only a matter of time. She gave his hand a brief shake and took a step backward. "Thanks, but I'm not the churchgoing type."

Stephen closed the gap between them. "Then perhaps you'll allow me to pray over you, to start the evening with God's blessing." His hands touched the top of her head.

Isolde ducked out from under him. "Thanks, but I really have to get ready now."

She escaped into the kitchen, heart pounding. Holy crow, what was Ellie getting into? They needed a heart-to heart ASAP. In the meantime, hopefully Noelle would explain to him about the flock of vultures that came after Grandma in her last couple of months. Including Stephen's predecessor, the Bible-thumping slimeball.

She wrapped four of Noelle's signature brownies in aluminum foil and went out the opposite door and upstairs. Low-voiced conversation came from the living room.

Fifteen minutes later she came downstairs in her red sweater, black stretch jeans, and flat, broken-in ballet shoes. Her black burnt-velvet skirt lay across the bed, a casualty of a last-minute wardrobe decision. As much as Stephen's lecture annoyed her, Isolde wasn't sure how long she could resist Gavin. Tight-fitting jeans would at least make both of them pause and perhaps think.

Stephen and Noelle still occupied different couch cushions. Isolde remembered the nuns from high-school dances admonishing couples to 'leave room for the Holy Spirit,' but she didn't trust herself to say it without laughing.

The doorbell rang as she took her oversized alpaca wool sweater off its padded hanger.

" 'Night, you two." She paused with her hand on the light switch. "I'll turn out this very bright overhead light for you. Don't get up."

She opened the door and slipped out, glad she didn't ruin Noelle's evening by telling her about the detectives questioning everyone on Tranquil Grove's staff about Edith Tarbell's and Ines Jeffrey's deaths.

CHAPTER TWENTY-ONE

Isolde smiled up at Gavin from the welcome mat. Her flat shoes shrunk her several inches below his head. "All set. Just let me lock the door and we can go."

As soon as she dropped her key into her butterfly-patterned purse, Gavin's arms were around her. "You look lovely."

He kissed her. Fortunately—did she really mean that?—it wasn't one of his brain-melters. He stopped after only a moment and they walked to his truck.

"I brought some of Ellie's Killer Brownies." She stepped on the running board and he closed the door for her. When he came around and buckled himself in, he said, "An interesting name."

"Some ice cream company copyrighted 'death by chocolate' so we used our back-up name. She makes this to-die-for homemade chocolate frosting and shortens up the cooking time a bit, so the brownies stay soft. You'll love them."

Gavin looked less than thrilled.

"You're not allergic to chocolate, are you?" She'd never considered that possibility.

He pulled away from the curb. "No; not at all. I was just thinking. Do large dogs make you nervous?"

"No; I love dogs. We keep thinking about getting one from the SPCA, but he'd be alone most of the day and sometimes the night. It wouldn't be fair to the dog."

"That's good." He reached over and held her hand. "I have a very large dog. He looks frightening—which is an asset—but when he's not on guard duty he considers himself a one hundred fifty-pound lap dog." He released her hand to make the right turn onto Summer Street, then groped for it again.

Isolde relaxed into the seat as Gavin stroked the base of her thumb. "This is too comfortable to be a truck. I keep thinking it should bounce and squeak over every bump and pothole." What an inane conversation choice. Next she'd probably talk about the Bridge Road repairs and how they affected rush-hour traffic.

He glanced at her. "Isolde, why are you discussing my truck?"

She slid her eyes sideways at him. Did the man read minds? Or was she that obvious? "Because you make me shiver when you touch my hand like that and you know it."

"So four-wheel drive and shock absorbers are a ploy to distract yourself?" He tightened his grip a smidge.

She gave up. "How can you reduce me to idiotic conversation in two minutes flat? It makes me doubt I'm a professional, taxpaying adult."

"Then I'll release you and you can marshal your thoughts. I need both hands for this turn anyway."

The Ram bounced down Friedenfels, but much less than Isolde's Prius would have. Sparse streetlights gave her glimpses of dark houses separated by stands of trees. "You live out where the buses don't run, Gavin."

"I like privacy. I need the room for my sculptures, as well." He turned right at the very end of the street and pressed the garage door opener.

"You have to show them to me."

Gavin shut off the ignition. "Of course. But first you have to meet Chayyliel."

She unbuckled her seat belt. "That sounds like the name of another angel I've never heard of."

He didn't say anything until he came around to open her door. His puzzled expression made her think she'd somehow been the queen of cluelessness.

He held her hand as she climbed onto the cement floor and didn't release it. "How did you know that?"

"I guessed. You said you enjoyed hunting obscure angels."

His mouth turned up in a half-smile. "Where have you been hiding?"

"In the nurses' break room at Tranquil Grove?" Isolde grimaced. "That was a terrible joke. I'll stop talking now."

"All right." Gavin pushed her against the door until it closed and kissed her again.

She could've wriggled away, but why? She stopped thinking about anything but the taste of mint on his tongue and the downward movement of his hand.

Barking. She heard barking.

Gavin finished the kiss and stopped his hand's progress. "Chayyliel's getting impatient. He heard the truck."

"Introduce me, then." She pressed her lips together, tasting lipstick and mint and followed him along the narrow slate path. "Did you plant the burning bushes?"

"No; I'm not a gardener. There's Chay."

Isolde put a foot on the bottom porch step and lamps lit on both sides of the front door. "Wow. Now that's a dog." Deep barks vibrated the wood under her foot.

"Come on." Gavin stopped them on the top step. "Sit, Chay." The dog obeyed, barking once more. "Let him get your scent."

Isolde held her right fist with the back of her hand up under Chayyliel's snout.

Gavin nodded. "You know the strange dog drill. Good. Chayyliel, this is Isolde. She is allowed in the house."

Chayyliel barked and licked Isolde's fist, then bumped it twice, chuffing. Isolde brought up her other hand and scratched the dog's ears, then the back of his neck and his chin. "That's a good boy. Where's that ear? Is that the spot? Yes it is. Yes, that feels good, doesn't it?"

Chayyliel butted Isolde's knees with his massive head and she almost fell backwards down the steps.

Gavin caught her. "Chayyliel guards me from Gow the Cow."

———

The wind rattled storm windows on Gavin's back porch every so often as the evening passed. On the flat-screen TV, a scrawny Tristan clashed swords with his rival, King Mark.

Isolde snuggled closer to Gavin. "He doesn't look old enough to grow that beard."

Gavin stroked her arm. "I'm glad you prefer older men."

"Aha. Come clean, sir. You learned my age at our first meeting." She batted her eyelashes at him.

Gavin paused. "I admit to being over forty. Is that too big an age difference?"

"Nah. Once you're out of college, ten-year gaps don't seem to matter so much." Isolde reached for her tea and sipped. "Ugh. Cold." She replaced it on the coffee table next to Gavin's mug and the remaining brownies.

Gavin pulled her across his lap. "What a perfect straight line. Ms. Connor, since your tea is cold, let me warm you up." He leaned her head on his arm and kissed her.

She forgot the movie. She forgot that Gavin wasn't thrilled with the brownies. His hand kneaded her neck and his tongue pressed against her lips, seeking entrance. She opened her mouth to him at the same time his other hand came to rest on her thigh.

Out on the front porch, Chayyliel barked once. On the screen, actors screamed and swords clashed. The string orchestra neared a crescendo.

Isolde moved her own hand up to Gavin's hair. It did feel as soft and thick as it looked. She wove her fingers in it and touched her tongue to his again.

His hand left her thigh and moved toward her chest. She stiffened—should she let him?

He whispered, "Stop thinking so much, Isolde."

A reckless impulse almost made her direct his hand underneath her sweater. Before she could give in, his hand encircled her breast—sweater and all—and his teeth caught and held her bottom lip. She sucked in a breath and her nipples hardened.

Jeans had definitely been the right choice. A colorful, detailed movie played in her head about what his hands would be doing with her in that skirt. Every inch of her wanted this man to take her to bed.

Her inner prude said in a pinched voice, *"Not on the second date."*

Isolde agreed with her inner prude, as much as any of her thought processes were functioning at the moment.

And then Gavin did reach under her sweater—when did his hand move? His mouth left hers and his tongue tickled the hollow above her collarbone and she breathed, "Gavin—"

He paused and looked into her eyes. The corner of his mouth curved upward the smallest bit. All at once he slid out from beneath her and she lay prone on the couch, looking up at him. He lay full-length next to her and ran his finger down one side of her v-shaped neckline and up the other. "Should I stretch this beyond repair, Isolde?"

Her mouth said, "I—no—I like this sweater…" while her head said, *"Yes, yes, who cares about a piece of cotton?"*

"All right. The sweater shall remain inviolate."

She giggled. It had a breathy sound. "Sometimes you talk old-fashioned."

"An occupational hazard." Gavin grasped the hem of her sweater and pulled it over her head.

A plaintive alto on the television sang about love and courage.

Isolde started to move one hand in a "stop and think" gesture. Gavin pushed her breasts together—too small, why couldn't they be bigger—and buried his face between them. His mouth kissed her inner curves. Her arm fell away; her hand grazed the wood floor.

"Do you trust me, Isolde?"

Speech. She had to form words. "Yes. Yes, I trust you."

His mouth moved on top of hers, then over her cheek until his breath heated her ear.

Was he saying something? She couldn't quite make it out. His teeth touched her neck and she shivered. He stopped moving.

Her mouth didn't seem to be obeying her. Her lips hung slightly open; an odd languor flowed through her arousal.

Gavin took a shuddering breath. "As ye wille."

Her ears were playing tricks on her... it sounded like he lisped that "s."

He kissed the shell of her ear, her earlobe, her neck.

CHAPTER TWENTY-TWO

Isolde's blood gushed into Gavin's mouth. His fangs almost lost their grip on her neck.

Her flavor... Sweet. Delicate... He swallowed. Like jasmine tea.

Heat seeped through his body. Isolde shuddered under his mouth in rhythm with the blood pumping into him. Christ, he wanted her.

He sucked harder. Something about the texture of her blood... He tried to place it, but couldn't think with lusciousness flooding every nerve and taste bud.

Stop. Enough blood for now.

He got a grip on himself and extracted his fangs. His tongue licked the minuscule openings clean. Her eyelids fluttered. He whispered in her ear again, his voice barely registering any sound.

He licked his lips. He was going to feast on this exquisite woman for years. If he had to change his name again and move her to the most crowded city on the planet, he would do it. Toronto. Seattle. London. He could hide her in an attic, in a cellar... he would keep her in graceful nudity and teach her every sexual and bloodletting delight he'd discovered over the centuries.

He snatched away his hands. Dear God, what was he thinking? He was not a monster. Serial killers, serial rapists thought that way. He was... what he was. He fed only for nourishment. He made love only with his wives.

This had been a mistake. If he had any inkling Isolde would be so delicious he would never have pursued her. She was dangerous.

No… the truth. Face the truth. He was dangerous. To her and himself, if he couldn't maintain control. And to consider Isolde as a surrogate Philippa, even for a moment…

Isolde stirred.

Tonight was over. Any possible relationship might be over, too.

But could he give her up?

"Isolde." He kept his voice a shade above a whisper. "Isolde."

Her lips closed. "Mmm?" She opened her eyes and saw him. "Mmm." Her brow furrowed. She looked down at her semi-nudity and her face flamed.

He kissed her. "I won't listen to one word of embarrassment." Her retrieved her sweater from the floor and turned it right side in. "May I help?"

"I can dress myself." Her voice was almost steady.

He sat her up and slipped the sweater over her head. "It's more enjoyable together. Stop looking like the woman caught in adultery. Chayyliel is not coming in here to stone you."

She didn't quite smile as she wiggled her arms into the sleeves. When she finished, he said, "It's past two. Perhaps we should call it a night."

Isolde nodded.

Gavin touched her hands. "But not till I'm sure you had a good time."

Isolde finally looked straight at him, and he saw Bambi eyes in real life. He stood and pulled her to his feet, schooling his voice to just the right shade of lightness.

"Ms. Connor, thank you for a delightful evening." He turned off the television. "Come say goodnight to Chay."

He walked her through the house to the front door. She still wasn't comfortable—shoulders tight, trying to keep her body from touching his.

He retrieved her coat-like sweater from the coat closet. "Isolde, what's wrong?"

She stared at the frosted glass in the front door.

He waited.

After a moment her shoulders squared and she turned to face him. "Gavin, I acted like a slut tonight. I can imagine what you think of me." She shoved her arms into her sleeves. "It won't do any good to say I'm not easy, because my actions say the opposite." She bit her lip. "I understand if you won't be calling me for another date." She wrapped the oversized sweater without buttoning it and held her arms tight against herself.

Lust—and bloodlust—cleared out of his head. He embraced her tight enough so she couldn't squirm away.

"Isolde, never call yourself names again. You and I simply enjoyed exploring each other tonight. Adults are allowed to do that."

He bent his head—awkward, since she didn't even have her flat shoes on yet—and kissed her. With closed mouth, since the last thing she needed was to taste her blood on his tongue.

Her tension eased a fraction. She worked her arms free and returned his embrace. "Thanks for not taking advantage of me tonight."

His conscience clubbed him with a physical pang. "I'd never do such a thing."

God and His angels must be laughing at that sentence. Were he to drop dead this instant at Isolde's feet, Satan himself would rise through the floor to drag him into Hell.

He turned on the porch light and lifted his keys from the hook. Chayyliel started to bark.

"Someone's waiting to say good night."

Isolde smiled at last. "Next time I'll bring him treats."

CHAPTER TWENTY-THREE

Gavin paced his living room, eyes closed, every taste bud on the prowl. When he returned from dropping off Isolde, he'd walked Chay for an hour to clear his mind. Then he paced his house. Upstairs. Downstairs. Out to the yard, but without touching the chainsaw.

The elusive element in Isolde's blood wasn't drugs or alcohol. It wasn't anything as simple as an overindulgence in horseradish or a temporary excess of Halloween candy.

That ruled out acid reflux and diabetes. He also knew it wasn't an allergy or an STD. The latter was almost ludicrous. Isolde certainly wasn't a virgin, but it had been a long time since he'd encountered someone with such a healthy set of principles. Combined with her responses to him, well, he hadn't pursued a meal ticket like this in ⎯⎯⎯

Stop it.

He'd had principles once. No. He still had principles. He worked hard to maintain them.

After four hours, the different element in her blood was a heartbeat away from giving up its secret. Perhaps something in her past had changed it. Of course. He scrolled through possible childhood diseases and the chemical makeup fell into place. Leukemia. A long time ago; before puberty, certainly.

Gavin clenched his teeth. What an upright example of humanity he was. Filling his stomach on an unconscious cancer survivor.

He walked to the piano, still without turning on a light, and opened the keyboard cover. His fingers played several fragments of ancient music. Nothing fit. He banged both fists on the keys, wincing at the discordant jangle.

He kicked away the piano bench. It overbalanced and crashed to the wood floor, scattering music from the opened lid.

Musical laughter assaulted his ears. Despite his distraction and self-flagellation, he recognized it. Philippa.

"If you're going to haunt me, love, now is a bad time to start." His voice was raw and guttural. Would her ghost recognize it?

He was losing his mind. He didn't believe in ghosts, anyway.

Philippa's voice—silenced five hundred eleven years before—said, "Coward."

Perhaps he was wrong about ghosts.

He retrieved his navy peacoat. Morning sun flooded the room. A new day. Task number one: feed Chay.

Chayyliel's chain clanked along the front porch and he gave his "Strangers! Strangers!" bark.

The doorbell rang.

CHAPTER TWENTY-FOUR

Gavin opened the front door with one hand while adjusting the tie on his plaid bathrobe with the other. A man and woman stood at the far side of the porch, the former dressed like a cold-weather refugee from *Miami Vice*, the latter in tailored black trousers and jacket with a striped Oxford shirt.

"Gavin Donne?" The man raised his voice above Chayyliel's barking.

"Yes." He grabbed the chain. "Down, Chay."

"I'm Detective Morgan and this is Detective Hill. May we have a few words with you?"

Gavin kept his jaw from dropping like an actor in a slapstick comedy. What on earth? "Certainly. Come in."

He scratched the dog's ears as the plainclothes cops walked past his other side and entered the house. "Feed you in a little while, boy."

Chayyliel barked once and settled by the stairs with an old rawhide chew.

"I apologize for receiving you like this, Detectives." His peacoat, socks, and shoes lay in a heap at the bottom of the cellar stairs. His barefoot, bare-chested look fit the image of a man sleeping late and scrambling into his jeans ands robe to answer the door.

Hill gave Gavin a formal smile. "Don't worry about it. It's early yet."

"Thank you." Until he knew what they wanted, he played it neutral. "Would you like to sit in here? Perhaps in the kitchen?"

"The kitchen would be fine. That way?" Hill walked through the living room, looking around with a casual air.

She wasn't subtle enough to fool Gavin. He watched her hazel eyes assess his furniture, piano, and bookcases.

Gavin had tossed the branch out back when the bell rang. The floor in front of the glass bookcase was spotless, thanks to his spit-shine cleaning. He'd pulled a splinter from his tongue when he swished and spat medicinal mouthwash. Couldn't have his breath give them a whiff of blood when he spoke.

Morgan pulled out a chair for Hill, who gave him an arch look. Gavin catalogued them: long-standing partners, easy with each other's quirks, possibly sleeping together, although he had an idea that Morgan preferred June Cleaver-type women.

He didn't offer them anything to drink.

Morgan adjusted a lapel on his forest-green blazer. "I understand you work for the Historical Society."

"Yes. I do genealogical research."

"Exactly what does that entail? Looking through old boxes in attics?"

"No; it's much more than that, although I do spend a great deal of time in attics and cellars." He contrived a friendly expression without smiling. They would expect him to keep them at a distance. "The Internet allows me to track down distant relatives without driving hundreds of miles or flying cross-country."

"But you also do face-to face interviews, is that correct?"

"May I ask what this is about?" The faster they all peeled away the polite layers, the better.

Hill leaned an elbow on the table. "Were you aware that there have been two deaths at the Tranquil Grove Nursing Home this past month?"

Gavin let his honest puzzlement show. "I'd heard of one from Ed King, the community theater director. His grandmother is a resident. He brings our high school drama class to entertain them on occasion."

Morgan's eyes unfocused.

"I'd interviewed a woman there about her great-granduncle. He'd been a missionary and had written a popular, if inaccurate, book about the Inuits."

"Edith Tarbell. You spoke with her mid-September."

"Yes, that was her. I'm sorry, I don't quite see—"

"Ines Jeffreys died on Sunday. The doctors said it was a heart attack, but her grandson insisted on an autopsy." Hill played an excellent 'bad cop.' Her attitude could freeze lava.

Gavin leaned back in his chair. "Maybe it's just early, but I still don't see your point."

"You interviewed Mrs. Jeffreys two weeks ago."

Gavin looked at Hill's stiff, belligerent face, then at Morgan's—perhaps—candid one. "May I ask you to state clearly what you're implying?"

Morgan took over. "We received a tip that you had a connection with both deaths."

Would Gow go that far? Probably. She was his only real enemy in town. Well, then, had she been stupid enough to lay her 'vampire' accusation before the police?

Gavin weighed the risk and decided the vampire bait was worth a trial cast.

"May I ask if your tip came from Miranda Gow?"

Hill didn't flinch, but Morgan blinked and tried to cover it by running a hand over his glass-smooth blond hair. Gavin focused on him.

"Did you know that she lobbied the Historical Society for months to get them to give her nephew the research consultant position?"

"I did. My father's on the board." Morgan stared past Gavin's shoulder. "And?"

"Then he might have mentioned the nephew was expelled from Harvard for plagiarism, among other things. The day the board offered me the job, they also brought Miranda and her nephew in for an exit interview of sorts."

Morgan sputtered. Hill shot him a dirty look.

"Yeah, I heard about that." Morgan returned Hill's look. "She ripped the chairman a new one—if you'll pardon the expression, Donne."

Hill, without moving, somehow shouldered Morgan behind her. "You think Gow has it in for you?"

She could be brought to Gavin's side with this. He saw it in the way the corners of her mouth relaxed. He risked a friendlier expression. "Did she tell you she thinks I'm a vampire?"

Hill's lips twitched. "She might have mentioned it in passing."

Morgan leaned across the table. "She told us to check the autopsy reports to see if the two vics had puncture marks on their necks. And if they'd been drained of blood."

Gavin wasn't green enough to fall for his 'I'm your buddy now' act. "She's been harassing me since I got the genealogy position." He sighed.

"Any idea where she got the bloodsucker fixation?"

Gavin conveyed the impression of a shrug. "I'm an actor. I also design costumes. Last Halloween I took part in a charity monster musical down in Boston. Many of the audience members complimented me on my Dracula portrayal."

Hill snapped her fingers. "I saw that. That was you singing 'Everyone Needs a Renfield?'"

Gavin rolled his eyes. "Guilty. Hal King talked me into it. It can be easier to yield to his salesmanship than to spend your energy fighting him."

"You were good, Mr. Donne." Hill turned to Morgan. "It was this big musical comedy at the Center. Dracula here sang that song with the Mummy and the Wolf Man."

Gavin inclined his head in acknowledgement. "Dracula was merely a role, Detective. Not a career choice."

Morgan looked at Gavin but said to Hill, "Good enough to send someone like Gow off the deep end?"

Gavin said, "There was a party afterward. Did you attend, Detective?"

Hill shook her head. "I had to pick up the kids from my ex's house."

"Well, my date and I wanted a little privacy, so we found an empty office."

"You mean Gow walked in on you?" Morgan slapped the table. "That's rich."

Hill didn't laugh. "And your point is?"

"My date insisted I keep in the stage fangs and bite her." He kept his eyes on Morgan, stud-to-stud. "She said the fantasy turned her on. Unfortunately, I got carried away and drew a little blood." Gavin began a smile on purpose and stifled it for the same reason. "We both heard this horrible screech from the doorway— we weren't able to lock it, of course. At first I thought Miranda was simply pitching a fit over our... er... activity in a public place."

"Why would she care? Boston's not the center of her web."

"I didn't know that my date was her niece."

"Ouch," Morgan said.

"Yes. Several things happened at once. My date saw the blood dripping over her evening dress, slapped me, and called me a few choice names. By that time Miranda had run down the hall to the party, screaming 'vampire.' "

"And everybody laughed?" Morgan's cell rang. He flipped it open and walked into the living room. "Morgan. Good. Give me the gist of it..."

Hill remained silent until Morgan returned.

"Digoxin and Calphron IV."

"What's that supposed to mean?" Hill moved her eyes sideways toward Gavin.

Morgan passed some type of signal. Gavin missed the specific body language, but Hill unbent a fraction.

"Mr. Donne, as much as disagreeing with a Gow is bad for my blood pressure, you'll be happy to know she's wrong about you."

"I'm sorry? Oh. The two bodies."

"Yep. No punctures, and all ten pints of blood intact." Morgan flashed his capped teeth at Gavin.

"Then they weren't murdered?"

"Did I say that?" Morgan tapped Hill on the shoulder. "Nine o'clock. Pastor's free."

Hill stood. "You might want to see who your next date's related to before you screw her in public, Mr. Donne."

Gavin didn't react to such a deliberate tactic. "Good advice, Detective."

"And watch out for Gow. She's worse than one of those little rat-catching dogs. The kind that never let go when they catch something."

"Terriers," Morgan said. "You know it. She's also got a bug up her ass about her new pastor."

Gavin stood and moved toward the living room. "I saw her interact with Stephen Oliver at last Saturday's fund-raiser. She seemed enthralled with his every word."

Hill gave a short laugh. "That's an understatement. She wants his church to be *the* go-to place in town. My aunt dragged me there for her birthday. They're into all that raising hands, prophesying, talking weird junk."

Morgan made a gagging noise. "Glad I'm an atheist. What's Gow's stake in pushing it?"

"Power behind the throne, of course." Hill took a set of keys from her purse. "Thanks for your time, Mr. Donne."

Morgan followed. "We might need to speak with you again. Is there a good time to stop by?"

Gavin opened the door and Chayyliel jumped up, barking. Gavin held him back by the chain, deliberately standing in a bright pool of sunlight. "Quiet, Chay. I'm at the Historical Society most days from ten to three, and in the evenings I work at the community theater." He made a 'gotta pay the bills' gesture. "You're most likely to catch me here after four."

Hill shook his hand. "Okay if we meet you at the Society after working hours? Traffic on the bridge is a bitch in the afternoon."

Gavin stopped at the front door. "No problem at all. Just call my cell." He looked at the bristling, growling dog. "I don't have any business cards on me."

"That's okay." Morgan took another step back from Chayyliel. "Leave a message for either one of us at the station."

CHAPTER TWENTY-FIVE

Gavin turned onto I-95 South and turned up the volume on his Nat King Cole Christmas CD. He dropped the octave with practiced ease, blending his baritone with Cole's smooth tenor.

"Caroling, caroling through the snow, Christmas bells are ringing."

Everyone said early November was too soon for anything remotely Christmas. Not him. As soon as All Saints' Day hit, Gavin loaded up his house and car stereos with his extensive Christmas collection.

He still remembered wassail and roast boar on Christmas Day. And sneaking sugared ginger from the kitchen on Christmas Eve, even though everyone was supposed to be fasting for Midnight Mass.

"Ding, dong, ding, dong, Christmas bells are ringing."

He rolled down the window despite the 45-degree weather. What got into him last night? This was the twenty-first century, not the fifteenth. Yet he'd succumbed to archaic guilt like an ignorant scullery maid.

Friar Antonius, all those canings worked. You beat the Faith into me forever.

"Joyous voices sweet and clear, sing the sad of heart to cheer—"

Give up Isolde? What an absurd idea. She didn't remember anything from last night, and why should she ever know?

Twenty miles to Marblehead and a dwarf jasmine tree from his favorite garden store. He'd set it on Isolde's porch tonight while she was at work. The quote on the card should be something from Donne, not Malory.

He reached into the storage compartment between the seats of his truck and brought out a stained washcloth. Without taking his eyes from the road, he pressed it to his nose and inhaled. Jasmine mixed with an earthy scent. His tongue touched the dark red smear on the terrycloth. If an aroma could be swallowed, he'd just accomplished that feat.

Two reasons to be grateful for those detectives coming to visit this morning. He'd splashed a little blood on his neck overnight and had to wash it when they arrived rather than lick it. Now he had this infinitesimal taste of Isolde to arouse him at will.

And almost as good—from them he learned that Gow had upped the ante. He wasn't going to turn a cheek to that harpy. The Newburyport *Daily News* was about to get its story of the year.

"Ding, dong, ding, dong, Christmas bells are ringing!"

CHAPTER TWENTY-SIX

"I am quite capable of administering an I.V., Ms. Emerson." Isolde hefted the orange in her hand, mentally aiming it at Emerson's head.

Lee made a surreptitious pitching motion with her own orange. Isolde relaxed her grip on the needle in her right hand before she snapped it.

The head nurse glared at them. "Every member of the staff is reviewing procedures today. Ms. Connor, Ms. Davis, please demonstrate the correct technique. Ms. Davis, please describe the process step by step."

"Blah, blah, blah," Lee breathed. Then in her regular smoke-roughened voice, she began, "First, wash your hands."

————

"Hey, Phoebe," Isolde said a few hours later, "I just finished setting up meds. Can you take them around? I have to get Stafford out of P.T."

Phoebe sashayed up to the meds cart. "I think I'll just double-check these." Her tight, false smile belied her fluting voice. "No one can be too careful around here." She took the chart from its hook.

Isolde choked on the insult Phoebe deserved.

Phoebe shook pills into her freshly manicured hand. "I heard everyone's assessment on Pleasant Street went through the roof.

Guess that's why you're working so much overtime. Those bills do pile up."

Isolde turned her back on Phoebe and met Ms. Emerson's thoughtful gaze.

The head nurse came all the way into the room. "Is everything on schedule?"

"Just finishing a double-check," Phoebe said in the same bright voice.

"You're welcome to triple-check the meds if you'd like," Isolde said.

Emerson glanced at the neat rows of paper cups, at Phoebe's smile, at Isolde. "I'm sure you two have things in hand. Carry on."

Isolde kept her back straight and her face blank as Emerson passed her and turned right toward her office.

"So are you going to administer meds?" Phoebe said.

Isolde breathed through flared nostrils. "I'm not feeling too well, Phoebe. I'm going to head home. Guess you'll have to do it."

Isolde dipped her long-handled spoon into the pint of Chunky Monkey ice cream and scooped up another mouthful. On the television screen, the singing lobster from Disney's *The Little Mermaid* failed for the first time to make her smile.

The ice cream wasn't doing its job either.

A chunk of fudge dropped on her brown yoga pants. She swiped it off, chewed it, and crossed her legs. It was weird being home at seven p.m. on the wrong week of the month. Isolde had never wanted to slap Phoebe more than when she'd poked her manicure into the med cups.

She shoved the cardboard lid onto the circular ice cream container and tramped into the kitchen. The spoon hit the sink with a *clank* and the freezer door shuddered from the impact of the half-empty pint carton. Porking out on ice cream and watching feel-good movies wasn't going to solve her problems.

From the other room, Ariel mooned over the unattainable prince in her lilting voice.

Isolde wanted Gavin.

For the tenth time in half an hour, she picked up the cordless phone to call him. And for the tenth time, she set it down without dialing.

They'd be talking about her in the break room. Lee would wonder if there was a connection between the cops and 'always there Isolde' suddenly getting sick. Phoebe would jump on that and tell everyone, "Hasn't Isolde looked a little—not that I harbor a smidge of suspicion myself—a little guilty lately?" Or she'd substitute 'suspicious' or 'furtive.'

Lecherous old Mr. Stafford might be the only one who'd speak to her tomorrow. Why couldn't the police have showed up on Friday and given everyone the weekend to get it out of their systems?

What if the police really did suspect Lee and Phoebe and her and everyone else on staff? Who'd want to kill these old people?

Now she was being stupid. The residents had money. They had to, to pay the fees Tranquil Grove charged. That also could mean they had greedy relatives who didn't want to wait for them to die naturally.

Her hand rested on the phone, fingers drumming. *No, Isolde.* No self-respecting adult woman goes running to the new guy in her life with every whiny little insecurity. Guys hate being bothered like that.

The Sea Witch's voice gave Isolde the creeps tonight. Isolde pressed two buttons on the clicker and shut her up. Man, but some of those villains gave her goosebumps. Give her the Disney princesses any day.

She turned the remote in her hands. Gavin wasn't scary at all. He liked to startle her, but she figured it was just his way. Guys and excitement—make the girl cling to you. But not too much— no one liked Velcro girls.

She wished Noelle would get home from church.

Church.

Who listened as well as a pastor? Stephen must be different from the leeches and shysters who'd come after Grandma's money—even if he was a little too hands-on for her taste. Noelle had good taste, plus she'd heard all Isolde's stories in painful detail. If she wanted Stephen, he must be worth trusting.

Before she could second-guess herself, Isolde slipped into her running shoes, grabbed her purse and keys, and locked the front door behind her.

CHAPTER TWENTY-SEVEN

Isolde turned the handle of the Newburyport Church of the Nazarene's front door. Unlocked. Weren't these people worried about thieves? She opened it onto a dark and deserted foyer. Maybe they'd quit for the night.

She walked in, the indoor-outdoor type carpet muffling her footsteps. A couch jumped in front of her leg and she shoved her face in its cushions to muffle her curses. Foul language in church wasn't the way to endear herself to the pastor.

When her shin stopped aching, she opened the double doors on the right. A vacant sanctuary. Even her breathing echoed. It must have a vaulted ceiling. Was there anything creepier than an empty church that should have a bunch of people praying and such?

She felt her way across the lobby until her sneakers squeaked on linoleum. Stale coffee and old popcorn odors hit her nose a second later.

Kitchen. Wrong way again. How high were their electric bills that they couldn't even leave a forty-watt lamp burning on a table somewhere?

She turned toward the lobby again. Now that her eyes were used to the dark, she saw a strip of light at the end of a long hall to her left.

"Just as I am, thy love unknown hath broken every barrier down..."

Isolde jumped, What kind of church meeting scared people in the dark like that?

She followed the song, waiting for her heart to stop dancing a jig.

"O Lamb of God, I come, I come."

A deep male voice spoke after the song finished. She couldn't make out the words, but she recognized it as Stephen's. Hopefully they were winding this session up.

"O for a thousand tongues to sing my great Redeemer's praise…"

She avoided a rickety table covered with papers, a kids' charity donation box, and a telephone. When the third verse started, she leaned against the wall just out of the light and sighed. By the fifth verse, she was drumming her fingers on her arms.

"…to spread through all the earth abroad the honors of thy name."

Metal chairs clanked and squeaked as the singers shifted position. Finally. Isolde raised her hand to knock.

A man started to speak. Isolde inched closer. What language was that?

"Praise Him for his great mercies toward us." A different man. "Let everything that has breath praise Him." That sounded like something out of the Bible. Maybe they were doing multi-lingual Bible Study tonight.

"When the day of Pentecost came, they were all together in one place."

That was Stephen. If he was one of those repetitious preachers, this might go on forever. Maybe she should just slide into the room and wait in a corner. A non-member's presence might make him keep it short and sweet.

She peeked inside. Six gray folding chairs in a tight circle held two men, a woman she didn't know, Miranda Gow, and Noelle. Stephen stood behind Noelle, his hands on her head, his eyes closed, his face toward the ceiling.

"…All of them were filled with the Holy Spirit and began to speak in other tongues as the Spirit enabled them."

Noelle raised her head and... sounds came out of her mouth. Like language, but Noelle didn't know any foreign languages. Unless being able to swear in French and Japanese counted.

Noelle raised her hands, palms up, and kept making the sounds. Tears started to run down her cheeks.

Isolde ground her teeth. What was Stephen doing to her? Some kind of mind control game? Damn all scheming pastors to hell.

Isolde had her hand on the door, ready to slam it open and wreck this cozy cult initiation, when Noelle stopped speaking and Gow leapt to her feet.

"Your holy people desire to do Your will, Lord. Give us power to serve You."

A chorus of "amens." Noelle clapped her hands over her mouth and looked up at Stephen.

He shook his head and urged her to her feet.

"Let it out. Don't be afraid to praise God with this gift He's given you, Noelle." He gestured to the rest of the circle to stand. "Rejoice with our sister in Christ, everyone."

Noelle raised her hands high and spoke those sounds again. Before Isolde could take a step forward, all six of them started making those language-y sounds.

Isolde stared like she was rubbernecking at a traffic accident. They didn't all make the same sounds, but no one said a single word in plain English. Noelle hadn't looked this ecstatic since... Isolde couldn't come up with a comparison.

She stared at Stephen for a moment, trying to block out all those distracting word-noises. He wasn't watching Noelle like he was making sure the mind-control was taking effect. He looked like... who was it... he looked like Isolde's oldest brother when he was ordained to the priesthood. Filled with an overwhelming happiness Isolde still couldn't fathom.

Stephen and Noelle and the rest of them were—praying, she supposed—with closed eyes and upturned faces. Gow's mouth made the noises too, but with eyes slitted open just enough to watch what everyone else was doing. Her smile didn't reach past her lips, either.

Gow's head turned toward the door and her eyes narrowed further. Isolde ducked out. Too late, she was sure—nothing escaped Gow on the prowl.

The noises went on. It was like tuning into a radio station from another country—Isolde had no idea what she was listening to. And Noelle was part of this unknown… thing.

Isolde heard Stephen's voice louder than the others, then softer. Then Noelle started singing in a happy, weepy voice. It didn't sound like Noelle. It wasn't Noelle—it was some force that had taken her over.

Gow's voice joined hers—hard and cold. Noelle laughed—not at Gow the Cow. She laughed with joy—and kept singing.

The hall was darker now that Isolde had been looking into the lighted room. She tiptoed to the far end and into the lobby, arms outstretched. Once she touched the couch, she ran around it and out of that nuthouse into a safe, normal night.

CHAPTER TWENTY-EIGHT

Gavin set the potted jasmine on Isolde's front porch and tucked a square white card into a forked branch. He hadn't considered this before, but he hoped she liked jasmine. Not because he was courting her. Women liked flowers. Simple.

Besides, jasmine was 'her' flower. He knew that without doubt.

The town hall clock struck nine. Isolde wouldn't be home for two hours, but the plant wouldn't freeze. The weather had mellowed and the night wasn't cold enough.

He wouldn't have been able to control himself if delivered this in person. She'd say some variation of, "It's beautiful; what a surprise; thank you." And he'd say, "If you really want to thank me, take me up to your bed."

It wasn't just her body he craved. Or her blood, which surprised him. He wouldn't need blood for three more days. It was her naiveté. Her humor. The way she baby-talked to Chay, who ate it up. The way she throbbed in his hands. He was starting to obsess; his control should be better than that. He should care only for his next taste of her blood, their next romp in bed.

He should go home right now.

As his foot touched the top step, Isolde pulled into the driveway.

He cursed. He should sneak away.

She didn't get out of the car. Her head rested on her hands at the top of the steering wheel. Her body shook.

Gavin shoved lust and cynicism aside and ran down the three porch steps to the driver's side door.

"Isolde."

She jumped back and screamed.

Gavin opened the door. "Isolde, it's me. What happened? Why are you home? Were you in an accident? Are you hurt?"

Isolde pushed him backwards. "Don't do that!"

He crouched next to her. "Answer me. Why aren't you at work? What happened?" She looked all in one piece, but her hands were trembling.

"I left early. It's bad over there. The cops are making us all suspect each other." She grabbed her purse and got out. "What are you doing here anyway?"

"I was—"

"Sorry. I'm really not in the mood for a date." She pushed past him, but he grabbed her arm.

"Tell me what happened at work to get you so upset."

"It's not just work. It's—forget it." She twisted and he released her. "I'm not a clinging vine. Go home."

He followed her anyway. "Isolde, wait."

She climbed the steps and pulled the switch on the porch light. "Look, Gavin, I'm really bad company tonight. The cops think one of us killed Ines and Edith and Noelle's gone all crazy over at church—" She saw the jasmine plant.

Her hunched shoulders eased a bit. "Is this from you?" She touched one of the blossoms, white and glowing in the moonlight.

"Yes."

"It's beautiful." She put her face into the center of the flowers and inhaled.

He cursed again. She was following the script. He would not tell her he wanted to kiss her lips, her breasts, her———

A flower came off into her palm. She tucked it above her ear with one hand and took out the card with the other. "'Send me some honey, to make sweet my hive/That in my passions I may hope the best.'" She looked up at him. "Well, Mr. Donne. What should I think of this?"

The strong scent of the flowers and the sight of the fragile white petals in her hair—and that last taste of her blood in his truck— Gavin yielded.

He pulled her to her feet and kissed her. Tonight she tasted of chocolate and bananas—how odd—and yes, the barest hint of jasmine.

Her arms clutched his shoulders and her hard—fearful?—kiss shredded his tenuous resolve. She was afraid of something other than him. She wanted him. Without hypnosis. She wanted him for himself.

He pulled back from her mouth and took her keys from her hand. In a moment he'd locked the door behind them.

"Gavin—"

He put his arms around her waist. "The correct response to a gift from a gentleman is 'Thank you.'"

Isolde caught a breath and smiled. "Thank you, Gavin."

His mouth came down on hers before he could say the next line in his fantasy script. She squeaked and her lips moved like she was trying to say something else.

He placed his hand between their mouths. "Belle Isolde," he murmured, "if you're afraid I'll think you're wanton," he tickled her ear with his tongue, "let me explain that between two adults," he sucked her earlobe and she gave a little whimper, "wanton is delicious."

Gavin pressed his lips on the side of her neck, her collarbone, along the collar of her sweatshirt. That wasn't enough of her skin. He wanted more.

He couldn't scare her. Couch. He'd with the couch.

He opened one eye and located its shape underneath the bay window. She couldn't see in the dark like he could, so he led her around the coffee table and onto the cushions.

She clutched his shoulders and kissed him again. Her fear was still there. She didn't kiss like this at the Halloween party or in the truck. Afterward. He'd get it out of her afterward.

He put his hands on her sweatshirt. "Shall I?"

Was she blushing?

"I'm, um, not wearing a bra."

Blood flushing her cheeks made her too tempting to resist. "Good." He pressed her backwards onto the couch cushions and covered her mouth with his.

He wriggled his hand between her legs, but her odd stretchy pants wrinkled under his fingers and he couldn't do much. Apparently Isolde didn't require much, because she responded in only a few moments.

Gavin kept his mouth on hers until her breathing slowed. When he raised his head, her eyes were open and not quite focused.

"Isolde."

He placed her hand on the rock-hard bulge in his jeans and she blushed again, but found the zipper pull.

She stopped.

"What?" He kept the frustration out of his voice.

"Church—I don't know what time it lets out."

"What? Who cares?" His encouraged her hand to pull the zipper down.

"Noelle." Isolde swallowed. "She could come home anytime."

The only part of his brain not clamoring for sex heard something wrong in the way she said 'Noelle' and 'church.' Later. He'd get details later.

"Bed, then, Belle Isolde." He pulled them both upright. "I want you right now. I'm going to get you naked and make you scream for more."

She bit her bottom lip and the mischievous look on her face surprised him.

"I dare you."

His zipper popped open two notches. God in Heaven.

She took a step toward the stairs. "Follow me."

CHAPTER TWENTY-NINE

Gavin didn't give Isolde a chance to turn on a lamp or take down the sheets. The half-moon shining through the open curtains filled the room with more than enough light.

They sat on the bed and he pulled off her sweatshirt, then his sweater.

Her dark, dark blue eyes appeared black in the moonlight; her blonde hair tangled around her shoulders. She glanced down and her hair brushed the top curves of her breasts.

Gavin stroked her hair and continued the caress down to her small, round breasts. "I love how you are shy and sexy at the same time."

He had to have her. He had to have her now.

He fingered her soft, clinging pants. "Lay back. I want to see you." He climbed between her legs and stretched her pants out over her hips—slowly. She looked at him through a curtain of hair and smiled.

The next moment, he bunched the material in his hands pulled it down to her knees, then over her ankles and off. Her socks, too.

Bikini underwear. Pink. He couldn't rip it—she didn't like to be scared. No violence.

When he started to remove the last barrier, she said, "Gavin, I'm, well…"

"Yes?" He kept easing her underwear off.

"I'm not a virgin. I mean, I haven't slept around, but—"

The thin bit of pink cotton reached her thighs.

"I'm not a virgin either, Isolde. Now that we've confessed all—" He flicked her underwear onto the floor and ran his hands in between her legs.

Isolde reached for his zipper. "Your turn." His jeans were around his knees before he knew what happened.

"You have to move or I can't take them off. Those plaid boxers, too. Thank you."

They hit the floor behind him and there he was, naked, with a flagpole an inch from Isolde's face.

He had to take control. She was supposed to be mindlessly moaning. He'd planned it that way. Then he stopped thinking, because her throat opened and she swallowed nearly all of his length. He panted and grabbed her hair and moved his hips in time with her mouth.

Soon, too soon, she pulled away, working her jaw from side to side. "I'm sorry, Gavin, my muscles hurt."

He sat on his heels. "Are you saying I'm too big?"

"Don't look so smug, mister. You had nothing to do with it. It's genetics."

He laughed. How long since he'd laughed during sex? Two hundred years, at least. "Are you complaining?"

"No."

"Good." He parted her legs and inhaled her scent. "Let's see if I'm too big for a different opening."

"Gavin, that's vulgar."

He laughed again. "Lady, you have no idea how vulgar I want to get with you. I'm going make your brain melt."

The best part of simultaneous sex and feeding was his inability to produce sperm. Only after the infusion of new blood did his testes produce sperm for a single day. Safe sex defined.

He stopped.

He drank her blood yesterday..

"What's wrong?" Isolde put her hands on his butt, urging him in.

He sat back. "I don't have a condom."

Isolde blinked.

"Do you or Noelle have any in the house?"

Isolde's head thumped into her pillow. "No. Not since last year."

"Damn. Damn." He could kick himself. He'd been so sure she would be at work. He certainly hadn't thought things would get this far this fast.

Isolde groaned. "That was incredibly bad planning, Mr. Donne."

Gavin wasn't going to waste this opportunity to tie her to him. He'd pleasure her and take three cold showers later if he had to. So he covered Isolde's naked body with his own and kissed her. "I'll make it up to you tomorrow, Belle Isolde. Tonight let me do what I can."

He spread her open and thrust his tongue in her mouth and his finger inside her. Her eyes glazed. He ran his tongue inside her mouth and across her lips, still pumping his hand. Small noises sounded in her throat and her muscles clutched his finger.

God, he wanted her.

He withdrew his tongue and opened her legs wider. Isolde made a frustrated whimper, but his mouth found the right spot and the whimper changed caliber. His finger still in place, he kept the rhythm for no more than thirty seconds. Isolde's body stiffened, then she cried out, bucking her hips against his face again and again.

A minute or so later, he removed his hand and lay next to her. "Until tomorrow, when I promise I'll be prepared."

Isolde took a deep, long breath. "No."

Gavin paused. "No?" What had he possibly done wrong?

"I mean, it's your turn. I'm not leaving you like that." She leaned on one elbow and dragged his hips over to her mouth.

Her head pumped in the same rhythm his hand had used on her; she sucked him harder, harder. The fraction of him that still could think remembered his girth was too much for her jaw to sustain long. When he reached the limit of his control, his body clenched, released, and he came. He clutched the comforter while his semen shot into her mouth, groaning as she swallowed the last of it. She sucked one final drop, then lay back, face still flushed, lips swollen, eyes languid.

Gavin flopped sideways next to her and pulled the other side of the comforter over them. She didn't speak, but he could read her expression: sated yet the smallest bit embarrassed at her own actions. He ran his hand over her breasts, hips, and thighs, caressing her. She purred when he ran his fingers over her lips.

A contradiction lay next to him. His contradiction.

He'd lost the battle. She was not going to be his next unending buffet. He would find a way to ease her into the knowledge of who and what he was. Times had changed. She wasn't doomed to be another Hannah.

But children were far into the future. Acclimating her to the terrifying part of himself, well, that was a different battle strategy. Tonight, now, he capitulated with grace.

"I'll pick you up here tomorrow at eleven-thirty and we'll go to my house and make love wherever you would like. The bedroom, the back porch, in front of the fireplace."

"Mmm. Power over a powerful man. I like that." She looked straight at him. "Gavin, are you sure I didn't—"

"Stop. Don't say it."

Hannah would approve of Isolde. So would Giacinta—Isolde was like both of them. Demure and erotic. How odd. How fascinating.

"Isolde, you amaze and delight me. Never forget that." He kissed her and sat up. "Before we go downstairs, fully clothed and respectable once again, may I use a washcloth?"

CHAPTER THIRTY

Gavin sat at the kitchen table while Isolde brewed coffee.

"Was the male detective dressed like he stepped out of an '80s time warp?"

Isolde set two mugs on the counter. "Yes. You know how on TV cop shows they talk about partners playing good cop/bad cop? He played the good cop. I kept thinking I should trust him but my gut told me it was all an act." She spooned sugar into one mug. "How did you know about him?"

"They paid me a visit early this morning. Of the two, I preferred the Ice Queen. She broadcast hostility in high definition."

Isolde didn't laugh. "Why did they come see you?"

"My bête noire, Miranda Gow. She never misses a chance."

The coffee stopped dripping. Isolde turned off the machine and poured. "What's up with her anyway?"

Gavin shrugged. "She wanted her nephew to have my job. She harassed the Board of Directors at the Historical Society for months."

"They didn't give in to a Gow? I'm impressed." She set a mug in front of him and sat kitty-corner at the table. "You must've wowed them with your résumé."

"I have experience." He wrapped his hands around the mug. The coffee smelled rich and mouthwatering. "It helped that Gow's nephew was expelled from Harvard for plagiarism. And hacking into the school's server to change his failing grades. And participating in a hate crime."

"Holy crow." Isolde sipped her coffee.

Gavin lifted his steaming mug, sipped, and swallowed. French roast. "Good coffee."

"Thanks."

He could manage to finish half of it to please her. "Is this where I say you have an abundance of talents?"

"Don't change the subject." She scowled at him. "Are you in trouble? Do they really think you're connected to the murders?"

"Not really. They interviewed me because no one ignores a Gow."

Isolde drank. "What did Gow say to them about you?"

"She told them I'm a vicious, undead monster who preys on the weak and drains their blood."

"That's ridiculous." Isolde stood and opened the refrigerator door behind him. "They paid attention to that nonsense?"

Exactly the reaction he expected from her. "Not really. Now, this being New England, if she told them I was a witch—"

Isolde closed the refrigerator, a quart of 2% milk in her hand. "Oh, please. This is the twenty-first century." She poured some into her coffee and held the carton toward him. "Milk?"

"No, thanks." His gut clenched at the thought.

She paused with her hand on the half-closed spout. "Wait a minute. You said 'Not really.' You mean the cops actually listened to her garbage?"

"I don't know." He gave her a censored version of the incident with himself and Gow's niece. "Detective Hill appeared to dismiss Gow's vendetta after I explained about the stage fangs. I'm not sure about Morgan."

Isolde put away the milk. "In other words, she's really the good cop? That'd make him the bad cop under his 'I'm a regular guy' attitude. I can see that." She kept one hand on the door handle, tapping her fingers. "I have an idea. Wait here a sec."

She ran upstairs and down again a minute later. "Here."

Gavin held out his hand and Isolde dropped a silver crucifix in it. Only centuries of training himself kept him from flinging it across the room before it singed his hand. That and his ingrained reverence for the Image it bore. Ten seconds later, his palm was still cool. How interesting.

"What's this?"

"It was my grandfather's. It's white gold but it looks like silver, doesn't it?"

He studied the half inch-long icon. "You're right. It looks like silver." That's why his hand wasn't smoldering. If it had been, what a rousing end it'd would've given to this conversation.

"You could wear it and if they start bugging you again, you could, I don't know, casually let it fall out of your shirt." She shrugged. "If anyone's stupid enough to believe the vampire thing, they'd know better when they saw you wearing that."

Gavin didn't move. Of course he could wear a crucifix. He'd done so for decades in different monasteries, albeit on the outside of a habit or cassock. Wearing one against his skin for longer than a few minutes, well....

"Don't you like it?"

He looked up at her insecure face.

She spoke before he could answer. "I'm sorry, Gavin. Are you Jewish or atheist or something? I didn't mean to offend you. I was just trying to help. I'll put it away." She tugged at the dangling chain.

He pulled her onto his lap. "I was just surprised. I'd love to borrow your grandfather's crucifix for the duration."

She shook her head. "No, no, I'm giving it to you. I mean, if that's okay."

What irony. He wished he could tell her his entire story. All five hundred plus years of it. But one look at his fangs and she'd run out of the house screaming.

"It's more than okay. Thank you. I was raised Catholic, although I haven't been to Mass in years." He held it up. "Why don't you put it on me?"

He bent his head as she draped the chain around his neck. The infinitesimal weight of the crucifix settled above his heart. So many memories. So many places and names and years of coping with Philippa's choice for him.

He had to stop obsessing about the past. This was now. This was Isolde.

He touched the crucifix and smiled at her.

That wasn't enough. He grasped her head and pulled her mouth down to his. He tried to make it a chaste kiss, but the spearmint mouthwash taste still on her lips reminded him why she rinsed her mouth earlier. His tongue touched her lips and she growled—yes, she did—and opened for him.

"Ahem."

Isolde's head jerked up. "Ellie—you're home."

Noelle set her purse on the table. "Why are you home, Izz? It's only nine-thirty. Hi, Gavin."

"Once the police left, you could cut the suspicion with a scalpel. I couldn't deal with four more hours of poison, so I faked emesis."

"Wow. For you to ditch work it must've been pretty awful."

Isolde took an unobtrusive deep breath. "How was church?"

Noelle's face practically glowed with happiness. "Amazing, Izz. Wonderful. Something I never expected."

Isolde's shoulders went rigid. Gavin rested a hand on one and kneaded it discreetly. Isolde didn't relax.

"Glad you had a good time."

Noelle didn't react to Isolde's stiff, wary voice. "I see you two are busy, so I'll make myself scarce. Just let me grab the rest of the coffee—is that okay?"

"I'm good. Gavin, you want more?"

"I'm fine, thanks."

Noelle poured it into a Winterfest mug and added sugar. "Don't stay up too late, kids. And remember to leave room for the Holy Spirit." She left the room, her laughter echoing behind her.

Gavin snuggled Isolde against his shoulder. "What happened at church? Were you there too?"

Isolde jumped off his lap. "Not here. I don't want Ellie to hear me. Come out to the porch—no, wait. It's too cold. What about your truck?"

"Isolde, if I get you that close in private again tonight, I will not be responsible for my actions." That earned him a real smile, not that tight, fake one she gave Noelle. "Don't you have a downstairs room with a door?"

"Just the cellar." She stopped as Noelle's footsteps went along the upstairs hall.

Gavin leaned through the archway between the kitchen and living room. "Noelle!"

More footsteps, and she leaned over the upstairs banister. "Yes?"

"What's the best room for Isolde and me to neck in without disturbing you?"

Isolde squeaked. "Gavin!"

Noelle laughed like a ringing bell. "The music room. It has a door and my room is separated from it by her bedroom and a bathroom."

"Thank you, ma'am. We're coming up."

"I'm disappearing." A door closed on another laugh.

"Gavin, what are you—"

"I am getting us a modicum of privacy in a warm environment. If you'll lead the way?"

CHAPTER THIRTY-ONE

Isolde closed the music room door.

This was ridiculous. Her job was hell, her best friend had turned into a religious nutbar, and she'd just acted like a porn slut on the third date.

She'd awakened in a parallel universe this morning. That had to be the answer.

Gavin raised the keyboard cover and played several chords on the harpsichord. "Excellent sound."

Isolde perched on the edge of the flowered armchair while Gavin examined the shelves of music and plucked the mandolin strings. He got her attention when he picked out "Puer Natus in Bethlehem" on the keyboard.

"You know some obscure music yourself."

"I told you. Research is like collecting baseball cards or playing the slots. Once the bug gets you, you're infected for life." He segued into "I Saw Three Ships."

"Isn't it a little early for Christmas?"

He looked embarrassed. "You've exposed my secret vice. I'm a Christmas elf. It's all I listen to from November first through January sixth." He started another verse. "Wait till you see the house decorations next week."

Gavin was beyond charming. If Isolde wasn't careful, she'd tell him she loved him.

Did she? Of course not. She'd known him less than a week.

Gavin finished the song and came to tower over her. "What are you thinking about, Belle Isolde?"

All the blood rushed to her face. What an idiot she must look like.

"I was, well, I was thinking about..." Oh, just say it. "Tomorrow night." Her ears sizzled, they were so hot. How could he want such an inexperienced, flat-chested, uptight old maid?

He squeezed next to her in the wide, sagging chair. "Isolde, you're driving me insane. You don't know how much you excite me."

"I think I can tell." She rested her hand on his—upper—thigh. Welcome to an evening with her inner slut. She was dying to get her hands on him again. And get his hands on her.

Well then, she should tell him. What was the point in keeping it to herself?

"I want you, too, Gavin." He kissed the back of her neck and she shivered. "Want you something wicked."

He kissed around to her earlobe and nibbled it. "Let's not wait till tomorrow. Come home with me tonight. The Rite-Aid is open late. We can stop for supplies on the way."

She could. She was an adult capable of making her own decisions.

He nibbled her shoulder through her sweatshirt. No other guy ever made her shiver like that. "Tell me how we clicked like this, Gavin. Tell me why."

He stretched her collar and kissed her bare skin. "I don't know. But I've learned not to argue with it when it happens." He brought his face up from her neck and met her eyes. "If it wasn't too soon, I'd ask you to marry me."

She swallowed. "If it wasn't too soon, I'd accept."

What did she just say? Had she lost her mind?

He leaned back into the chair. "What am I saying? You could be a possessive, domineering spendthrift for all I know."

She poked a finger at his chest. "You could be a psycho ax murderer in disguise."

"Or a vampire."

"Nope." She hooked the pointing finger in the chain around his neck. "You're a good but lapsed Catholic, just like me. Of course, you could be a closet transvestite." She let the chain drop. "That reminds me—no promises until I look through your underwear drawer."

He laughed. "Noelle told me that story. I wish I'd been there."

Gavin put an arm around Isolde and angled them sideways in the chair, hip to hip. "Tell me what happened with Noelle tonight."

Once Isolde started, it all came out in a rush. The dark church. The tight circle of chairs. The not-language. "It was like something took over Ellie and she loved every minute of it. It scared me, Gavin. Church shouldn't be scary." She tried to shake off the creepiness. "Or it shouldn't be unless you're waiting in the Confession line and you've done something that ten Hail Marys and ten Our Fathers won't fix."

Gavin stroked her hair. "Sweetheart, sometimes church is the scariest place you'll ever see."

She turned her head and kissed him. She shouldn't be so comfortable or secure in his arms. They'd only met five days ago. Life didn't hand you that kind of gift.

He put his hand over her lips. "If you do that again I'm going to rip your clothes off and take you on that comfortable-looking throw rug. So please don't." He clenched and released his fists. "I can tell you what happened at that prayer meeting tonight. It's called speaking in Tongues."

"You mean like on the Jesus-freak channel? I saw it once: they had this gaudy stage set and a woman in a long dress was rolling around on the floor, shouting something. I thought she was just from a different country."

"I can't vouch for the TV types, but it's a legitimate phenomenon. I've seen it for real in churches like Stephen's. Very low-key, not meant to impress anyone." He got a faraway look in his eyes. "I wonder what it would be like to be invaded by God like that."

"I don't." He didn't seem to hear her. "Earth to Gavin."

He blinked. "I heard you. It can be frightening to watch until you understand it."

"I don't understand it. You're right about that. Do you think Stephen is trying to control her with this ultra-religious stuff?"

"No. He's one of the few pastors I've met who care more about God and his parishioners than about power and increasing the Sunday morning head count."

Isolde sighed. "I'll have to talk to her about it tomorrow morning. Maybe she'll be less glowy at seven a.m. Did you see her face when she came in?"

"That's a normal reaction to an intense religious experience. The initial rush will settle into the task of incorporating her new dimension into everyday life."

"Yeah, well, I liked the old three-dimensional Noelle."

Gavin laughed. "Did anything else trouble you tonight that all-powerful Gavin can fix?"

She started. "I almost forgot. Gow was at that prayer meeting, but she acted different from the rest of them. They all looked like they didn't know anyone else was in the room, like it was only them and God." She swallowed. "Man, Gavin, that's just creepy. Anyway, Gow looked more like she was studying everyone else on the sly."

"Learning a part?"

"Yes. Just like that."

"I wonder. Good Cop and Bad Cop said that Gow was trying to make Stephen's church into her personal power trip. This could be her way of getting into his good graces." He made a spitting noise. "Faking spiritual gifts for power. The woman always finds new ways to disgust me."

Isolde leaned into his chest. "Can we stop talking about Gow and how she's screwing with both of our lives?"

Gavin put his arm around her. "Absolutely. Let's talk about you getting into my truck and coming home with me."

Isolde traced patterns on his leg. "I want to, Gavin. But this little voice is telling me we're moving too fast."

"Hit your inner mute button."

She laughed. "Seriously. I get this feeling that if I go home with you tonight I won't want to leave."

"Good. I have a large, comfortable bed, lots of closet space, and Chayyliel already likes you." He laced his fingers into hers. "Unless you expect me to marry you before you move in."

People didn't have this kind of *Alice in Wonderland* discussion on the third date. Isolde and Gavin were definitely in a parallel universe. So she should come right out and say what she was thinking. "Actually, yes. One of the lessons drilled into me was 'marriage before cohabitation.'" Isolde traced a different pattern with her free hand. "Another one was 'no sex before marriage,' but times change."

"All right. I'll talk to Stephen and see if he's free next Saturday."

She laughed. "Of course. Why not? I promise not to sign up for overtime."

He wasn't laughing.

She looked him in the eyes. "Are we really having this conversation?"

He still didn't smile. "Yes, we are."

Now she was weirded out again. He couldn't be serious.

She squirmed out of the chair. "I think we should call it a night, Mr. Donne. We've strayed from the path of common sense."

He stood and stretched. "If you say so, Ms. Connor. Will you see me to the door?"

They walked down the stairs in silence and Gavin kissed her in the foyer—a plain, simple, friendly kiss.

Later, Isolde lay awake in her bed that hadn't retained even a faint impression of Gavin's body or a trace of his aroma. That last kiss had proved their talk of marriage and weddings and moving in was just banter. All right. Probably for the best. Then why not indulge in a physical relationship with a hot, intelligent man? Especially one who respected her enough to sheathe his weapon.

Despite cops at work and weirdo church people, her luck was in.

CHAPTER THIRTY-TWO

Isolde stirred peppers and onions in the medium cast-iron skillet. How Noelle could eat this for breakfast was beyond her.

She chopped tomatoes and gave the scrambled eggs another whisk. Seven forty-five. The noise of the shower upstairs stopped. Isolde emptied the skillet and poured in the egg mixture. Just as she flipped the omelet, Noelle walked in.

"Izz? What are you doing up?"

"I'm feeling domestic. Sit down. This is just about ready."

A sesame seed bagel and a piece of toast popped from the toaster. Isolde spread cream cheese on the former and buttered the latter.

"Your petit dejeuner, mademoiselle." Isolde set the plate in front of Noelle and poured coffee.

"Mmm." Noelle spoke through a full mouth. "This is great. What's the occasion?"

"I need to pick your brain." Isolde bit into her bagel.

"At eight o'clock in the morning?" Noelle slurped coffee. "I wonder if Stephen knows how to make a western omelet?"

"You're already thinking about breakfast with him?" Isolde shook her finger. "O ye of loose morals. What would the blue-haired grannies say?"

"They'd be jealous." Noelle cut another forkful of omelet. "And you know we couldn't sleep together before marriage." She chewed and swallowed. "And even if I would, Stephen wouldn't."

Isolde leaned across the table. "Are you saying he asked you?"

"No. But I'd say yes in a heartbeat." She put down her fork. "All right. I'm sorta awake. What's up?"

She plunged. "After I left work yesterday I was sitting here stewing over everything and wishing you were home to talk to. Then I thought of Stephen—pastors are supposed to be good listeners, right? So I headed over to church looking for both of you."

"I didn't see you."

"No. I saw you, though. You were in that little room, you and Stephen and Gow and the others." Isolde took a calming breath. "What were you all doing in there?"

"Praying."

"It didn't sound like any prayers we learned in school."

Noelle's face changed from reserved to joyful. Isolde almost backed away from her.

"It was incredible, Izz. Stephen's been teaching me about the Spirit and the Gifts and the history of the early Church and how that passion still exists today, we just need to open ourselves to it."

"Passion for what?" Isolde held her coffee like a barrier between them.

"For Jesus to fill you with His life and love and—it's hard to put into words, Izz, but when Stephen prayed over me—did you see that?"

Isolde nodded.

"I sat there, trying to be open and reverent and trying not to feel too disappointed if nothing happened, because it doesn't a lot, you know? That's what he told me earlier. And then *whoosh*—it was like a wind blew through my whole body and then my mouth opened and the words came out."

Her eyes were shining now, like she was going to cry. But she wasn't sad. Isolde got the crawlies.

"You don't know any foreign languages, Ellie."

"I know, I know. It wasn't me speaking—it was the Spirit speaking through me. I can't explain it, Izz—it scared me a little at first. Then Stephen told me not to be afraid and we all stood up and everyone was praying like that and then someone stated singing—"

"You. You started singing. You don't remember?"

"Did I?" Noelle beamed at her. "I didn't plan to. It wasn't me anyway, Izz. I mean it was and it wasn't. That's what's so amazing, incredible—humbling about it. I'm just a conduit."

Isolde set down her cup. "Okay, prove it. Do this conduit thing in front of me so I can see it. Prove it wasn't just you getting caught up in the whole emotional moment of the thing." She crossed her arms. "That's what it looked like, Ellie. One big group high."

Noelle's face closed. "I can't. It's a gift, Izz. I can't turn it on and off like a light switch."

"Oh, come on, Ellie."

"No. It's not a talent. It's prayer. You know I don't like to pray in front of people."

Isolde's patience snapped. "Why are you shy in front of me and not in front of Gow? You did this praying thing with her and in the room last night."

Noelle said in a small voice, "Because Miranda believes and, and, you don't."

Isolde shoved back her chair. "It's Miranda now? Spare me. You know she's only out for power. She'll use Stephen and you and anyone else to be Unofficial Queen of Newburyport."

"You've got it all wrong, Izz. It doesn't matter that I don't like Miranda, or that she might be trying to use Stephen to boost her prestige." Noelle stood and gathered her dishes. "What matters is that the Spirit's touched her."

Isolde snatched plate, cup, and silverware from her. "I never thought I'd hear Christian-speak from you."

"If you'll let me try to explain—"

"Not now. You'll be late for work." She slammed the dishes into the dishwasher. "If those detectives interview your shift today, watch out for the man more than the woman. They hit Gavin's early this morning and talked to the whole night shift yesterday. We both think the man's the deep one."

"Why did they go after Gavin?"

"Because Gow told them he drained the blood from Edith and Ines with his vampire fangs."

"You're kidding."

"No. She's a psychotic, manipulative bitch, and you know it." Isolde spoke to the dishwasher rack. "What Spirit did you say Gow had, again?"

"Oh, Izz."

"Forget it. Go to work, Ellie."

Instead, Noelle walked over to Isolde and closed the dishwasher. "No. Listen, Izz. I know you think I've changed forever—I saw it in your face when I came home last night. But I haven't turned into some weirdo Jesus-freak Hallelujah-screamer like on TV. I've simply been given an amazing gift and I'm so happy I could bust." She hugged herself.

Isolde bit the inside of her cheek to keep from either crying or snarking at her.

"Look, I can prove things are still one hundred percent normal around here," Noelle said. "Did you see Miranda buttonhole Stephen after the meeting?"

"No, I bailed after you all started singing in those languages."

"Right. I found some busywork to keep me there. I wasn't going to let her monopolize my man all evening."

Isolde smiled for real. This was the old Noelle. "Your man?"

"You bet. Listen. She got all in Stephen's face about rooting out evil and how it was her family's duty to maintain the legacy of 'their' Jonathan Edwards."

"Speaking of screaming Jesus-freaks." Isolde tried to remember any other sermon besides his famous one. "Or was he just a hell-and-damnation freak?"

"Both, maybe. Anyway, Stephen didn't yes-ma'am her, he just asked her to call him to set up a meeting. He told me later that he's got to bite the bullet and tell her to learn to be a humble follower of Jesus or he'll ask her to find a different church."

"Whoa. Standing up to the Gow. Good for him."

"You know it." She looked at the clock. "I gotta go. Listen. After she left, Stephen took me into that little garden out back with the gazebo and all the flowers in summer, like a Thomas Kinkade painting. Then he kissed me," Noelle twisted her fingers around themselves, "and told me that my own spirit was what he loved about me, and even if the Spirit of God had chosen not to bless me with this gift, he knew that I was the gift God had given him."

Isolde's heart melted. "Oh, Ellie. What a Prince Charming."

Noelle hugged her. "He's wonderful and I love him and he's going to ask me to marry me, I know it."

"How can he resist you?" Isolde released her. "Holy crow, it's twenty of nine. Get out of here."

Noelle ran into the living room and grabbed her shoes from the boot tray. "Breakfast was great, Izz."

"I might be cooking breakfast for Gavin."

Noelle jerked upright. "Really? Do you want to? Are you sure?" She threw on a winter jacket.

"If I told you that he stopped himself yesterday because he didn't have protection with him, what would you say?"

"Ooh, I'd say 'knight in shining armor.'" She opened the door. "Are you coming home tonight?"

"I don't know. Maybe not."

Noelle ran back and squeezed her. "Be careful, don't get pushed into anything, and make sure he's worth it."

Isolde squeezed back then pushed her toward the open door. "Yes, mom. Go to work."

CHAPTER THIRTY-THREE

Gavin opened the front door of the Newburyport *Daily News*, carrying a bulging leather portfolio under one arm.

The receptionist gave him a professional smile. "May I help you?"

"I have a nine o'clock appointment with Allen Cooper. Gavin Donne."

"If you'll have a seat, I'll call him."

Gavin read the framed front pages lining the walls so he wouldn't have to stare at the bland lobby. Back when he wrote and set type and printed his hamlet's twelve-page paper, the all-in-one space was cluttered and frantic and saturated with paper dust and ink. He still loved that smell.

The giant web presses must be hidden in the basement, because he heard no rhythmic thump-hiss-thump-hiss of the rolls of paper feeding through the machine. No, he wouldn't choose this profession again. Too sterile nowadays.

The elevator doors to his right hissed open and Kolchak the Night Stalker stepped into the lobby. The original one from the '70s TV show. Of course it wasn't, but if ever two people were separated at birth... Gavin bit down on the laughter. Who dressed this man and where did get that hideous, ill-fitting, pale blue suit? The headshot under his weekly bleeding-heart column hadn't prepared Gavin for this.

"Mr. Donne? Allen Cooper." He held out a chapped hand.

Gavin shifted the portfolio and returned the handshake. "Pleased to meet you."

"If you'll follow me, I'll take you to my state-of-the-art gray cubicle."

Gavin stopped. "I'm afraid this requires an office with a door we can close. Perhaps a meeting room?"

The man's ears pricked like antennae. "The big conference room has the Friday FUBAR meeting." He leaned over the blond wood semicircular desk. "Iris, is anything free?"

The receptionist tapped several keys. "Third floor funeral parlor is open till the ten-thirty copyeditor interviews."

"Great. Could you block it off for an hour?"

"Only if you buy a new suit."

Cooper laughed. "Only if you volunteer to strip this one off me."

Iris snorted. "In your dreams, paper boy." She hit 'Enter.' "Room's yours till ten."

"You're the best. This way, Mr. Donne."

———

Gavin stood in the doorway of the small conference room. Filmy floor-length drapes covered the tall windows on the east and west walls. The recessed ceiling lights and the burgundy carpet added to the gloom.

"What did I tell you, Mr. Donne?" Cooper closed the door. "All it needs is a vase of hothouse flowers."

"You're right." Gavin would run from the building screaming if he had to spend more than an hour in this haunted house atmosphere.

Cooper flipped up his laptop screen and sat at the imitation mahogany oval table. "You said you had a story that would put the tabloids to shame?"

Gavin sat opposite Cooper and unlatched the portfolio. "Let me show you." He drew out a manila folder and turned it so Cooper could read the top page.

"Port: Charleston... Brig Providence... 12 May 1807." He raised his eyes to Gavin's. "A two hundred-year-old ship's manifest?"

Gavin didn't reply.

Cooper pulled the folder closer. "Master: Jonathan Gow." He started. "Consignee: Ethan Edwards. Slaves: Sam, male, aged twenty, race: black. Harry, male, aged eleven, race..." He took his hands away from the manifest and sat back in the chair. "Holy shit."

Gavin took a large, water-stained Bible from the portfolio and opened it to the family birth and death records in the center. "Fourth branch from the top on the left-hand side."

Cooper sniffed. "Somebody used to smoke expensive cigars."

"Somebody had the money."

Cooper traced the family tree with a fingernail. "Jonathan Gow married Ada Edwards. Really? No wonder... Martha married Ezra. Abigail married William. They had four, six, nine kids. That's all those women did back then."

"And milk cows, educate the children, sew the clothes, preserve fruit and vegetables, clean the house, do the laundry—should I continue?"

The reporter inclined his head. "I get your point. And here we have another Jonathan and," his fingernail traveled to the right, "his cousin Ethan." He leaned across the table. "Slave trading. Holy shit. Donne, tell me these documents are real."

Gavin leaned toward Cooper until their foreheads almost touched. "First let me tell you my conditions. One: You will not reveal the provenance of these documents. Two: You will not use my name. Three: Everything I'm showing you stays in my possession. No photocopies. If you want this story, you have until one o'clock today because I have a one-thirty appointment."

Cooper's mouth worked. Gavin lip-read a few choice swear words before Cooper threw up his hands. "Fine. I agree. Before I get the editor-in-chief up here, tell me where you got these."

"The family records in the basement of the Historical Society."

Cooper whistled. "No wonder you wanted them kept out of it. How'd you get all this?" He opened a new document on his laptop and started typing.

"The Society hired me to do genealogical research."

His fingers banged the keys. "What else have you got?"

"Three wills, a diary, bills of sale—"

"For people?"

"Slaves are lumped in with horses, furniture, and silverware. The color of the horse and the color of the slave's skin seem to affect the value of both."

"Fuck me." Cooper picked up the phone. "Susie, honey, I need a favor... come on, babe, you know I'm good for it... I need you to interrupt the FUBAR meeting and tell the boss to come to the funeral parlor now... Yes, I'm serious... Well, crack the door and see if they're winding up." He sandwiched the receiver between his ear and shoulder and spoke to Gavin, still typing. "The editor-in-chief has to give the go-ahead or I'm wasting my time." He hit 'Save.' "If the terrorists don't blow up something important between now and midnight, my byline is gonna be on the front page above the fold... Yeah, Susie?... Fantastic. You're a doll. Dinner tonight in the Marketplace, my treat. I'll tell you why later."

He hung up the phone and typed a line, deleted it, typed another. "Donne, this story is a reporter's wet dream. Why'd you call me? I mean, I'm in your debt forever, but what made you choose my name?"

Gavin began laying out several sets of papers. "Your columns on Essex County history and legend this past summer. You have the right voice to give this the treatment it deserves."

The door opened and a tall, thin, black man in a three-piece gray suit walked in.

"Cooper, since when is a human interest column important enough to interrupt my schedule?" His cultured tenor voice filled the small room.

"Read this opening line." Cooper angled the laptop toward him.

"The city of Charleston shall thereupon grant a permit to Maser Jonathan Gow for unlading such negro, mulatto, or persons of colour, to be put on shore for the purpose of selling said persons at auction on Tuesday fortnight."

Silence.

The editor-in-chief looked at Cooper, then at the fragile paper at his elbow, then at the computer screen again.

"Our Gows? As in Miranda and William? As in stockholders of this newspaper?"

"As in Great-Great-Granddaddy Jonathan, the slave trader." Cooper gestured at Gavin and the Bible. "Show him the ancestry."

The editor appeared to notice Gavin's presence in the small room for the first time. Gavin brought the open Bible to the other side of the table and pointed out the relevant branches on the Gow family tree.

"I also have Jonathan's Last Will and Testament, in which he disposes of twenty-three human beings in the same manner as his silver and bed linens."

The editor met Gavin's eyes. "Authentic?"

"As I explained to Mr. Cooper, these items have been stored in the Historical Society's basement for more than a hundred years."

The editor sat in one of the uncomfortable wheeled chairs, never taking his eyes off Gavin. "Who and why?"

"My name is Gavin Donne. Do you need to know the reason I've brought you this story? I have the evidence, which you may use until one o'clock today."

"What? But we need copies, we need to—"

"No." Gavin closed the Bible. "Mr. Cooper has agreed to my conditions. Are you willing to publish the truth about Miranda Gow's family?"

The editor stared at the shipping manifest. Gavin wondered if he was calculating the increase in sales versus the loss of potential advertising revenue. Or perhaps the possibility of a lawsuit. Or the potential riot at the next shareholders' meeting.

Cooper stopped typing. A minute passed.

With an abrupt motion, the editor snatched the phone and punched four numbers. "Susie, tell everyone to clear out of the conference room. No, wait. Tell Mac and Angie and Rhys to stay. And cancel anything else I have till—" He looked at Gavin. "One o'clock?"

Gavin nodded.

"One o'clock. And ask the new kid to get us coffee. Lots of it. Thanks."

He hung up the phone and closed his eyes. A minute later, they flew open and he jumped out of the chair. "Cooper, you parasite, why aren't you typing? Mr. Donne, is it? Donne, we're moving this into the second-floor conference room. I hope you're ready for us to pick your brain. Move it, Cooper, it's already nine-twenty."

CHAPTER THIRTY-FOUR

"Hey, Connor, didja hear the latest?" Nuncio said to Isolde before the entrance door had closed behind her. "This place is like a living soap opera."

Isolde logged in. "Now what?"

"Those cops have been here all day, dissecting everyone." He opened a fresh Diet Coke.

"Oh, God."

"Don't worry. They left at three. Said they'd be back tomorrow to finish up." *Slurp.* Lee's royally pissed. I'd keep away." *Slurp.*

"Great. Thanks for the warning."

Isolde pushed open the break room door. A minute later Lee banged through the outer door.

"Cigs aren't strong enough. I should be smoking my ex's weed." She yanked open the refrigerator door, pulled out an energy drink, and slugged half of it. "I hate cops."

Before Isolde thought up a soothing reply, Lee turned on her.

"Only one of them died on my shift. Why the hell aren't the cops crawling up your ass as well as mine?"

Isolde ignored the obvious implication. "Old people die. That doesn't mean we're trying to cut our workload by killing them."

Lee snorted. "Not according to Ms. Bitch and Mr. '80s. They're checking everything. They even asked me if I was having trouble making rent since my divorce." She paused and eyed

Isolde. "Phoebe said your assessment skyrocketed just before you got all cozy with Jeffreys."

Isolde stared at Lee's calculating face for a long moment. "No wonder your husband left you," she said, and walked out.

———

"Ten-thirty, Mr. Wilson. Time to get ready for bed."

Isolde braced herself. This one patient was why she hated three west. Where was Geoff? This was not a one-nurse job.

She called through the half-open door, "Are you ready for me to come in?"

"Yes."

Uh-oh. His feeble voice. That meant he was primed for a fight.

She took a deep breath and opened the door, prepared for six feet of buck-naked former steelworker. But unlike last time, when he'd stood there shimmying his flaccid privates at her, he was lying in bed watching a hockey game on the wall-mounted TV.

"I'll just get these around you, and you can enjoy the rest of your game in peace." Isolde pulled the first padded strap across his chest and started to buckle it.

Wilson expanded his chest and the belt slipped through.

"Mr. Wilson, the sooner I finish, the sooner you can watch the Penguins beat the Islanders."

He farted. She held her breath and tried again. This time he shoved her away and laughed. Without speaking, she shifted to the strap at his ankles. He kicked her arm.

"Mr. Wilson, you know you can't be wandering the halls at night. Now stop making this harder on both of us."

If she let on that he hurt her he'd jump out of bed and cackle and applaud himself and she'd have a real struggle to get him in again. He might be too senile to live on his own, but he was lucid enough to treat the nurses like sparring partners. Where the hell was Geoff?

She tried the ankle strap again and succeeded. Two to go. She moved to the hip strap and he grabbed a fistful of her cap and hair and yanked her backwards, laughing.

Son of a— Isolde pushed her cap straight and snatched the hip strap. The old man punched her shoulder and tried for another hair grab, but she cinched the belt and jumped away.

Wilson blew a raspberry at her.

She walked around the other side of the bed and picked up the end of the chest strap. If he got out, he'd hurt himself. He'd done it before. He was senile. He couldn't help himself.

She kept repeating this as she pried the belt buckle from his hand while he tried to elbow her in the ribs. Panting, shouldering him away, she pulled the strap through and pinned his upper arms to his chest.

"Good night, Mr. Wilson." Isolde pulled the sheet up to his neck. She tried to be nice to all these senile old people, but Wilson was just so easy to hate.

She'd made it to the door when his tremulous voice said, "Look."

Isolde turned around. Bright yellow urine was spreading in an irregular circle on the sheet over Wilson's crotch. He smiled as the reek of ammonia hit her.

She walked out of the room, closed the door, and stalked to the nurse's station at the end of the hall.

Lee, on desk duty that evening, said into the phone, "I'll call you back." As she hung up, she gave Isolde the once-over. "What happened to you?"

"Wilson's in rare form tonight. Any idea where Geoff is?"

"Bathroom." The sound of a toilet flushing reached them, then running water, and a muscle-bound male nurse came out of a small room behind the desk.

"Hey, Lee, tell maintenance there's no more towels in that bathroom, would you?" He saw Isolde. "Whoa."

Isolde stifled everything she wanted to say and stuck to the facts. "Geoff, I just went three rounds with Wilson, and now he's peed the bed." She headed back toward Wilson's room.

Geoff scooted around the desk and caught up with her. "No problem. I can handle him while you clean up. You okay?"

"I'll live. Let's go. I have a date tonight and I'm not staying one second later than eleven."

CHAPTER THIRTY-FIVE

Gavin pulled into Isolde's driveway and parked in front of the garage doors. Had she changed her mind? Should he give her the ring before or after they made love? Would she accept it?

He stepped out of the truck and walked up the steps. He hadn't been this nervous since Hannah. Giacinta and he had wrestled for domination for fifty years. He smiled. Those had been good years.

Isolde opened the door and stepped out next to him in the glow of the porch light. "Hi. Shh. Ellic's asleep. I'm all set." She stopped with the key in the lock and looked up at him. "That is... I mean, we are going to your house still, aren't we? Because if you changed your mind and were just coming to tell me thanks but no thanks, I'll go back inside."

Gavin put his hand over hers and they pulled out the house key together. "I already have a fire built and the bed turned down."

Her wide, happy smile caught the light. "Unless I prefer the hearthrug."

"Whatever you wish, Belle Isolde."

———

"Listen to the wind in the pines." Isolde paused on the path between Gavin's house and garage. "It's freezing, but the trees sound beautiful."

"They're one of the reasons I bought the house." He led her up the stairs and inside.

Chayyliel jumped on both of them, barking and slobbering. Isolde took a package of Snausages from her purse.

Gavin laughed. "Isolde, he'll worship you for life."

"Good. Want a treat, Chay? Want a treat?" He barked and sat at attention, tongue out, and she fed him two from her hand.

When she closed the bag, Chayyliel put his huge face between his huge paws and whimpered like a puppy. Gavin and Isolde laughed and she tossed two more treats to the dog, one after the other.

Gavin clapped his hands. "That's enough, boy. Go on, now. We want some time alone."

Isolde rubbed Chayyliel's face before he loped into the kitchen. "I think I should wash my hands. Unless you're attracted by the aroma of Snausages."

"It's not my first choice." Gavin took her quilted red jacket. "The bathroom's that way, just off the kitchen." While she found the bathroom, he rearranged the logs in the fireplace to increase oxygen flow.

She'd dressed for him. Her long burnt-velvet skirt swirled around her legs when she walked. Her Kelly green blouse invited him to unbutton it. The fire crackled. He hadn't put a different hearthrug out, though. He wanted to take her to his bed. Perhaps he would stand behind her here, with the fire warming her smooth skin, and unbutton her blouse.

"Should I offer a penny for your thoughts?" Isolde's arms wrapped around his waist and she kissed the back of his neck.

"They're rated R."

She laughed—a happy laugh, not quite relaxed, but not stressed. Eager? A touch nervous? He set the poker in its stand and put his hands over hers. "Has scheduling this evening ruined the romance of it?"

"No—tonight's been on my mind all day. Thoughts of it helped me through an awful shift at work."

He pounced on the important point in that statement. "What happened at work? The detectives again?"

"I missed them, but they're doing a great job making us wonder which of our coworkers might be a murderer. To top it off, I got the Alzheimer floor tonight." She shivered. "If my mind goes, someone I love has permission to push a pillow over my face until I suffocate."

"That's morbid."

"You haven't worked with these sad people. It's the scariest sight on the planet. Anyway. I had to strap senile Mr. Wilson in for the night and he was having one of his punching bag days."

"What?" Gavin pulled Isolde around in front of him. "He hit you? Are you hurt? Did you report it?"

She put up her hands. "Stop. He's not too bad. I've got a couple bruises, that's all." She wrinkled her nose. "The last straw was when he peed the bed as soon as I got him strapped down."

Gavin tried to process the surge of anger and the simultaneous desire to protect her. Foolish of him, the latter emotion. She didn't need protecting from someone's addled grandfather. She had experience—and apparently muscles—enough. But from spinsterhood and unscrupulous suitors and anyone besides himself holding her for the rest of her life? He could and would shelter her from those.

"Isolde." Too many ways to say it jostled for priority on his tongue. "Isolde—"

"Yes?"

Gavin dug the ring he'd bought that morning out of his pocket and dropped to one knee. Looking up at Isolde's surprised face, he picked up her left hand and placed the ring on the tip of her fourth finger.

"Will you marry me?"

CHAPTER THIRTY-SIX

Isolde stared at the ring, then at Gavin's hopeful, determined face. She opened her mouth, but surprise had vacuumed her brain cells clean.

"You meant it?" She should slap herself. What a moronic thing to say.

"Every word." The ring stayed poised at her fingertip.

Her inner old maid screeched and scolded and prophesied doom. Isolde had always hated that shrewish voice. Her mouth widened in a smile so complete her eyes crinkled half-shut. She'd known her answer for days. Despite his questionable use of medieval quotes, despite his touch of scariness—no, of excitement. Absolutely—

"Yes."

Gavin slipped the ring onto her finger and got to his feet. "I love you, Isolde."

Her mouth and her brain didn't want to sync. "I, I, love you, Gavin."

He raised her left hand and kissed the palm.

Oh, she remembered that kiss. The first night at the Halloween party, over the rickety counter of their craft booth. Last week. Not even last week. Six days ago.

"We've lost our minds, Gavin."

He turned her hand so she could see the ruby with its four surrounding pearls. "Do you like the ring?"

She tried to concentrate on something other than what his lips were doing to her. "It's beautiful… Stop kissing my hand like that. I can't think."

He spoke into her palm. "Do you mean that?"

"Yes… no… Stop it, Gavin."

"No. I don't want to know what you think of the ring. It was just a ruse to let me start kissing you."

His lips traveled up her hand, her wrist, her inner elbow. Shivers ran over her body in waves. The fingers of his other hand unbuttoned her blouse's first button. Her knees folded.

Gavin caught her waist. "I'm taking you to my bed, milady."

"I think that's a good idea." What she wanted to say was: "Yes. Now. I want you to finish everything you wouldn't yesterday."

"What a good wife you'll make. You're so agreeable."

"Gavin." She had to silence that last, nagging doubt. "Do you mean it?"

"Belle Isolde, if I can talk Stephen into it, we'll be married next Saturday."

She shook her head. "It's like a Disney movie, but without the obligatory witch trying to spoil true love."

"You're a Disney fan?" He put her at arms' length. "Maybe this isn't such a good idea. Those movies give me hives."

He was joking. She didn't need to panic, just answer him in kind. "I still haven't seen your underwear drawer, mister. If you're a cross-dresser, the deal's off."

"All you'll find in there are boxers and plain white undershirts. Promise."

She nodded. "Good. Besides your deficient taste in movies, are there any other deep, dark secrets I should know?"

"We can work around the movie issue. How do you feel about the Marx Brothers?"

"I own every DVD."

"See? True love conquers all."

She giggled. "You said 'true love.' "

He kissed her that brain-melting way, with his expressive lips. "I did. Come with me, my lady. I have an overwhelming need to see more of that lacy undergarment I glimpsed a moment ago."

CHAPTER THIRTY-SEVEN

Gavin knew he'd chosen a king-sized bed for a good reason. That reason now lay on his dark green cotton sheets in barely-there pale green underwear. The forty-watt bulb in his nightstand lamp made her eyes look almost black. Her breath came a little fast and her jugular pulsed like an invitation.

Thank God above he didn't need to feed tonight. Her long, golden hair fluffed on his pillow, her breasts stuffed into that push-up bra, her legs open slightly, revealing how little those panties covered—he'd have fallen on her veins the moment he pulled off her skirt.

And that would drive his Disney princess in terror into the night. She apparently didn't notice he hadn't answered her joking question about other secrets. He took the bra's single front hook in his fingers. "Where did this come from?"

She colored a little. "Do you like it? I bought it today."

Warmth filled him. "You bought sexy underwear just for me?"

"I wanted you to like what you see."

"Isolde, never doubt that looking at you is a pleasure." He put her hand up to his crotch. "See what I mean?"

She bit her bottom lip. "Take your jeans off for me."

Gavin dragged down the zipper and tugged them off his hips. Isolde raised her eyebrows. "Is that silk?"

"It is." He wriggled out of his jeans and pushed them off the foot of the bed. He couldn't wait anymore. He had to bind them together. No hypnosis, no blood-sharing, just her, just Isolde, to just him—Gavin.

Love. He'd been a fool for one hundred and three years to think it would never happen again. He sat cross-legged next to her and unhooked her bra one-handed. She inhaled—did she know her breasts would just about burst free from that diminutive undergarment with every breath?

"God in Heaven—" He jerked the cups away and grasped her naked breasts. His mouth covered one then the other, her nipples hard, his tongue flicking them, his teeth nibbling each in turn.

"Oh—oh—yes—"

He raised his head to see her eyes—unfocused, half-lidded. Before she could say anything, he crushed his mouth on hers. His tongue didn't ask for entrance this time. When she sucked on it, his silk boxers stretched.

Isolde pulled back from him. "Give it to me." Her voice was lower, husky.

"Let me get the condom."

"No. Not yet." She raised herself on one elbow. Her other hand pulled his waistband out and down.

"Isolde…" Then she swallowed him. He groaned. She toyed with it and sucked it and licked its length and girth.

"Ow." She pulled back and rubbed her mouth with one hand. "I'm going to have to practice. Get my muscles in shape."

She was much too coherent. He wanted her as lust-crazed as he was.

"I'll show you the reward of seductive underwear." He pushed open her thighs and pasted his tongue on the crotch of her panties. Wet. Steamy. She gasped and her hips jerked. He closed her legs long enough to strip the silky green material off them. Then he spread her open with both hands and sucked. Somewhere above him, she squealed.

Wrong kind of squeal. He looked over her thigh into Chayyliel's big black eyes.

Isolde wiped her hand on the sheets and laughed. "Chay, your nose is cold and wet. We seem to have an audience, Gavin."

Gavin pounded his forehead on the mattress. "Chay, you load, get out of my bedroom."

Chayyliel yipped.

"I don't have any treats right now Chay." Isolde brushed her hands against each other in an "all done" gesture.

Gavin scooted from between Isolde's legs and onto the cold wood floor. "Chay. Out." He pointed to the kitchen.

The dog huffed and padded through the doorway. Gavin locked the door.

Isolde smiled. "I think he got lonely."

Gavin climbed back into bed. "Too bad." He frowned, but Isolde's smile changed, a subtle invitation. The mood wasn't completely broken, then. He parted her curly golden hair. "Now where were we?"

"You were... oh, oh God, Gavin..."

She swelled and moistened under his fingers. He hardened again. *Now.* He pushed a finger inside her. She squealed—the right kind. He thrust it in and out, his thumb rubbing at the same time. Her hips bucked and she drenched his finger, her folds throbbing, her muscles pulsing. He nearly came with her.

As her orgasm passed, Gavin moved his head to rest on her stomach. Out of nowhere—or out of depths he'd repressed for decades, his lips formed an old prayer.

"Mittere sanctum Angelum tuum de caelis, qui sua custodiat... Send Your holy angel from Heaven to watch over her... sua protegat, sua vistet, atque defendat omnes habitantes in hoc habitaculo... to protect her, to abide with her, and to defend all who dwell in this house."

CHAPTER THIRTY-EIGHT

Isolde wove her fingers in Gavin's hair. He was saying something. She couldn't quite hear the words. Hadn't that happened on his porch the other night, too? Man, he shorted out her brain waves something fierce.

"Gavin."

He tipped his head back without moving from her stomach. His eyes were darker in this light... or maybe it was her vision. She sure wasn't thinking or seeing or hearing clearly.

"Please, Gavin. I want you now."

He pushed off her. His long arm stretched toward the nightstand and he manipulated a foil-wrapped condom into his hand. "Will you do the honors?"

"It's been forever, but it'll come back to me." She ripped open one edge and extracted the smooth beige circle. Her fingers trembled a little. Not from nerves anymore, no—from the thrill of what he did to her. *Start it. Nope; wrong way. There.* "I've got it." She unrolled the slick latex.

As soon as she finished, he propped her on two pillows and straddled her. Her heart skittered. Her body tensed. No going back.

"Now, Isolde, Belle Isolde."

She opened for him and he plunged straight into her, shoving her into the pillows.

"Aaaah—" Every part of her fixed on the sensations from his thrusts.

Gavin grunted and panted and fell on top of her. "Give it to me, Isolde."

Lisp... he didn't lisp this time... "Yes—aaah—"

Through her moans, she heard his harsh voice. "Mine—you're mine—"

Her muscles clutched him again. She clawed at his back and their sweat-covered chests slapped together.

Gavin cried out, then his shoulders and legs relaxed. His breathing slowed and her own breathing fell into his rhythm. She stroked his hair.

"Stay still." Gavin pulled out and peeled off the condom. When he dropped next to her, he grasped her left hand. "Tell me you're mine." He kissed her palm.

"Mmm. If you keep doing that I won't be able to tell you anything."

He gave her a lopsided grin. "Should I object to that?"

She laughed. "Men." Then she snuggled against him. "You asked a question."

"I did."

"Despite its prehistoric implication, yes, Gavin, I'm yours." A rush of happiness filled her. "But don't think that means I'm going to stay barefoot, pregnant, and in the kitchen."

He chuckled. "I'm willing to discuss it." His feet kicked the sheet and blanket toward his hand, and he covered both of them. "Goodnight, Belle Isolde."

CHAPTER THIRTY-NINE

Isolde wrapped one of Gavin's bath towels around her. If he still wanted her without makeup and in last night's clothes, she'd take it as proof this wasn't a fling.

She was being paranoid. She stared at the ring. It was real. He was serious.

The ruby sparkled red and pink and rose in the mirror lights. The pearls matched it—they had a pinkish cast, or maybe pale rose. She wouldn't have thought of pearls or rubies for an engagement ring, but these were beautiful. Perfect.

Who would've thought she'd go all goopy over a man and a ring? People thought she was silly, maybe, because of the princess movies thing. But practical was her real middle name. Except with Gavin.

She found a comb and worked it through her wet hair. How simple all this was. Comfortable. His shower, his toiletries. His bed.

Isolde opened the door wearing the towel tucked around her chest but not quite covering her butt. Gavin was leaning against the wall in a loosely tied plaid bathrobe.

"All yours." She moved aside to let him enter, but he blocked her way.

"I know." He plucked at the twisted towel ends.

"Hey. I meant the bathroom."

"I meant you." His fingers tugged one corner and the towel slid to the floor.

She pulled his sash and his robe opened. He was naked under it.

Isolde wanted him. Earlier that morning she lay in his arms wanting him; wanting to see if it was true that men woke up erect, wanting to give it a little help. She didn't have enough guts to take the plunge. "You said you had a ten-fifteen appointment." Her hands slipped inside his bathrobe and up to his muscled shoulders. She liked those muscles.

He kneaded her butt. "It's only five after nine. I thought of an alternative to breakfast."

She pressed against him. "Breakfast is overrated."

CHAPTER FORTY

Gavin walked to the west side of the Church of the Nazarene. A small sign next to the door listed the pastor's office hours. He rang the doorbell below it.

Stephen opened the door a minute later. "Gavin. Come in." He led them through a narrow hall into a claustrophobic office. Gavin wondered how they would both fit. Packed bookshelves lined two walls. An outdated photocopier sat on a pitted and gouged grade-school desk. He navigated the tight path between that and Stephen's working desk.

Two Bibles, a Strong's *Concordance*, a yellow legal pad, and a coffeepot covered the top. The morning paper hid most of a black telephone. Its headline, if Gavin's typesetter's eye still worked, screamed BLOOD MONEY in 96 point Helvetica Black. He pointed to it. "May I? I haven't seen today's paper yet."

Stephen's linebacker shoulders fell an inch. "Brace yourself."

Gavin skimmed the front page. Excellent copy; accurate but not inflammatory. The facts took care of that. He turned to page two. The recreated manifests and wills looked almost like photocopies.

He read one line aloud to hear the sound of the old-fashioned prose. " 'Item, I give, devise and bequeath unto my daughter, Mary Gow, wife of Isaac Gow, one Negro woman named Mariah and her increase to her and the lawful heirs of her body forever.'"

Enough of that. Stephen's face was worried enough. He replaced the paper on the telephone. "Scandal-mongering, Stephen?"

Stephen slumped into his fraying office chair. "Unfortunately, no. I called Arthur Lawley as soon as I read it. Sorry. Do you know him? He's editor-in-chief at the *News*." He waved at an armless typing chair. "Sit, please. Lawley said his sources were unimpeachable. He wouldn't reveal them, and I didn't ask."

"And Miranda Gow is a member of your congregation." Gavin turned the chair backwards and straddled it.

"Yes. We'll be packed tomorrow. Even if all of them come only to worship—and I'm not that naïve—half will spend the entire time watching her. The other half will be taking bets on what kind of sermon I'll preach."

Gavin pulled out his wallet. "I'll give you five to one on 'The children of grace shall not be punished for the sins of the fathers unto the third and fourth generation.' "

Stephen almost smiled. "Have you ever been accused of clairvoyance?"

"It's simple logic. Although I won't weep over her disgrace, Miranda's not responsible for how her ancestors made the family fortune." Gavin pocketed his wallet unopened.

"I'm afraid too many of the good citizens of Newburyport won't think the same." Stephen drank from a 'Jesus beat the devil with two sticks' mug. "Blech. Lukewarm." He topped it off from the pot and added two spoons of sugar. "Coffee?"

"No, thanks."

Steven closed one of the Bibles around the legal pad. "You didn't make an appointment to listen to my sermon woes. What can I do for you?"

Gavin rested both arms on the back of the chair. "Feel like performing a wedding ceremony next Saturday?"

"Let me check my calendar..." Stephen piled the *Concordance* on top of the other Bible and opened a monthly planner. "Choir rehearsal's at nine, the Pioneers meet in the basement from nine-thirty to eleven. The sanctuary's free from eleven to two—"

His head jerked up, one finger still on the date square. "Whose wedding?"

"Mine and Isolde's."

Stephen stared at Gavin for several seconds. "You're serious."

Gavin grinned. "I am."

"I thought you just met last week."

"At the Halloween fund-raiser, yes." His grin stretched. "So, will you marry us on the fourteenth?"

Stephen's finger hadn't moved. His eyes hadn't left Gavin's face.

Gavin nodded, more to reassure himself than Stephen. Isolde hadn't been this gobsmacked when he proposed. More proof they'd made the right decision. She knew. He knew.

Stephen groped for a pen. "No."

Gavin opened his mouth. He could coerce him.

"I won't marry anyone on a week's notice, Gavin." He circled the fourteenth, twenty-first, and twenty-eighth. "It's irresponsible of me as a pastor." He turned the page and wrote 'G + I' on Saturday, December 5th. "You're not giddy teenagers—"

Gavin snorted.

"But you're still taking a lifelong step. That requires three pastoral meetings."

"Stephen, I can assure you—"

"Don't try. If you want me to marry you, you and Isolde will be here at," he wrote on the calendar, "nine-thirty," drew an arrow down three squares, "for the next three Saturday mornings. Choir starts then, so I'm not needed. I'll have you out by ten-thirty at the latest."

Gavin crossed his arms. Three sessions was a small compromise. He wouldn't take Isolde out those Fridays after her shift ended, so she'd be awake enough for the appointments.

"Shall I presume that these sessions are a formality? She and I have taken care of the big questions: We're not sexual innocents, we want children, and our finances are satisfactory. She has a problem with church, but I believe that's baggage, not a current issue." He leaned on the chair back again. "I'm not a weekly churchgoer anymore, Stephen. What are your expectations?"

Stephen drank a swallow of coffee. "What denomination are you?"

"I was raised Catholic. So was Isolde."

"If I marry you, it won't be recognized by the Catholic Church."

Gavin shrugged. "I don't care. I doubt Isolde does, but I'll ask her." He reached out and tapped the nearest Bible. "Just because the Catholic Church thinks it has a monopoly on salvation doesn't mean it also has the monopoly on Revealed Truth."

Stephen spluttered. "Just what my congregation needs: A heretic. All right, here are my conditions: Both of you show up for church tomorrow. After that, both of you show up at least once every six weeks." He set down the mug. "I understand that getting back into regular worship may be difficult. Several of our people are recovering Catholics—their term for it—and they're adjusting." He blew out a breath. "I'm working for change. The elders here demanded the resignation of the previous pastor. He liked power and money a little too much."

"Money isn't a bad thing in itself."

Stephen slapped the newspaper headline. "That depends on the way it's acquired and how it's used afterwards. My vision is to see this church mirroring the early church in Acts. Helping people. Showing the love of Christ in words and actions. By our own joy leading people into His grace."

Gavin stood. "It would be a refreshing sight."

Stephen looked up at him. "But you doubt it can happen."

"I've seen a lot of corruption. Let's say I'm cynical."

"Come help us, then." He stood and headed down the short hall. "Oh, that's right—now you have to." He burst into movie-villain laughter as he opened the door. "I'm blackmailing you, Gavin. Now that you're getting married here, you'll be part of the team."

Gavin held out his hand. "I enjoy a challenge."

Stephen clasped it. "I'll take you up on that. Don't forget: Ten o'clock tomorrow morning. I won't demand you show for nine-thirty praise, but I'm glad you and Isolde will be here tomorrow. I'm going to need to see unbiased, friendly faces in the seats."

"I'm not unbiased, Stephen. If Miranda Gow dropped off the face of the earth today, I'd throw a party."

Stephen laughed, then looked guilty. "I was going to speak to her about several things before I read the paper this morning. Now I don't know." A muffled ringing came from the office. "Probably another horrified parishioner." He started to close the door, then called, "And congratulations!"

CHAPTER FORTY-ONE

"Detective Pacione will be with you in a few minutes, Mr. Donne." The desk sergeant closed the gunmetal-gray door to the eight-by-six cinderblock office.

Gavin sat on the edge of a gray metal desk and fought off claustrophobia. He hadn't been in a police station since that time he and Giacinta had been caught robbing the thieves who'd stolen their week's theater receipts. Five days in a narrow, filthy cell below the waterline in Venice before the bureaucratic chaos had time to hear their case. And he couldn't feed without revealing his nature to the four other wretches in the cell.

Not in Italy in the 1600s. Anyone could have been a spy for the Inquisition.

He paced the Newburyport Police Station cell—no, not a cell. Just narrow, ugly room that smelled of antiseptic and old cigarettes. No screams of tortured prisoners assaulted his ears. No rats fought for space in the moldy straw. He was not caught in the Catholic reign of terror.

The door opened and a short, curly-haired brunette entered, carrying an ashtray.

"Sorry to keep you waiting, had a meth dealer get crazy on us." Her sensible heels clicked on the linoleum before the scrape of the heavy metal chair legs obliterated the sound. "Please sit down, Mr.—"

Gavin took a deep, steady breath and walked the four steps to the desk. "Donne. Thank you for taking the time to see me." He pulled out a smaller gray chair and eased onto its hard cushion.

"How can I help you?" She tossed an open pack of Kool Lights on the desk. "Do you mind if I smoke?"

"Not at all." He detested that chemical reek, but it was worth it to have her receptive and relaxed. "I'd like to report a case of, I believe, statutory rape."

Detective Pacione set her lighter next to the pack and inhaled on her cigarette. "Why don't you start at the beginning?" She opened the center desk drawer and brought out a legal pad and a mechanical pencil.

Gavin explained the community theater, the acting class, Halloween, the pot.

"Just a minute. You smelled it on these kids?"

"Just on Judith. Her brother indicated it wasn't the first time."

She twisted more lead down the barrel of the pencil. "Go on."

"I've been to cast parties with Hal. It's a habit of his to leave at least once and return smelling of pot smoke. I once caught him after a rehearsal doing lines—is that the right phrase?—of cocaine."

Her brown curls bounced as she looked up. "And friends don't turn in friends for possession?"

Gavin shrugged one shoulder. "That only happened once. Hal's funds are tight since his divorce. Pot is a cheaper high."

She sucked on her cigarette. "Yeah. All right, you think he's dealing."

Time for harsh words to bring the focus back to where he wanted it. "I wouldn't go that far. I think he's giving it to Judith and raping her when she gets too high to resist."

Her voice remained neutral. "Details, please."

"At the end of last Monday's class, Hal made a point of helping Judith with her long black poncho. He used the chivalrous gesture to fondle her underneath it."

She wrote for a moment. "How could you tell?"

Gavin kept his face expressionless. "I'm an adult male, Detective. I recognized those particular motions."

She flicked ash into the tray. "And?"

Now for the big lie. She was interested but controlling her anger, being a professional. Perhaps she had a daughter at home. All points in his favor. He certainly couldn't tell her he knew all this because of the extra hormones he tasted in Judith's blood.

"I've also seen Hal pick up women in Boston bars. He goes after dark girls who look like jailbait." That was true. "After he left Monday with the whole class in his Explorer, I followed in my truck. He kept Judith until last. He drove to the community theater—the opposite direction of her house. I parked half a block away: my truck is dark. They rolled down the windows a crack and smoke drifted out."

The detective tapped her foot against her chair leg and twisted the pencil again.

She believed him. Excellent. "I left my truck when all the SUV's windows fogged up." He could show a touch of disgust now—also quite true. "When I came within a car length of them, I could hear talking." He paused. "This is repellent, Detective."

She stubbed out her cigarette. "I'm a big girl, Mr. Donne."

He took a slow breath. "Ed was saying, 'Ready for me to fuck your hot little pussy, Judy, babe?'"

The detective's pencil point snapped.

Gavin repeated Judith's most telling lines: 'Make me come,' and 'Tell me you love me, Hal.' He watched the lead dig into the thin legal paper. The detective had a teenager at home—or she'd done something stupid in high school herself.

The world had changed in five hundred years. In the fifteenth century, girls Judith's age would be married and raiding their first-born already. And society would wink at tomcats like Hal, as long as he limited himself to the servants and peasants. Gavin had never thought twice about it until he joined the Bergerac monks. So many cast-off girls weeping on the next-door convent steps. So many abandoned babies left in the chapel.

And those babies had the sweetest blood he'd ever tasted.

Gavin kicked that memory to the curb. His sins could bury him in a circle of Hell unseen by Dante. This minuscule aid to justice might move him a millimeter closer to Redemption.

———

Half an hour later, Gavin walked away from the police station, breathing the cold November air like it was a Hawaiian breeze. Freedom. God in Heaven, he hated police stations. Ridiculous of him when there were so many worse dangers.

Well, not in modern times. He no longer had to fear mobs with torches and stakes or the Inquisition. Or adventure-hero wannabes who needed to impress an eligible heiress. Besides, he hadn't killed to feed since that Bastille guard. Gavin Donne fit into Newburyport like any forty-year-old bachelor.

The meter showed ten minutes remaining, so he waited for his truck's cab to get warm before heading home. Detective Pacione and a member of the Narcotics department promised to investigate Hal. Because Gavin's story was technically hearsay—he hadn't actually seen them *in flagrante*—no court would admit it. They needed to catch Hal in the act with photos or an eyewitness. He didn't envy them the job of lurking by the theater on rehearsal evenings.

Judith's brother would be in for a hard time when Hal went to jail. Gavin wouldn't want to share a house with Judith on sex and drug withdrawal. But she was better that way than pregnant and abandoned. Hal would jettison Judith without a second thought—Hal's career came before everything: family, friends, loyalty, love, conscience.

Gavin signaled and pulled into traffic. Would Isolde want children with him when she found out what he was? Would she want him? Surviving cancer and fighting incontinent old men weren't the right kinds of preparation for something like this..

"Isolde, remember how I said I was older than 40? You may have underestimated how much older." He grimaced. Humor wasn't the right approach, but he might as well face it: There wasn't a 'right' approach. She might not even believe him since he wore her grandfather's crucifix with no ill effects. He might have to reveal his fangs to convince her. Shit. Maybe he'd have to try a session of stronger hypnosis. Why did she have to be a Disney princess?

He pushed the CD changer and tried to lose himself in Mannheim Steamroller's *Fresh Aire Christmas.*

CHAPTER FORTY-TWO

"Sit down, Ms. Connor."

Isolde sat on the edge of the only free chair in the family conference room. She'd never been in here—'family conference' was a euphemism for 'doctors suggesting it's time to pull the plug on your great-grandmother.'

If the pale blue walls and Monet garden posters were supposed to soothe grieving relatives, they weren't working for Isolde. Detective Hill scowled like an evil grade-school principal. Detective Morgan faced away from Isolde, writing on a phone screen. Isolde thought Hill was supposed to be the nicer one. No way.

Morgan tapped his screen and spoke without looking at her. "We'd just like to ask you a few more questions."

"Of course."

"How long have you been a nurse?"

"Seven years."

He poked his phone's screen with the stylus. "I understand you nursed your grandmother full-time. When was that?"

"She passed six years ago. I took care of her for two years before that." What was he getting at? If he knew about Grandma, he must know when she died.

"You were already a qualified nurse?"

"I was already an LPN. Afterwards, work took the place of full-time school." She resisted the temptation to wipe her hands on her uniform. TV cop dramas always showed guilty people sweating when the cops questioned them.

"What exactly did your grandmother die of?" More pokes with the stylus.

"Colon cancer that metastasized into her lymphatic system. May I ask what this is about?"

Hill shifted position, but Morgan said, "We're just checking some facts. You were your grandmother's only nurse?"

"Yes, once she left the hospital. She wanted to be home and with family, not strangers."

"And you administered all her medications?"

Isolde's forehead crinkled. "Of course."

"Did you adjust dosage on painkillers or calcium supplements or heart medication?"

"Of course not. I drove her to her doctor's and he wrote her scripts." In a minute she'd rip that tippy-tappy stylus out of his freckled hand. "When the pain got bad toward the end, her doctor came to the house with more meds and instructions."

Morgan's reddish-blond eyebrows rose. "Wish I could get my kids' pediatrician to make house calls."

"Doctor Holcombe knew Grandma from when he and my brothers were little kids. His mother insisted he make her his only house call patient." How he'd cringed at Isolde knowing he was still a mama's boy.

Hill leaned back in her blue vinyl chair. "Must've been tough paying for college and the mortgage on that house you and Ms. Robins share."

Snake, Isolde thought at Hill's cynical face. "My grandmother left me the house in her will. The mortgage was paid off in the mid-eighties."

"So you had no unexpected expenses, no student loan debt, nothing that required an immediate source of cash before your grandmother died?" Hill's cell phone started to play 'The Liberty Bell March.' She left the narrow room before she answered it.

Morgan's stylus tapped like a court reporting machine.

Isolde bit the inside of her cheek so she wouldn't say the angry words forming in her head. So that's why these two showed up here at ten o'clock at night. They probably knew she was working overtime and hoped she wouldn't be hitting on all cylinders when they insinuated she might've killed Grandma for money. And therefore she might've killed Mrs. Jeffreys and Mrs. Tarbell. Because of course Grandma had been practice for her next murders. *Bastards.*

Morgan looked up. "Ms. Connor?"

Isolde's teeth released her cheek. "No, I had no unusual expenses. No, I didn't need a lot of money right away. Then or now. Our paychecks cover taxes and expenses quite well." She wanted to tell him to shove his stylus up his butt. "Is there anything else you need to know?"

Hill came over to Morgan's chair and he turned his screen toward her.

"Thank you, Ms. Connor." Morgan tucked the stylus in its slot. "I understand Tranquil Grove is short-staffed tonight, so you're free to go."

Hill was already making another call.

CHAPTER FORTY-THREE

Two hours later, Isolde lay in Gavin's arms and tried to stop shivering. He'd pulled the couch up to the fireplace and added crème de menthe to a cup of hot chocolate for her.

"It was the way they looked at me when they asked the questions." She sipped the chocolate. Its warmth was almost as good as Gavin's arms around her. "And the time of day they picked to talk to me. Like all they had to do was wait for me to slip because I was so tired from all the OT."

"How long do you think that will go on?"

"People pretending to call in sick? Not long. Nobody's rich enough to skip more than a few days. Our sick time policy is lame, too." She drank more chocolate and set it on the table. "How much alcohol did you put in this?"

He rubbed her arms, pushing her three-quarter sleeves up and down. "Half a shot-glass. Didn't you eat anything tonight?"

"Too busy, and then I lost my appetite after the session with Morgan and Hill."

"Don't work tomorrow night. You need at least one day off."

Isolde snuggled against him. "I already promised my supervisor. She asked before I left at eleven. Did I tell you three families took their old people home?"

"I thought the nursing home was keeping things quiet."

"Like they could. All the staff's talking about it. It was bound to get back to the families that the cops are involved."

Chayyliel barked twice from the porch.

"Gavin, shouldn't you bring him in? It's cold out there."

He shook his head. "Chay is a guard dog. Gow hasn't left crosses or stakes or bats on my porch since I told her he's on duty."

"Hey—I almost forgot. Did you see today's paper?"

"Stephen had a copy on his desk when I went to see him today."

"The town's going to crucify her." Isolde reached for the hot chocolate. "I suppose I should feel bad for her."

"I don't."

"Why does she hate you so much? And where did she get the vampire idea?"

Gavin paused. "Isolde—"

She yawned. "That's right—the Halloween cast party. Never mind about Gow. Why am I wasting our time talking about her?"

He took the half-empty cup from her. "Agreed. Who are you replacing tomorrow night?"

"Lee again. She called my cell when she knew I'd be on break. All wounded dignity, whining how she couldn't bring herself to cross the threshold while she was under a cloud of suspicion."

Gavin laughed. "Sounds like she's read one too many historical romances."

"She devours them by the truckload, even though you wouldn't think it to look at her. But she's got no romance in her real life."

"Unlike a certain nurse I know." Gavin tipped Isolde's head back and kissed her.

Where did he learn to kiss like that? The way his mouth moved… the way his tongue tasted the mint and chocolate on her lips. When he moved his lips off hers, a bit of the chill had finally left her blood.

"Stay here tonight. If we set the alarm for seven, I can get you home in time to change for church."

"Oh, Gavin. I can't. I shouldn't even be here now. I'm going to fall asleep cleaning bedpans tomorrow if I don't hit the sack soon."

Gavin wrinkled his nose. "A fate worse than death."

"It's your fault, mister. I can't sleep in because you committed us to church tomorrow."

"You were supposed to have weekends off." He raised her arm and kissed her wrist. A light kiss, just enough to brush her skin. "Besides, I don't want to get married at City Hall." More kisses along the inside of her arm.

"Don't do that. It shorts out my brain."

"Good."

Isolde sat up, out of his arms. "Stop. Getting married in Stephen's church is a great idea, but I need at least five hours of sleep before I can deal with the whole group worship thing."

"You'll have me for moral support." He looked over her shoulder. "It's only twelve-thirty."

"Only? Oh, man, Gavin, I've got to go."

His arms reached around her. "Ten minutes. Fifteen. I want to see what you're wearing under that practical nurse's uniform."

She made a 'blech' face. "It's boring and practical and the farthest thing from sexy."

He reached under her A-line dress. "Now I'm intrigued."

If she didn't stop him now, they'd end up in bed together. She had to get some sleep, so she pushed his hand away. "I'm going to remain a woman of mystery." She got off the couch, wanting to do the exact opposite. "I really have to go home."

"Why didn't you warn me about your practical side?" He stretched his back.

"It was bound to come up sooner or later." She put on her coat as he walked her to the door.

"Then I'd like to put in a request for several hours of your time after work tomorrow. You'll have all Monday morning to sleep. That is, if I can't interest you in other activities."

She gave him a chaste kiss on the lips. "Come eleven-thirty, I'm all yours."

CHAPTER FORTY-FOUR

Isolde and Gavin stood at the back of the Newburyport Church of the Nazarene, staring at the standing room-only crowd. Three hundred people packed into a sanctuary designed for two hundred at most.

"It's only nine forty-five." Isolde lowered her voice. "Is this all to see if Stephen humiliates Gow? He'd never do that."

"You and I know that, but schadenfreude is a powerful draw." He scanned the benches. "We might be stuck back here."

That didn't bother Isolde. She wanted to sit in the darkest back corner. It was as close to invisibility as she could get in this small sanctuary.

"I see space in the third row." Gavin pointed down the center aisle. "Come on. Stephen said he needs to see some friendly faces today."

"Only for you."

"Think of it as practice for December fifth."

He held out his arm and she took it. Heat covered her face as they walked up the aisle.

She was being silly. They weren't not looking at her and Gavin. They were too busy gossiping about yesterday's big story.

Just as Gavin stopped to let Isolde enter the bench first, a fat woman and three iPod-wearing teenagers jostled past her and wedged into the limited space.

Gavin and Isolde sidestepped in after them and squeezed onto the padded seat. There was just enough room for both of them at the end, if Isolde didn't breathe too much. Since honeysuckle oozed like invisible ectoplasm from the woman, Isolde didn't feel much like breathing.

"If you don't have enough room, my lap is available," Gavin whispered.

"Shush." She pretended to slap his hand. "We're in church."

It was a plain church; nothing like the baroque Catholic edifice she grew up with. Off-white walls, clear glass windows, plain wood benches with dark blue cushions. No kneelers—of course not. She looked up to the apse. They didn't need kneelers—no Tabernacle.

She called it an apse out of habit, but it didn't look like any apse she'd ever seen. It was simply a platform running the width of the room. No altar rail, no statues, no high, carved chairs for the priest and altar servers. Just two steps along its length raising it so the people in back could see the pastor.

And the music: A drum set, speakers, and an upright piano jammed the corner below the right side of the apse. Six stands for sheet music, guitars, and possibly a saxophone crowded around them. Four benches in two rows took up that end of the platform. The choir's seats, most likely.

A plain wooden cross hung on the wall behind an equally plain lectern. A coffee table had been pushed against the wall beneath the cross. Right, for the non-Catholic version of Communion.

Isolde leaned into Gavin. "Do you have any idea what this will be like? I've never been in here before."

"The choir will sing, Stephen will pray, there'll be more singing, a reading or two from the Bible, and Stephen will preach. Then more singing and that's it."

"What do we do?"

"Sing if you know the words. That's it."

Isolde remembered the new Noelle. "Do you know if they'll do that Tongues thing?"

Gavin put an arm around her and squeezed. "I don't think so, but don't worry. It's just prayer."

A door opened on the left side of the apse. Three men and two women in slacks and button-down shirts entered and went over to the instruments. The choir followed in long blue robes with white triangular collar insets. When Miranda Gow entered, the low noise of hundreds of voices stopped like someone had flicked a switch.

Then a baby somewhere to Isolde's right started crying and stage whispers filled the room.

Two women across the aisle to Isolde's left: "She looks mad." "No she doesn't, she looks scared." "Bull. She's pulling that stiff upper lip crap."

The bald man and blonde woman in front of Gavin: "I always hated that pushy rich bitch." "Don't swear in church. It's not her fault what her great-great-grandfather did."

Two high voices—sisters? Mother and daughter?—just behind Isolde: "I hope Pastor rips her a new one." "He wouldn't." "She deserves it. She knew where her family's money came from."

A loud voice near one of the windows: "She should give it all to the NAACP in reparation."

And the worst, two older male voices Isolde thought she recognized: "My family traced our roots to slaves in South Carolina. I'd like to see her whipped and forced to work someone's farm till she died." "Yeah. Maybe then she'd stop shoving her prestige in everyone's face."

Isolde didn't look around. Was there such a thing as 'church rage'? Would Stephen have to use his football muscles to subdue his congregation?

Miranda Gow stood in the front row of the sixteen-member choir, near the window. People stopped whispering here and there as her narrowed gaze roamed the packed room. Then she saw Gavin. Her perfectly made-up face flushed tomato-red. Her stare sizzled with hate.

Isolde grasped Gavin's hand in both of hers. "Why pick on you? I'm glad she doesn't have a gun."

Gavin broke his gaze away from Gow and looked down at Isolde. "She does look homicidal." He smiled. "Don't worry. She's just using me as a focus for all her anger and humiliation."

"I'm not worried. But I wish we didn't have to sit in the same room with her for the next hour."

Gavin raised their hands to his mouth and kissed hers. "Who cares about her? We're here to enjoy the singing and send positive vibes to Stephen."

When Isolde looked to the front of the church again, Gow's laser eyes were aimed at her.

"Uh-oh. Looks like I'm on her hate list now." Isolde smiled at Gavin. "Life will go on."

Stephen entered through the same door. The band played a two-bar introduction and the choir began a song Isolde didn't know.

It was simple, and she was singing along by the second chorus. Even the three teenagers pulled out their headphones and joined in. The lyrics were theologically sound. One of the benefits of having an older brother in the priesthood had been proofreading his theology thesis. And arguing with him about whether the Catholic Church had really changed its 'our way or the highway to Hell' attitude.

Huh. Her first time in a church in years and she was already dissecting it as though she planned to return. Well, if Gavin was willing to do this for their marriage, it wouldn't kill her either.

That song was growing on her. 'Here I Am to Worship' might be the title. However, they could stop repeating the chorus any time now.

As though they'd heard her thoughts, the song ended after one more round.

Stephen stepped to the front of the platform. His eyes had bags under them, but otherwise he looked like nothing unusual was happening in his church this morning.

"Good morning, and welcome to all our visitors." His clear, deep voice didn't need a microphone. "Let's begin with a prayer."

CHAPTER FORTY-FIVE

Isolde didn't realize how tense she'd been until after Stephen's sermon. Only when he sat in a chair at the side of the Communion table and the choir began another song did she feel the cramp in her shoulders.

She knew this song—'It is Well with My Soul.'

Gavin whispered, "Good hymn choices. Calculated to make the angry mob stop and think."

"Good sermon on forgiveness and personal responsibility, too. Think it'll do any good?"

"When they calm down, perhaps. And if Miranda refrains from screaming at everyone."

————

The ushers preceded the crowd to the foyer after the final song. Half the people followed them, voices overlapping like startled bluejays. When the men opened the front doors, the children nearest them cheered. Two inches of snow covered the stairs, sidewalk, and grass. Every woman stared at her fancy Sunday shoes.

"We'll get the shovels, folks. They're just in the shed out back." The ushers squeezed back through the crowd and headed down the hall to the back door.

"Hey, lovebirds, come out of this mob." Noelle took hold of Isolde's and Gavin's sleeves and steered them through the kitchen into the nursery.

Isolde got a whiff of fresh coffee before she walked into a cloud of baby powder. A pale redhead made silly faces at a plump baby on a changing table as the baby tried to wriggle out of her frilly pink dress. Three toddlers banged on a plastic workbench with toy hammers and screwdrivers. Two older children pushed bigger babies in walkers around the floor.

"It's always chaos in here." Noelle nudged them into a meeting room opening off the nursery.

Isolde propped herself on a long table that looked like part of an antique dining room set. "That could've been worse, Ellie."

"Church for you or the whole 'My granddaddy was a slave trader' debacle?"

Isolde laughed. "Both. At least she didn't go postal."

"Thank God." Noelle sat in a metal folding chair. "Gavin, Stephen wanted me to ask you to wait till the place clears out."

Gavin leaned against a cartoon poster of David and Goliath, hands in pockets. "Why?"

"He wanted to thank you for the sermon help, I think."

Gavin shrugged. "I didn't do anything."

"Yes, you did. You showed him that not everyone is ready to judge Miranda on what her family did two hundred years ago."

Twin four-year-olds ran squealing into the room and out a second door. The redhead appeared in the nursery doorway, baby on her hip.

Isolde pointed. "That way."

"Thanks. April! June! Time to go!" She wormed through the throng gathering in the short hall connecting the meeting room and the kitchen.

Stephen appeared in the nursery doorway. "Someone hide me."

Noelle put an arm around him and closed the door. "Izz, get the other one, would you?"

The man who'd wanted Gow's money to fund the NAACP said from the kitchen, "Anyone see Pastor Oliver?"

Isolde closed the hallway door. "If they break it down, we'll hide you under the table and beat them off with Bibles."

Stephen laughed. "Thank you, Isolde. I appreciate the sentiment." He sat down in a Quaker chair. "That could've gone worse."

"That's what I just said."

Someone knocked at the door to the nursery. "Pastor?"

"He'll be out in a minute," Noelle said.

"Thank you, Noelle." Stephen leaned back until the chair rested against a bookshelf holding paper and art supplies. "I know people mean well, but when the fifth person asked me if I could still accept Miranda now that I know what she is, I had to get away or lose my temper."

"What she is?" Noelle tipped his chair forward and massaged his shoulders. "Was her father a space alien? Is she a secret government android prototype? What a stupid thing to say."

Stephen reached up and held her hand, but looked at Gavin. "As stupid as Miranda pulling me aside by the Communion table and asking why I let a vampire into the House of God."

Isolde stamped her foot. "What century does that woman think we live in? Look—" She reached into Gavin's shirt collar and pulled out the white gold crucifix. "Maybe we should drag her in here and show her this. He can't wear a religious image repellent to vampires and be one at the same time. So much for her delusions."

Gavin laughed. "I'd like to see her face."

The hall door slammed open.

CHAPTER FORTY-SIX

Miranda Gow, perfect hair askew, plum-colored suit rumpled, stalked up to Gavin and aimed a slap at his face. Gavin caught her hand before it made contact. Stephen jumped out of his chair and took a step toward them.

Half a dozen gawkers crowded the other end of the hall. A teenage girl giggled and an older woman elbowed her.

"Keep your hands to yourself, Miranda." Gavin dragged down her arm, Gow fighting him for every inch.

"Filthy liar. Son of Satan." Though her teeth were clenched, she pronounced every word with precision. "You defile God's house."

Gavin hadn't cherished such a vehement hate for someone since Father Matias, the Master of Novices, made all their lives the seventeenth-century version of unending Hell. He raised an eyebrow at Miranda. "It appears God's representative disagrees with you."

Gow struggled to free her hand. "Pastor Oliver, order this creature to release me."

Stephen closed the short distance to their tableau. "Miranda, your behavior is inappropriate."

Her gaze snapped from Gavin's face to Stephen's.

"My behavior? Every minute he stands there is an insult to God."

"Miranda—" Stephen took a deep breath and focused on Gavin. "Gavin, please let her go. Miranda, you will not strike anyone in my church."

Gavin inclined his head to Stephen and released Gow's hand. What a miserable, bitter harridan. Did she sit awake nights worrying that someone, somewhere, was enjoying life?

The six immobile onlookers remained silent. The teenager and an older man grinned at each other.

Gow stepped nose-to-chest with Gavin. "How do you do it, vampire? Why aren't you screaming in agony every minute you stay in this holy place? What powers did Satan give you?"

Gavin laughed and Gow tried another slap. He blocked it. "Miranda, if you do that again, I'll forget we're in church."

Stephen put a hand on Gow's shoulder. "Miranda, it's been a difficult morning."

She shook it off. "Pastor, how can you stand there while—"

"Miranda. Stop it." Stephen pulled her away from Gavin. "Please go home now. Come to my office tomorrow and we'll discuss everything that's happened. Ten o'clock."

Gow didn't break eye contact with Gavin. "Only if the ushers throw this creature out."

"Miranda."

This time she looked at Stephen.

"I am the pastor here. Not you. I will discern who does and does not have a place in this church." He glanced at the rubberneckers in the hall. "Is your nephew here?"

"He's waiting in the car."

"Noelle can take you out the side door to meet him."

Gow drew herself up. "I am not a criminal trying to escape justice."

Stephen sighed. "That's not what I meant."

Gow straightened her suit and patted her hair into place. "I suggest you email copies of today's sermon to the rest of your congregation. The 'Christians' here this morning need a refresher course in *agape*."

"As do we all on occasion, Miranda." Gavin kept his voice light and neutral.

A sneer distorted her plum-painted lips. "I am being vilified as though I were the Gow who stooped to human trafficking. The years and money I've dedicated to humanitarian causes have been conveniently forgotten." She moved closer to Gavin and said into his ear, "I know you're responsible for the newspaper article."

Gavin began a smile. When she seethed he stifled it, slowly, to prolong the moment.

Her voice trembled when she finally said, "I do not suffer slander lightly."

"Is the truth considered slander, Miranda?"

Gow actually hissed. "Your time is coming, monster."

Stephen took Gow's arm. "Tomorrow at ten, Miranda."

"Yes. We have a great deal to discuss." She disengaged herself and walked down the hall through the select audience. The grinning man laughed until Gow glared at him. When she turned the corner, they followed at a distance.

Stephen dropped into a chair. Noelle whistled.

Gavin changed his smile into a reassuring one for Isolde. "She's all hot air under that wig."

Isolde gulped. "That is a wig, isn't it? I had no idea."

"She can afford the best. By the way, Stephen, I think you should congratulate me."

"For keeping your temper?" Stephen held out a hand. "I do, wholeheartedly."

Gavin shook it. "No. For not giving into the temptation to knock that perfect hair off her imperfect head."

Stephen groaned. "Praise God you didn't."

Isolde pecked Gavin's cheek. "You win the 'act like an adult' prize."

Noelle closed the hall door. "Izz, I won't ask how you liked your first time here."

Stephen groaned again. "I forgot this was the first time for both of you. It's not like this every Sunday, I promise."

Gavin put his arm around Isolde's waist. "We didn't think it would be."

"Thank you." Stephen's pointed at Isolde like he was trying to pin her to the wall. "I was supposed to ask you something. Ah. Did Noelle talk to you about playing for Thanksgiving?"

"Yes, but—"

Noelle gave Isolde a calculating look. "Now that you've survived one Sunday, why not?"

"I don't know..."

Gavin put his mouth by her ear. "I will if you will."

She looked up at him. "You play?"

"A few instruments. We can make it a duet."

"Well, I suppose so."

Stephen stood and shook Gavin's hand again. "Wonderful. Best news I've heard today."

"We'll have a short list for you to choose from this Saturday." Gavin raised his eyebrows at Isolde. She scrunched her face at him, but nodded.

Someone knocked at the hall door.

"Just a minute," Stephen called. "Gavin, is there a short explanation of Miranda's vampire obsession?"

Isolde rolled her eyes and Gavin gave Stephen a truncated version of the Halloween musical aftermath. Noelle and Stephen laughed.

"I needed that," Stephen said.

Isolde snapped her fingers. "Gow didn't see the crucifix just now, did she?" She nudged it out between Gavin's buttons. "It was hidden."

"Probably for the best." Gavin tucked it back in place. "Why confuse her beliefs with facts?"

Stephen put one hand on the doorknob. "Noelle, if you'll look into the nursery, I'll field the rest of the adults."

"Of course." She kissed him, but he held her when she went to move away.

"Meet me in the sanctuary after everyone's gone."

"Okay." She grinned at Isolde on her way out the other door.

Stephen beckoned to Gavin. "How did you ask Isolde to marry you?"

"Down on one knee, the ring on the tip of her finger."

"I like that ring idea. Mind if I use it?"

"Be my guest." He feigned wide-eyed innocence. "Will you be attending three pastoral counseling sessions?"

"Touché. If I survive the gauntlet in the lobby, yes." He opened the door and three people said, "Pastor, if you have a minute—"

Isolde drew Gavin behind the door. "I'm starving. Want to come to my place for lunch? I got up too late for breakfast."

Gavin kissed her temple. "Can't. I'm meeting Hal King at twelve-thirty. He wants me to design the costumes for his new play."

"What an industrious husband you'll make."

He kissed the top of her ear, her earlobe, her neck. "If you're going to be barefoot, pregnant, and in the kitchen, I have no choice."

She stuck out her tongue. "We have some serious discussions ahead of us."

"You mean about how many children we should have?" He reassumed the innocent look.

"Aargh." Isolde pushed him away.

Gavin drew her arm through his and they walked down the now-empty hall. A handful of adults lingered in the foyer. A mother and daughter stared at Gavin and whispered to each other after he passed.

CHAPTER FORTY-SEVEN

"Gavin, I know Newburyport is full of witchcraft and Puritanism and H.P. Lovecraft history, but this is nuts. Hey—"

Isolde jerked forward-back-forward-back as Gavin pumped the brakes. The Ford hatchback in front of them skidded into the curb.

"Idiot." Gavin cut around the car's back end. "Why do people panic at the first snow? Look at them. They drive like they've been teleported direct from the Sahara."

The light changed at the next intersection, but a junker Pontiac ran it. Gavin slammed the brakes and cursed.

Isolde waited for her pulse to return to non-panic state. "I'd like to survive to marry you, Gavin."

His hand groped for hers. "You're safe in my hands."

"Only if they're both on the wheel."

"Nag."

"Road hazard."

"Me? I beg to differ—Hang up and drive!" Gavin turned hard left onto Green Street. "Cell phones are an invention of the devil."

"But a convenient one." Isolde lifted her foot from the imaginary brake.

"I saw that." Gavin skimmed through the Green and Harris intersection and turned right onto Pleasant.

"Instinct."

"I am not driving like a maniac."

"I didn't say anything."

He pulled into her driveway and slammed the gearshift into 'park.' "I am a skilled, competent driver. I regularly transport humans and other cargo without incident. Unlike the congenital idiots who shouldn't be allowed to drive anything more complex than a go-kart."

Isolde pinched her lips together, but the giggle burst out.

"What?" Gavin killed the ignition.

"I'm waiting for sparks to fly out of your ears. I didn't know you had a thing about being contradicted."

For an instant, Gavin looked at her with Gow-like hate.

Isolde stopped breathing. She was marrying this man in a month. Maybe she should know a little more about him. Maybe they should wait.

Gavin's face became his own again. "I'm sorry. A touch of road rage on top of the Gow incident."

Isolde backed away till she hit the door and remembered to breathe. "I guess it wasn't the best time for a joke."

"Isolde—"

"Hey, it's already twelve-fifteen and you have a meeting. I'll see you tonight." She was glad he didn't ask her to finish her earlier thought about Newburyport somehow attracting evil.

She opened her door and he snatched her arm.

"Stop."

His eyes were different. Darker. Intense. His voice, too.

"There's no reason to be afraid of me, Isolde."

She believed him. Almost. Yes, she did believe him.

He maintained his hold. "Sometimes my temper gets the better of me."

"Sure."

"I'll call you at the end of your shift."

"Sure."

He released her.

Isolde didn't want to leave him like that, but she didn't know what to say. 'You made me nervous just now' were not the right words. So she leaned over and kissed him. His answering smile proved she'd chosen well.

CHAPTER FORTY-EIGHT

Hal King pushed a black three-ring binder across Gavin's kitchen table. "It's the exact opposite of *300* and *Troy* and all those epics."

Gavin heard the central heat kick in and shivered reflexively as he opened the binder. Outside, the first snow of the season couldn't make up its mind whether or not to settle in for the day. Sleet pattered against the window above the kitchen sink, the sun appearing for an instant afterward.

Two beers sweated on Gavin's kitchen table, one in front of Hal, the other next to Gavin's sketchbook and box of pastels.

"How are you going to come up with enough backers?" Gavin studied the list of properties. "Marble-faced columns and a working sacrificial fire? A two-horse chariot?" His finger stopped at the last item. "A Mount Olympus that opens to reveal the underworld. Hal, you'll have to rob every bank in town."

"Gav, it's in the bag. Trust me."

"Forgive me for being cynical, but I've heard you say that before."

Hal downed half the beer. "This is different. I told you. My grandmother is dying to see her favorite grandson take his big step on the road to Broadway."

Same shtick, different play. Gavin knew better than to cast more doubt on Hal's Great American Drama.

Hal opened a thicker, white binder. "Forget the sets for a minute. I've got four main characters and two minors. Main are the younger brother, mother, father, and the girlfriend. Minor are the older sister and the mentor." Hal turned a thick stack of pages. "Plus three—five—six smaller double-up parts."

"Mentor: male or female?"

"Male, of course. I'm not creating a powerful female in Ancient Greece. Anachronisms distract the purists and make for bad reviews."

Gavin turned a page. Hal's usual rendition of his dysfunctional family might work in a classic setting. It had failed as a Western, an avant-garde minimalist experiment, and as theater of the absurd. That last attempt... he still remembered the scathing review in the *Daily News*.

"How open are you to defining each character by color?" Gavin flipped past several filled pages in his sketchbook. "The father in gray. Charcoal, I think." He chose that color from his box of pastels and sketched a human shape wearing a chiton. "Pale blue for the mother, red for the girlfriend. Like this."

A figure with drooping shoulders and a grayish-blue chiton took shape next to the upright charcoal sketch. Next to them grew a smaller, red-clothed form with upswept hair and all the right equipment.

"Awesome, Gav." Hal skipped several pages farther into the script. "Here's the mentor's first scene."

Gavin scanned the lines. "Olive green. A quasi-military look."

"I don't know. I was thinking burnt orange for contrast and conflict."

Gavin shook his head. "Not according to these opening lines." He turned back to the beginning. "Here—the curtain rises with the father onstage beating the daughter as the mother advises her to accept it quietly." He pointed a pastel-smeared finger at Hal. "Does he attack the main character's girlfriend later?"

"In every scene they're together."

Gavin smudged the charcoal figure. "He should be the one in burnt orange. Keep the girlfriend in red. It'll clash visually while they're clashing physically."

"What about the younger son?"

"Not yet. The daughter first. Is she three-dimensional or just a vehicle for the father to abuse?'

Ed finished the beer. "She's Lorraine, Gav. Potential squashed by a clueless mother and a bulldozer father. But I'll show her how to tap that potential."

Gavin's artistic zeal crumbled at the memory of the last acting class with Lorraine and Judith in Hal's sights. More sleet hit the window as Gavin remembered how much he wanted to castrate Hal.

"In the last act, when the father tries to kill the mother for supporting the son, the sister has her big scene." Hal pushed the binder aside. "All that promise we saw in her will make the audience weep. I've outdone Sophocles—she'll outdo Antigone. She stands up to the father and he stabs her."

"Cliché, Hal." Gavin sketched random set pieces in blues and grays.

"Yes, yes, the idea is, but not her speech. It's more than pathos. It's worthy of Sydney Carton at the guillotine."

"Burgundy or maroon, then. Not as vibrant as the girlfriend and foreshadowing the Big Speech."

"Yes, yes, yes." Hal clapped Gavin on the back. "What a team we make."

Gavin resisted the urge to pick up Hal's hand with two fingers and return it to the table. "Who's playing the girlfriend?"

"Judy, of course. She at that intense, smoldering age. A perfect foil to the younger brother."

"He's not intense?"

"Of course, of course, but in a positive, change-the-world way. She's sexually intense."

"Of course."

"Gav, don't be such a downer. Look at the archetypes I've written: Power, sex, innocence, anger, righteousness. Act three is a forty-minute thunderstorm."

"Not more special effects."

"No, no, not weather. My cauldron of boiling emotions explodes in fury and murder."

Gavin sketched the stage as he thought of ways to get Hal out of his house. He couldn't use his work schedule; it was Sunday. It was too late for church, and the Patriots were playing the Bills down in Buffalo. The Celtics were away this weekend, too.

Perhaps a veiled question. "No onstage sex, I hope."

Hal managed to make his smile look sleazy. "Of course there's sex. Look how it worked for *Rent*. The younger son and the girlfriend go at it behind the fountain. I told you about the fountain, right? The mentor catches them in the act."

Gavin closed the sketchbook. "Hal, it can't be done. Not if Judith's playing the role. She's fifteen."

Hal waved that aside. "Who cares? She looks the part. She can act the part. She'll do what she has to to get away from her lousy home and nagging family." He slapped the script. "This is her ticket out and my ticket up. Design my costumes and sets, Gav, and you're in on the ride."

Gavin could think of few things he wanted less than permanent association with Hal King. If God was good, Detective Pacione was already tracking Hal like a terrier after a rat.

"Certainly I'll design for you." He didn't add, "I wouldn't mortgage the farm that you'll stay out of jail long enough to hold the first read-through, child molester."

Now that he'd pretended to seal this deal, Hal would go. Then Gavin could concentrate on the important issues: Isolde and his flash of temper and how to tell her about his rare nutritional needs.

"I knew I could count on you, Gav. I can't ask you to play the father, though. I'm playing the younger brother, and we're too close in age."

Gavin shook his head. "Recipe for disaster, Hal. Never act and direct in the same show."

Hal held up a hand. "Heard it. Know all the gloom and doom lectures. Who else can direct my play but me? Who else can star in it but me, who lived it?"

Gavin opened his mouth, but Hal forestalled him. "No, my dad didn't murder my sister. You know what I mean."

"Act in it if you want Hal, but…" A lightbulb appeared in Gavin's head. "What about the Antichrist?"

"The Boston theater stiletto bitch? God forbid."

"She's a great director."

"If you enjoy post-rehearsal notes that rip you a new orifice every night. No, thanks." Hal looked at the clock next to the refrigerator. "One-forty already? Damn. I'm supposed to be schmoozing Grandma at two."

"Is she ready to sign the check?" The poor woman. Surely she had no idea that her favorite grandson was a future convict. In the very near future, if Gavin had pushed the right buttons on Detective Pacione. "Hal, didn't you say she had Alzheimer's? Is she competent to sign checks?"

"Mom hasn't filed the power of attorney papers yet, so it doesn't matter. This is my moment." He grinned. "Mom won't fight me over this. Read my script and you'll see her lifelong motivation: Peace at any Price." He patted his breast pocket. "Check's right here. Grandma signs, I shoot it into the ATM tonight, the funds get transferred at open of business tomorrow morning, and dear ol' Mom won't see the statement till the end of the month. It'll be too late to fight it then."

Gavin took the empty beer bottles to the sink. "Good luck, then."

And may he rot in the devil's gullet for eternity.

Hal picked up the script. "It's charm and planning, Gav. Luck has nothing to do with it."

CHAPTER FORTY-NINE

Isolde emptied bedpans and changed sheets like a robot. Those tasks required no thought. Gavin and marriage did. Specifically, marriage to Gavin.

She shouldn't be spooked by a little show of temper. She wasn't a sick, frightened child cowering in a hospital bed listening to her father scream at her mother over how she was neglecting the rest of the family because of Isolde's chemo treatments.

Adults lose their tempers. She sure did. Even Noelle, that paragon of equanimity, did.

It was Gavin's eyes.

Isolde rinsed and dried the fifth bedpan and set it on the shelf.

His eyes got darker when he was angry. When he was aroused, too. She squirted antibacterial soap into her hands and slid them over each other. She liked his dark eyes hovering over her when they were in bed.

She was being silly. A Disney princess without the spine to attack the wicked witch. Even Giselle had guts. Floofy ones, but guts nonetheless. And neither suitor in *Enchanted* could compare to Gavin.

Nuncio opened the door. "Hey, Connor, the Gestapo says to goose-step your overworked hiney to one east and serve dinner."

Isolde leaned her forehead against the shelf. "Bite me, Nuncio. Where's Geoff?"

"Baby puked, Tina panicked, he rushed to the rescue."

"Crap." Isolde's opinion of Geoff's whining, pampered wife plummeted further.

"Nah, that's what I'm rescuing you from." He blew her a kiss.

"Thanks loads. Don't expect a twelve-pack of Diet Coke out of it."

"Nobody appreciates me." The door slammed.

Isolde rinsed and dried her hands. God, she was tired. Only five o'clock and all she wanted to do was sleep. Although she wouldn't resist a little physical relaxation with Gavin. She could change into that dark blue teddy hidden in the back of her closet.

A half-smile formed on her mouth. Guess she wasn't so worried about his temper after all.

———

Gavin touched his fingertip to the sharpened end of the stick. "Ouch. You're playing with fire, Donne."

He eyeballed the width of the 'fishing pole' and switched out the cordless drill bit for one a size up. The snow began again as he squatted at the base of his carved six-foot fishing bear. Fluffs of sawdust mixed with snow fell to the ground beside him as he widened the hole. A minute later he switched off the drill and tested the fit. The stick squeaked, but with a little English he snugged it in.

Gavin looked up, a fat wooden belly obstructing his view of the snout. "Welcome to the world, bear. Next summer some rich tourist is going to snap you up. I'll carve you a fish next week. Perhaps a hat as well."

He hung the drill and his whittling knife on the tool grid in the shed. Time. He dug into his jeans pocket, but his cell phone was in the house. He dashed into the back porch through stinging clouds of icy flakes and checked the DVD clock.

Four-thirty. Six and a half hours until Isolde's shift ended. What an idiot he'd been to lose his temper like that. Stupid drivers and Gow in a frenzy were no excuse. Isolde required delicate handling and a gradual acclimation to the possibility that not all fictional ideas were indeed fictitious. She must be eased into the concept that frightening only applied to the unknown. Since she knew him, there was therefore no reason for fear.

Fine. He had six hours to compose the perfect opening sentence. If only this all didn't sound like one of those 'make a tabloid headline out of these words' games.

Marriage. Serendipity. Vampire. Disney. Forever.

Well, 521 years so far. Like Stan Freberg said, 'Close enough for jazz.'

CHAPTER FIFTY

Isolde buttoned her boiled wool coat and waited for the computer to log her out. Nuncio wasn't behind the front desk at this hour, but he'd left two empty Diet Coke cans by the phone. She tossed them in the break room recycle bin.

"Hey, Isolde, you need a day off something wicked." Bethann, the overnight nurse, said as she closed the fridge. "Your eye bags have eye bags."

"Thanks." Isolde yawned. "Tell everyone to stop faking sick and I will."

"If you're seeing that hot guy tonight, try cucumber slices on those bags for ten minutes. Works for me."

"I am and I will." Isolde frowned at her. "How'd you know about him?"

"Phoebe, who else? Next to man-hunting, gossip is what she lives for."

"Don't I know it." Isolde opened the door. "Check on Stafford, will you? He's been in the dumps lately."

"Sure thing. I might even let him almost pinch my rump. That'll make his day." Bethann adjusted the cap on her wiry black hair. "How's what's-her-name King adjusting to the Alz floor?"

"Not good. It's—"

"Doctor Blau. Doctor Blau to 304."

They stared at the recessed ceiling speaker.

"That's Mrs. Holden." Isolde was already at the door when Bethann caught up to her. "I'll get the crash cart."

CHAPTER FIFTY-ONE

Gavin lifted his hands from the piano keys and the final chord of "Rhapsody in Blue" faded.

Was that Chay? No; couldn't be. He didn't whine like that. Must be one of Petrie's overbred poodles, although it was little late to be walking a dog.

Late. What time was it? He tossed the sheet music into the bench and flipped open his cell phone. "Eleven-ten? Damn, Gershwin, if Isolde's annoyed, it's all your fault." He punched in Isolde's number.

Blinding pain crushed the back of his head. His nerveless hand dropped the phone. The sound of the second ring faded and the room went black.

————

Thor and Hephaestus were playing bongos in Gavin's head. He'd never liked bongos.

Fluffy bits of cold struck his face. He tried to raise his hand, but it didn't obey him. Something constricted his chest, as well.

He had to open his eyes. If he was outside, it'd be dark. He unglued them a fraction and bright light stabbed him. He jerked away and hit his head on a hard, lumpy... something. The bongos tripled their pounding.

He shouldn't have listened to his brain. If he wasn't outside, had someone opened all his windows? But if strangers were in the house, why wasn't Chay raising hell?

He slitted his eyes against the light. Too bright and steady to be torchlight.

He was being an idiot. Torch-wielding mobs didn't burn people at the stake anymore. Of course: a flashlight. One of those big halogen lantern types. He ignored the sledgehammers in his skull and opened his eyes all the way. Two oversize flashlights on the ground lit him like opening-night spotlights. He turned his head away. Duct tape. Wide strips of gray duct tape along the length of his body held his arms against his sides and his legs against—

He bent his head. The bongos from hell increased their tempo

Round wood, like a pedestal. If he was in his backyard and not falling over from the combined weight of himself and whatever he was taped to, that meant he was standing on... his bear. Right. The rebar held the fishing bear in place. And him.

Maybe whoever taped him out here was ransacking his house right now and he could start to work free. He tried to wiggle his fingers. His left hand didn't respond, but the top joints on his right hand complied. He twisted that hand and discovered that the tape covered it only as far as the knuckles. Those fingers touched a rough, curved surface. The belly. That meant the hard point poking the top of his spine was the snout. Gavin didn't think whoever coshed him tied him out here for the absurdity potential.

A male voice beyond the spotlights said, "He's awake, Aunt Miranda."

CHAPTER FIFTY-TWO

Isolde shivered in her Prius as the engine struggled to warm the interior. Even her cell was slow to start.

"Thank God it wasn't another death—murder—no, no, just plain death is enough." Her cell finally showed decent reception and she punched in Gavin's number. Three beeps, then dead air.

She stared at the screen. "Who are you talking to at midnight? And if you're calling me, hang up."

———

Miranda Gow stepped into the halogen lit circle.

"Did you think this would fool me, vampire?" She held up the crucifix Isolde had given him.

A surge of rage swamped Gavin's initial rush of fear. He shoved it away and brought up a wave of calmness. He could let her gloat at his humiliation and trade insults with her. But he had to postpone physical violence until he worked himself free.

"Does Stephen Oliver know you're a thief as well as a liar, Miranda?"

She took another step. "What do you mean, vampire?"

Not good. He had to re-humanize himself in her mind. The longer she called him 'vampire' instead of 'Gavin', the more she'd work herself up to murder. He expanded his chest a millimeter, but it didn't loosen the overlapping strips of tape. "How long do you think you can pretend to have the Gifts of Tongues and Interpretation? How long before God reveals your sin?"

"My sin?" She crossed the remaining space between them and slapped him. "You are an abomination in the sight of God. You murder without remorse. You glut yourself on the blood of the innocent."

His cheek stung. Blood glistened on Miranda's ostentatious diamond wedding ring—his blood. His fangs threatened to descend. Her sour blood would make him retch, but he wanted to bite her, hurt her, make her gibber—

Gavin made a show of raising his eyes to Heaven. "Miranda, has your family ever suggested a psychiatrist? I might know one who could help you."

She backhanded his other cheek.

Another gash. Warm trails of blood dripped down his cold face.

His whole body yearned to suck her, drain her, kill her—

No. He was not a killer. Not a monster. He was... differently nutritioned. There. He almost smiled. Miranda looked puzzled.

"Come on, Aunt Miranda. Make him do it so we can get out of here. It's cold."

Gavin had heard that voice before.

"Be quiet, Jonathan."

Gavin looked over Miranda's head. A tall man in a leather jacket slouched at the edge of the light. Jonathan Gow, still expecting all-powerful auntie to fix everything for him.

"Look, it's snowing, I'm tired, and you wouldn't even let me search the house for cash." Jonathan stopped his bored whine with a drag on a cigarette.

"You don't need spending money, Jonathan. Soon you'll have his well-paid position at the Historical Society." She held out her hand. "Give it to me."

A gust of wind rattled the shed roof. Goosebumps rose on Gavin's body under his Henley and jeans. Just then Miranda shielded her face from the needles of snow and he pulled his right index and middle fingers free of the tape.

The wind changed. Miranda lowered her outstretched hand. "God hates all who do evil. God destroys all who speak falsely."

Gavin concentrated on stretching the piece of duct tape around his right hand. "Move away, then, Miranda. I don't want to be in range when lightning strikes you."

A jab to his chest silenced him. For an instant he couldn't breathe: Miranda held a stake over his heart.

———

Isolde shifted into park and tried Gavin's number again.

Busy.

She grasped the keys, but hesitated. It was already twelve-twenty. Should she drive over there? She needed an infusion of his calm strength before those cops showed up tomorrow. They'd be crawling down her neck as soon as she arrived, all because she doled out meds the night Mrs. Holden decided to have a reaction to her new dose of thyroid hormone.

"If she'd died, I'd be toast. I may be toast anyway." She glared at the phone. "Gavin, why don't you answer?"

CHAPTER FIFTY-THREE

"Want me to help, Aunt Miranda?"

"No, Jonathan. I will eliminate this evil with God's help." Gow lowered the stake.

Gavin breathed again.

"Yeah, right." Miranda's nephew came fully into the light and stood next to her. His uncut hair fell into his eyes; his pudgy cheeks needed a shave. "So, Donne, you gonna resign the cushy Historical Society job and recommend me? My loving aunt," he stooped to squeeze her shoulders, "guarantees she can ram it through this time."

"Fuck you."

Jonathan punched Gavin's mouth.

Gavin hadn't expected him to move that fast. He spat blood off to one side and tried to clench his fists. The duct tape stopped him. "Big man, aren't you, with crazy Aunt Miranda by your side?"

Jonathan drove his fist into Gavin's nose. The cartilage snapped. Staggering pain crashed into the pounding at the back of Gavin's head. Blood gushed over his mouth and down his chest.

Jonathan shook out his hand. "You're in my way, Donne. I'm a Gow. People get out of our way or they get plowed under." He stepped back and crossed his arms. "Which is it?"

Gavin swallowed a mouthful of blood. His nose started to repair itself, but he spoke as though the blow had done permanent damage. "You suffer from short-term memory loss, Gow? I'll repeat it: Fuck you."

With one more tug, his right hand would be free. He just had to drag this out a little longer.

Jonathan raised his fist again, but Miranda stopped him.

"Jonathan, this isn't only about earthly justice."

Gavin shoved aside pain and fury and fear and laughed in her face. "What do you know about justice, Miranda? Your family lives in luxury stolen from the lives of slaves."

She adjusted her grip on the stake without answering him.

Gavin's body chilled, and not from the November wind.

Gow raised the stake.

———

Isolde threw her coat on the arm of the couch and kicked her shoes in the direction of the boot tray. Noelle had left the stove light on for her. Isolde set her phone on the kitchen counter and opened the fridge.

Was that her ringtone? She poked her head out of the crisper.

She was imagining things. Too much overtime. Her synapses were misfiring.

She rummaged under a pile of tangerines for a Cortland apple.

Her ringtone? She flipped open the phone.

She was hopeless. She wasn't hungry, either. It was twelve-forty and she should go to bed. She set the apple back under the tangerines.

Isolde hefted her phone. Twelve forty-one.

To hell with it. Isolde switched off the light, walked with deliberation into the living room, grabbed her coat, and shoved her feet into her old duck shoes. If Gavin was asleep, she'd pound on his door till he woke up. Or let Chay bark the whole neighborhood awake. Whatever worked.

The wind blew open her coat as she ran to the garage.

———

Gavin's heart held its breath. God in Heaven, she was holding the bear's fishing pole.

He looked down at the point he'd sharpened a few hours earlier, then up to Miranda's face. Her eyes. Her smile. The face of a fanatical prophet.

"Murderers and destroyers the Lord abhors." Gow balanced the stick in her hand.

Jonathan stared at her. "Aunt Miranda?"

Gavin stared at the stick he'd chosen for his bear. Miranda wasn't strong enough to stake him. Was she? Her nephew was. Would he help her? Gavin only had the one hand free. He needed more time.

"Rise up, Lord God!" Her cultured voice shrilled in the snow-muffled night. "Raise your arm!"

Gavin tried to wrench free, but the thick layers of tape held him.

Miranda rammed the stick into his chest.

———

Isolde's car skidded on black ice when she turned onto Summer Street. Winter driving in New England sucked out loud.

She tapped the brakes and slowed to thirty-five miles per hour.

———

Gavin screamed as white-hot pain blinded him. Blood spurted from the thumb-sized hole and his fangs sliced through his tongue. The stake hung, quivering, supported by his ribs.

"What the fuck?" Jonathan's voice.

Gavin closed his mouth. He had to hide the fangs. God, the pain—

"Are you nuts, Aunt Miranda? We came here to intimidate him!"

The roaring in Gavin's ears distorted Jonathan's voice, but the shock and horror came through.

Miranda's voice, cool and triumphant: "We came here to destroy evil, Jonathan."

Gavin lunged against the tape and closed his mouth on another scream. Blood soaked down his shirt. The world dimmed, then brightened.

He smelled their blood faintly through his own. His fangs ached with hunger and hate.

"You murdered him!" Jonathan replaced shock with panic. "The cops'll find our fingerprints on the doors and that stick. We're screwed."

Gavin's vision blurred as another wave of agony pounded him. Jonathan tried to drag Miranda away, but she planted her feet in the mud and slush at the base of the pedestal. The eerie smile still distorted her face.

"The morning sun will burn him to ash, Jonathan. There will be no traces. The stake will fall and his remains will mix with the sawdust." She pinched a bit next to Gavin's feet and watched the wind blew it away. "We've sent a monster to eternal torment. We've done God's work, just as our ancestor brought God's Word to New England."

Gavin tried to laugh, but his mouth wouldn't obey him. His head sank and his ears rang. So weak, so fast.

"Jesus Christ, Aunt Miranda, this isn't the Great Awakening or whatever that shit was you keep yapping about. This is a goddamn horror movie." He fumbled out a cigarette, but dropped it. "Fuck the job and fuck the family name and fuck this shit." He scooped up the soggy cigarette and stuffed it in his pocket. "I'm going inside to wipe our prints. If you want a ride home, you better hurry."

Jonathan's footsteps squished across the yard, slapped on the deck, and faded into the house.

Miranda came closer to Gavin's bowed head.

He glared at her, but kept his fangs hidden. If there was any chance he might escape this, his secret had to stay intact.

She held up Isolde's crucifix. "Perhaps your Jezebel will find this and wonder what became of you. But she'll meet you in Hell soon enough."

Gavin grunted with the effort not to move. He wasn't going to squander precious energy railing at the bitch. He had to free himself. She was not going to get her murdering hands on Isolde. He flexed his stomach muscles and the stake pierced deeper. The world tilted. He kept the scream in his throat as blood dripped down his jeans and onto his socks.

Miranda placed the crucifix between his feet and carried both spotlights into his house.

———

A white Lexus ran the red light at Bridge Street and skidded on a patch of black ice. Its taillights dwindled in Isolde's rear-view mirror.

"Slow down, dummy. It's nearly midnight. What's the rush?" She turned left onto Friedenfels.

———

Gavin's ears lost the sound of Miranda's Lexus driving away on the icy street.

He was still breathing. Impossible.

He listened to the blood pulsing onto his shirt.

Pulsing.

Beating.

A feeble laugh dribbled from Gavin's lips. Miranda missed his heart. Stupid cow. The Inquisition would've used her for target practice.

He tried to draw a deep breath, but cold, relentless pain engulfed him. He had *to* stay awake. It was his only hope. He coughed, reawakening the hammers and anvils pounding in his head. No one was going to find him before morning.

Hadn't he called Isolde? Her remembered dialing her number… No. Gow's nephew knocked him out before she answered.

Hard to breathe. Nose must've stopped healing. He should've fed today. Smart of Gow to choose his weakest day to play Van Helsing, or dumb luck? The latter. Some Internet research and a few Hammer films and she dubs herself the Hand of God.

God.

This would be his judgment day. Would Jeremiel sprinkle him with holy water? Would he be counted among the Redeemed? Had he relied on grace or works?

He wished Isolde's music box was out here. He strained his eyes, but couldn't see the tiny crucifix at his feet.

No one would pray the Burial Service over his ashes but him. If God had accepted Gavin's years as a priest, then perhaps He would accept his prayers now.

"From everlasting death, deliver my soul, O Lord. Lord, hear my prayer, and let my cry come unto Thee." His voice was barely a whisper.

Gavin tried to move again. The stake scraped against his ribs and he dug his fangs into his lip to hold in the scream.

Snow and sawdust blew into his face. He coughed. Fire scored his chest.

No more time.

A phantom cello played in his ears. "Drop, drop, slow tears..."

His singing voice sounded ghastly—an echo from a haunted graveyard. He couldn't feel his hands or feet anymore.

"And bathe those beauteous feet..."

———

Isolde parked in front of Gavin's garage and looked toward his dark house. Duh—it was just after midnight. Gavin was probably in that king-sized bed, sound asleep. Maybe with Chayyliel making a huge dent at his back.

She set the keys in her open purse. The wind tried to drag off her coat her when she got out of the car. This had been a dumb idea, but, she might as well go all the way and make a fool of herself by waking up Gavin. He was just a few steps and one doorbell ring away.

When the automatic porch lights kicked on, Chayyliel shuffled up to her and rubbed his face on her uniform skirt. Isolde crouched and wiped his face with another part of her skirt.

"What happened, Chay?" His eyes watered, the fur on his face and snout was matted, and he whimpered with every other breath. She touched his fur and smelled her fingertips. "Pepper spray. That's cruel. Who'd do that to a guard dog?"

Thieves would. Isolde jumped up and tried the door. Unlocked.

"Gavin?" She opened it all the way. "Gavin?" What was she waiting for? He could be lying in there hurt or bleeding.

"Chay, I'll clean you up as soon as I find Gavin." She ran through the house, turning on lights as she passed them. "Gavin? Are you in here? Gavin?"

———

Isolde's voice.

Gavin raised his head a few inches.

"Isolde." Just a whisper. She couldn't hear a whisper. He cleared his throat—hurt—burned—so thirsty.

"Isolde." A croak.

Lights appeared in the upstairs windows. She was still in the house.

"Come to the porch, Isolde. Come out on the deck. See me."

———

Nothing upstairs. Nothing downstairs. Nothing in the cellar. Isolde stood in the middle of Gavin's living room and stamped her foot.

Couch. Fireplace. Chairs. Door to deck. Bookshelves. Lighted bookshelf. Piano—she dived under the piano and snatched Gavin's open cell phone. She pressed 'send' and the list of calls appeared. Her number was the last one. She set it on the piano.

"Gavin!"

He could be unconscious, but where in the house was he? There was no blood anywhere. Could he have crawled away after an attacker?

The back porch.

She ran. Nothing inside. Oh, no—not the backyard. He'd freeze out there.

She turned on the deck floodlights. The bear carving moved.

———

The outer edge of the deck lights just touched Gavin. He took a careful, shallow breath and raised his head.

"Isolde."

CHAPTER FIFTY-FOUR

"Gavin!"

Isolde ran across the yard, kicking up clods of mud and slush.

"Oh, my God—" She touched the five-foot stick protruding from his ribs and he hissed.

She almost wept. "You're not dead. You're not dead."

"Take—it—out." He rasped the words through gritted teeth.

Isolde stood to one side to allow more light onto Gavin. She had to focus. Catalog his injuries. His nose was bruised but not broken. She touched it. Swollen, that was all. His lips were turning blue. Cold combined with blood loss. How much blood loss? She palpated the skin around the wound and Gavin hissed again.

"You've lost some blood, but it looks like the stick missed your major organs." She studied its upward angle and gauged its depth of penetration. "Gavin, I think you're bleeding internally. If I remove the stick, you could bleed out." She met his dark, desperate eyes. "I'm calling 9-1-1."

Cell phone—purse—damn, it was in the car. Wait—she groped in her coat pocket. Yes. She'd put it there on her way out of the house.

"Isolde."

She stopped with her cell phone half out of its case.

"Take—it—out—now."

"Gavin, listen—"

"Now—" His rasping voice broke.

She could do it. She had the strength, she'd just have to cut the... duct tape? What kind of sick bastard— "First tell me where the scissors are so I can cut the tape after."

"Office. Next to. Living room. Desk drawer."

Isolde ran into the house, snatched them, and ran out, leaving a slick, muddy trail on the floor.

"All right." She wrapped both hands around the stick, close to Gavin's body. "Are you ready?"

No answer.

"Gavin?"

She held one hand against his heart. Sluggish. His pulse. Shallow and erratic. No more time.

She wrenched out the stick.

––––––

Gavin roared as the stake chewed through his chest. Isolde screamed with him as he slumped within duct tape.

Too late.

His legs moved. Isolde must have cut the tape. She was saying something.

"You're almost free. I'll catch you. Don't worry."

The bands around his chest opened. He had nowhere near the strength to hold himself upright. Isolde cut the last strips around his shoulders and with a sticky, tearing sound he collapsed on top of her.

––––––

Isolde landed flat on her back. Gavin's weight squashed her into the cold mud.

He wasn't dead. He couldn't be dead. She got here in time.

She rolled him off her, toward the house, keeping her arms around him. Her soaked uniform slapped against her legs as she eased him onto his back. More light reached here, illuminating his gray, sunken face.

"Gavin, talk to me."

He breathed faster now, but not deeply enough. His teeth chattered and his forehead was clammy. Shock. She stripped off her coat and covered him with it. Thank God for her training. She rubbed his arms and his legs, working heat from friction into them.

He coughed and his body convulsed. Relief made her hands shale as she pulled her phone out of her coat pocket again. "I'm calling 9-1-1."

"No." His arm flailed and knocked it out of her hand.

"You have a hole in your chest, Gavin. You're in shock. You need surgery and a transfusion." She reached across him for the phone.

He clutched her arm. "No."

What was wrong with his teeth?

———

Skin. Naked. Short sleeves? Veins. Blood—

Gavin yanked Isolde's inner elbow to his mouth and punched his fangs into her cephalic vein.

———

Isolde gasped. Blistering pain shot up her arm as Gavin gulped her blood.

Gavin.

Sucking.

Her.

Blood.

CHAPTER FIFTY-FIVE

Sweet, hot blood flowed down Gavin's throat. In less than a minute it spread throughout his body and the cold vanished.

He shoved his face deeper and his fangs tore apart the skin. The hole in his chest began to heal.

———

Her voice stuttered in her head: Get off get off get off

"Gavin—" Only a gasp. "Gavin—"

His—fangs—pierced deeper.

Stop stop stop

"Stop!"

Isolde hit Gavin's head. Again. He didn't budge.

"Stop!" She punched everything she could reach. His temple. His forehead. His ear. His temple again.

Those sounds. A milkshake. A mouth slurping a thick milkshake through a straw. Her vision dimmed. Her ears buzzed. She hit his head. Harder. Again.

Get off get off

He paused to breathe. She ripped her arm out of his mouth, scrambled to her feet, and ran.

———

Gavin's heart beat stronger with every swallow. His fingers and toes tingled. His cheeks filled out. His chest expanded. The shredded muscles and flesh inside the hole repaired. The ragged edges closed.

Something hit his head.

He filled his mouth again.

What was hitting his head—ouch—

He took a quick breath. The fountain vanished.

———

Isolde slipped in the mud, flailed on her hands and knees, then regained her feet on the deck. Her left arm throbbed. She couldn't feel her fingers. She ran through the house, slipped again on the kitchen floor, stumbled down the porch steps, and locked herself inside her car.

Oh my God oh my God

She touched the place where the—monster—pierced her vein. The thinnest trickle ran down her forearm. She banged at the overhead light till it lit. Two quarter-inch slits spaced one inch apart violated her inner elbow. The edges were already bruising.

Why wasn't there more blood?

Why did they look like teeth marks?

Gavin just—Gavin just drank—

Isolde fumbled with the lock, pushed open the door, and vomited onto the driveway.

———

Gavin stared up at the fishing bear's round belly. Cold, wet mud soaked him from the back of his head all the way to his heels, but he wasn't shivering any more. He fingered the thick wool lying on top of him. Then he worked his hand underneath and felt ripped, wet cotton. But his skin was whole, if a bit tender.

Who put a coat over him?

Whom had he fed from?

CHAPTER FIFTY-SIX

Isolde found a tissue in the glove compartment and wiped her mouth. The cold air cleared her head. Her hands shook like she had Parkinson's. She couldn't drive home like this. She'd hit more black ice and skid into the river.

She looked at her arm again. The slits were closing.

Her body shivered so hard the steering wheel rattled. She had to leave. Had to get out of his reach. She had to get steady enough to drive.

"Angel of God my guardian dear to whom God's love commits me here ever this day be at my side to light and guard and rule and guide." Where did she dredge that up from? And her voice trembled almost as much as her hands.

A practical voice in her head overrode the childhood prayer and gave her orders. Say it. You're afraid. What if he's—it's—in the house? What if—it's—already at the front door? Coming for you? Leave, Isolde. Start the car and drive. Get out of Gavin—of Gavin—of the—monster's—reach.

She needed help. 9-1-1. That's who you called for help.

She upended her purse. No cell phone. She flung pens, scrunchie, comb, wallet, gum, flashlight all over the front seat.

Where was it? Where? She always had her cell.

Oh, God. It was in the backyard. The monster hit it out of her hand.

She couldn't get it back. Wouldn't. Wasn't going near it—him—it.

She could cancel the contract in the morning. That meant a couple hundred bucks' penalty.

So what? She'd pay it.

Leave. Go.

The keys were in the ignition when she heard a pitiful bark from the front porch.

Chayyliel. She couldn't leave him with the monster. It might—bite—the poor dog tomorrow.

Dear sweet Jesus in Heaven, they were supposed to get married in three weeks.

Isolde's stomach somersaulted, but she'd already emptied it.

Chayyliel barked again. She had to help him. She could do it. Unlatch his chain, lure him into the back seat, drive away.

She'd do it. Gavin—it—he—didn't know she was still here. She would save Chayyliel and get out. She wouldn't have to get near him—it.

Isolde's knees buckled only once on her way up the stairs. A small, clinical voice in the back of her mind said, 'Why aren't you weaker from blood loss? Did he put something in your blood?' But that thought made her want to run screaming for home, and Chayyliel needed her.

He whimpered and licked her hands as she felt for the clip on his collar. The moment he was free, he galloped down the steps and around the house.

Isolde ran after him. "Chay! Come back! Chay!"

He went straight for the monster. His huge snout nuzzled—it—between yips.

She inched toward the dog.

The monster laughed.

CHAPTER FIFTY-SEVEN

Gavin licked his lips. Jasmine.

God in Heaven, He'd fed from Isolde. She'd be petrified.

He leaned on his elbows. Chay licked his face and stuck his cold nose in his ear.

Gavin laughed in a voice that was almost back to normal. "Chay, Stop it. I'm all right." He sneezed. "Come here, boy. Give me your face."

He sat up, Isolde's warm coat sliding onto his lap. He grasped the dog's head, sniffed, and sneezed again.

"Pepper spray? Who—Gow." That psychotic bitch and her thug nephew. "At least they didn't stake you, too, boy."

Gavin shuddered. Old wives would say that someone had just walked over his grave. But he wasn't dead. He wasn't damned. Isolde had saved him.

Chayyliel bumped Gavin's shoulder and barked. He loped toward the side of the deck and returned to Gavin. Another bump.

"I'm not one hundred percent yet, boy. What is it?" He looked in the same direction as Chay. "Isolde?"

The dog bounded toward her and grabbed her arm in his teeth.

She jerked back. "No, Chay, no. Come away from the monster. Come on, boy."

Her voice sounded one step away from complete hysteria. She tried to pull Chay toward her, but the dog worked her closer to Gavin a foot at a time.

Monster. From Isolde. Gavin could have wept. Isolde's hair and uniform were clotted with mud and—yes—blood on her left sleeve as well. He had to be gentle. One abrupt move and she'd bolt. Not that he was capable of 'abrupt' yet.

He held out his hand. "Belle Isolde."

She jumped and her sleeve ripped. Chayyliel held on.

"Isolde, it's me."

She shook her head over and over—short, tight movements. Tears streaked her face. She dug in her heels against Chay's pull and the bottom of her sleeve ripped away. Chay skidded backwards and Isolde fell on her rump. Slush and mud squished up around her.

Gavin got to his knees. A little woozy at first, but it passed. Chayyliel barked and his giant paws came down hard on Gavin's shoulders. Gavin fell sideways, but caught himself with one hand.

"Down, Chay. Give me a minute."

Three feet away from him, Isolde tried to get purchase in the slush. Her shoes slipped. She clawed up a handful of mud and flung it at Gavin, but it fell short.

Chayyliel leapt for the mud ball. When he couldn't find it in the rest of the mud, he trotted over to Isolde and sat, eager and panting.

Gavin used the bear for leverage to pull himself upright. Strips of duct tape caught at his sleeves. He peeled them off and took a wobbly step toward Isolde.

———

The monster—Gavin—it—was coming for her.

Isolde slid backwards in the muck, her soaked uniform weighing her down. He was getting closer. He was going to open his mouth and attack her with those teeth. Fangs. With those fangs. She sneaked a glance at her arm. The holes had closed and they didn't hurt at all. That freaked her more than if she'd been bleeding out into the mud.

What was he—a human mosquito? No, then he'd have foot-long nose like a bendy straw. Besides, her arm didn't itch.

She giggled. The high, breathy sound of her own voice scared her.

She'd lost it. The monster was coming for her and she was sitting here like a clueless B-movie heroine. All she needed was a diaphanous white nightgown and marabou slippers.

Chayyliel licked her face and she revived. She put her arms around the dog and squelched to her feet.

The monster was only a few feet away. He moved slowly, like a convalescent.

Run.

But if she ran, Chayyliel would grab her again. She was trapped.

––––

When Gavin was close enough to touch Isolde, he stopped. "Isolde, it's me. Gavin."

She stared at him, white rims around dark eyes, skin pale as ivory. Then she sneezed.

"Sweetheart, we're both freezing. Come inside and I'll light a fire." He held out his hand. She stepped back.

Chayyliel trotted behind Gavin and bumped the backs of his legs with his massive head. Gavin lost his uncertain balance and fell to his hands and knees at Isolde's feet. Isolde yelped.

Gavin looked up at her with a wry smile. "I'm not quite myself yet." He sat on his heels in the muck and wiped his hands on his jeans.

Isolde whispered, "What are you?"

"Not what, sweetheart, who. I haven't changed."

"You have—you did—" She sneezed again.

"Isolde, come in the house before you catch pneumonia." This time he sneezed and pain scored his chest. He doubled over, gasping.

Isolde knelt beside him and held him steady.

"Not—quite—healed." He breathed through the fire clawing his chest.

Why was she holding him? She must have reverted to nurse mode and forgotten what he'd just done to her.

She probed his ribs. "Let me see." Then she snatched her hand from beneath his shirt and backpedaled into the deck. "That's impossible."

Gavin took a slow breath. "Not impossible, just unusual." He leaned on the deck and tried to stand. "I could use a little help getting inside."

He regained his feet, but she didn't move near him. Tears rolled down her cheeks; her right hand clutched her left arm, covering the bite. Her breath came in short, sharp pants.

Gavin closed the distance with a hint of his usual speed and put his mud-covered hands on either side of her face. She flinched.

"I'm not going to hurt you."

She stared at his mouth.

Gavin brought her thumb to his lips. She tried to pull away, but he kept her there. She blinked away more tears and surprise crossed her face.

"Don't cry, Belle Isolde. It's okay. Feel." He ran her thumb along the base of his upper teeth. His fangs had retracted as soon as he gained control of himself underneath the bear. "Okay?"

She jerked away her hand. "No. Not okay." She stared at her uninjured thumb and tried to back away again.

Gavin dropped his hands to her shoulders and held her there. "Tell me."

Her whole body started to shake and Gavin caught it like a disease. He had to get them both to a fire and get nourishment into Isolde. He risked a bit of force.

"What kind of nurse are you, ma'am, to leave two injured people outside in this weather? Inside the house, please."

Isolde finally looked into his eyes. "Who are you? What are you? What happened here?"

Heavier snow started to fall. Chayyliel snapped at the big, puffy flakes.

"How can you wear my grandfather's crucifix if you're… if you're…" She brought up her arms and broke his hold. Her eyes caught her torn sleeve and healed bite. "No. No. Not possible."

Snow cascaded off Gavin's hair and into his eyes. *Enough.*

"Yes, it is possible. I'll explain if you get inside. Now." He hustled her into the back porch before she could run away again. Chayyliel followed.

CHAPTER FIFTY-EIGHT

Isolde stood shivering just inside the sliding door on Gavin's back porch. Her teeth chattered. Her soaked hair dripped cold water down her back. Her ruined uniform clung to her like a refrigerated body glove.

Chayyliel planted all four feet on the mat and shook himself from shoulders to tail.

"Chay! I'm wet enough." She sneezed.

Gavin stumbled in from the living room. "What happened?"

Chayyliel lay flat on the floor and put his nose between his paws.

Isolde didn't answer. Gavin looked so normal. Like he really was a regular guy who liked obscure music and dogs and tall, thin blondes. But he wasn't. He wasn't. He was—

"Chay, you inconsiderate load of fur." Gavin opened a storage chest next to the mat. "Stand up." Gavin rubbed him down, and used the wet towel to wipe the pepper spray residue from his face. "Look how wet you got Isolde. Say you're sorry."

A semi-fluffy Chayyliel flopped at Isolde's feet and whimpered.

Isolde smiled into his huge black eyes. Who could resist a vicious guard dog who thought he was a giant puppy made for love? She reached down to pat him and he popped up to slurp her hand.

"Good boy, Chay."

He reared, thumped his paws on her shoulders, and licked her dirty face. Isolde laughed.

He sniffed her left arm and the laugh choked off. Then he pasted that huge tongue over the tender, closed punctures.

She was deluding herself. This wasn't normal. This was parallel-freaking-universe abnormal. She edged toward the door while Gavin balled up the towel and set it on the mat. Outside, the wind whipped the heavy snow into glittering mounds. Where was her coat? Oh… she'd put her coat over it—Gavin—when she cut him free. Her cell phone would be near it. She wasn't quite as freezing now. If she took off her shoes, her toes would be able to grip the mud through her stockings.

Her big toe hooked into the back of her smooth, practical nurse's shoe. There. Easy. One shoe off.

"Come on, Chay." Gavin led the dog into the kitchen. "Isolde, I'll be right back."

Second shoe off. She slid the door open a crack.

———

Gavin came back into the empty porch and ran for the open door. "Isolde, wait—" He tripped over her shoes. She was barefoot in the snow? Was the woman insane?

He crossed the deck in two strides. Snow clung to his mud- and bloodstained socks. He dragged them off and left them there. Now that her blood had brought him back to near-total strength, wet feet were nothing.

He reached her as she fought to extract her coat out of the swamp around the fishing bear. One hand gripped the collar, the other a sleeve and her cell phone. Gavin freed the coat with a single tug.

"Isolde, please get back inside. Your immune system can't handle this. You need to replenish your blood."

She snatched the coat and swung the cell phone at him. "What did you do to me?"

For the first time since he regained consciousness fastened to the bear, Gavin breathed easier. She'd said 'you.' Not 'it' or 'monster.'

He caught her hand. "Please, Isolde. You have to get dry and warm. Come sit in front of the fire. I'll make you hot chocolate with crème de menthe."

"Tell me who you are." Cold and fatigue overpowered the fear in her voice.

"I'm the man who loves you enough to put up with marriage counseling and Disney movies."

She almost smiled.

CHAPTER FIFTY-NINE

Isolde curled in the corner of Gavin's couch in front of the fire and sipped spiked cocoa. On the hearthrug in front of her, Gavin wiped Chayyliel's face with a wet cloth.

"There you go, boy. Let me see your eyes."

The dog jerked his head away from Gavin's fingers and knocked him on his back.

Gavin laughed. "You're welcome, Chay." He tried to block the dog's enthusiastic tongue. "I'm glad I'm still here, too."

Isolde smiled at Chayyliel's slobbery delight and scratched her feet through Gavin's wool socks without much effect.

Gavin turned his wet, happy face to her. "Isolde, let me wash the mud off your feet."

"No. Thanks. I'm fine." She held the mug in front of her to keep her inner arms out of sight. Some shield.

"If you don't want me to touch you, at least take a hot shower."

Apparently she was Miss Transparent tonight. "No. Thanks. Really." She looked away from his regular green eyes. What did that mean? Was his eye-color changing thing all her imagination? If it wasn't, did he have some kind of hypnotic hold over her?

She had to stop thinking like that or she'd run home barefoot, and to hell with her immune system. A week in the hospital on oxygen and IV antibiotics or... Or what? Ask him if he used some kind of Vulcan mind-meld on her? She wanted to ask. She was too scared to ask.

That's why she couldn't take a shower here. To be naked and defenseless in its—his—house was scarier than, scarier than... Alzheimer's.

Yet he was the soul of thoughtfulness. He'd set his Patriots sweats—how odd, how funny, he really was a Patriots fan—in the bathroom for her to change into. He didn't touch her. The sweats were two sizes too big for her, but they were thick and soft and absorbed the heat from the fire like she was toasting her freezing skin. Her still-muddy feet swam in his wool socks.

Gavin gathered the cloths and towels from Chayyliel's cleanup and headed for the kitchen. On his way he tossed them down the cellar stairs and they landed with a plop.

"Isolde, can I make you something to eat?" Water ran into the sink, followed by lots of splashing. He came back into the doorway drying his face and hands. "Soup? Buttered toast?"

She indicated the mug. "This is fine."

He wasn't eating or drinking, and he'd been out in the snow longer than she had. Plus he was injured. Had been injured.

The mug started to shake. Every time she was sure she'd gotten a grip on herself, something shattered it.

His long hand reached around her and took the mug. She tried and failed not to flinch. He set the mug on the end table and himself at the opposite end of the couch.

"Where should we start?"

The chorus of 'Hakuna Matata' sounded from the kitchen.

Isolde scrambled to her feet. "My phone still works." She ran into the kitchen, sliding twice on the wood floor in the oversize socks. "Hello?"

"Izz? It's Ellie. It's nearly two."

"I didn't realize it was so late. Why are you up?"

Noelle yawned. "I wanted to talk to you, but I fell asleep. Are you at Gavin's?"

Isolde leaned against the doorframe. To keep an eye on—him—or to show him she wasn't running away? She didn't want him to chase her again.

"Izz?"

"Sorry." She gulped. "Yes, I'm at, um, his house."

Noelle's voice sharpened. "You two having a fight?"

"Not exactly. What did you want to talk about?" Anything to get Ellie off the subject of her and—him.

"Feel like postponing your wedding a few weeks?"

Isolde gripped the little phone. Bad question. What to say? Ellie would catch— wait. "Why?"

"Stephen asked me to marry him."

Isolde squee'd and threw aside all the evening's craziness. "When? Where? How did he ask? Did he give you a ring?"

Noelle's voice tripped over hers. "This afternoon, after everyone finally quit drooling over Miranda's family scandal. Oh, Izz, he was so romantic. He got down on one knee and everything."

Isolde blinked through sudden tears. She'd been that giddy a few days ago. "Ellie, I'm so happy for you."

"Stephen's the one who thought of the double wedding. He's checking with his friend in Rockport to see if he'll perform the ceremony on New Year's. Or better yet, on Christmas Eve. Doesn't that sound wonderful?"

"It does." She would not cry. Crying was weak. She had to stand up to—him.

"So is Gavin right there? What does he think?"

Isolde cleared her throat. "I'll ask him later."

Noelle stopped chattering. "Are you fighting?"

"I have to go now, Ellie."

Noelle didn't answer for a moment. Then in a different, serious voice, she said, "Signor Ferrari thinks it might just be possible to get an exit visa for you."

Isolde bit the inside of her bottom lip. If she said, 'Round up the usual suspects,' Noelle would come over and extract her with their 'Bad Boyfriend Excuse.' In high school, it was emergency babysitting. As adults, it was emergency overtime.

She watched Gavin watching her.

It was now or never. She had to trust yourself and trust him, or run.

She stared at his eyes. Not dark, not intense. Normal. If the word meant anything anymore. Her voice said, "We are only interested in two visas."

Noelle exhaled. "Okay, Izz. You coming home tonight?"

"It depends. Don't worry about me. Call your mom and use all your rollover minutes."

"Already did. Ask Gavin about the double wedding, okay? Talk to you tomorrow."

Isolde closed her phone and picked at the dried mud on the side keys.

Gavin said, "That sounded like code."

CHAPTER SIXTY

Isolde's hands clutched the phone and the ringtone tripled in volume. "Oops. Hit the wrong button. Sorry."

Gavin cursed himself as she brought the song back to an average level. He'd forgotten for a moment. Slow and patient. She had a brain. She could handle it if he didn't frighten her again. What would make her laugh? Ah.

"Did you use that extraction signal the night your dinner date went into his apartment a man and came out a woman?"

She snorted. "He was so weenie I didn't need help." Her wide eyes met his and her voice dropped to a whisper. "How did you know about that?"

"Noelle told me."

Her shoulders un-hunched. "Oh." She glanced at the front door, then step by slow step returned to her end of the couch.

Gavin clenched his fists so he wouldn't reach over and caress her face. Between the blood loss—how much had he taken from her?—cold, and fear, she looked almost translucent.

She reached for the cocoa, but saw the healed teeth marks and pulled her arm back.

He smiled. "We can't sit here all night ignoring the elephant in the living room."

Isolde tucked her knees against her chest and wrapped her arms around them. "I don't know where to start."

Gavin knew where: With her leaning against him on this couch, listening to him say that he owed her his life. That she was his gift from God. That he would spend her lifetime in her service for that debt.

Her lifetime. His throat tried to close. Sixty more years, in all likelihood. With him unchanged and her with gray hair, wrinkles, and arthritis at the least. And what if her cancer returned?

"G—Gav—" She swallowed. "Why are you crying?"

"I am?" He wiped his hand across his face. He hadn't cried since Hannah's last, disastrous childbirth. One hundred and three years. Alone. Skimming the surface. Existing.

He blinked, but Isolde still wavered in his watery vision.

To hell with fear.

Gavin stretched across the couch like Mr. Fantastic and dragged Isolde into his arms. She opened her mouth, but if she meant to scream, his kiss swallowed it. She squirmed in his grip. He kissed her harder. She shoved at him and kicked his leg, then something crashed.. They both looked over to the tipped mug spinning on the tabletop and cocoa splashing onto the hearthrug.

He pulled her tighter against him. "Isolde, you saved me. I would've died by morning if you hadn't come."

She still struggled.

"I'm sorry. I'm so sorry, sweetheart. I was working on how to tell you. I didn't expect Gow to attack me like that." He kissed every place he could reach: forehead, eyebrows, cheeks, wondering in an abstract way whose tears he was tasting.

"Let go—let go—"

He opened his arms enough for her to push away. Her eyes had that trapped-animal look again, but to a lesser degree. She rubbed her lips with one hand but stayed on the couch.

"Gow did that to you?"

"Her and her nephew." Like the worst kind of cliché romance hero, he ached to hold her. He wanted to kiss her hands and tell her a hundred times how much he owed her.

She stared at his mouth, inhaled, and said, "Show me."

"Who are you and what have you done with Isolde who hates all things scary?"

Her nails dug into his sweatpants. "I have never been so scared in all my life, but right now I think I'm going mental, so terror is a better option."

He rested a hand on her leg. "Isolde—"

She swept it off. "Don't."

He nodded. "All right." It took an act of will since he was full to bursting, but he opened his mouth and extended his incisors.

––––––

Isolde whimpered. Her rigid hands clenched the Patriots sweatpants till her nails threatened to poke through.

Oh, God, she was sitting twelve inches away from a, from a… "It's impossible."

His—fangs—retracted and his teeth returned to normal. This wasn't happening. Vampires didn't exist. There. She said the word.

She dragged her gaze away from his teeth and met his eyes. They were dark again, forest-green flecked with emerald. Tears still lurked in their corners.

"Why are your eyes dark? No, wait. Why are they changing back to emerald green again?"

Gavin smiled. "I thought only animated heroes had emerald-green eyes."

Isolde closed hers. "Don't smile at me. I forget what you are when you smile."

"Sweetheart—"

"Don't call me that! You're not a man—you're a walking nightmare—you ripped my arm open and drank—" She choked trying to disguise a sob. "How can you exist? How can you look so normal and act just like you always do when you're a, you're a—" She clutched her healed arm with her other hand and the sob escaped. "You're a monster." But her voice made it sound like a question.

––––––

Gavin ignored Isolde's earlier warning and embraced her again.

"I'm not a monster, sweetheart. I'm not going to attack you. I'm never going to hurt you again."

Her body shook like she was still soaked and freezing in the backyard, but she wasn't trying to escape. He kissed her tangled, dirty hair. *Thank You, God. Thank You.*

When she quieted, Gavin turned her around and tucked her against his chest. "First rule for the rest of our lives together: Do not be afraid of me."

"No, first rule is find me a tissue."

Gavin laughed and sat her up. "I'll be right back." He paused after his first step toward the bathroom. "Isolde?"

"I won't leave."

He sprinted there and back and set the box on the coffee table. She hadn't moved. While she blew her nose, he rearranged the logs in the fireplace and added two more. She almost didn't flinch when he snuggled her against him again.

"Have I told you that you look warm and fuzzy and adorable in my Patriots sweats?"

A shiver.

He rubbed her arms, and a memory clicked. "Did you try to warm me like this after you pulled out the stake?"

"Gavin." Her voice shivered as well.

He kissed her. "You said my name."

"It's... hard."

"Sweetheart, that you're still here is equivalent to climbing Everest."

He sat her up again and slid to his knees on the floor. Her lips parted in surprise—not fear, he was almost sure. He took her hands and kissed them.

"Isolde, I owe you my life. My service is yours until the day you die. You are God's undeserved gift to me."

She looked nonplussed and a little charmed. Then her expression changed. "Why not until the day you die?"

He didn't answer.

"How old are you, Gavin?"

He exhaled slowly. "I was born in 1489."

CHAPTER SIXTY-ONE

Isolde practically heard her synapses short out. This was more surreal than the evening in her music room when Gavin talked about getting married after knowing her only five days.

"Tell me you're kidding. Tell me I'm not here. That it's all a sausage pizza nightmare. That tomorrow I'll find a message from you on my cell phone saying you tried to call but forgot to charge your battery." She looked down at her hands, clutching his like the cliff she was hanging from was physical instead of mental.

He gave her a crooked smile. "Look at me." His fangs appeared.

"Oh, God—"

He switched the positions of their hands faster than she could follow. Her eyes snapped up to his face again and he spoke with a slight lisp.

"Listen to me. You have nothing to fear from me. Ever." The fangs contracted, leaving straight white teeth. He turned her hands palm up and kissed them.

She remembered that kiss. His lips felt the same as always. His hands did, too. He smelled the same, under the dried mud. Now that he wasn't reenacting a horror movie before her eyes, he was the exact same Gavin she'd agreed to marry.

She wasn't dreaming. She had to face it. Bang in the center of her average life in this average small town in plain old America, the stuff of fiction knelt at her feet. If he were a real man, she'd be in romance heaven.

He was a real man. He'd proved that in bed.

Zzzzt. Another short. She'd slept with him.

"What are you thinking, Belle Isolde?"

A dozen ideas fought for priority on her tongue. The most inconsequential, but perhaps the most telling, won. If he answered this— "Did you know Malory?"

He laughed. "No. He was dead by then. My uncle knew Caxton, though, and was wealthy enough to own one of his first editions. My cousins and brothers and sisters and I spent three very long winters reading it. Blackletter was never easy on the eyes."

Zzzzt. "You mean it. All of it. You're telling the truth."

"Yes." He raised his eyebrows and his eyes caught the firelight. "What other proof can I give you? You have to believe me."

Snatches of prayers tumbled through her mind yet she realized she wasn't hang-from-the-ceiling freaked-out anymore. But the prayers reminded her of something else.

"Church. My grandfather's crucifix. How?"

"I told you I was raised Catholic. I've also been a Benedictine monk in France and a Jesuit priest in Spain." He gripped her hands. "I believe, Isolde."

She slid one hand free and tweaked open a button on his ruined shirt. "It's not there."

"What?" He reached into his collar. "Damn. Where did it— Gow."

"Gow took your crucifix?"

He was already up and moving toward the back porch. "She took it off me and provoked me with it, but I think she left it here. By the bear, maybe. I'll be right back."

Isolde sank into the couch because she didn't think her legs would hold her. At least her brain had stopped shorting out. That was one good thing. Gavin didn't seem to think she'd bolt like a scared rabbit this time. Was that a good thing? Did it mean she was in his power somehow? Or did it mean that despite the—

teeth and the blood and, well, everything, that he was still Gavin who loved her? And was that truth unchanged within her as well?

The sliding door closed and Gavin's feet stamped on the mat in the back porch. When he came into the living room, his hair and shoulders were covered with more fluffy snowflakes.

"By the bear's feet. I remember now. She put it there and went inside after her nephew."

"You have to tell me what happened."

"I will, but not before I prove myself to you."

He draped the chain over his head and the white gold glimmered against his shirt. Then he picked up the crucifix and kissed it.

His lips didn't scorch. His body wasn't incinerating. He didn't look hurt at all.

Isolde threw up her hands. She couldn't argue with Gavin as Gavin—not as shrieking, blazing monster—right in front of her.

"I'll clean up the cocoa before it damages the table further. Then I might take you up on your offer of food." Her stomach rumbled. She had the feeling she'd been this hollow for awhile and just hadn't noticed. She reached for the fallen mug.

Before she could touch it, Gavin crushed her to his chest and kissed her again and again.

CHAPTER SIXTY-TWO

Gavin could've watched Isolde eat peanut butter sandwiches and chicken soup for hours. She was still here. She believed him. She—he prayed—still loved him.

"The church forbade marriage between first cousins, but Philippa and I sneaked around for a year. I thought only the grace of God kept her from getting pregnant. Birth control methods weren't so reliable then."

Isolde shook half her sandwich at him. "Two horny fifteen-year-olds thinking with the wrong parts of their bodies. Always a recipe for disaster."

Gavin shook his head. "Not that way. You'll see. The manor church was named for St. Thomas the Apostle, so July third was always a big feast day. A long Mass, of course, but afterwards a banquet and entertainment and dancing till the small hours."

She moaned. "The instruments."

"Yes. I would have loved to see you play an original viola da gamba." Inside, Gavin rejoiced. Even if Isolde was focusing on inconsequential details of his story, it still meant she was becoming comfortable in his presence again.

"Toward the end of the dancing, Philippa and I sneaked away to the room she shared with my sisters. We knew we were safe, because both of my sisters were singing a duet to end the evening and had gone to the wine cellar to practice."

He reached over and wiped a crumb of sandwich from the corner of Isolde's mouth. "Philippa liked to be on top, and especially liked to nip when she kissed me. That night she was more enthusiastic than usual, and when she climaxed, she bit into my neck. I remember pain first, then ecstasy, like a second orgasm. I wasn't thinking at all. When she didn't take away her teeth after a few minutes, the ecstasy changed into worse pain than before. I thought my blood was cooking inside me."

He didn't like to remember this. Hadn't thought about those three days in at least a decade. His neck muscles twitched.

"I shoved her off and she growled at me. My blood smeared her mouth like overdone theater makeup and I saw her fangs. Then she tried to kiss me."

Isolde wrapped one arm around him.

"I threw her onto the floor and yelled and ran down to the great hall."

"Naked?" Isolde's hand massaged his neck and shoulder.

Gavin crooked a smile. "Completely, and shouting 'gole' and 'deuel'. The music stopped. No one moved or spoke for a moment. Then my father and Friar Antonius pushed through the dancers and we ran upstairs. Philippa must have hit her head when she fell, because she was lying on the floor, rubbing the back of her head with one hand and scraping the blood from her lips into her mouth with the other. We all saw the fangs."

"What happened?" Her voice was soft and quiet, as though he were the one who needed gentle handling.

"Friar Antonius lifted up his big silver crucifix and advanced on her, just like in the movies. She screeched and tried to back away, but he straddled her legs and slapped the crucifix on her face." Gavin put his hand over Isolde's hard-working one on his shoulder. "She sizzled like grilling meat and her voice could've shattered glass. Friar Antonius shouted one paternoster after another as my father threw Philippa's dress over her naked body. They dragged her downstairs and two of my father's knights helped lock her in an empty storeroom. She fought and screamed and clawed at the knights. Her fangs still hadn't retracted and everyone in the hall saw them."

"But why didn't anyone notice you?"

"You mean, my bite marks? By the time Philippa was locked up, I'd put on my shirt. When I wiped the small amount of blood off my neck, the marks were already healing."

Isolde glanced at her left arm. Gavin ran his fingertips along her life-giving vein and she flinched. "Um... not comfortable with that yet."

He kissed the smooth, almost scar-free place on the crook of her elbow. "Isolde, you never have to fear me. Never." He wrapped her arm around his waist. "Friar Antonius barged into my bedroom when I was putting on my hose. He was a happy old man who loved honeycakes, and his waistline showed it. But he shouted, 'Appropinquabit enim judicium Dei,' shoved me against the wall, and pressed his crucifix into my face. I was too scared to say anything, even though Christ's head dug into my cheekbone."

"You had no reaction at all?"

"None. He removed it and inspected my face, then had me recite the paternoster with him."

"To prove you weren't—one—as well."

She still wasn't saying the 'v' word. "Yes. When we finished, he called in my father and his knights and I told them the whole story. My father boxed my ears for sleeping with my cousin, and the knights grinned at me behind his back. Philippa was quite the siren. Then I showed them the minuscule bite marks and Friar Antonius praised God's mercy for my escape." He chuckled. "At which point, I fainted."

Gavin looked sideways at Isolde. She looked overloaded again. Break time. He gathered her dishes. "I'll be right back."

She stood with him. "Let me help."

He scowled at her. "What part of 'you have to get your strength back' did you miss? Sit."

Gavin set the dishes in the sink and ran water in them. This ruse was so transparent you could read fine print through it. The pragmatic vampire needs a moment to collect himself before he tells the timid Disney princess about his shining moment of cowardice.

Back in the living room, he passed the couch and opened the fireplace grate.

Isolde's outwardly calm voice stopped him. "Gavin, you're stalling. Come and finish your story. The fire's fine."

She was right, of course. He returned to the loveseat armrest and she curled next to him. Isolde did look cute in his clothes. He disliked 'cute,' but for her he had no problem making an exception.

"I spent the rest of the night vomiting and with a raging fever, but my brothers forcibly walked me to morning Mass. Everyone watched me swallow the Host and drink the wine, and not spontaneously combust. That was the only time I've heard a collective sigh. My mother started to cry and my father recited the gloria patri.

"Friar Antonius began Philippa's trial in the storeroom right after Mass. It was just a formality. Philippa screamed and cursed throughout it, because the knights had entered the storeroom armed with crucifixes to force her into a corner."

Isolde said in that soft voice, "Did they involve you?"

He nodded. "I had to tell my story before my father, his steward, and the bailiff. I lied about how much blood she'd taken from me and never said a word about the way the bite marks healed. Philippa stopped cursing long enough to say how she planned for us to be together forever. My father clubbed her with the hilt of his sword. When she was unconscious, Friar Antonius opened her mouth. Her fangs had descended partway from the pain of the crucifixes, and they condemned her to be burned at the stake at dawn the next day."

Isolde frowned. "Why do you still feel guilty? It wasn't your fault."

"Around midnight that day the fever vanished. I was hungrier than I'd ever been, but I could've threshed an entire field or shoed all the horses by myself. That's how terrific I felt. I went to the buttery and stole some bread and chicken from supper and wolfed it down. Five minutes later I threw it all up. I ate too fast, I thought. I took more bread and a skin of wine outside, to catch a breeze."

"And you couldn't hold that down either."

"No. I was frightened and starving and didn't know what to do. Then a mouse ran over my foot and I snatched it. People weren't supposed to be able to move that fast. It tried to bite me and I broke its neck. I smelled its blood and stabbing pains shot through my incisors. Then my mouth was on it and I drained it."

Isolde didn't say anything.

"I looked at its flat little body and tasted wheat and berries on its blood. Half of me wanted to throw up and the other half thought it tasted better than mulled wine on Christmas Eve."

Isolde started.

"What?"

Her head moved right and left on his chest. "Later. I just remembered something I was supposed to ask you. Go on."

"I ran for the chapel and was sure the sight of the crucifix would immolate me. When it didn't, I prayed at its feet the rest of the night. Sometime toward dawn I fell asleep and dreamed of Judgment." He pulled Isolde closer. "I floated between Heaven and Hell. Fire billowed up from Hell and engulfed the damned, but the Redeemed rose into a sunlit Heaven. Demons tormented the damned and angels flew with the Redeemed."

"That's traditional."

"I know, but wait. In between those two groups, on a stone floor magically suspended in the air, were crowds of repentant sinners. Don't ask me how I knew, I just knew. They lay flat on their faces at Jesus' feet. An angel dipped a stalk of bearded wheat into a chalice filled with holy water and sprinkled the water over the prostrate sinners. Demons tried to drag them to Hell, but the holy water burned them and they flew away empty-handed. Jesus said, 'Jeremiel, your work is done.' He touched those people and they rose, Redeemed."

"Mm. That's a comforting dream."

"Don't patronize your elders." He kissed the top of her head. "Friar Antonius found me there when he came to say a private pre-dawn Mass. I told him about it and he said God had given it to me to remind me that Heavenly love is our true love."

"Talk about patronizing."

"The world was different then. Simpler. Demons tormented, angels helped, the Church knew the perfect will of God. I believed Friar Antonius. He let me assist at his Mass and once again I took Communion as though nothing had changed. Then we went out to burn Philippa.

"Friar Antonius asked her to repent and she cursed him and the Church. Everyone—my family, Philippa's family, villagers, servants, adults, and children—recited a final paternoster. Then the knights lit the wood. In less than five minutes it reached Philippa's gown. When she saw me, she laughed. She knew. She stared at me until her gown itself was a torch."

Isolde had laid his hands over her stomach and was stroking them with gentle fingers.

"She stopped screaming after a few minutes and we let the fire burn to ash. I lasted another week at home. When I tried to bite one of the kitchen maids, I ran away."

"Gavin—"

"I let Philippa die alone when I should've burned along with her. We were the same kind of creature, Isolde, but I was too much of a coward to admit it."

"Gavin—"

"I've done terrible things, but I've spent most of my five hundred years trying to make up for them. I know the limitations of medieval theology, but I've held onto the Judgment vision. I believe God gave it to me to strengthen my hope that I won't be damned when someone finally stakes me."

She continued to stroke his hands. Did she believe him? Was she thinking of the best way to return his ring? Hannah had been the last one to hear his story, and she had understood.

Isolde said in a quiet voice, "Young, scared, your body betraying you, and family chaos around you. We have more in common than you'd think." She tipped her head back, apprehension in little lines around her mouth. "You said outside that cold and, and blood loss would wreck my immune system. Was that merely a generic concern?"

He wouldn't lie to her, but he could be selective with the truth. She wasn't ready to know everything he did to her that night on the back porch. If he could ever bring himself to tell her.

"I tasted the leukemia in your blood."

She inhaled sharply.

"You had it as a child—correct?—and beat it, but it altered your blood enough for me to tell."

"That's creepy, Gavin."

He shrugged. "I've always been able to analyze blood that way. Not that I thought of it in those terms at first. I've met a few others who have the same ability."

She put up a hand. "Stop. Let me get used to you, yourself, before you hit me with Masonic Templar Vampire secret societies."

Gavin kissed her. "You said 'vampire.'"

She gave him a tentative smile. "It was time to kick the elephant out of the living room. Besides, it wouldn't leave room for all the Christmas decorations you claim to have. Oh—" She wormed out of his embrace and sat up. "I almost forgot. Stephen and Noelle are getting married, and they want to know what we think of a double wedding on Christmas Eve. New Year's is the second choice if Stephen's friend can't swing Christmas."

Gavin's still-intact (thanks to Isolde) heart pounded. "You're still going to marry me."

"You said you'd put up with my Disney princess obsession. How many men would be willing to do that?"

"'Men.'"

She shrugged in turn. "It's like learning a new instrument. I'm working on fitting its rules into my current body of knowledge."

She met his eyes, a ghost of fear lurking in hers. "I'm trying to get my balance. It's not here yet."

Gavin kissed her hand. "It will be my business to balance you."

"That sounds either like a trapeze act or like kinky sex."

He turned her hand over and kissed her palm. "Now, fayre lady, what wold ye I shold doo in this matere?"

CHAPTER SIXTY-THREE

Isolde searched her memory for a *Morte Darthur* quote. Before she found one—Malory's Isolde didn't have nearly enough good lines—Gavin lifted her hair and planted kisses all along her neck.

Only a brief flinch, and she hid it. She hoped. She didn't want to run. She wasn't really scared anymore. Just a little bit, like that tiny flinch when his lips had pressed the extinct bite marks.

"Gavin... will you need to... bite me? Regularly, I mean."

He stopped kissing her and laid her head over his heart. "If you don't want me to replenish from you, I can continue as I have been."

She dug her nails into her palms. "Tell me."

"I've trained myself to need approximately half a cup every four days. I also use simple hypnosis, so the person remembers nothing and suffers no ill effects."

She put a handbreadth of distance between them. "You've done that to me, haven't you?" The closing credits song from the Tristan movie played in her head. "On the porch, the night you didn't like the brownies."

He looked like a kid waiting to be called into the Principal's office. "Yes. How did you remember?"

"The lisp. You said a word with an 's' in it then, like you said just now when you showed me your, um, fangs." She shook her head. "This is the most surreal conversation I've ever had. Is that when you, um, tasted the old cancer?"

"It had been four days and I had to drink." He grasped her hands again. "You taste like jasmine, Belle Isolde. Delicate and fresh, light within rich depths."

She blushed at the extravagant compliment. "You are dangerous. You're seductive and charming and frightening—you know you are—and logical on top of it all. And you will not be talking like this about any other woman while you're married to me."

When had she made the choice to stay with him? The words had come out of her mouth hard on the flare of jealousy at the idea of Gavin that intimate with another woman.

Gavin's eyes lit—bright, clear, no darkness in them at all. He grasped the ruby and pearl ring on her finger. "Say it, Isolde. Tell me you're still going to marry me."

And she found the right quote.

"Myn own lord, I maye none other wyse doo."

CHAPTER SIXTY-FOUR

Gavin plumped the spare comforter around Isolde. His maroon cotton pajama top made her look paler and more vulnerable than she had on the couch.

"Are you warm enough?" The matching pajama bottoms twisted around his waist; he straightened them.

"My fingers and toes are chilly, that's all. Gavin, stop treating me like an invalid." She raised herself on one elbow. "I've given blood before."

"This was different."

"Only in atmosphere."

He stopped adjusting the covers to stare at her. She was smiling—he had indeed heard it in her voice. "You're amazing."

"Just practical."

Gavin climbed into the down cocoon and lay next to Isolde. He traced the curve of her breasts under the smooth cotton and threw a leg over hers. Chayyliel had been banished to a rug outside his bedroom door. There would be no damp dog-nose interruptions tonight. Rather, today: his nightstand clock read three-fifteen. He yawned.

Isolde yawned a moment later. "Do I want to know what time it is?"

"No. May I suggest you call in sick today?"

"The world might come to an end."

"Let it." He unbuttoned her top button. "Nothing is more important than me talking care of you today. We're going to sleep until noon and I'll order take-out for you. My pantry is limited."

She smiled. "Mmm... was that a joke?"

"No. Oh, I get it. No one's ever stayed here before. I only keep food with a long shelf life, and I'm not a creative cook."

"I'm really the first woman to stay here?"

He tickled her ear. "You are."

She snuggled deeper into the comforter. "I'm a decent cook. I'll see what you have when we get up."

He liberated another button. "This is your first test of wifely obedience, Ms. Connor. I refuse to let you perform any work today other than somewhat strenuous lovemaking."

"Mmm..."

"Was that 'mmm' an indication of agreement?"

Silence. He switched his attention from her buttons to her face.

"Isolde, are you awake?"

Silence. He smiled down at her. The circles under her eyes bothered him, but she looked healthy otherwise. Food and wine would erase her pallid skin tone. He reached backwards and turned off the nightstand light. Then he settled beside her, her long hair tangling in his chest hair, her breathing calm and even.

"Ego dedi vestri ancilla vobis, Isolde," Gavin whispered. "Servo suus obviam malum et planto mihi dignus suus."

CHAPTER SIXTY-FIVE

She runs through bogs that suck at her high-heeled shoes. Her diaphanous white nightgown flutters behind her.

The monster is coming.

She trips over a rotting tree root and splashes into the muck. She can't get up.

The monster is there.

She throws her marabou slipper at it. It laughs. The entire top row of its teeth stretch into razor-edged fangs.

She screams. It licks its lips. Her other shoe is in her hand, but the monster knocks it away.

She clutches her gauzy collar.

The monster falls on her neck and its fangs shred the useless material. She screams again as it slices through her jugular vein.

―――

"Isolde, wake up."

She opened her eyes. The monster's face hovered above her, lit by a grayish dawn. She sucked in a breath, but before the scream came out he put a finger over her lips.

"You were dreaming, sweetheart. It's all right. You're safe now."

"Gavin." Now she knew where she was.

Isolde snuggled against his warm chest. Gavin would protect her from the monster.

CHAPTER SIXTY-SIX

Isolde climbed back into Gavin's bed. The bathroom floor had chilled her feet and she tried to keep them away from him.

"Good morning." His voice wasn't sleepy at all.

"Don't scare me like that! I was trying not to wake you up."

"I took Chayyliel for a walk at eight."

"Are his eyes all right?" Isolde traced figure eights through Gavin's soft chest hair.

"I gave them another rinse. He wasn't happy, but he'll do anything for Alpo Prime Rib."

"Mmm." She lay her head next to his on the pillow and crossed one leg over his. "Gavin, your legs are bare."

"Indeed." He drew their heads together and kissed her. One of his long kisses that tingled all the right parts of her body.

"Perhaps you should call work."

Isolde checked the digital clock. "Ten-thirty already. You're having a bad influence on me, encouraging me to call in sick when I'm not."

"Let's say you're taking a mental health day."

She sighed. "I have to get out of this warm, comfortable bed again."

"No, you don't. I brought your cell phone in here after I fed Chayyliel. It's next to the lamp."

She snagged the phone. "The service here is impeccable."

"We aim to please."

She giggled and dialed Tranquil Grove. "Nuncio? It's Isolde. I won't be in to work tonight... Yes... Let Emerson know, would you?... Thanks. 'Bye."

Gavin brushed aside her hair and kissed the back of her neck.

"Gavin, I can't concentrate if you do that."

"Good." He kissed down her spine through the pajama top.

"Stop. I need to let Ellie know what's going on." She dialed home. "Ellie? It's me... Yes, I'm still at Gavin's... Stop it... No, not you, Ellie. Listen. I called in sick... I know, hell is freezing over... I'll be home later... oh, wait a sec." She turned and put her hand over Gavin's busy lips. "Christmas Eve?"

He nibbled her fingertips instead. "Christmas will be perfect."

"Ellie? If Stephen's friend can swing Christmas Eve, that'll be great... Gavin, stop... No, Ellie, I'm not telling you what's happening right now... Yes, everything's fine... I'll see you tonight."

She closed the phone just as Gavin's hands closed over her breasts. "Oh—" She aimed her hand at the nightstand. Gavin pulled her on top of him and the phone landed somewhere in the comforters.

"Now, lady, I'm going to reduce you to mindless ecstasy."

"O—okay." Gavin kissed her neck, his fingers unbuttoning the pajama top much faster than a few hours earlier. He reached her nipples and used his lips on them like they were her mouth.

She purred and moaned, needing the preliminaries to be over. "Gavin, I want you."

"Are you ready?"

"Yes—keep doing that—yes, I'm ready."

He paused so long, she opened her eyes. He was staring at her with those dark eyes, darker than his normal green. "I'll get a condom."

She put a hand on his arm. "Why?"

Did he look ashamed? "I fed from you last night. My body is replenished. That includes sperm. After twenty-four hours they'll be inactive again."

This wasn't the time to say she wanted to study the medical aspects of all this. "That's all right. You don't have to."

"You could get pregnant."

Just nine hours ago she cringed at the thought of him touching her. She'd have to analyze all this later, like maybe every day for a month. "You said you wanted me barefoot, pregnant, and in the kitchen." She teased his curly chest hair. "Seriously, Gavin. Is your sperm more potent than other men's?"

He shook his head. "Less, actually. Something to do with the three-day hiatus."

"That's fascinating. I want to study that." Her brow wrinkled. "Sorry. Professional instinct. Never mind that. We're getting married in a few weeks. Would you hate it if by some chance we conceived before then?"

He bit back a wide smile. "You know I want children with you."

"Good. Because I want to see you go all goopy over our babies." She took his hand away from the nightstand and put it onto her breast.

"Are you sure, Isolde? I mean, now, without protection?"

She looked at him through her eyelashes. "Did you forget? Last night I said I'm yours." She was sure. She knew it the same way she knew she'd say 'yes' when he got down on one knee to propose. "Give me all of you."

He opened her legs. "Last chance." His teeth met in her bottom lip. "No going back."

His voice alone aroused her. She dragged her fingernails down his back. "Do it, Gavin. I want you. Do it."

He plunged into her. Her inner walls grabbed him and he groaned. Her hips moved against him and their skin slapped together.

"Come, Isolde." He fell on her breasts and sucked like he needed nourishment from them.

"Oh, God—oh, God—" She wasn't afraid—she'd never be afraid of him again—she—her thoughts fragmented.

Gavin closed his teeth on the inner curve of her breast and she froze. *Was he going to—*

His teeth left her skin. "I'm not going to bite you, Isolde."

He rolled onto his back, taking her with him. She moaned and gasped and rode him.

"Going to come." His voice roughened.

She wanted it. She wanted everything. "Yes."

Her body thrashed, she drenched him, and he climaxed. Spurts of semen pumped into her. His cry blended with hers and she collapsed on top of him.

CHAPTER SIXTY-SEVEN

Isolde sat at the table with the sleeves of Gavin's Patriots sweatshirt rolled to her elbows. She hadn't realized how ravenous she was until the Chinese take-out arrived.

Gavin leaned against the kitchen counter, tossing a wine cork back and forth. Isolde dipped a spring roll in duck sauce and tried to remember to swallow before she spoke.

"What was your name?"

Gavin appeared to follow this non sequitur. "Gerard Deyncourt."

"Exactly the name for the hero of a romance."

He shrugged. "It wasn't anything special. One son in every generation was christened Gerard for the d'Incourt who of course came over with William the Conqueror. His son Anglicized the surname when the Conqueror gave him the manor and surrounding farmland."

She nabbed a strip of gingered beef with her chopsticks. "You were farmers?"

"Among other things. Our lands were considerable. We had a village to support."

"Talking to you is like having my own personal time machine." The warm, spicy beef was just what her mouth wanted. "And you don't have to tell me I'm focusing on irrelevant details. I'm getting my head around everything in little steps." She reached for her glass of pinot noir. "I've never had wine at this hour of the day before."

"It's nearly twelve-thirty. Pretend it's a businessman's lunch." He pushed off the counter and pulled out a chair next to her. "How do you feel?"

She looked up from a straw mushroom trying to elude her. "I'm fine. What's the matter?"

"You're not dizzy or nauseous? Your forehead isn't damp?" He touched it with the back of his hand.

She set the chopsticks across the corner of the foil container. "What are you hinting at?"

He took her hand. Guilt and worry covered his face. She steeled herself for something panic-inducing. "I'm not sure how much blood I took from you last night, out in the yard."

"Oh. You thought I might have a blood-loss reaction? Why didn't you just say so? I'm a nurse, remember? I know the signs." She played with one of the chopsticks. "Besides, I don't think it, um, lasted that long."

"Why?"

"After the first few seconds, well, I started hitting your head so you'd, um, let go." The beef didn't look quite so appetizing anymore.

"You what? Wait." His touched the side of his head. "You punched me here more than once, right? I thought I remembered something like that."

She straightened her shoulders. "I'm not going to apologize, Gavin."

He shook his head. "No, no, you shouldn't. I was... not myself."

He was so sweet. But it was so all-out nuts that she was sitting here eating take-out with a man who could only eat...

Isolde traced a circle around Gavin's knuckles. "About that. When will you need, um, any more, um—"

"Not until Thursday."

She exhaled. "I wasn't sure I'd be ready yet."

He handed her the wineglass. "Drink. We'll talk about it Thursday. If you don't want to, I can find another avenue."

She stared at his hands, but a rush of muddled emotion had her full attention. "Tell me why I just got neon-green jealous at the idea of you, um, drinking from other people."

"I don't—"

"Because I should feel violated. I did feel violated last night, when I got away from you. I looked at my arm and saw the blood, and saw how the—marks—were already healing and, well, I puked my guts up." The chopstick tapped the table, the staccato beat rattling the other one off its perch. "When I stop to think about how unreal everything is, part of me thinks 'freak out' but part of me knows it's just you, and that makes it okay. It shouldn't, should it? But it does."

He kept silent.

She looked into his eyes. "Tell me what happens when it's, I don't know, just another... meal."

"Don't think of it like that." Gavin dragged her chair toward him across the ceramic tile floor and then dragged her into his lap. "Animals are 'just another meal.' You are my wife—you will be my wife by Christmas. You're my partner."

As much as Isolde wanted to lean against him—she was more tired than usual—she watched his face instead. There was nothing of the predator about him. She'd dated men who were more ruthless in trying to get into her pants than he was merely talking about his... nutritional needs.

"Partner, how? What's my role in—the act?"

His hand stroked up and down her back. "When—if—you let me sustain from you, it will be part of lovemaking. It will give you pleasure like you've never experienced. I promise."

"That sounds like a good trade. But you said when Philippa bit you, it hurt." She huddled into the extra-large fleece. "Out in the yard, when you first bit my arm, it burned."

"I'm sorry, sweetheart." He kissed her. "I wasn't in control, remember? When I take only what I need to survive, it's different. When Philippa bit me, she deliberately tried to bring me to the point of death, then turn me into what she was. That caused the overwhelming pain."

"That's too much information again." This time she did snuggle into his chest. "And you're not a what. You're Gavin. You're a human being." She raised her head. "Are you? Technically, I mean."

"Define human being, and I'll be able to answer you."

She smiled. "Touché. You're a human being in every way that counts."

"And you're a stubborn woman who's not eating enough to rebuild her red cells." He handed her the wineglass. "Drink, please."

CHAPTER SIXTY-EIGHT

Isolde explored Gavin's face in the bright bathroom light.

"The cartilage is intact and there's no swelling around the orbits or cheekbones. Are you sure Gow's nephew broke your nose?"

"Positive. I've had it broken a few times over the years. You don't forget that kind of instant pain."

"It healed along with your chest, then."

"Yes." He kissed her inner wrist. "I have so much to repay you for."

She wasn't ready to concede the many layers of debt Gavin was committing to. "I'll work up a program of classic Disney movies for us to watch together."

Gavin did his best puppy-dog eyes imitation. "All at once?"

Isolde laughed. "Stop trying to manipulate me."

"Caught. I hang my head in shame. However, I also do laundry. Your uniform should be dry. I'll be right back."

Her laughter bounced off the tiled walls. "You win."

———

Isolde held up her almost-clean uniform. Only about two percent of the mud stains remained, but faded reddish-brown lines streaked the left sleeve. The new, ragged hem shortened that sleeve by two inches.

Gavin gave her a sheepish smile. "It'll get you home, at least."

"Yeah, but it's toast." She slipped into her still-warm underwear. "Thanks for washing it. I would've had even more to explain to Ellie." She turned her back and he zipped the dress for her. "Are you sure you shouldn't go to the police?"

"What would I tell them? That a fifty-year-old woman and her chain-smoking nephew strapped me to one of my carvings and left me outside all night to frighten me into ceding my job to him? I have no broken bones and the stake wound is healed. Anything I say would also bring you into it."

He led her out to the back porch and presented her with not-quite-cleaned shoes. "Gow sounds like a candidate for a padded room whenever she says the word 'vampire' to people. That's my biggest advantage. I'm going into work for an hour today like nothing happened. If I know her, she'll be in the director's office hinting that I'm unreliable because I didn't show up this morning."

The shoelaces were damp, but she managed. "Do you need to leave now? I can lock up."

"No, we'll leave together. What Gow doesn't know is I often don't go in on Mondays. The Board doesn't care where I do the work as long as it gets done. I want my appearance to either terrify her into silence or goad her into such a public display of hate that her family has to take steps."

"She'll flip her wig when she sees you."

"I'm counting on it." He checked the lock on the back door. "Please don't change your mind and go to work."

"I won't. I think I need to sleep for about twelve hours anyway."

"I'll stop by after I make my appearance at the Society. What are you going to tell Noelle?"

"That Gow and her nephew broke in, clocked you on the head, tied you up, and left you outside to freeze. I came over when the cell phone wouldn't connect, found Chayyliel all pepper-sprayed, and went to look for you." She walked into the living room. "I don't have to remember anything because it's the truth."

"Just edited."

"Exactly." She looked around the foyer. "My coat?"

271

He opened the closet and hid the coat behind his back. "You don't want to see it."

She peered around him and pretended to scream.

Gavin adopted Chay's 'I'm guilty but too lovable to be mad at' look. "At least it's not wet anymore. Dry cleaning should save it. I think we trampled it last night."

"Gavin Donne, are you going to be a high-maintenance husband?"

"I expect nightly foot rubs, my own private concert once a week, and an endless succession of seductive undergarments." He helped her on with the coat. "Would you like me to email you a list?"

Isolde aimed a fake slap at him. He ducked and ran out the door, calling for Chayyliel. She followed.

CHAPTER SIXTY-NINE

A white Lexus pulled into the Historical Society's postage-stamp sized parking lot and parked against the stone wall.

Gavin looked up from the volume of bound 1880s newspapers he had open on a reading table. Miranda. What impeccable timing.

What would the murdering bitch do if he opened the window and called her name? Scream? Faint? If she fainted he could drive her to her tasteful mansion on High Street. Would she put a good face on it when the butler told her who brought her home? Just a Boy Scout helping the little old lady across the street. He laughed and closed the volume.

The Lexus's driver door opened. Gavin flung on his coat and waved to the grandmotherly secretary. He opened the front door in time to make Miranda stop dead at the bottom of the steps.

A slow smile covered his face. "What brings you to the Society on such an inclement afternoon, Miranda? Surely not to plant the idea that the research position may be open again. Because there's no way you could have come by that knowledge."

Her face paled so that her tasteful blusher stood out on her cheekbones like clown makeup.

"You—you—"She leaned a gloved hand on the snow-covered balustrade.

"You really should work on your poise. This isn't the proper way to answer an unexpected greeting." Gavin descended the steps and took her hand. It flopped in his grasp, the supple leather cold around her trembling fingers. "I owe you a great deal, Miranda. And I mustn't forget to repay your charming nephew as well."

He kissed her fingertips. "May I accompany you inside? I just finished my day's work, but there's always something more to research."

When he released Gow's hand she scuttled backwards. Her mouth hung open still, as though she were trying to finish the sentence she began with 'You.'

Gavin tilted his head a fraction. "No? Then I'll leave you here. I must say I prefer the silent treatment to your misplaced prophecies of damnation." He walked closer to her and she backed away down the front walk. His smile returned. "Good day, Miranda. We'll meet again soon."

CHAPTER SEVENTY

"No, no, no. B-natural." Isolde flexed her left hand and repositioned her fingers on the cello fingerboard. "All right, let's see. Pickup to measure thirty-three." Sixteenth notes filled the music room.

Isolde knew this was just another avoidance technique, like cleaning out the fridge when she got home. She'd begun the score to *Beauty and the Beast* on the English horn, but that gave her too much freedom to think. The 'Londonderry Air' was another mistake—too emotional. Bach had been the only sensible choice. Her fingers were already sore when she started his 'Little Fugue.'

She loved Gavin. He loved her. He was not scary like those bad CGI-fests on the SyFy channel.

Her finger moved an eighth of an inch in the wrong direction. "Argh. Stupid accidentals."

Those movies always made her jump, no matter how much Noelle laughed at the fake monsters. Gavin was not a monster, because his character was stronger than what he did the previous night in a moment of fear and pain.

Crescendo. Forte. Her fingers raced up and down the strings. She loved this piece.

———

Did someone call her? Apparently not. She broadened her bow strokes for the last few measures.

Bang. Bang. The door opened. "Isolde, didn't you hear me?" Noelle beckoned. "We've got company."

Isolde's bow scraped. "Augh, I messed up the final chord."

"That doesn't matter." Noelle took the bow from her hand. "Those detectives are downstairs. Come on."

"What? Why?" Her fingers jangled on the strings. She laid the cello on the rug and followed Noelle downstairs.

"Good afternoon, Ms. Connor." Morgan flashed his too-white smile. "We'd like to ask you and Ms. Robins a few questions."

"Uh, sure."

Noelle nudged Isolde. "May we take your coats?"

"Thanks." Morgan handed Noelle a camel-colored London Fog special.

"Thank you." Hill placed her wool herringbone in Isolde's outstretched hand. A purple splotch had ruined the sleeve, making Isolde think of a kid waving around a PBJ. The idea of Hill with small children just didn't compute.

Morgan sat on the arm of the couch. "We stopped at Tranquil Grove but were told you called in sick, Ms. Connor." His voice didn't quite ask why she was up and running around.

"More of a mental health day." Isolde chose the armchair rather than share the couch with Morgan. Noelle brought in the telephone chair and set it next to Isolde.

"I see." Hill made even two small words sound like an accusation. She hitched up her black trousers and sat next to Morgan. "Since Ms. Robins' shift had finished, we thought it would be easier to talk to you both here."

"Of course. How can we help you, detectives?" Isolde tried to remember which one had been the Bad Cop the last time they talked to her. Was it Hill who acted the part but Morgan's All-American Boy charm that hid things?

Morgan brought out his phone. "There's been another death at Tranquil Grove."

Isolde slumped. "Not Mrs. Hudson? We got the crash cart there in plenty of time."

Noelle said, "No, she's still okay. It was Annabelle King."

Tap tap tap went Morgan's stylus.

"What?" Isolde looked from Noelle to Hill to Morgan. "I just fed her dinner last night. She was fine. Well, physically, anyway."

Hill crossed her legs. "Please explain."

"She's got Alzheimer's. It got so bad they had to move her from two east onto the Alz floor."

"It has bars on the windows and the hall door is locked," Noelle said, "so they don't wander around at night or hurt themselves."

Tap tappity tap. "Other than that?"

Isolde shrugged. "She was eighty-seven, but except for heart and diabetes, she was in pretty good health. Nothing special in her diet, right, Ellie?"

Noelle shook her head. "Nothing."

"She fell last week," Isolde said. "Broke her nose and cracked a tooth. Her grandson took her to the dentist to get fitted for a crown." Isolde watched Morgan's busy stylus. "She couldn't swallow pills so her doctor gave her painkillers in an IV. He added calcium to help her bones along."

"And you administered this?"

"Me, Lee, Bethann, Geoff—anyone who was on duty when her IV needed replacing." Isolde ordered herself not to scowl. "What did she die of? Or can't you tell me?"

Tap taptap tap.

Hill spoke over the tapping. "Did she have many visitors over the past month?"

Isolde chewed her lip. "Her grandson came once a week. I think some of her kids showed up for her birthday in June."

"She's not really a nice person." Noelle grimaced. "I mean, she wasn't a nice person. She liked to complain, and most of the residents avoided her."

The doorbell rang. All four heads turned toward the noise and Isolde leapt at the temporary escape.

Gavin stood on the welcome mat. "You look good." Before she could say anything, he took her in his arms and kissed her. For a long moment she forgot about murders and fear and police in the living room.

He released her and said, "'Cello grrl?'"

She looked down at the front of her hoodie. "Grandma thought it was cute. Gavin, the police are here."

His smile vanished. "Why?"

"Come in before we all freeze." Isolde closed the door. "One of the Alz patients died today."

"And what can that have to do with you?"

"Mr. Donne?" Morgan was on his feet. "Glad you're here. I forgot one question the last time we talked."

Gavin walked to the couch and shook Morgan's hand. "Your family tree?"

"Damn." He looked down at Hill's deadpan face. "All right, I'll tell you about it later."

She flipped open her cell phone and dialed.

Gavin sat on the arm of Isolde's chair. "I'll email you a list of the information I need to begin. May I ask what happened at the nursing home?"

"Another death."

"And you're here because?"

Hill held her phone away from her ear. "May I ask why you're interested?"

Gavin smiled down at Isolde. "Ms. Connor is my fiancée."

"I see." Morgan tapped his screen.

"Annabelle King, Gavin. That old lady with the slimy grandson."

Gavin stared at Isolde. "King."

The tapping stopped. After several seconds of silence, Morgan said, "Mr. Donne?"

He ignored Morgan and said to Isolde, "What does her grandson look like?"

"Um… phony smile, long face, dark floppy hair."

"God in Heaven." Gavin stood. "Detectives, may we speak somewhere in private?"

Isolde and Noelle looked at each other. "The music room?" Isolde pointed. "Just up the stairs."

Gavin shook his head. "Your office would be better."

Morgan glanced at Hill, who punched one more button on her keypad and closed the phone. "Certainly."

Hill stood. Morgan slid his stylus into its silo. Noelle retrieved their coats from the closet.

"Thank you for your time, Ms. Robins, Ms. Connor." Morgan buckled the belt on his coat. "We'll be in touch."

"If we need any further information." Hill's lowest button popped off. She made a frustrated noise and shoved it into her pocket.

"I'll follow you there." Gavin waited until Noelle closed the door on Morgan and Hill and pulled Isolde to her feet. "I'll call you tomorrow. Get some sleep tonight."

"Gavin, how do you know anything about this? What do you have to do with Annabelle King's grandson?"

He shook his head. "When he's behind bars I'll tell you the whole story. It's a case of a criminal talking too much."

CHAPTER SEVENTY-ONE

"Mr. Donne, this is a serious accusation." Detective Hill picked up the telephone handset and pressed zero.

Gavin paced the cinderblock room. "I know that. Can you get me to a computer terminal, please? If I write all this down I'll be able to show you the progression of events that led me to this conclusion."

Hill spoke into the telephone, "Can you send Chen into Room C with his laptop, please? Thanks." She hung up. "Mr. Donne, an officer will be here shortly to take down your statement."

Morgan looked up from his phone. "Mr. Donne, would you like a chair?"

Gavin turned and walked the seven steps to the far wall. "No, thanks."

The door opened and a buzz-cut uniformed officer entered. Morgan gave him his chair at the metal desk and the officer opened his laptop.

"Mr. Donne, if you'll give us the details, Officer Chen will type them up."

Gavin nodded to Morgan. As soon as Chen opened the form template, Gavin described Hal King's history of failed plays. When he reached Hal's latest effort and his confident predictions of funding, Morgan set down his phone.

"He's been saying for weeks that his grandmother will bankroll this play because he's her favorite, because she wants to see him make it to Broadway. But yesterday afternoon he said his mother was going to have power of attorney over his grandmother's money. He had a check ready for his grandmother to sign." Gavin stopped in front of Morgan. "Do you know if the grandmother was competent to sign? Do you know to whom she left her money?"

The light tapping of the keys stopped a moment after Gavin's last word.

Morgan waited for silence. "We'll know tomorrow morning."

"All right then. Listen: If the power of attorney was about to become official, and if Hal's grandmother was too far gone to sign…" Gavin resumed pacing. "I spoke to Detective Pacione last week about Hal and one of his acting students. She's fifteen. You get the picture? My point is that Hal isn't overburdened with scruples."

Hill leaned forward in her chair. "Is he resourceful? Intelligent?"

"He's been DialSource's top salesman more than once. He stopped bragging about it when I told him my number was on the national Do Not Call list."

Hill wrinkled her nose. "I hate those people worse than my ex-mother-in law."

Morgan laughed. "That's saying something."

Gavin got in Morgan's face. "Do you know how Hal's grandmother was killed?"

"Yes." Morgan poked keys and turned his screen toward Gavin.

He leaned over the desk. "Calphron? What's that? Digoxin is—heart medication?" He looked up at Morgan. "Did you mention something like this the day you came to my house?"

"We did, but it's not important to you." Morgan took back the phone. "Despite your mistrust of me, Mr. Donne, I do not consider you a suspect." Morgan scowled at Hill's questioning look. "And I'd appreciate it if you could convince Miranda Gow that you are not a card-carrying member of Bloodsuckers International."

Chen snickered, but cut it off.

"Oh gods, did she call again?" Hill slid down in her chair.

"Late afternoon, in controlled hysterics. Damn desk sergeant routed it to me because I got stuck with her before when she came in person."

Chen tried to turn another laugh into a cough.

Gavin rubbed his temples. "What did she say this time?"

Morgan poked his screen. "Chen, if you laugh once more, I'll put you on the undercover prostitution sting in drag." He squinted at the tiny screen. "After she grilled the desk sergeant on his church attendance, Mr. Donne, she said, 'I have it on good authority that Gavin Donne is dead.' When I asked how she knew, she said… uh… 'Because he is a vampire and one of God's Righteous drove a stake through his heart last night.'"

"She said 'righteous' with a capital R, didn't she?" Gavin kept annoyance on his face and in his voice.

"She did." Morgan glared at Chen, who typed with slower, deliberate keystrokes.

Hill took a pen from the black plastic holder on the desk and began clicking it. "Is it permissible to hate a Gow in this town?"

"If it isn't, Detective, I'm in trouble." Gavin decided this was the right time for a little self-humiliation. "I think I'd better tell you what happened last night."

When he finished his Bowdlerized version, Chen was beet-red. Gavin didn't mind. Let them laugh. It deflected any iota of suspicion they might be harboring from watching too many horror movies.

Morgan said, "Leopard-print hot pants, Chen."

Hill cleared her throat. "Why didn't you file a complaint, Mr. Donne?"

Gavin looked shamefaced. "It doesn't say much for my manhood to admit that an old lady and her useless nephew hit me from behind, duct-taped me to my own carving, and left me helpless in the snow."

"Until your fiancée came to your rescue."

"Precisely."

"Why did Gow say you were dead?" Morgan tapped the stylus against his mouth.

Gavin unbuttoned his shirt, furtively scratching his left side with a fingernail as he did so. "This is her idea of righteous justice. She tried to stab me with the stick I used as a fishing pole for my bear carving. Fortunately it was dark and snowing, and this is all the damage she did."

Hill pinched her lips together, but the laughter snorted out of her. "My apologies, Mr. Donne, but Gow actually tried to stake you? Like what's-his-name in the Dracula movies?"

"Van Helsing," Chen said.

"We could—ha ha ha—charge her with assault." Hill took several deep breaths and finally stopped laughing. "I meant that, Mr. Donne. Chen can open the proper form right now."

Gavin rebuttoned his shirt. "She's a Gow. It's not worth the aggravation. It's my dog I'm angry about."

"Contact PETA, then," Morgan said.

Gavin raised both hands. "Please, no. My life doesn't need two sets of fanatics."

Morgan stood and hovered over Chen. "It's your choice not to press charges, of course.

"She's not important." Gavin smiled when both detectives laughed. "True. What Gow doesn't think the world revolves around them? Have I given you enough information about Hal King and his grandmother?"

"You have. Chen, are you finished?"

"Yes, sir." He handed the laptop to Morgan, who transferred it to Gavin.

Gavin read the transcript. "Well done. Do you need me to sign anything?"

Hill plunked the pen in the cup and stood. "No; we have what we need."

Morgan opened the door. "We'll call you if anything else comes up, Mr. Donne."

———

Gavin brushed off his windshield while the truck warmed up.

He hadn't received a summary dismissal like that since he was the Comte de Fourquin's vassal before the Revolution. Had Morgan and Hill taken him seriously? The two other nursing home deaths could easily have been Hal's dress rehearsals for the big show: killing his grandmother for her money.

Gavin spat in the slush. Money. Ego. Fame. And Hal thought they were worth murder.

He threw the brush behind the front seat. What should he expect from a thirty-five-year-old man who was using a fifteen-year-old girl for free sex?

CHAPTER SEVENTY-TWO

"Just a minute!" Isolde closed the oven door on a nearly done chicken pot pie and ran out of the kitchen. She'd slept till eleven and here it was, noon already. Her empty stomach needed food before she could face eight hours at Suspicion Central.

She opened the door to a cold, cloudy day and a bakery take-out bag at her eye level.

"Almond croissant, ma'am?" Gavin followed the bag inside and closed the door.

"How'd you know?" Isolde snatched the bag and opened it, inhaling. "Oh, yes. I can't wolf this. It must be consumed with proper ceremony. Follow me."

She set the bag on the counter and poured water into the one-cup coffeemaker. "You don't have to bring me something every time you come here." Isolde set her Ariel mug under the filter and turned on the machine.

"The Little Mermaid?" Gavin's voice sounded pained.

"I warned you." She sniffed the milk and set it next to the coffeepot.

He pulled out a chair and sat. "There are conspiracy theorists who say Disney is the root of all evil."

Isolde blew him a raspberry. "Love me, love Walt."

Gavin laughed and pulled her into his lap. "I haven't laughed this much in years."

She kissed him. "I'm obviously a good influence."

He prolonged a second kiss.

The coffeepot hissed. Isolde squirmed off and added milk to the full mug. With her head in the refrigerator as she put the carton away, she said, "Did the detectives listen to you yesterday?"

"I wasn't sure at first, but they called me this morning to check some facts."

Isolde brought the coffee and croissant to the table. "Ellie and I couldn't get our heads around it. Why would Annabelle King's grandson kill her? And is there a connection to the other murders or are there two killers? Three?" She sipped the coffee. "This would be cool in a movie but it sucks in real life."

"It'll all be over tomorrow, if I understood everything Hill and Morgan weren't telling me in between all their questions."

"That means they'll leave you alone, too, now." Isolde bit into the croissant. "God, these are good. Do you want a small bite?"

"Perhaps I'll taste it when I kiss you later."

Isolde stared into her coffee, knowing her face just turned hot pink.

"Why are you blushing?" Gavin's thumb stroked the back of her hand.

She shrugged.

"Are you afraid I'll think you're not a lady?"

She raised her eyes. "I'm kind of embarrassed at how easily you get me all hot and bothered."

Gavin grinned. "I don't see a problem with that."

Isolde slumped. "Men." Her face cleared. "Let go of my hand so I can give this croissant the attention it deserves."

"Haven't you eaten anything today?"

She tipped her head toward the oven. "Breakfast is cooking. I slept late."

He nodded. "All right. To answer your earlier question, Hill and Morgan didn't divulge anything specific, but I got a definite impression that they were targeting only one suspect."

Isolde wet her fingertip and picked up slivered almonds and shards of icing from the plate. "I want to say that at least it's not one of us—at Tranquil Grove, I mean. But it's still miserable.

He—if it was Annabelle's grandson—killed Edith and Ines too. For what? Ines was the sweetest little old lady."

"I expect the *News* will have all the lurid details on tomorrow's front page."

"Ugh. If they come to interview us, I'm hiding in the bathroom." Isolde let the last bite of croissant linger in her mouth. "Forget them. Gavin. What about Gow?"

"What about her?"

"What if she comes back?" There. She'd said it. The spiked ball of fear in her chest eased a bit.

Gavin took her hand. "Are you worried about me?"

Isolde exhaled a short, sharp sigh. "Of course. What did you think? She's going to see you around town. She could freak and come after you again."

"Sweetheart, if Gow tried to stake me on High Street on my way to work, I think that'd take care of our Fearless Vampire Hunter problem."

"It's not funny."

"It is, because I caught her at the Historical Society yesterday afternoon."

Isolde choked on her coffee. "You—just a sec—you—"

Gavin came around behind her and patted her back till she stopped coughing. After she blew her nose on her napkin, she said, "What did you do?"

"I said good morning and chastised her on her lack of manners."

"On her what?"

"She was rendered somewhat speechless by my appearance."

Isolde pushed back her chair and turned off the oven. "Gavin, you can't blow off a Gow like you can the rest of the townies."

"I can and I have. Remember, she thinks I'm the epitome of evil. You should've seen the look on her face."

"Gavin—"

"She's no longer important." He wrapped his arms around her. "She's a fanatical old lady with connections, yes, but what do you think she can do now?" He kissed the shell of her ear. "She knows I won't be taken by surprise again. Her nephew is a cipher without her prodding." He kissed her throat.

Isolde leaned her head against his chest and he kissed more of her exposed skin. "I've survived worse than an enraged Gow, Isolde. She's laughable by comparison." His hands roamed upward. "I can think of better ways to spend our time before work."

Isolde's stomach growled.

Gavin paused, then snorted. "That wasn't the reaction I wanted."

Isolde jerked out of his arms. "The pot pie." She grabbed two hot pads and took the cookie sheet out of the oven. "Good. It's not burned. Sorry, Gavin. That croissant didn't make a dent."

He pointed to the food. "Eat. I suppose I can control myself till tonight."

She opened the foil collar and poked the crust with a fork. Savory steam escaped and her stomach gurgled. "At least you didn't tell me again that I have to regain my strength."

Silence. Isolde looked over her shoulder. "Busted! You were just about to say it, weren't you?"

"Guilty."

"I knew it. Look, I know how the human body works. I'm doing what I need to maintain my health." She set the pot pie on the table, a hot pad beneath it. "Are we going to have to set relationship ground rules?"

Gavin swept an imaginary hat off his head. "Ma'am, I bow to your know-how. The subject is closed."

"Good. What time do you have to be at work?"

"Two. Shall I pick you up tonight at eleven?"

She blew on a forkful of chicken and veggies. "I'd rather come home and change first. Sometimes I get body fluids on my uniform."

"What an appealing occupation you have."

Isolde popped the food in her mouth and gasped. Gavin poured her a glass of water while she waved her hand in front of her panting mouth.

"Was there a warning label on that package, Miss 'I know how to take care of myself'? As in, 'Caution—just-baked pie is hot'?"

Isolde gulped half the water. "Oh, shut up. Haven't you ever burned your mouth on food—Oh." She drank the rest. "Sorry. I wasn't thinking."

"The way you blush at the least thing is both charming and tantalizing, Belle Isolde."

She met his eyes. He did look aroused. "Um… thanks, I think." This was going to take a lot of getting used to.

Gavin stood. "Come walk me to the door while your pie cools enough to eat. Would you like me to get take-out for tonight?"

"Is there anything you can eat with me?"

"My stomach can process a few bites of most food."

Isolde aimed a kiss at his cheek. "Never mind, then. I'll grab something at work. Gotta remember your life works differently than mine."

He squeezed the breath out of her for a second. "You have no idea how happy you make me when you say things like that."

"That I'll eat at work? No, don't explain, I know what you meant." She snuggled against him. "I'm getting the hang of this in bits and pieces. I don't promise there won't be any more kinda-sorta-freak-out moments, but I'm trying."

"Then I'll make a concerted effort to watch a Disney movie with you."

"Who could ask for more?"

CHAPTER SEVENTY-THREE

"And Nuncio said Phoebe told him that her new boytoy found out—"

Isolde unscrewed the cap on her iced tea. "I don't want to hear it, Lee."

Lee waved an unlit cigarette at Isolde. "Yes, you do, because it lets all of us off." She coughed, setting off echoes in Tranquil Grove's empty break room. "Damn, I gotta get outside and light this. My throat's raw. Listen. Phoebe's guy said that old man Sargent's family didn't take him home last week because they thought TG was dangerous."

Isolde refrained from sighing. She wasn't going to get out of here until Lee unburdened herself. At least Lee wasn't treating her as Suspect Number One tonight. And Isolde sure wasn't going to say word one about Annabelle's grandson. Even the Candystripers would know it by tomorrow if Lee got hold of that tidbit.

"So why did they take him out of here?"

"Because," Lee scooted her chair closer to Isolde, "when Sargent was a teenager, he did time for murder."

Isolde set down her tea. "What?"

Lee wagged her eyebrows. "Got your attention now? He worked for one of the bootleggers during Prohibition and one night the Feds tried to intercept a shipment. There was a shootout—just like on the History Channel. Lots of guns and blood and the story is he and his partner shot one of the Feds."

Isolde shook her head. "It's too pat, Lee. Phoebe's boyfriend's been watching the movies instead of managing the theater."

"Uh-uh. Her guy said he combed the Net for info on everyone who got sprung from here."

"I can imagine how Phoebe repaid that favor."

"No shit." Lee fingered her lighter.

The door squeaked open and Geoff appeared. "Isolde, come on, it's time for Stafford's and Wilson's baths."

"Yeah, okay, two minutes." The door closed and she stood, taking a long drink of iced tea. "Why are we supposed to think Sargent killed them? The short version."

Lee tapped her cigarette on the table. "He's losing it, right? Going back to his childhood. Well, what if he thought those old broads were, I dunno, undercover Prohibition Feds?"

"Doesn't follow, Lee. They didn't shoot at him." She tucked her tea bottle in a slot on the refrigerator door.

"I know, but—"

"I've gotta help Geoff. Wilson's having one of his PITA days. When do you get off shift?"

"Half an hour. God, I'm sick of everyone dogging it. I never thought I could get too much OT, but this shift-and-a-half crap sucks." She pushed out of her chair and opened the outside door. "I'll tell you the rest when you clock in tomorrow, if the cops haven't hauled Sargent to the nut house before then." She flicked her lighter before the door closed behind her.

―――

Isolde yawned and stretched while the computer updated her timesheet file. Eleven p.m. on the dot. Five minutes to get to her car and warm it up, ten-ish to get home. Ten more to shower and change. She could smell urine on her clothes, even though she was sure she hadn't splashed any out of Martin's brim-full bedpan. The man had a bladder the size of a watermelon.

She retrieved her quilted jacket from the staff closet. That reminded her—the dry cleaners said her wool coat should be ready tomorrow morning. She walked down the dim, empty hall, fiddling with the zipper to get it past the broken tooth halfway up. It stuck as she pushed open the door.

First things first: she turned on her cell and stuffed it into her jacket pocket. The closing door bumped her and she stepped aside, still coaxing the stiff zipper pull.

Dazzling light burst behind her eyes. Pain followed an instant later. Then darkness.

CHAPTER SEVENTY-FOUR

"O tidings of comfort and joy, comfort and joy. O tidings of comfort and joy."

The song ended and Gavin checked the dashboard clock. Eleven forty-five. Isolde should've been out before now. Her house had been dark when he pulled into the driveway, but that meant nothing. She would've used only a few lights so as not to wake Noelle.

Bing Crosby sang, "Mele Kalikimaka is the thing to say on a bright Hawaiian Christmas Day."

Gavin got out of the car and peered through the rectangular garage windows. Isolde's side was empty. Maybe she broke down. No. She would've called. Maybe her phone died.

He stared at the house's dark second floor.

He put his back to the wind and opened his cell. No messages, so he dialed Isolde. Four rings and straight to voice mail.

He crossed the lawn and climbed the porch steps, fighting wind and the last of the autumn leaves hitting him like missiles.

"Sorry, Noelle." He rang the doorbell. Nothing.

What kind of bell did they have... right. One of those Big Ben imitations. He pressed it, waited thirty seconds, pressed it, waited another thirty seconds, pressed it again.

A light came on upstairs, casting a dim glow through the frosted glass in the door. Two minutes later Noelle's voice called from the other side, "Who's there?"

"It's Gavin, Noelle. Is Isolde home?"

The door opened. "I thought she was going to your place." She clutched her bathrobe closer. "Come in. What time is it?"

"Nearly midnight." He shivered in the sudden warmth of the foyer.

"Did you call her? Maybe she had to cover for an emergency."

"No answer. I thought you had to turn your phones off at work because of the machines." Gavin opened his cell again.

Noelle rubbed her eyes. "She'd go outside to call you."

He held the ringing phone to his ear. "Three. Four. Voice mail."

'La Vie en Rose' played from somewhere in the house. Noelle's head whipped around. "That's my phone."

———

All of King Louie's monkeys from *The Jungle Book* were banging a hollow log in Isolde's head. Did she fall asleep with the DVD on?

She pried open her eyes. The monkeys played harder.

Dim lights. Good. Her head liked dim right now.

Those blobs were her feet. She was looking at her feet? She was standing, then. No, she wasn't. Something was holding her up. That was why her neck had a wicked crick.

She straightened it a fraction. Not that bad. She raised it an inch. Another.

———

Gavin was one step behind Noelle when she pressed the phone's 'receive' button.

"Hello?"

Gavin should've been able to hear the caller, but he was whispering. A man. Not Isolde.

Noelle pressed the cell to her ear. "Isolde? Speak up. I can't hear you."

Gavin leaned his ear closer to Noelle's phone.

"Call 9-1-1."

———

Isolde blinked several times, trying to focus through the brutal pounding in her head. The room she was in looked backwards, like she was seeing it from the wrong angle.

She tried to feel her head. Her hand wouldn't move. She bent her neck—ouch. Why couldn't the monkeys take five?

Rows of dull gray strips held her arms to her sides and her legs to… what?

She looked—slowly, slowly—over her shoulder. An off-white wall. A narrow piece of polished wood behind her. She looked—slowly—down. More wood. A coffee table?

The pounding backed off a degree or two.

Coffee table. Wood on the wall. She looked out. Benches. No, pews.

Wait. The long gray strips swathed her body and extended another foot onto the wall. She shifted her arm a millimeter. The fine hairs on her forearm stuck to them.

Oh, shit.

CHAPTER SEVENTY-FIVE

"Who is this? What's wrong?" Noelle's voice had caught Gavin's worry.

Gavin stopped himself before he snatched the phone out of Noelle's hand.

"Shh. Call 9-1-1."

Static distorted the whisper. Gavin pressed his ear to the back of the phone.

"We're at that church on Fairview."

"Who is this?" Noelle whispered too.

"She's got the vampire's girlfriend."

Gavin was out the front door before Noelle's "Wait!" reached his ears.

"Call them!" He yanked his phone from his pocket as he jumped down the steps. On his first try he fat-fingered the contact menu, but pulled it up on the second and dialed Hill's number. "Pick up, dammit. Pick up."

"Hello?" Sleep furred her voice.

"Detective Hill, this is Gavin Donne." The anger and fear in his own voice unnerved him. "Call Morgan and meet me at the Church of the Nazarene on Fairview. Do you know where that is?"

"Uh... yes... Donne? Why are you calling at this hour?"

Gavin started the truck. "Wake up, Detective. Miranda Gow kidnapped my fiancée and took her to the church."

A beat, and Hill's voice snapped awake. "Where are you?"

"Heading east on Pleasant."

"Call 9-1-1, they'll—"

He took the corner too fast. "We did. They might get there in time to stop me from ripping that bitch's heart out, but don't count on it."

"Donne, hold on, I'm calling Morgan."

Gavin turned left onto Prospect one-handed, adrenaline constricting his head. He remembered now. After Gow tried to stake him Sunday night, she said something about Isolde meeting him in Hell. He pressed down the accelerator but the wheels caught ice. The phone hit the floor as he turned into the skid. Just in time, too: the passenger side tires scraped the curb but didn't jump it.

"Damn. Dammit to hell." Gavin braked and groped for the phone. "Detective? Are you still there?"

Silence, then a *beep*. "Donne? Are you still there?"

"Yes." His pulse throbbed in his ears.

"Listen. Morgan's on his way. I can't leave till my mother gets here to stay with my kids. Don't do anything stupid."

"If she touches Isolde, I'll—"

"Donne!" Hill changed from reasonable adult to cop-with-power. "Don't. Do. Anything. Stupid. Morgan lives on Beck. He might even get there before you, so don't pile into a tree. I'll be there as soon as I can."

Gavin hung up on her and threw the phone against the passenger seat. To hell with reason. He hit the gas and slid halfway across the empty street. At last the tires found purchase and he sped through the next stop sign.

That must've been Gow's thug nephew calling Noelle's phone. Had the thieves fallen out? Who cared, as long as he got to Isolde in time because of it?

———

Miranda Gow, in a long black dress like a Jane Eyre bridesmaid, stood in the middle of the sanctuary aisle. Her eyes were closed, her hands raised, and her lips moved. She would've looked like any church member indulging in late-night prayer, if she wasn't holding a three-foot long dowel in her hands.

Isolde swallowed. One end of the dowel had a pencil-sharp point.

———

Gavin fishtailed onto Oak. He'd lost count of the red lights he'd run. Didn't matter. He was nearly there.

Right on Withington. Left on Graham. Ice everywhere. Where the hell were the salt trucks?

Left on Fairview and he saw the church. Lights shone behind the curtained sanctuary windows. He bumped over the curb into the parking lot and slammed on the brakes. With jerky movements he turned off the ignition and leapt out of the truck. As he ran for Stephen's office, a high-pitched beep-beep-beep warned him that he'd left his keys in the ignition and the door ajar.

Now that he was near Gow, all he wanted was to make her die screaming in terror and agony. He could disguise his method. He'd perfected that in Inquisition-riddled Rome. No, no, wait: the cops were coming. If he couldn't do it soon, he'd have to settle for getting her arrested.

Laughter reached his ears. Whose?

Stephen's office door was locked. Where had Gow entered? Gavin ran around the back of the church, his slow heartbeat pounding in his ears. There—the hall door. He touched it and it swung in.

CHAPTER SEVENTY-SIX

"The Lord examines the righteous, but the wicked and those who love violence his soul hates." Gow lowered the dowel and smiled at Isolde. "If you were a God-fearing woman, vampire whore, I would tell you to pray for mercy." She walked closer to the altar platform. "But that would be a waste of time."

Isolde's mouth turned to dust. Gow had finally gone off the deep end. She tried to conjure moisture from her tongue to lick her lips. It didn't work.

Keep a straight face, Connor. You don't show fear to a batshit crazy religious fanatic who thinks you're a vampire.

Isolde's mouth quirked.

Batshit crazy. Perfect. They should be in a decaying cathedral with bats flying above her and ghosts of nuns in the choir loft chanting Latin.

Without expecting it, Isolde laughed. Oh, no. She shouldn't laugh at the nutter either. That made her laugh harder. Maybe not nuns. Maybe monks wearing huge silver crosses and carrying pieces of firewood sharpened at one end.

She stopped laughing.

Gow climbed the platform steps and slapped Isolde hard enough to bang her cheek against the polished cross. Her lip split and blood trickled down her chin.

"Sacrilegious tramp." Gow balanced the dowel in her left hand and prodded Isolde's ribcage.

Isolde looked down. The tape strips squashed her breasts, left her next five ribs free, and started again just above her waist.

She had to distract Gow. The longer it took to work herself into vampire-killer frenzy, the more likely someone would show up. If anyone knew where she was.

She wouldn't think about that. She'd think about Gavin wondering why she wasn't home from work yet. She'd think about him searching for her.

"You can't run Stephen's church when you're in jail for murder, Gow." Isolde kept the quaver out of her voice, even though she was shaking like Wile E. Coyote on Earthquake pills. "How are you going to explain all this to him tomorrow morning?"

"You can't deceive me." Gow unbuttoned the exposed section of Isolde's uniform. "No one will ever know we were here. We'll open the drapes when we leave," Gow swept her hand toward the tall windows, "and God's own sunlight will fill the church and burn your dead body to ash."

She tried to pull Isolde's sturdy uniform apart, but it was made to withstand lots more than one old woman's attack.

"Jonathan, come here." Gow spoke over her shoulder and didn't break eye contact with Isolde. "I checked the weather before we came for you. It's going to be sunny tomorrow." She raised her voice. "Jonathan."

An unshaven man with lank hair hanging in his eyes climbed next to Gow. "Aunt Miranda, you gotta stop . You gotta let her go. This is nuts."

"Jonathan, you're letting fear of man supplant fear of God. Please rip apart this material for me."

"Aunt Miranda—"

She looked at him this time. "Jonathan, since you're so concerned with your status in the world, remember that you helped me execute the first vampire."

Isolde said, "But you didn't—"

Gow slapped her again. "Shut up, whore of Satan." She turned away from Isolde and stood toe-to-toe with Jonathan. "Remember that I can lay the blame for his death on you anytime I please. I have social standing and power. You have only me to support you. Whom do you think the world will believe?" She cuffed the back of his head. "Obey me, Jonathan."

He opened his mouth, but closed it without saying anything. Then he grabbed the sides of Isolde's button placket and ripped.

CHAPTER SEVENTY-SEVEN

Gavin ran down the unlit back hall. The sanctuary doors were closed, but a long, thin rectangle of yellow light shone through their center gap onto the hall rug. If he remembered correctly, the doors had those soundless hinges.

If they'd harmed her, he would kill them.

He opened the left-hand door a crack.

Voices, still calm.

He widened the gap enough to see in the room. Only the track lights above the altar platform were lit. Gow stood directly beneath one with her back to him. Isolde—God in Heaven—was taped to the bottom of the five-foot cross like he'd been taped to the bear. The lights dimmed, then brightened, then dimmed again. A faulty dimmer switch, or the nephew working it like a stage show? No—there he was, walking up the left aisle. He climbed the steps and spoke to Gow.

When she replied, Gavin caught her voice, but not her words. Then Isolde said something and Gow slapped her.

Gavin's nails dented the edge of the door. Wait. Wait. Don't move too soon.

Gow hit her nephew on the back of the head.

Out of the corner of his eye, Gavin saw Morgan come through the back door. Then he heard cloth rip and switched his gaze back to the tableau before the cross. The center of Isolde's white nurse's uniform gapped, revealing her bare skin. Jonathan backed down the steps.

Bastard! Gavin leapt at him with a roar that made the drum set rattle.

Jonathan spun around and shrieked like a girl. "You're dead!"

In a single movement, Gavin crashed into him and bent him backwards over the end of the first pew. He smelled nicotine and scotch and fear; Jonathan's jugular vein pulsed like the clapper on a dinner bell. Gavin's fangs appeared. He gripped the long, oily hair and yanked Jonathan's head over the side of the bench, exposing six inches of pallid throat.

Miranda screeched, "Vampire!"

Gavin stopped a heartbeat away from the feast. He remembered who he was. Who was trapped on the Communion table. Whose throat he really wanted to shred. He closed his mouth over his fangs.

Beneath him, Gow's nephew blubbered. "Miranda, you fucking lying bitch, you didn't kill him. Oh, God, you're not dead. Get away. Get away from me. Aunt Miranda, get him off me. Donne, I don't want your job, I don't want anything, just please, please let me go."

"Say an Act of Contrition." Gavin heard the fang-lisp in his voice. It didn't matter. He was talking to a dead man. His appetizer. "You're going to Judgment." He ripped the front of Jonathan's sweatshirt like he was peeling a banana. Jonathan screamed.

Isolde said, "Gavin?" in a voice thick with controlled fear.

He jerked up his head. Gow had pushed a stake against Isolde's exposed skin. Gavin's hand dug into Jonathan's scalp. "Get away from her, Gow."

"Release my nephew, vampire."

"Get away from Isolde first."

Jonathan's hair started to slide through Gavin's fingers. He closed his fist on it, scraping bits of scalp under his fingernails. Jonathan stopped moving.

Miranda gave Gavin that crazed-prophet grin. He remembered it from Sunday night. "You are the son of the Father of Lies. God is a fire in me. God guides my arm to do His works."

Gavin forced his fangs into hiding. "Gow, back off of her."

"Release my nephew."

She pressed the stake—a dowel this time?—deeper. Isolde sucked in a sharp breath. Blood trickled down her skin.

Gavin dropped Jonathan's head. He reached the steps in two strides and leapt them in one.

"Gow, you have one chance." He leaned over her, inching his hand toward the dowel. "Drop the stake and I'll let you live."

She laughed and batted his hand away. Gavin's heart clenched as the harsh noise devolved into a titter.

"You have no power over me. Once I realized you hadn't died, that meeting you yesterday wasn't a trick of Satan's, I wrestled all night in prayer and God revealed my sin. I thought too much of worldly things in your yard on Sunday: Jonathan and status and power. That's why He allowed Satan to deflect my hand. But you won't pollute Newburyport much longer. God has shown me the way."

Gavin heard Isolde's quick breathing above him as he began the same slow upward movement of his right hand. He couldn't reassure Isolde; he couldn't break eye contact with Gow. She might push herself over the edge any minute.

A footstep near the door. Morgan. Hopefully he heard Gow's last speech.

"Who the fuck are you?"

Gow's head jerked to the right an instant. Gavin followed it and saw Morgan standing over Jonathan, gun pointed at his head.

"Go into eternal darkness, vampire whore!"

Gavin wrenched his head around and flung up his right arm to deflect the stake as Gow plunged it up and in.

Isolde screamed.

CHAPTER SEVENTY-EIGHT

Blazing agony ripped through Isolde's side. The sanctuary vanished behind a red haze. She screamed again and tried to move away from the source of the pain, but the tape kept her immobile. Rushing sounds filled her head. The room reappeared, only to tilt and spin around her.

She heard male voices she didn't recognize; Gow shrieking; Gavin yelling. She gasped for a breath and pain blazed through her chest. Warm wetness slid down her stomach.

Blood.

Her heart stuttered. Gray fog filled her vision.

———

Gavin pounced on Gow. His nails hooked into her throat.

"Donne! Let her go!" Morgan's voice.

Gavin blinked. Gow grinned up at him—a rictus of death.

"I'll rejoice from Heaven at your damnation, vampire. You'll follow her to Hell."

Gavin drove his nails deeper into her throat. Her laughter died in a gurgle.

"Donne, back away now. Let go of her. Help's coming. Think of Ms. Connor."

Gavin listened to his hate: Slice her. Bite her. Glut yourself on her foul blood. Avenge Isolde.

Morgan's voice, firmer. Louder. "Ms. Connor's not dead. Don't do something stupid."

Alive? Gavin shuddered. He retracted his fangs and disengaged his nails from Gow's wrinkled flesh.

"That's it. Stand up. We'll take care of her. Right, Hill?"

Hill's out-of-breath voice reached Gavin. "Right. Come on, Donne. Leave her to us."

A siren wailed outside, growing louder and closer. Pulsing red lights glowed on the long drapes.

"Ms. Connor needs you, Donne."

Gavin dragged in a long breath and got to his feet. He steeled himself for the sight of Isolde dying, despite Morgan's reassurance, and turned.

No. God in Heaven, no. All that blood.

————

A hand touched Isolde's face and she dragged open her eyelids. Gavin wavered in front of her, blurry but recognizable.

"Isolde, I can't take it out." His voice grated, harsh in her roaring ears. "You'll bleed to death."

"What's..." She swallowed and tried again. "What's your angel of mercy's name? Forgot." She couldn't get her voice above a whisper.

Tears streamed down Gavin's face. "Jeremiel."

The white noise in her head and the voices in the sanctuary overwhelmed her. She breathed in and nearly fainted. "Maybe he'll... holy water over me."

Gavin gripped her shoulders. "Close your eyes." He lisped the last sibilant.

She squinted, trying to see him clearly through the fog. Was everything fading again or did his eyes darken? The lights hurt. Breathing hurt.

Gavin's breath warmed her cold neck. Neck. Lisp. Isolde gasped and opened her eyes wider. Gavin's fangs were a whisper away from her jugular.

"No, Gavin."

He froze. "I'll be as quick as possible. The pain won't last long. Trust me."

"No." Her eyelids fluttered.

"I have to." His fangs broke her skin.

"No!" She jerked free. Oh God it hurt—

———

Isolde's body sagged in the restraints. Pain stabbed Gavin like a stake.

"Isolde?" His fangs retracted. "Isolde, please. Isolde."

Was her heart still beating? He couldn't hear it over the turmoil in his head. His palm couldn't feel a heartbeat.

"Sir, please move." An EMT set a bag on the Communion table and another one started slicing through the tape at Isolde's feet.

"Isolde, wake up." Gavin pulled at the tape around her shoulders.

The first EMT pushed Gavin aside with gentle but firm pressure. "Sir, please let us do our job. Detective, could you give us a hand here?"

A different hand grasped Gavin's arm and led him down the steps.

Behind Gavin, one of the EMTs said, "Hold onto that stick, Andy. Got it? Cutting the tape around her shoulders now."

Gavin's head pounded. He couldn't breathe. He couldn't see. Someone sat him down.

"Get her flat on the table. Pulling it out on three. Ready? One. Two. Three." The light wood rattled onto the Communion table. "Bleeding's bad. Gauze. More. Give me some pressure."

Gavin dropped his head into his hands and tore at his hair.

"Mr. Donne, look at me." Hill's voice.

Gavin glanced over at her. Her short, efficient hair was disheveled and her shoulder holster had rucked her Pink Floyd t-sh' ↄ one side.

EMTs transferred Isolde to a gurney and wheeled her aisle.

Hill said, "Come with me. I'll drive you to the ER."

Two uniformed policemen hustled out Jonathan as two different police officers entered.

"Over here." Morgan gestured the men to Gow, who sat muttering on the top step, cuffed hands raised to the ceiling.

Gavin started out of the pew toward her.

Hill shoved him back. "Control yourself. We're taking care of her. Now come with me willingly or I'll cuff you and drag you out to my car."

Gavin almost laughed. As if this woman could control him. Through the open doors he heard the ambulance drive away, siren blaring.

Isolde. He had to get to Isolde.

Gavin stood. "All right, Detective."

CHAPTER SEVENTY-NINE

"De profundis clamavi ad te Domine; Domine exaudi vocem meam. Fiant aures tuae intendentes in vocem deprecaionis meae."

Gavin paced the narrow surgery waiting room like it was a cell.

He'd actually tried to turn Isolde. God in Heaven, he was a monster. Selfish. Evil. Panicking at his own loss.

No. Not a loss. She wasn't dead. They were repairing the injury right now. He hadn't been able to deflect the stake all the way, but he'd done a little. Gow missed her heart.

He'd done as little as possible; too concerned with attacking Jonathan and Gow. Isolde should've been his only concern. Instead he embraced revenge and bloodlust while Gow murdered her.

No. She wasn't dead. No.

"De profundis clamavi ad te Domine; Domine exaudi vocem meam. Fiant aures tuae intendentes in vocem deprecaionis meae."

The yellowed wall clock read two-forty. She'd been in there an hour already. He kept pacing.

"De profundis clamavi ad te Domine; Domine exaudi vocem meam."

Footsteps clattered down the deserted hall. He faced the doorway as Noelle and Stephen hurried into the room.

Noelle took one look at Gavin and slumped into one of the hard plastic chairs. Gavin couldn't imagine what his face looked like, but the sight of it erased the fatigue from Stephen's.

Compassion and fellowship replaced it, along with an unspoken offer to share the burden. Gavin knew that look—the face of a priest who truly cared for his people. He'd been in Stephen's place often, comforting people, praying with them. Praying that God would listen to his prayers, and if not, that he could lead them to accept God's will.

But Gavin wasn't a priest any longer. He was nothing more than a creature driven by hate and bloodlust. He couldn't raise his soul to pray those prayers.

He stared into Stephen's eyes. Whatever he might have said, the only words that came were, "Veni in altitudinem maris, et tempestas demersit me."

Stephen put his hands on Gavin's shoulders. Gavin yielded to despair and sobbed.

He didn't know how long they stayed in that position, but Gavin's tears finally stopped and he took a deep breath; the first in hours. The weight on him had lessened.

"Thank you, Stephen."

Stephen smiled. "Just doing my job."

Noelle handed Gavin a tissue. He honked into it, took another, and wiped his face. The clock read two fifty-five.

A surgeon came to the doorway and cleared his throat. "Mr. Donne?"

"Yes?" His measured heartbeat quickened.

"Your fiancée is in recovery. The weapon missed all major organs and we repaired her internal injuries without a problem. She lost quite a bit of blood, so she's on her second transfusion now. We'll keep her here for a few days to make sure there are no complications, but she'll be back to normal by Thanksgiving."

Gavin's knees buckled, but Stephen caught him. "I—I—" He inhaled and tried again. "Thank you, doctor."

The surgeon smiled. "She'll be transferred to a regular room when she wakes up. Why don't you check with Admissions to see where they'll put her?" He looked at the chairs bolted in a row against the wall. "You'll be more comfortable waiting upstairs."

Noelle flung her arms around Stephen and Gavin. "I'll go check. Stephen, you want some coffee? Gavin?"

Gavin shook his head.

"Yes, please, Ellie." Stephen kissed her. "One cream—"

"One sugar. I know. Back in a few."

Stephen plopped into the nearest chair. "Ugh. That doctor wasn't kidding. While we wait for Ellie, can you give me the complete scoop on what happened in my church tonight?"

CHAPTER EIGHTY

Beeps. Even, rhythmic ones. Isolde sniffed. Hospital disinfectant. Ugh. That meant she was hooked up to at least one machine.

Why was she here? And why did the left side of her chest feel like all thirteen of Erma's cats had attacked it at once?

She forced open her gummed-up eyes. Whitish drop-ceiling. Dim light above her head. Tube in her right arm. Oh, this sucked big time.

She turned her head to the left. Gavin half-sat, half lay in a mustard-colored vinyl recliner, asleep. Dark circles ringed his eyes and his hair looked like cats had targeted it as well.

She tried to reposition her numb butt. "Ow." Bad idea. Her breathing quickened. Another bad idea. Holy crap, she hurt.

Gavin leapt out of the chair and pressed the call button. "What hurts?"

"Everything. Who put my chest through a shredder?"

"Don't move. Try not to inhale too deeply. "

"Hello to you, too." She smiled, then winced. "Why am I..." Like zapping through a DVD, everything in the church came back to her. Gow, the tape, the nephew, the dowel—

"She tried to kill me." Isolde moved her free hand to the bandages on her ribs. "She missed?"

Gavin caught her hand in both of his. "It's my fault. I went after Jonathan, then all I could think of was killing her. I should've hit the stake out of her hand sooner."

The door opened and a gray-haired nurse entered. "Good morning. Glad to see you're awake. Got some pain? Thought so. A dose of Demerol will take care of that."

Isolde watched Gavin watching the nurse. He looked quite possessive. How funny.

The nurse pressed a series of buttons on the infusion pump attached to Isolde's IV port. A moment later, chilled liquid flowed into her vein. The nurse checked the readout. "Later this morning I'll adjust the flow and you can self-med at regular intervals. The police want to talk to you and the doctor will be in to see you in a few hours, too." She took Isolde's temperature. "One-oh-one. Very good. Would you like some ice chips? That's all I can offer you."

Isolde's mouth dried out further at the word 'ice.' "Yes, please."

"Be right back."

After the door closed behind her, Isolde said, "Gavin, what were you talking about?"

"I could've stopped Gow."

She shook her head. "No, sir. No way. She's off her nut. You can't do anything with them when their minds go. Trust me; I work on the Alz floor."

"You're too forgiving. You don't understand."

The Demerol hit her brain. Lovely. All the cats ran away to claw at something else.

Amusement replaced the desolation in Gavin's eyes. "You look more tranquil."

"This is good stuff." Her eyes started to close.

Gavin squeezed her hand. "Isolde?"

She opened them in slow motion. "Mmm?"

He smiled. "Never mind. Sleep now. I have to leave for awhile, but I'll be back soon."

"Mmm."

CHAPTER EIGHTY-ONE

Gavin led Detectives Morgan and Hill through the artist's entrance of the community theater.

"I followed Hal from his lawyer's office to the funeral parlor to the high school, where he picked up Judith," he said quietly.

Two voices reached them from the stage area and they stopped walking. A man, then a woman, footsteps, then the man again.

Gavin led them into the wings, keeping behind the side curtains.

Hal and Judith stood stage right, reading from looseleaf scripts.

"I promise you, Olivia, that my army service will raise me above my father's status in the city." Hal's voice, pompous.

"I know it will, beloved." Judith, lilting like a romance cliché. "Will you not formally wed me before you leave?"

Pages rustled.

"I have promised you that I would. Your father has arranged your dowry and the feast is being prepared."

Footsteps.

"Prove your faith in me, Olivia."

Papers hitting the floor.

"Anything you wish, my lord." A pause, and Judith's normal voice returned. "Hal, are we really going to, you know, do it on stage?"

"Only to a point, Judy." Pompous Hal still had the stage. "The tutor's going to interrupt, but we're going to wake up the Boston theater crowd before he does."

Gavin inched forward. Hal's hands were on Judith's shoulders, Judith's head tilted up to his, her version of a seductive smile on her lips. Gavin beckoned the detectives to come next to him.

"Ready for some method acting, Judy?" Hal kissed her, his tongue slurping her lipsticked mouth.

Gavin glanced at the detectives, but Morgan held up a hand, then pointed to the stage.

Judith raised her arms and Hal stripped off her sweatshirt and sports bra. She unbuckled his belt and removed his jeans. Gavin winced at how fast she yanked them over the obvious bulge in his crotch.

"This air mattress will be covered with turf. I'll have trees on three sides of it. It'll be 'our' grove where we escape the pressures of family obligations."

Judith giggled. "Turf'll tickle my butt."

Hal shook his head, at the same time moving his erection into Judith's waiting hand. "We'll lay my chiton over it. Come on—ooh, yeah, it's ready for you, baby—I'll show you." He flung a bedsheet over the mattress and sat Judith on it.

Hill angled in front of Gavin. The sudden change in her expression would've made small children cry. When he turned his head toward the stage again, Judith was naked on the mattress and Hal held a joint to her lips.

Morgan crowded next to Hill and put a hand on her arm. Hill nodded tightly.

"Another toke, Hal, c'mon." Inhale. Slow exhale. "Ooh, so good." Giggle. "Fuck me now, future Athenian archon?"

"You know it, baby." Hal set the joint on the edge of a plastic chair and straddled Judith. He thrust forward once.

Morgan stepped on stage. "Newburyport police, Mr. King. You're under arrest."

CHAPTER EIGHTY-TWO

Low voices nearby woke Isolde.

"How did her father react?" That was Gavin.

"Rage, shame, tears." A female detective… Hill. "Where was all that concern when she started running around with that bastard?"

"Mother's dead; he works two jobs. He's just lucky she's not pregnant. We won't know about STDs for a couple of days yet."

The Demerol haze had lessened and Isolde could think. If one voice was Hill's. that made the other voice Morgan's.

"Before I forget, Detective Pacione says thank you." Hill's voice definitely grinned. "We promised to share the charming Mr. King with her."

"That will make three murders—" Gavin paused, "sorry, alleged murders—distributing drugs, and statutory rape."

Tapping noises. Morgan and his stylus. "Child molesters don't do well in prison."

"I won't lose any sleep at the thought." Gavin's voice was hard.

Isolde started to turn over, but thought better of it.

Gavin appeared at her side. "Good evening." His smile transfigured his tired, lined face.

"Already?" Isolde tasted her palate. "Don't come too close. I have death breath."

Hill approached. "Good to see you in one piece, Ms. Connor."

The tapping stopped and Morgan joined Hill. "Welcome back. Before you take another hit of the drug they're feeding you, we'd like to ask you some questions."

"Sure." She looked at Gavin. "Ice?"

He picked up a Styrofoam cup from the nightstand. "Open, please."

The ice melted immediately. Water never tasted so good. Gavin fed her three more, and she nodded at Hill. "What do you want to know?"

"We got most of the church story from Mr. Donne, but we need to fill in a few blanks. When did the Gows kidnap you?"

Isolde told her about the exit door and her stuck zipper and the crack on her head. Morgan's stylus sounded like a telegraph key.

"I don't know how they got me to the church. I didn't wake up till after they duct-taped me to the cross."

Gavin laced his fingers into hers.

"Your purse was in the trunk of their Lexus," Morgan said. "Moving on, what did she say to you in the church?"

Isolde closed her eyes to concentrate on something other than an image of her body stuffed in that small space. "I might've got her mad. In church, I mean." She wriggled her stiff shoulders. "Ow. This is really annoying."

"Ms. Connor, do I need to point out how lucky you are?"

She grimaced. "I know. I just hate being the patient. It's a hazard of the profession. Her eyes were hot. Fever. All she wanted to do was go back to sleep. "What was I saying?"

"You made her angry." Hill tapped her fingers on the bed rail.

"Oh, yeah. She was scaring me, so I went on the attack, sort of. I told her that she couldn't run Stephen's church if she went around killing people."

Hill snorted. "Did it work?"

"Too well. She swatted me and poked that stick into my chest."

"That's where your fat lip came from."

Isolde extracted her hand from Gavin's and felt her mouth. "No one show me a mirror for a week, okay?"

Morgan said, "What came next?"

"She quoted the Bible at me and called me... a vampire whore." Gavin's fingers grasped hers again. "You have no idea how tired I am of that word."

Hill said, "You and me both. She's been ranting ever since they locked her up. I drew the short straw and tried to get a statement from her. Fat chance."

"She's really crazy? Officially, I mean?"

Hill snorted. "Unofficially, she's a fruitcake. Officially, the family'll hire a fancy lawyer and a tame shrink who'll tie everyone up in knots with their jargon. That and money will get her sent away to some pricey foreign 'spa' for the rest of her life."

Morgan tapped away. "Right. We've got the rest from the nephew." He looked over the phone at her. "The nephew stole your phone and hit the first number in your speed dial list when Gow was distracted. Told your housemate where you were."

"Oh. That's how everyone found us."

"Yep. And that's," a few more taps, "that. You look all in." He tucked away the stylus and caught Hill's eye. "Anything else?"

"Not for me." She nodded at Isolde. "The nephew will stand trial eventually, but the Gows will delay it as long as possible. Forget about it and enjoy your honeymoon. You might be diapering your first kid before jury selection begins."

Isolde blushed. "Thanks. And thanks for saving the day."

Morgan shook his head. "Donne here did that. We just mopped up. Ready, Barb?"

"Let's go. The kids are probably driving my mother up the wall."

CHAPTER EIGHTY-THREE

The door closed behind Hill and Morgan. Gavin couldn't delay any longer—the weight was almost physical. He squeezed Isolde's hand in both of his. "Isolde, I—" The words clogged his throat.

She looked up at him with bloodshot eyes. Her lips were bruised and swollen, her hair looked like leftover Halloween straw, and her face was ashen.

He'd caused this.

"What's the matter, Gavin?" She winced. "You're crushing my hand."

He loosened his grip. "Isolde, I'm sorry. I'm leaving. You won't have to see me again." She had intelligence and common sense. She wouldn't think he was deserting her.

"Gavin, what are you talking about?"

Was he not making sense because he was tired or because she was ill? He clenched his jaw. Isolde's delectable blood, Isolde herself—in all her contradictions and warmth and innocence and fascination—would never be his again. The most ignorant beggar, throwing away an ancient coin because he didn't recognize its value, was not as profligate as he'd been last night.

Isolde groped for the pain pump button. "Gavin, if you want to go home, that's okay. I feel like roadkill and this'll put me out a minute after I press it. Drugs hit me like a brick."

She still didn't understand. He opened his mouth to try again, but she was still talking.

"You stayed here all night, didn't you? I bet Chay is starving, and you couldn't have gotten any rest in that Godawful chair."

"That's not what I mean." He stepped back from her bedside. "You were right. I am a... monster."

She started to speak, but he held up a hand.

"I tried to turn you last night." Grief lodged in his throat and he couldn't swallow past its rock. "It took me a hundred and ten years and ordination to the priesthood to forgive Philippa. Despite my promises, I was about to put you through my hell."

Isolde gathered herself with an effort. "Gavin, tell me slowly, in words of one syllable, exactly what you're saying."

"Gow attacked you because of me. I didn't protect you. I didn't save you. I nearly stole your salvation." He backed away another step. "Goodbye, Belle Isolde."

She clutched the bed rail. "Don't you dare."

Gavin stopped as she pulled herself up an inch, but sagged back onto the mattress.

"Ow-ow-ow, dammit, this hurts. For someone with as much experience as you, Mr. Donne, you sure haven't thrown off the Catholic guilt trip. Why on earth would I blame you?"

"Because if she hadn't connected you with me, she would've left you alone."

Isolde snorted. "Ow. Spare me. And what's this about— turning me? Is that what you said?"

Gavin slumped. She didn't remember. He could've kept quiet. He could've kept her with him to feast on and bear his children... No. His soul was black enough.

"After she tried to stake you, I thought you were going to die. So I tried to keep you with me forever."

Isolde's eyes unfocused. "You said... it would hurt but you'd be quick."

He nodded.

"I felt your fangs in my neck." Her gaze sharpened again. "And that's why you look like someone just ran over your puppy?"

A smile tried to usurp Gavin's frown. "Isolde, you don't understand."

Isolde gripped the Demerol button but didn't press it. "Gavin, you threw me a life preserver when you thought I was drowning. Just because I refused doesn't mean you did something Utterly Evil." She bit back a groan. "I have to press this. Sorry."

He shook his head. "You're wrong: it was evil. I know evil."

"Yeah, and so do I. Its latest disciple just tried to kill me. That would be Gow. Not you." Isolde's body relaxed. "Oh, yes."

Gavin moved back to her bedside. "Better?" What an inane remark; cover for of the thoughts clamoring to be uttered.

"Yes." She scowled at him with dilated eyes. "If you want to break it off because you don't love me, that's one thing. But if you're just being a martyr to your hyperactive conscience, then the minute I get out of here I'll suborn Chayyliel with Snausages, sneak into your house, and tie you to the bed until you agree to drag yourself out of the fifteenth century. Or was it the fourteenth? No, the fourteen-hundreds were the fifteenth century. That's right."

"Isolde."

"Don't apologize again. I'm feeling much too floaty to argue now." She smiled. "So tell me you're not leaving."

He took a deep breath. For a moment he wanted to worship this woman above the Almighty. Now that would be evil.

"Only as long as it takes to feed Chayyliel. Then I'll be back."

"Good answer."

CHAPTER EIGHTY-FOUR

Noelle came into the room with Gavin after Isolde's supper of chicken bouillon and green gelatin.

"Are you awake?"

"Awake and not loopy at the moment," Isolde said.

"Cool." A flower arrangement wider than the narrow hospital bed muffled her voice. "These are from everyone at work. The Tinkerbell doll on the bottom is from Stafford. I drove out to Peabody for it just to shut him up."

Isolde remembered her stitches and suppressed a laugh. "He's a sweetheart."

"He's a pain in the butt. Gavin, this vase weighs a ton. Can you grab it?" She dropped it in his hands and sagged into the vinyl recliner. "I haven't been this tired since I pulled all-nighters in college."

"Didn't you get any sleep?"

"Stephen dragged me home around six a.m." She set Tinkerbell on the windowsill. "I called both of us in sick and showed up around noon to give everybody the news."

Gavin came out of the bathroom with the vase full of water. "Were you the highlight of the day?"

Noelle pushed out of the chair. "Better than the Jerry Springer Show. Just let me shove all this stuff off the nightstand… There. Plenty of room." She worked the gigantic bouquet into the vase and arranged daisies, roses, lilies, freesia, and a few exotics Isolde couldn't identify into something like a symmetrical pattern.

"They're beautiful, Ellie."

"You're going to have a ton of visitors, so be prepared. Nuncio actually stopped sucking on a Diet Coke for twenty minutes while I told them all how Gow kidnapped you and taped you to the church's cross and stabbed you." Noelle stopped playing with fern leaves, took a shaky breath, and burst into tears. "Oh, Izz…" She bent over Isolde and rocked them both. "When I called Stephen last night he took forever to get to the house and when we passed that ambulance on the way to the church I thought the worst, I couldn't help it, oh Jesus, Izz, I'm so glad you're okay."

The Demerol wasn't strong enough to combat Noelle turning Isolde into a rocking chair. "Ellie? Stop shaking me."

"Oh—oh—sorry, Izz, I wasn't thinking." Noelle laid her down like she was something antique and fragile. "When'd you take your last dose?" She snatched three of the truncated hospital tissues and blew her nose.

"Just before you came in." Isolde breathed carefully. "I'm okay if I stay still."

"I'll wait till it kicks in before I yell at Gavin."

"What? Why?"

"Because he scared me half to death last night while you were in surgery." She punched Gavin's arm. "The look on his face nearly gave me a heart attack."

Gavin smiled slightly. "I apologize."

"Izz and I have led a pretty boring life till now. I didn't think I'd miss it, but man, Gavin, could we work in the excitement in little batches?"

"Ma'am," he swept an imaginary cowboy hat off his head, "you can tie to me."

"Speak English, cowboy. Halloween's over."

"It means 'I'll do my best.'"

"Good. I'm trusting you with my best friend, and I'd better not regret it."

Gavin plucked a pink rose from the vase and presented it to her. "I promise you won't."

CHAPTER EIGHTY-FIVE

Isolde leaned her head against her cello's fingerboard. "I came in too soon on the pickup to 71 again."

She looked over her shoulder as sleet rattled against the music room window. The crimson drapes and warm light in the room helped her maintain the illusion that it wasn't the end of November. That is, until Gavin played an arpeggio from the music they were supposed to play in church on Thanksgiving.

Gavin flexed his fingers. "Stop being so nervous."

"You rope me into playing on a holiday when the church'll be packed, and insist I can play a Gibbons song I've heard exactly once before."

"You can play it. You have much more difficult music on your shelves."

"Fine. Once more from measure 65, please."

Gavin's arrangement of Gibbons' 'O Clap Your Hands' for two voices bounced and rang around the room. This time Isolde and Gavin finished the song, her soprano holding the C two octaves above his baritone F as they played the final chord.

"See?" Gavin stood and stretched. "You'll be fine tomorrow."

Isolde set her cello on its side on the oriental rug. "I'll only be fine because I hate making a fool out of myself in public." She put her hands on the small of her back and stretched, but her left side twinged. With a grunt, she bent over and pressed her hand to it.

Gavin's arms were around her before she heard him move. "Are you all right? Is playing this piece on the cello too much for you?"

She patted his hand. "It's just a stitch. I'm fine. The scar'll stop pulling in a month or so. Just in time for our wedding night."

He slid his hands beneath her sweater and stroked the ridged, circular scar bisected by the three-inch incision scar the surgeon made to sew her insides back together. "I have plans for when you're able to move freely again."

"Mmm." Isolde shimmied her hips against him. "Gavin, tell me the truth now. Do you need, um, nourishment tonight?"

Gavin's hands stopped moving. "No."

Isolde turned in his embrace. "I said the truth."

"Truly, no. I took care of that yesterday."

"Then why didn't you 'take care of that' with me?"

Gavin kissed her forehead. "You're not strong enough yet."

"Who's the health professional here?" Isolde put both hands against his chest. "You're using your guilt and my recovery as an excuse, and you know it."

A wave of sleet crashed against the window and they both turned toward it.

"Suddenly I'm cold," Isolde said.

Gavin kissed her neck. "I'll warm you up."

"On one condition."

"Name it." He mouthed her earlobe.

"On Saturday night, you take mine."

Gavin's arms tightened. "You know I want to taste you again. But—"

"No 'buts.' I'm ninety-nine percent recovered. Everything else in my life is back to normal except this." She smiled. "I seem to have redefined 'normal' since I met you."

"You're not afraid?"

Isolde shook back her hair, exposing the skin her v-neck sweater left bare.

Gavin inhaled sharply. "Don't do that."

"Or?"

"Or I'll strip you naked and take you right here on this throw rug."

"Gavin, you lisped that 's.'"

He looked away. "You wreak havoc on my self-control."

She traced his lips with her finger. "Lose it, then."

The next second, he grasped the back of her neck and crushed his lips on hers. While she was distracted, he backed her against the wall between the bookshelves. When his lips pulled away, she opened her eyes. His fangs gleamed in the light above her music stand.

"May I taste you, Belle Isolde?"

Her heart stuttered once, then beat fast and steady. He looked wild and aroused, but not evil. She'd known that; she just needed this last confirmation.

She tipped her head back against the wall. Then the warmth of his mouth and a prick on her throat. She gasped, waves of pleasure flowing through her as Gavin pulled her close, closer.

A few minutes, an hour, a timeless moment later, his tongue caressed her neck and he raised his head. A few drops of her blood clung to his teeth and he licked them clean. His fangs retracted as she watched. His tongue moved around inside his mouth and his eyes rolled back in his head for a moment.

"I will never get enough of your taste." His eyes returned to her. "Tell me you're not afraid."

She raised her head and kissed him.